from London, with love

EM HARDY

*To anyone who may look at their life and think,
'This isn't where I thought I'd be.' You don't have
to have it all figured out just yet.*

From London, With Love

Playlist

Iris - The Goo Goo Dolls
No Place - Backstreet Boys
Feels Like Home - Chantal Kreviazuk
Slow Dancing in a Burning Room - John Mayer
Can't Help Falling In Love - Kasey Musgraves
London Boy - Taylor Swift
You and Me - Lighthouse
Heaven Is - Kasey Musgraves
What Was I Made For - Billie Eilish
Lay All Your Love On Me - ABBA
That Don't Impress Me Much - Shania Twain
I Knew I Loved You - Savage Garden
Half Grown - Zach Bryan
Heaven - Calum Smith
Worst Way - Riley Green
The Girls - Megan Moroney

Chapter 1

Lara

"If I have to hear 'but she bit me first!' once more this week, I may very well bite her myself."

The picture in front of me freezes. I hear Mia giggle and what I can only assume is Harper choking on her mouthful of coffee. It takes a few seconds before the video buffers and reconnects. While it may be 5:00pm here in Brisbane, it's only 7:00am where two of my favourite people reside; the same two I happen to be FaceTiming right now.

It's Friday afternoon, and we're on our 'Weekly Debrief' call—code for 'let's talk shit about the week that was', even though the girls still have Friday to get through. We started our Weekly Debrief calls over a year ago now, and they're still the highlight of my week.

"Lara, the children can't really be *that* bad, can they?" Harper asks, having recovered from her near-choking episode.

"Oh Harps, you've got no idea," I say while plucking my wine glass off the coffee table and leaning into the comfort of my couch. It's emerald green in colour, made from a beautiful suede that's soft to the touch. This couch is the only piece of furniture that would even border on the edge of luxury within my tiny, suburban apartment, and even that would be a stretch.

Through the screen of my laptop, Mia and Harper sit side by side on their bay window. Although it's morning, London in December means the sun doesn't begin rising until at least now, if not later.

Thankfully these two are 'morning people', so they don't mind waking up earlier for our calls. Well, mostly. I say 'morning people' because when it comes to the girls, it's more of a varying degree of morning. Harper is up by 5:30am most days, whereas Mia's idea of an early rise is around now.

The contrast between the two of them has me holding back a giggle. Mia is dressed in one of her signature oversized track-suit sets, looking as though she just rolled out of bed. Her long blonde hair is tied in a messy updo on the crown of her head. She attempts to stifle a yawn with the cuff of her soft pink sweater but fails miserably.

Harper, on the other hand, is the portrait of sophistication. Immaculately dressed as always. Today's outfit of choice pairs a pretty white blouse with a billowing teal green skirt. At least, that's how it appears in her seated position through the small frame on my screen. Harper's brunette lob is in salon-perfect waves, and her curtain bangs fall softly over her face as she sips what is probably her second cup of coffee.

Today I'm Team Mia, as I too am in my pyjamas. This evening's attire consists of a navy satin short set, the day's makeup hanging on for dear life, and my hair still holding Monday's curls like an absolute champ.

I've spent the past nine months working in administration at the local primary school, during which time I've overheard all sorts of bizarre excuses and explanations for why children do the things they do. Who would've thought biting was still a concern at age ten? Not me, that's for sure.

Don't get me wrong, I don't dislike children. But working around them for the rest of my life? Add it to the list of "I don't fucking think so", which includes the likes of working in the local supermarket deli, barista-ing, and Uber driving. I haven't actually done the last one, but I'm quite positive it's not the career for a socially anxious introvert.

Mia's cheerful voice interrupts my inner thoughts. "Well Lars, unfortunately I can't relate to the biting or the tough week." Despite the fact she's probably been awake all of 15 minutes, Mia is as animated as ever.

Her eyes gleam with enthusiasm as she continues. "I came up with a new cocktail, and I must say, it's divine! I haven't completely decided on a name for it yet, but I have one front-runner I need to run by the two of you."

For the past few years, Mia has worked at The Bookend, a quaint old bookstore-turned-pub a little further in towards Covent Garden, and spends her free time creating cocktails inspired by her favourite thing: fictional men.

"Ooh I'm intrigued, what's in this one?" I ask, rubbing my hands together in anticipation.

Most recently, she's introduced us to two of her latest creations. The Icebreaker—relating to Hannah Grace's novel of the same name—is a frozen variation of the popular Porn Star Martini, aptly named after the delectable Nate Hawkins. Mia also has her own personal take on the classic hot toddy: The James Toddy. Inspired by none other than *the* Cassius James, of Brittanee Nicole's *Loving Whiskey Duet*, this standard hot toddy with the addition of freshly ground cardamom is the perfect winter cocktail packed with spice.

One night, while Mia and Harper were visiting me in June, Mia made an entire cocktail night agenda so I could have the pleasure—*her* words, not mine—of sampling each of her signature Fictional Men cocktails. Each was displayed impeccably, with subtle hints referencing their origins.

The Longwood—derived from Hailey Dickert's *The Sister Between Us*—was given its beautiful shade of red thanks to the sweet raspberry syrup and displayed with a single tulip; Mia had insisted on three, but sadly a standard cocktail glass just wouldn't allow it. A cocktail jug, however? The perfect size.

Similarly, one of her personal favourites, The Spicy Slade—a nod to Lauren Asher's *Throttled*—was always presented in the sleekest of glasses. The chilli-rimmed beverage was a huge hit with the locals and tourists alike, especially those who were familiar with the man behind the name.

Whipping out a notebook from lord knows where, Mia clears her throat before continuing, "It's quite possibly my best idea to date." Mia flips to a previously bookmarked page and reads aloud. "The Screaming O: Hunt Athalar's Version. Think of it like Taylor's Version; something we all know and love, recreated by someone with even more experience."

The wineglass in my hand is no longer safe as I burst into a fit of laughter. With my eyes squeezed tight from the sheer force of my laugh, I can't see the girls, but I hear them. We must look and sound like crazy people; one of us almost squealing while another has her mouth wide with no sound coming out. That happens to me on occasion, but only if I'm laughing incredibly hard. Given we're all *very* familiar with the scene behind Mia's latest inspiration, this is one of those occasions.

Managing to recover the fastest, Harper claps her hands with joy. "Alright, let's hear it—What this Week!" 'What this Week' is a little segment in our call where we talk about what we're currently watching, listening to, and most importantly, reading. The three of us are huge readers, and have books to thank for bringing us together from opposite sides of the world.

Eighteen months or so ago, I decided I wanted to join the

Bookstagram community as a bit of a creative outlet and to talk about my books with like-minded people. I love that so many of my friends and family read, but we don't share my particular taste in books. Said taste being the likes of decidedly spice-heavy novels, or questionably dark romances.

One of the first accounts I started interacting with was one belonging to two high school best friends who lived in England. The three of us quickly learnt we shared many favourite books, and we'd find ourselves talking most days. We discovered we shared a lot of common interests as well; training in the gym, baking, and failing to spot the red flags so obviously being waved by the men we interacted with.

As the months went on and we got to know each other better, the conversations became less about books and more about keeping each other updated on everyday life. Having a large time zone difference made it difficult to keep conversations fluid, and so the Weekly Debrief calls were born.

"I'll go first!" Harper seems overly enthusiastic, sitting up straight and on the edge of her seat, so Mia and I let her take the stage. "I'm currently watching, and absolutely *living* for, Bridgerton. Lars, you were right—this show is crack. Don't even get me started on the Duke."

Mia laughs whilst trying to speak, making her hard to understand. "Harps, I hate to break it to you, but neither you nor Lara have ever even had crack." Her laugh is a particular breed of unique, a hybrid of sorts. There are sections of witch-like cackles interspersed with an almost wheeze. The longer she goes on, the more prominent the wheeze becomes.

Harper feigns shock. "Miss Mia, is this your way of revealing you're a secret crack addict?"

"So what if I was?" The prominent lift in Mia's eyebrows is a silent challenge.

"Mia honey, we've watched you struggle to use a Vicks

inhaler. I think it's safe to say none of us are secret crack users," I respond, grinning wickedly at Mia through the screen. "Harper, please proceed!" This gets one final snicker from Harper before she continues.

"This will come as no surprise, but I have been listening to true crime podcasts."

As if planned, Mia and I dramatically roll our eyes in unison.

"Harper, you do know there's a wonderful thing called music you can listen to instead of gruesome murder retellings, right?" Mia's tone is playful, a small smirk tugging on her lips as Harper turns to face her with a huff.

"Okay ladies, let's play nice," I tease. "You can listen to anything you want, Harps, as long as you tell us what we really want to hear; what are you reading?"

"The absolute literary masterpiece that is Give Me More by Sara Cate." She beams, holding up her paperback triumphantly, not dissimilarly to the way Rafiki holds baby Simba. The familiar face of a half-naked man appears in my line of sight, his 'come fuck me' eyes staring right into my soul.

When it comes to smut, I'm partial to a cutesy illustrated cover rather than a male model shot. However, there's something about the tattoos and leather jacket sported on the front of Give Me More.

I lock eyes with Mia through the screen and watch her eyebrows raise the same way mine do. Her expression of surprise reflects mine. A moment passes and smiles stretch across our faces as we look back at Harper.

"She sees the light!"

"It's a Christmas miracle!"

Mia and I excitedly talk over each other, a regular occurrence on these three-way calls. We're all easily excitable, which is both entertaining and chaotic. The three of us could never be allowed in a library together; the havoc we'd cause would be tremendous.

We've spent the past several months trying to goad Harper over to the dark side and dip her toes into this series, but she was reluctant, to say the least. Of the three of us, she'd be labelled as the more conventional one when it comes to romance novels and their contents.

While Mia and I lap up the smut, Harper was never as exposed to that genre the way we were—we'd been the 16-year-olds secretly reading the Fifty Shades series and convincing our mothers it was a "teen series". Imagine my mother's shock when she watched the movie several years later. After that, she didn't dare ask too many questions when it came to the books I was reading.

Having read Praise and fallen in love with the Salacious crew immediately, we knew Harper simply had to read it too. She was hesitant at first, but I strongly believe she has a closet praise kink, and this book brought her out of her shell. Needless to say, we're overjoyed with the progress she's made of her own accord through the series. Soon the apprentice will become the master, and we'll be going to her for smut recommendations rather than her coming to us; what a moment in history that'll be.

"I hate to admit it, but the two of you were right. This series is sensational. Who knew you could have a healthy balance of smut *and* storyline?" Harper returns the book to her lap before turning toward Mia. "You're up."

"Embracing my overachiever archetype, I've been rewatching a TV series and a movie series this week, and I have no regrets. Bridgerton continues to hit quite sensationally the second time around, as does the Fifty Shades trilogy. Really, I'm getting the best of both eras for sex and smut."

Stifling a grin, I playfully roll my eyes at Mia as Harper smacks her on the arm.

"Must everything revolve around sex when it comes to the two of you?" Harper shakes her head ever so slightly as she speaks.

"Yes," Mia and I respond in unison, causing us to burst into hysterics. Harper fails at maintaining a straight face and joins in. If the girl's neighbours weren't already awake, they certainly would be after hearing this raucous.

"The sex doesn't stop there!" Mia exclaims with a wide grin. "Harps, you might need to prepare yourself for what I've been reading this week—Pucking Around by Emily Rath."

Harper reaches over and grabs the book off Mia's lap; her brows pull together slightly as she lifts it into view. "This book has sex? This cute little cover doesn't portray that. Where's the half-naked model shot?"

"This book *is* sex Harps. We're talking about one woman, three men, absolute filth." The smile splitting the lower half of Mia's face is downright devilish. Harper's expression? Quite the opposite. I've never seen her look so confused.

"Honey, let me break it down for you." Mia turns to Harper, levelling with her. "Girl meets three boys. Girl likes three boys and they like her, and each other. Said three boys proceed to fuck the girl in a loving manner, resulting in some of *the* hottest sex scenes you'll read. I'm going to assume the look on your face means I don't need to spell it out any further?"

She's displaying a look of astonishment, crossed with . . . No, it couldn't be. Is she *impressed*? Colour me shocked.

"I've seen this book on almost every surface of our apartment the past week, and I never would've guessed it contained such *dirty* content." The small grin on Harper's lips is trying oh so hard to remain hidden, but it's there.

"I'll be finished it by this evening." Mia bumps her shoulder into Harper's as she promises, "I'll leave it on the bench for you."

Harper's cheeks turn pink, and I stifle a giggle.

"I'm quite alright with my current read, thank you." Harper's cheeks turn a slightly deeper shade of pink. "But I may take you up on that once I finish."

"Of course you will, you little hoe." Smirking, Mia continues, "To finish off, I've been listening to the excellence of Tchaikovsky."

That takes me by such a surprise that I fold in half, tears springing to my eyes as I laugh. I wipe away those that escape down my cheek and look back to see the girls in a similar situation.

"We truly never know what to expect when it comes to you," I say. I'm still recovering from my outburst as the girls tell me it's my turn to share. "I'm still bingeing The Bold Type. If the two of you haven't jumped on that bandwagon yet, I'm not going to be mad, just disappointed."

"Prepare to be disappointed because we completely forgot about it. Again." Harper looks at me briefly before lowering her eyes and feigning guilt.

"It's honestly amazing, and the girls remind me so much of the three of us when we're together. As per usual, I'm on a Shania kick and absolutely *devouring* every album she's ever made."

For as long as I can remember, I've loved Shania Twain. My grandmother was her self-proclaimed number-one fan while I was growing up, so we'd always have little dance parties when I visited her. We've stayed true to Shania over the years, and always celebrate her new album releases with a wine and 'Shania on Repeat' night.

"As for books, I'm rereading and annotating Tangled in Tinsel by Queen Trilina and loving every second of it."

"Oh Lars, you and that bloody book." Harper shakes her head at me. "Was once not enough? Actually, don't bother answering because *clearly* it wasn't."

A cheesy grin expands over my face, which I direct right at her. She knows me well enough by now to understand once is never enough. Harper is yet to read this one, but I plan to convince her soon enough.

"May I remind you that Tangled in Tinsel is a holiday classic. By not indulging in this highbrow literature, you are not only doing yourself a disservice, but you are also breaking the hearts of millions around the world." I cross one leg over the other, clasping my hands around my knee, and let out a small sigh.

Mia says nothing; she doesn't need to. Appreciation shines through her eyes; smut lover supporting smut lover. God, I love my friends.

"Okay Lara, I understand this book means a lot to you. You don't need to use the grand speech on me." Amusement lights up Harper's face as she continues. "Mark my words, I'll read your Bible before December ends."

Cheers erupt through my apartment; Mia and I the only source of the chaos.

"Christmas has come early!" Her promise has a feeling of elation washing over me.

But as I sit watching my friends laugh together, I'm hit with a sudden and unexpected wave of sadness. It's been six long months since I've hugged the two of them, and right now, I'd give almost anything to squeeze them again.

I have a small but close-knit group of friends here in Brisbane who I love dearly, but recently it's become more and more prevalent that I'm in a markedly different time of my life than they are.

My closest friends are several years older than me. One is

about to be married, another is in the midst of building a family home, and the other is preparing to move interstate to follow her dreams. I couldn't be prouder of the three of them, but my life is a stark contrast to any of theirs.

I've been single for the past two years, agonisingly navigating the sewage waters of online dating. My career prospects are few and far between. The only thing I've got going for me is my books, and unfortunately it isn't an option to marry inanimate objects.

A phone rings on the other side of the screen, dragging me out of my self-pity spiral and back to the present.

"Sorry Lars, I have to take this," Mia says with a tight smile, glancing up to meet my eyes after checking the Caller ID.

"Everything okay?" I ask Harper once Mia is out of earshot.

"Mostly. Just the ongoing issues with Satan. That was her calling."

Satan is the girls' other roommate. I'm sure she has a real name, but I couldn't tell you what it is. To me, she's always been Satan. The girls found her on a roommate website earlier in the year when they first moved into their Camden townhouse. She'd listed glowing reviews from supposed previous roommates, but it was obvious early on they were nothing but lies.

"It baffles me why she won't move out when she obviously despises living with you guys." I take another sip from my almost empty glass as Harper continues to sip her coffee.

"Trust me, it baffles us even more."

As I rise from my couch to grab myself another moscato, Mia reappears through the kitchen entryway, looking several degrees less smiley than she was five minutes ago. I hastily sit back down, not wanting to miss the story behind her expression.

"Well ladies, Harper and I are simultaneously fucked and freed," she announces as her face re-enters the screen, and she dumps her phone onto the nearby throw cushion.

Harper's face turns down, the disappointment obvious. "She didn't."

"She did indeed. Happy Friday to us."

"Guys, what am I missing?"

The girls open their mouths and at the same time mutter, "She's moving out."

"She's given us three months' notice, since that's when her one-way ticket to Peru is booked for," Mia continues.

The confusion in my expression morphs into frustration. "How can she bail on the lease like that? I know she's awful, but this isn't right! What will you two do? The rent is hardly—"

"Lara, hon, take a breath." Mia interrupts my babbling. "We're big girls. We'll find another flatmate, and all will be okay."

"I'd rather move in myself than risk you two inviting another Satan to live with you."

I'm not sure what response I'd expected, but it wasn't their answering silence. In sync as always, the girls face each other, sharing a look. When they look back at me, they're wearing expressions I can't quite place.

"You two are worrying me, what's the scheming look for?"

"Lara, that's possibly the best idea you have ever had," Harper says as Mia nods enthusiastically, causing her blonde bun to bob all over the place.

"Okay, you've lost me. I didn't have an idea?"

"Move in with us!" Mia exclaims.

"Ha! Oh, Mia. You know it was a joke, right?"

"It doesn't have to be," Harper responds. I look between

their conspiring faces, trying to determine what on earth is happening.

"You know I love you both, but I can't up and move halfway across the world; that's insane."

"Why not?" the girls say in unison. "Lara, please know I mean these next words with nothing but love. What's keeping you in Brisbane, or Australia, for that matter? You don't like your job, you're single, and the only ties you have are your parents and brother," says Harper.

"Ouch Harps, brutal. True, but brutal." I wrap the cream throw adorning the couch around my shoulders, feeling a little cooler after the theoretical cold shower that was Harper's words.

"You should definitely think about it, Lara. I mean, can you imagine the mischief the three of us could create if we were in the same country?" Mia replies with a wink. A cheeky grin breaks out across her face, causing her dimples to pop.

"Oh bugger, it's seven thirty already. Sorry Lars, we have to cut it short this morning because Harps has a meeting," Mia's voice is laced with regret as she announces the end of my favourite Friday tradition.

Harper, in my opinion, is the epitome of adulthood success and represents everything I want to be when I grow up. She'd be offended if she heard me say that since she's not even a year older than me. At 28, Harper is in her dream field, working towards her dream career—she's a senior accountant at one of London's top accounting firms, with the dream of one day taking the reins as CFO. Being the headstrong person she is, I have no doubt Harper will achieve her goal in no time.

Meanwhile, Mia and I are still trying to figure out what the fuck we want to do with ourselves and our futures. I have the thought, 'I am not qualified to be an adult', at least twice a week; I imagine Mia has it even more frequently. We aren't immature by any means, but we're also incomparable to Harper and her assurance.

"Goodbye, my girls. Have a wonderful Friday!" The girls say their goodbyes and blow kisses to me through the screen.

Those three distinct beeps signal the end of the video call, but I don't move to stand. Instead, I settle into the lounge, empty wine glass in hand, and think about the unimaginably crazy direction that conversation went. *Me*, move across the world to the UK? I couldn't possibly. Could I?

Chapter 2

Carter

"Fuck!"

With more force than anticipated, I pull my helmet off my head and flinch.

"Too slow, little brother," Teddy gloats. "Is that fancy new Ninja unable to live up to the hype, or is it perhaps a user error?"

"Screw you, Theodore," I throw the mirth-laced words at my brother as we walk our motorbikes back to the sheds. Teddy's deep belly laugh rings out around us while the smell of rubber-marred asphalt encases my nostrils. It's quiet when we reach the shed; the past hour of wind that threatened to whistle straight through my eardrums now nowhere to be seen.

Theodore Lawrence, affectionately known by our family as Teddy, is practically my twin. We're the spitting image of each other despite the fact he has two years and two inches on me. The latter is a fact he'll tell anyone who'll listen. He loves it when we're mistaken for twins; it makes his old arse feel younger than his thirty-one years.

"It's alright, bud, someone has to lose."

The fucking *cheek* of this guy.

"Keep shit-talking, old man, see what happens."

Teddy throws his head back, that distinctive sound filling the air once more. We remove our racing gear, place the items into the dry-cleaning bags hanging overhead, and head into the rooms to change.

It's a typically dreary December afternoon, and we've just finished our bi-weekly Saturday race. We frequent many of the British circuits, but Brands Hatch is a personal favourite of both of us.

The Lawrences of the 1910s were a founding family of the British Motorcycle Racing Club, and the men in our family have been members every generation since.

I'd never admit it to him, but unfortunately my brother is right—my head isn't in it, and my racing was garbage at best. Teddy is a good rider, great even, but it's a rare occurrence for him to beat me. Most days, I absolutely thrash him on the track, and he knows it.

"What's going through that little head of yours, Carter?" My brother turns to face me as we head through the shed into the common room, each grabbing a beer from the mini-fridge. "You looked sloppy out there."

Absent-mindedly, I bring the beer bottle to my mouth. Resting it against my bottom lip for a moment, I drag it away again. Apparently, I'm too lost in my own head to remember to take a sip. "The past few weeks have caught up with me since the announcement in the executive meeting yesterday and, *fuck* man, it's a lot to process when it hits you all at once."

The crease between Teddy's eyebrows softens.

He places his beer on the bench we're leaning against. "Of course it's a lot, Carter. You're twenty-nine years old and being placed in charge of the largest law firm in England." Teddy levels with me. "But Father wouldn't have asked this of you if he didn't believe you were more than capable of handling not only the role, but its responsibilities."

The breath I wasn't aware I was holding escapes me. Raking my fingers through the dark locks of hair atop my head with my free hand, I take a long sip of my beer as I replay Teddy's words in my head.

I'm 29 years old and being placed in charge of the largest law firm in England.

I've spent many years knowing I'd one day take over as CEO of J. L. & Sons Attorney and Law, but what I didn't know was how soon that day would come.

For the past five years, I'd been working as a criminal law barrister. Criminal law was all I'd ever wanted to specialise in; I'd never even thought about a backup because, to me, that was it. The days were long, the nights often longer, but I didn't mind. I loved it, lived for it even.

Over the years I encountered many awful crimes, but I always knew that was part of the job. In order to help victims, I couldn't be spared the gory details. After a while, you build up somewhat of an immunity to the crime scene pictures and witness recounts.

I'd thought my immunity was unbreakable, until it wasn't. The last victim had been a little girl, aged four. She'd been killed in a horrific car accident caused by her own mother, who was driving under the influence.

The case hit too close to home. After the mother had been sentenced and justice was served, I had to take a step back. Many nights were spent lying awake, wishing I could've saved that innocent child. Logically, I knew there wasn't anything I could've done, but it didn't stop the thoughts.

A few weeks later, I made the decision to hang up the criminal law boots. Upon speaking with my father, he shocked me with the revelation that he was wanting to step down from his CEO duties in the coming years.

When I queried where this had come from, he'd said, "Son, I'm not as young as I once was. I've dedicated most of my life so far to this company; now it's time to dedicate the rest to your mother."

Who was I to argue?

Flash forward a couple of weeks, and it was settled. Which brings us to here, in the shed's bar, contemplating what the fuck I've signed myself up for. Although the oldest, Teddy has never been interested in the family business. While I finished college and went straight into Cambridge's Law School, he dropped out at 16 and joined the British Army.

Taking a moment, I look at my brother—*really* look at him. Fifteen years on, and he's a Military Educator training new recruits, retired—*for now*—from his role within the Intelligence Corp.

Rain begins to patter against the tin roof, suggesting it's time for us to depart. The petrichor scent drifts in through the slightly agape steel door. I breathe in deeply, savouring, as a wave of calm washes over me. It always has a way of grounding me; the smell, the sound, the feeling of the droplets on your skin.

Beer bottles empty, we dispose of them before grabbing our bikes once more, locking up and returning to the car park. Thankfully, what was previously a downpour is now a mere sprinkle. Once the bikes are safely stowed in their respective trailers, Teddy rounds the hood of my Audi, pausing in front of me. His brows knit together ever so slightly. A hand raises a fraction, before he drops it back to his side.

"You can do this, Carter. You're a born leader. We have that in common, but I was never meant for the corporate world; you are." Teddy takes a deep breath, and I find myself mirroring him. His face softens. "You know you're not going to be alone through this either, right? I'll be in your corner, as will Mother, Father and Emilia. Always"

Appreciation swells within me, stinging my eyes with gathered tears. I close the gap between us, enveloping my big brother in a tight squeeze. His body stills for a moment. A second passes before he wraps his arms around my back, returning the hug.

Over almost as quickly as it begins, we release each other and take a small step apart. Teddy reaches out to squeeze my shoulder, something he's done since we were young boys. A small gesture that always made us both feel grounded and safe.

"We should get out of here before this storm hits." He gestures above us, where the clouds have darkened to an ominous shade of grey.

I nod. Teddy gives me a small smile. The familiar feeling of looking in a mirror surfaces as I return his smile. "See you Friday?"

"Considering our parents would have my head if I missed our little weekly bonding dinner, yes." Teddy responds with a chuckle, strolling towards the driver's side of his Jeep. He gives me a salute and hops in, disappearing from sight behind the window's tint.

I follow suit, climbing into my own vehicle as the rain begins to fall with force. Soaked to the skin, a wave of goosebumps overcome me as I make quick work of turning the car and heater on, the plush leather seats warm me from the inside out. Fervently rubbing my palms together, the goosebumps dissipate.

Raindrops splat on the windscreen as I follow Teddy down the circuit's driveway and out to the main road. We convoy for a while before Teddy takes the exit that eventually leads him into Surrey, and I continue on to Kensington.

When I stroll into my flat, my gaze immediately falls to the luxurious six-seater black lounge that sits sunken in the lounge room. It then sweeps over to the timber dining table and its seven mostly unused chairs. The size seemed perfect at the time, but the empty spaces cause a twisting feeling deep within my stomach.

I'm hit with an uncomfortable and not uncommon thought —*this place is too big for one person.*

I purchased the penthouse almost five years ago now, after landing my first big role. At the time, I didn't think I'd still be alone five years later, but time has a way of surprising you.

Walking into the kitchen to raid the fridge, I survey the place as if for the first time. Black cabinetry with gold details lines the space behind me, topped with an oversized granite benchtop. The black and gold marbled splashback is one of the reasons I love this kitchen so much.

Childhood memories of cooking with my parents and siblings are some of my favourites. I always wanted a kitchen that would allow me to recreate those memories with my own family one day. Only I didn't realise how lonely it would be when most nights it's just me.

Sweeping my eyes over the lounge room, they land on the fireplace I installed shortly after moving in. I love the cold, as long as I can keep warm. I couldn't install a real fireplace, so electric was the next best thing. Snuggling up with Winnie in the ridiculously oversized lounge is one of the best ways to spend an evening when Teddy brings her over.

Although excellent company, she happens to be four years old and my niece. I love her dearly, but sometimes I think it would be nice to have someone my own age to snuggle with and keep me company.

Deciding on last night's lamb roast leftovers for tea, I pull the tray from the fridge and dish myself a plateful. My mind drifts to the conversation with Teddy as my food heats, and I wander to the bathroom to shower off the remnants of today's race.

I'll be in your corner.

The words had struck a chord somewhere deep inside. Although he denies it, he's one of my biggest supporters. I may never have graduated law school if I hadn't had him breathing down my neck to finish assignments instead of drinking myself into oblivion over them.

When I was sworn in, he was the first to crash-tackle me in congratulations, closely followed by our baby sister Emilia, much to our parents' amusement. He's been through some hard shit—shit no one should have to go through at the age he did—but he's never broken. Teddy continues to have the biggest heart of anyone I know, and our family is everything to him.

Turning the shower to my preferred temperature of Satan's arsehole, I strip out of my jeans and tee. When the water is on the verge of scalding my skin, I get in.

Feeling much fresher, I pull on a pair of grey sweatpants before heading back to the kitchen. I pour myself a glass of my favourite Chateau Palmer 2016 that I stocked up on during my visit to Margaux last year, and inhale the scent deeply. Black cherry cassis aromas invade my nostrils, reminding me of the beautiful French vineyards. Contentedness washes over me. Glass in one hand and plate in the other, I make my way over to the lounge to settle in for the night.

The fireplace blazes with warmth, but I reach for the throw out of habit. Growing up, we had throw blankets on every bed and lounge; one could never own too many. The burgundy knit throw living on the arm of my lounge was unsurprisingly part of a housewarming gift from my mother.

I grab the remote off the coffee table to turn on the surround sound system, decreasing the volume until it's just audible over the crackling of the flames. Leaning forward, I pick up my copy of *Crime and Punishment* lying on the table. Hitting shuffle on the remote, the southern drawl of Morgan Wallen fills my apartment.

I let out a content sigh, opening the book to find where I left off. Wine, books and country. It's the simple things.

I awaken with a jolt. Eyes darting around the room, I take in the scene—my empty glass lies by my legs, and my plate is on the table in front of me. The throw that was over me is now discarded on the floor, along with *Crime and Punishment*. Morgan has long since stopped singing, and I realise I must have fallen asleep mid-chapter. Glancing at my watch, my brows raise faintly when I see it's 3:00am.

Collecting up my mess, I turn the fireplace to sleep mode and head to the kitchen. I place the wine glass and plate in the dishwasher. Switching off the lights, I walk down the hallway towards my bedroom. The door glides over the carpet with a soft swish. The curtains are already drawn, which means I forgot to open them this morning.

Depositing the book onto my bedside table, I head into the ensuite. The double vanity with large oval backlit mirrors looms to the side, but my favourite feature sits a few steps higher than the rest of the room. A freestanding black stone tub is parallel to the floor-to-ceiling window, allowing for uninterrupted views of some of Hyde Park and Kensington Palace. Feeling slightly more awake than I'd like to be in the middle of the night, I clamber into bed. As I close my eyes, the week's events replay behind my lids until sleep takes over.

"Are you ready for this, Son?"

The weight of my father's hand on my shoulder reminds me

to breathe. Truthfully, I feel far from ready. But is anyone ever really ready for change?

"As ready as I'll ever be."

"That's my boy." He gives me a small smile before turning with outstretched arms to address our executives, who are currently seated before us in the expansive boardroom of J. L. & Sons. "Ladies and gentlemen, thank you for joining us today." My father's voice ceases the chatter, all eyes now on the head of the table. "As you're all aware, I've made the decision to step down from my duties as CEO. It brings me great pleasure to announce that effective January 1st, my son, Carter—who you are all very familiar with—will be taking over as CEO."

In the brief moment of silence that follows, I survey the faces around the room. There are gaping jaws, a few gasps, but not one look of disappointment or displeasure. Is every single person truly happy about my appointment as CEO? The chorus of cheers and claps following that thought answer the unspoken question. That is, until I notice one older barrister along the back of the room—a look of utter displeasure marring his features.

Despite the bundle of nerves still tumbling around my stomach, I allow myself a moment to enjoy the atmosphere. If my father thinks I can do this, and our team of executives agrees, I'd have to have some audacity to disagree. My thoughts momentarily linger on the disgruntled barrister. I'd put money on him having seen the tabloid headlines and accompanying photographs. Those who matter know the truth, but as others don't, it opens the floodgates for judgement and criticism. I can't say I blame the older gentleman; I'd do the same thing if I didn't have context.

"I will spend the coming weeks preparing him for my departure, but I have no doubt he's exactly what the firm needs in this next chapter," my father continues, his hand once again resting on my shoulder. "I trust you will allow him the same respect you've given me and will show him some grace during this transition period."

The claps start again, but I'm removed from the moment as images of magazine front pages and newspaper clippings flood my vision. I'm well aware that my actions and choices are the reason these exist, and I'd do it again in a heartbeat, but I can't help but wonder—will this new chapter bring with it a fresh start? Has enough time passed that I could let this persona go in the hopes that I might be seen as more than the Oxford Street Playboy?

Chapter 3

Carter

The heavenly aroma of coffee beans swirls in the air around me. It's 9:00am, and I'm sitting at my father's favourite table at Spoonful, a quaint local cafe. We never sit anywhere other than the round table in the back right-hand corner of the cafe, adjacent to the window overlooking the many activities of Hyde Park. It's the perfect place to people-watch.

There are several marshmallow-looking children playing in the playground, dogs running off leash in their fenced-off area, and a few couples and families rugged up from head to toe enjoying their Sunday strolls. Despite the fact it offers little warmth, it seems everyone is enjoying the rare bout of winter sunshine.

Inside the cafe, the radio plays softly beneath the chatter of baristas and cafegoers alike. The ring of the bell above the door has me turning my head in its direction. I raise a hand to signal my father, although it seems unnecessary as he's already heading my way.

"Carter," my father says as he reaches the table. "Good to see you, son."

I stand, embracing him in a brief hug. "Good to see you too."

If my father were twenty-five years younger, there's no doubt he, Teddy and I would look like triplets. With his dark, salt and peppered hair—no doubt from the efforts of helping my mother raise my siblings and me—and deep green eyes flecked with shards of gold, there's no mistaking who we belong to.

My father pulls his chair out, the wooden legs scraping lightly on the timber floors. We both take a seat. Neither of us need the menu to know what we'd like; we've ordered the same thing for years—a large Americano and an eggs Benedict each.

The waitress, a pretty blonde, approaches our table with a small smile. "Hello, gentlemen; the usual?"

A chuckle escapes my father. "Do we really come here that often?"

Grinning, the waitress replies, "I think your visits and my shifts happen to coincide often." She turns to me, and a faint blush pinkens her cheeks.

"The usual will be perfect, thank you, Kate," I respond, reading her nametag. If she knows our orders, the least I can do is address her by name.

"Won't be long." The apples of Kate's cheeks deepen in colour before she returns to the counter.

My father's eyes bore into me. "Yes?" I ask, amused.

"Oh, nothing." He raises his brows, a smirk on his lips.

"Spit it out." This turns the smirk into another chuckle.

"Our lovely waitress, Kate, seemed quite taken with you," he responds.

It's my turn to raise my brows as I give my eyes a small roll. "This again?"

My father beams widely at me, his dimples on full display. "Don't be like that, Son, I'm trying to look out for you. If your mother were here, she'd already have given young Kate your number."

"In that case, thank god she's still away at her girls' weekend retreat," I reply with a smirk.

My father's smile grows smaller, his eyes now less vapid. "Carter, you've been single for almost four years now. Don't you want to share your life with someone? The support would be of great benefit to your impending life changes."

I let out a small sigh, unnoticed by my father. This isn't the first time I've heard this speech in some form or another, nor is it the last I'll hear of it. Since separating from my ex, both of my parents—and occasionally one or both siblings—often bring up my relationship status, or lack thereof. I haven't been in a committed relationship since. Although they're all aware of my reasons, I suspect they'd like me to find my 'person'.

I look him in the eye, giving him a small smile. "I appreciate your concern, Dad, I do, but I promise you I'm happy."

We were raised to address our parents as Mother and Father, but I decided to call him Dad when it's the two of us.

His gaze roams over my face, searching for a flicker of anything other than happiness. I hold my smile while he does so. Seeming to have found what he was looking for, his eyes soften at the corners when he locks them on mine once more.

"You didn't answer my question though, Son."

I pause. He's correct; I purposely evaded the 'don't you want to share your life with someone' part because I simply can't lie to him. I would love to share my life with someone, but that someone won't be found by having my family attempt to chat them up on my behalf. Despite my dad's best efforts, these things can't be rushed.

"I know."

He gives a small nod, and it's the only confirmation I need to know he understands. We had many difficult conversations over my teenage years. Difficult in the sense I offered up very little, and my father was left to work the rest out on his own. The benefit of that is now he knows what I mean, even when I don't say it.

A different waitress brings out our coffee and meals, and we eat in comfortable silence. I'm finishing the last of my eggs when my father softly clears his throat.

"Do you remember your mother and my friend, Annette? From university?" My father pauses, waiting for my affirmative response. "Her daughter Molly is a couple of years younger than you and has recently returned to the UK after studying abroad."

I look blankly at him, so he presses on.

"Molly has recently started teaching at Winnie's school, and she recognised your brother at pick up yesterday. The two of them had a quick catch-up and the topic of your relationship status came up."

I groan inwardly, retaining the blank expression on my face.

"Any who, Molly seemed quite interested in hearing about the grown-up Carter once Teddy mentioned you hadn't. She gave him her number in the hopes you'd contact her if you were interested in seeing her."

Molly is beautiful, there's no denying that. She was one of those cute children you *knew* would grow up to be something remarkable. That's where my knowledge of her ends. I haven't known Molly since we were children. I only know what she looks like because of the handy little thing that is social media.

Being well known in the media, whilst beneficial for my law career at the time, has its downfalls. I have women throw themselves at me all the time, but it's only ever really for one reason: money. This is partly why I haven't bothered to form anything real these past few years. You can never truly tell if someone is interested in you as a person or what your bank account holds.

Annette is a lovely woman, and I imagine anyone raised by her would be nothing less. Do I really have anything to lose by agreeing to a date with Molly?

"I'll have Teddy pass on her number," I say in a somewhat resigned tone and hope he doesn't catch it.

My father almost jumps from his seat as he rips his phone from his trouser pocket. "Oh, this is excellent! I must tell your mother."

"Calm down, old man, you'll give yourself a heart attack."

This earns me a well-deserved slap to the shoulder. I flash him a megawatt smile in return.

"You can be such a pest sometimes, Carter."

Still beaming at Dad, I rest my elbows on the table, placing my chin against my clasped hands. "I know."

The waitress who served our food returns to clear our table. We say our thanks and pay before heading towards the door. My father places a hand on my shoulder as we walk. The bell chimes once more as we exit onto the street, and my dad receives a text as we begin wandering down the footpath. He looks up at me with a sad smile. "Son, I'll have to cut this morning short. That's your mother saying she's arrived at Annette's."

Pulling each other in for a quick hug, we say our goodbyes. As my father's figure retreats down a cobblestone street, my phone pings in from within my pocket.

I chuckle to myself as I read the incoming message.

BIG TED

Excellent choice, brother.

The message is accompanied by a number. I should've known Dad would get to him before I had a chance. I fight the urge to roll my eyes at Teddy's message.

Fuck it, I've got nothing to lose.

ME

Hey Molly, it's Carter Lawrence. If you're not busy on Saturday morning, perhaps we could grab a coffee?

I hit send before I can change my mind. As I go to put my phone in my pocket once more, the text tone sounds again.

MOLLY

Hey Cart, so lovely to hear from you! I'm free Saturday; it's a date x

I take a deep breath.
I have a date on Saturday.
This is a good thing, right?

Chapter 4

Lara

The day the girls told me Satan was moving out was the day I made the decision I would move to London. More specifically, I'd move in with Harper and Mia —they just didn't know yet.

I'd always known my father was born in the UK and therefore a citizen, but he moved to Australia as a child. I'd never thought much of it, especially given our rocky relationship, except how cool it must have been.

Not once in my twenty-seven years did I think my dual citizenship would benefit me by allowing me to move there myself. I've loosely planned to live there for nine months, but with no set return date, I'm open to going wherever the wind takes me—who knows what might happen over time. As the girls aptly pointed out previously, I don't have much keeping me in Australia. I'm ready for a fresh start, and hopefully London will provide that.

As I sit on my bed, waiting for the girls to join our Weekly Debrief call, I go over exactly how I'm going to deliver the news.

Does it matter that I've already done this approximately ten times in the hour leading up to this, as well as countless times over the past two months? Absolutely not. Do I continue to agonise over it until the last second, when none of the planned words will come out, and instead, I'll blurt it out at the first opportunity? Absolutely.

The familiar sound of a FaceTime call rings out through my quiet apartment, and the nerves shoot around my body. With a slightly shaky hand, I answer.

"Lara! Hi!" The girls beam at me through the screen of my phone, and I mirror their smiles.

"Hello, my loves," I respond, taking them in. They're both in pyjamas, which is odd. Harper is always dressed by the time our calls happen, normally having been to a pilates or boxing class prior.

"Harps, are you sick? You're still in pyjamas at seven in the morning."

The girls' smiles falter. They exchange a brief look before turning back to me, locking eyes through the screen and the thousands of miles separating us.

My brows furrow. "Is everything okay?"

A weak smile returns to Harper's face, but it lacks her usual fervent. "We're okay."

"Well, we aren't *really* okay," Mia interrupts, "but Harp's isn't unwell. We only have a month until Satan leaves, and we have no prospective replacements for her."

My heart thumps quicker in my chest, but I say nothing.

"I've taken the day off so we can look into other apartments. It's seeming more and more likely we'll need to find somewhere else to live without a third person."

Seeing the sadness in their eyes makes me want to cry for them. The girls love their apartment. I can only imagine the heartache this is causing them. Luckily for them, I can fix this.

"But if you had a third person, you could stay, *right*?" I ask hesitantly.

This time it's Mia who gives me a sad smile. I want to reach through the screen and squeeze her tight. "We could, but Lars, we've spent two months searching, and we can't find anyone."

"I might know someone."

"You know other people?" Mia questions. Harper lets out a loud chuckle as I feign hurt.

"Ouch Mia, do you really think I'm *that* much of a loser?" Laughter ripples through me as I fail to keep a straight face.

"I was asking if you know other people in *England*, you knob."

A chorus of laughs rings out through my little apartment, momentarily making me feel less alone.

"No, I do not."

The girls tilt their heads slightly, the way dogs do when they're trying to understand what the fuck you're attempting to convey. As if hearing my thoughts, Harper speaks.

"Lara, what are you trying to say?"

"Well, when I say I may know someone, the someone I'm referring to may or may not be the person you're talking to right now." I grin despite the severe anxiety gnawing at my insides as I await their reactions.

I watch their faces intently, witnessing the moment my words sink in. A pause to process. Then, as expected, they both have completely opposite reactions to one another. What surprises me though is they each have the reaction I expected from the other.

Harper, ever the picture of poise, *squeals*. A full-blown, ear-splitting squeal that's sure to startle anyone within a 5km radius. Jumping up from her spot on their bay window, she disappears off camera. She hasn't gone far though, her excited cheers still blasting through my speakers.

Mia, on the other hand, appears to be shocked into silence. A look of pure dumbfoundment covers her facial features as she stares at me.

"Mia, are you still with me?" I ask loudly, fighting to be heard over Harper, who's reappeared in the frame.

Before Mia can respond, Harper pulls her into the most passionate bear hug ever witnessed. Caught off guard only momentarily, Mia bursts into hysterics, her smile wide.

I have to fight to blink back the tears threatening to surface as I watch the ecstasy on the girls' faces. It cements that I've made the right call; I'm moving to London.

Once all composures are regained, Harper and Mia proceed to question me on every major and minor detail of my decision, including my family's reactions to the news.

"So you've mentioned your mum and brother were super excited for you, once your mum got past her initial concerns, of course. Have you told your dad?" Harper asks, a small note of hesitation in her voice.

I smile weakly at the girls before answering. "No, not yet. It's been a while since we've spoken. I'll tell him when he calls next." Even as I spoke the words, I didn't truly believe them.

The girls return my smile, nodding slowly in understanding. My father and I, while we love each other, have somewhat of a strained relationship. We have since I was old enough to understand the breakdown behind my parents' divorce. You can't help but see someone in a different light after learning the way in which they broke your family.

Sensing the negative turn of energy, Harper chirps up and suggests we book my ticket to London right here on the call. The buzz of excitement we all feel right now is palpable. Fifteen minutes later, the call ends, and I have a one-way ticket to Heathrow.

Three months passed in a whirlwind of chaos. Between Christmas festivities, New Year's Eve celebrations, farewells, and too many hangovers to count safely, time flew by in a haze.

As March rolled around and my departure date loomed, I began to pack. Thanks to Mia, I had a part-time job lined up for me at a new and used bookstore near my new home. I'll be starting there a few days after I arrive. I still have *no* idea what Mia told the owner in order for her to hire me, but when we spoke the other week, she seemed elated to have me.

You'd think it would be difficult to pack up your first apartment, but I didn't experience that. Mum insisted it was because I still used my bedroom at home as a storage facility, but I prefer to believe I've succeeded in living minimally.

Except, of course, when it came to my library. Packing those suckers was an absolute nightmare, and I'm still concerned they won't all make it to the UK safely. Bubble-wrapped and nestled between every sweater I own, four of the five suitcases accompanying me on my travels are filled with books. It was a challenge, but the smut made it on the plane.

Sitting in the departure lounge of Dubai Airport, I still cannot *believe* the adventure I'm embarking on—one hell of a whim decision.

The chime over the speakers pulls my wandering mind back to attention.

"All remaining passengers of Emirates flight EK31 to London Heathrow are invited to board through Gate 52. Thank you."

Looking down at my boarding pass, I take a deep breath.

This is it.

London, here I come.

Chapter 5

Carter

"Well, good morning, sir."

"Dex, you bastard, cut your shit."

It's been two months since I took over as CEO of J. L. & Sons at the start of January, and I've had the absolute displeasure of beginning each of those days with my best friend greeting me as 'sir' the second he sees me every morning. I'm all for a bit of a dom/sub vibe every now and then, but preferably not from my best mate.

I turn my chair around and see him leaning against my doorframe, a cocky grin on his face. His piercing blue eyes glint with his grin; most women would kill for the thick lashes that line them. Having grown his beard out to a style reminiscent of Captain America in Avengers: Infinity War—and given that he shares the same hair colour as Chris Evans—my best mate looks every bit the heartbreaker. He's 6ft 2 inches of muscle, so he practically takes up the entire doorframe.

"You're very good-looking Dex, but you're simply not my type," I say calmly as he moves to enter my office. I close the diary I'd been meticulously filling out with the day's meetings and to-do list.

"Yeah right arsehole, I'm everyone's type," Dex responds with a smirk, strolling in. He takes the seat across from my desk, propping his foot up on the corner like he owns the place.

What I wouldn't give to wipe that smug expression off his face.

"You are one cocky son of a bitch," I say with a grin, throwing his foot off my desk.

"Alright boss, what's new?" Dex supports himself on his elbows, chin resting on his fists like an enthralled child.

Since my first day in charge, Dex has come to my office every morning to check in on me. Our meetings—using the term loosely—typically feature some shit-talking, followed by a review of the previous day's work. We finish off with a rundown of what's happening in the firm at present and then grab a coffee from the Pret down the street.

Dexter 'Dex' Ford, also known as *major pain in the arse*, and I met during our first year at Cambridge. We spent many nights studying and drinking, one more so than the other during the early years.

He's now one of the best lawyers on our staff, which is one of the many reasons I plan to promote him. He's worked his arse off to be the best lawyer he can be, and it's pretty fucking cool that my new position gives me a chance to reward that.

We go through the cases each of our staff is currently working on, checking progress and updates from each associate. Once Dex has finished going over his current client cases, I decide there's no time like the present to bring up the promotion.

"I know you've had a massive caseload these past couple of months since I stepped away from cases, but you've also had an excellent track record. How are you finding it all?" I watch the ghost of a smile pass over his face at his acknowledgement of my complimentary words.

Dex straightens up, removing his elbows from the desk and placing his folded hands in his lap. He's sensed a shift in the conversation, and I appreciate how he's slid right into business mode.

"Honestly man, I've loved every second."

I don't doubt he means every word as he replies.

"I've been busier than ever, and some days are tougher than others, but I love this shit. I love my job," Dex adds. The way his face lights up as he speaks about his job cements that what I'm about to propose is the right decision for both Dex and our firm.

"Your passion for your career doesn't go unnoticed." I offer my friend a gentle smile, which he returns.

"Thanks Carter, that means a lot. I'm always grateful for your father taking a chance on a law grad, and I'll always bust my arse to prove he made the right decision."

"I know you will, Dex. That's why I'd like to offer you the position of Senior Associate, as well as being the Manager for Junior Associates. I know it's a lot of responsibility and an even bigger commitment, so please take your time to think it over." From the corner of my desk, I locate a manilla folder and remove the contract I had Anna from HR make up in my second week as CEO. I've never doubted Dex.

Handing Dex the contract, our eyes lock briefly. Admiration and gratitude shine in his gaze. I don't say anything, afraid of ruining the moment. Dex's smile widens as I grin at him.

"You're serious?" he asks, his mouth slightly agape as he tries to determine the level of sincerity.

"Dead serious, brother. You're one of our biggest assets, and it's time you stepped up. I need a faithful lackey by my side." My grin morphs into more of a smirk, and Dex lets out a chuckle as he swipes at my still outstretched hand before he grabs it and shakes.

"As long as I can still call you Sir, I'm in."

"I never told you to call me that, you dick. You made that decision all on your own."

"In that case, the decision stands. Pleasure doing business."

And with that, Dex rises, flashes me a devilish smile, and leaves my office. The door closes with a soft click, and I smile to myself.

The rest of the day flies by in a blur of financial reports, meetings, and catching up with each of our associates. Before I know it, it's 5:15pm and Teddy's calling to see where I am. We made plans to grab a drink after work and I was supposed to meet him down the road fifteen minutes ago.

"Teddy, sorry, lost track of time," I say while placing my brother on speaker so I can pack up for the night.

"You sure you're not trying to stand me up?" Teddy asks, and I hear the smile he's wearing through his voice.

"Positive. Besides, you have too many friends in high places. I'd be a fool to piss you off."

Teddy's deep rumble of a laugh makes me smile.

"Correct. So, are you on your way?"

I gather up the last of my files and paperwork as I respond. "About to be. I'll see you in five."

Teddy says a quick goodbye before hanging up.

Five minutes later, I'm walking through the pub door. I spot my brother ahead on a table with high bar stools talking to a tall, pretty blonde who I don't recognise. Teddy is mid-conversation when he spots me near the door.

Leaning in, he places his hand on the small of her back. He

whispers something in her ear before placing a light kiss on her cheek. Smiling at him, she gives him a small nod and walks away. Teddy ushers me over with a wave of his hand.

I walk over to my brother, clapping him on the back and pulling him in for a quick embrace. "Who's the lucky lady?" I ask, a smirk on my lips.

Teddy gives me a sly grin, turning towards the bar. He raises two fingers in the direction of Olly, the bar owner, who nods before grabbing our usual beer pick and wandering over.

"Here you go, lads." Olly's northern accent thickens on the last word. We thank him, receiving a salute in response as he makes his way over to the next customer.

"Wouldn't you like to know," Teddy finally replies in a sing-song voice.

I stare daggers at my brother, which only causes him to chuckle. Knowing I won't stop until I get an answer, Teddy lets out a sign before he continues. "An old friend I haven't seen since high school. Her name is Margot, if you must know."

"Interesting." I take a sip of my beer.

"Interesting?" he questions, another laugh on the tip of his tongue. "What the fuck is that supposed to mean?"

"Nothing, brother. You looked quite cosy, considering you haven't seen each other for about 13 years."

"You want to play that game, little brother?" Teddy takes a swig of his beer. "How's Molly?"

I've been waiting for this question. My first date with Molly was awkward at best, at least for me. The conversation felt stilted, and I had no idea what to talk to her about.

Molly, apparently, felt differently. A few days later, she'd asked me if I wanted to grab a drink, and I almost felt obligated, given how shit our first meeting was. It had been a little while since I'd been on a real date, and it showed. We caught up, I apologised for the terrible date, and we laughed it off.

"I wish I knew how to answer that question," I respond honestly, rubbing my thumb along the neck of my beer bottle. Teddy narrows his eyes on the action.

"You're doing the thing, Cart. What's up?"

I exhale a small breath before looking at my brother. "Molly is great Teddy, she is, but something is off. We've been on numerous dates these past few months, but it's nothing more than friendship on my side." It feels good to give a voice to my thoughts. "She's nice enough, and obviously beautiful, but there's no *spark*." I continue.

"Hmm," Teddy hums, his eyes boring into me like he can see through my skin and directly into my thoughts. A man of few words at the most inconvenient of times. Feeling a little vulnerable, I break eye contact and instead take in my surroundings.

The pub's stone wall interior reminds me of a cottage; the fireplace below the mantle really sells the vibe. The heavy wooden door is adorned with wrought iron features, looking like it came straight from a Scottish castle. The bar runs the length of the left-hand side, and bottles of every spirit under the sun line the wall behind it. Provincial-style wall sconces provide a majority of the light, giving it the sort of ambience you'd expect in the Cotswolds. There's just something about the cosy pub that brings me comfort.

My eyes return to Teddy. With his arms crossed on top of the table and brows dipped in thought, he looks every bit the wise older brother in this moment.

"Any words of wisdom, or just hums?"

Teddy straightens before leaning into the low back of his stool. With his arms now crossed against his chest, he gives me a small smile.

"She could be the most wonderful person you've met, but it

means nothing if you don't feel a connection on a deeper level, Cart."

Damn him and his fucking wisdom.

I suppress a laugh. Not because what my brother said is funny, but because he's unnervingly spot on.

Trying to lighten the mood, as usual, I respond, "Shit, Theodore, no need to go all therapist on me."

My words have the desired effect: Teddy's facial expression warps into a harsh scowl. It's not that he doesn't like his full name; he just prefers Teddy when it comes to the people he holds close. Theodore makes him feel like he's in trouble.

The scowl pointed in my direction only deepens when I let out a chuckle.

"Way to deflect, you shit."

My chuckle turns into a deep belly laugh at this, and it only takes a few passing seconds before Teddy joins in.

Sitting at my very empty dining table the following morning, I rest my head in my palms, running my hands over my face once, twice, before clasping them together and resting my chin on them. An internal deliberation begins to take place between my head and my heart.

The last thing I want to do is lead Molly on, but I fear that's exactly what I'll be doing if we continue to see each other.

But on the same token, the old saying goes, 'good things take time', right?

What if Molly and I could have something special, and I'm about to fuck it up because I didn't let it play out long enough?

Five minutes later, I come to a decision. There's a 50:50 chance I've made the wrong one, but at least I've chosen.

She answers within three rings.

"Hey Carter, how are you?" Her tone is light, the smile evident through her voice, and I'm hit with a pang of guilt over the impending conversation.

"Good thanks Molly, yourself?"

This conversation already feels uncomfortably stiff.

"Excellent to hear. What can I do for you?" Molly asks. I'm thankful she's managed to be direct when all I'm currently capable of is small talk. I rub my hand over my jaw, contemplating how to proceed. Fuck, I should've thought about this before I hit call.

"Would you perhaps like to grab a coffee on Monday morning?" Restless with anxiety, my knee bounces up and down of its own accord. "My first meeting isn't until ten, so we'd be able to sit and have a chat."

"As lovely as that sounds, unfortunately I'm not able to on Monday," Molly responds. Before I can reply, she continues. "If by *a* chat, you happen to mean *the* chat, I think we're on the same page."

I'm taken by surprise at Molly's admission. We chat for the next few minutes, and by the time I'm hanging up the call, a weight has lifted off my shoulders.

It turns out Molly had been feeling the exact same way but didn't know how to call it quits when it was her who'd instigated this in the first place. We laughed at how silly we both sounded, too scared to communicate with each other. Let this be a lesson on the importance of communication.

We wish each other the best, but neither of us utters the classic "let's stay friends" phrase. Frankly, it's unnecessary. There's little chance we'll see each other again. We don't see one another organically out and about.

Feeling lighter than I have in weeks, I bring up the text thread with my siblings. The current conversation between Emmy and Teddy brings a smile to my face.

BIG TED

Em, are you trying to kill me?

EMMY

What's troubling you biggest brother?

BIG TED

You know very well "what's troubling me",
you heathen. You sent my daughter home
with the highest of sugar highs!

EMMY

In my defence, she's quite hard to say no to.

BIG TED

ME

I hate to break up this sibling bonding, but
I've got news

The speech bubbles pop up a second after I hit send. Two replies come through at the same time.

BIG TED

What did you do?

EMMY

Lord have mercy. What have you done?

My eyes threaten to roll back into my brain. They always assume the worst. *Arseholes.* I lean my elbows on the table and type out a response.

ME

Why do you both assume I've done
something?

Don't answer that.

BIG TED

Did you do something?

ME

Well yes, but not the point

I ended things with Molly

EMMY

I'm proud of you Cart. If it wasn't working, it wasn't working. We just want you to be happy, right Teddy?

BIG TED

I wouldn't mind marrying him off fairly quickly, so perhaps he'll annoy someone other than me. But yes, I suppose we do want you to be happy too, little brother.

I let out a groan, but my lips pull into a smile. Siblings really are simultaneously the best and worst things in existence.

ME

Emmy, I love you.

Teddy, you're a wanker.

BIG TED

EMMY

Aren't you a little old for emojis?

BIG TED

I laugh as I lock my phone and place it on the table.

Chapter 6

Lara

This still doesn't feel real. Have I really just landed in *London?* Is it truly my new home for the foreseeable future? These questions play on an endless loop as I slowly make my way through customs and security with the other thousand people arriving in London today.

Moving almost robotically, like cows in a milking line, the masses make their way through the welcome doors ahead of me. As I pass over the threshold, an overstuffed backpack over my shoulder and two books in my arms—because one is *never* enough—I hear shouting.

From a distance, the shouting is indiscernible. I'm continuing my leisurely stroll into the terminal when the shouts sound again. I'm closer this time and can make out the word.

"Yoohoo!"

Who the fuck bought the guy from *Frozen?*

The shout comes again, louder still. Curiosity gets the better of me. I look around the arrivals hall, and that's when I see it. Harper and Mia are standing on a bench near the back of the room. Above their heads in lettering I'm certain would be visible from Mars is a sign reading 'THAT'S MY GIRL' in hot pink glitter.

A squeal rings out through the airport when Mia's eyes find mine, and all eyes turn towards my ridiculous friends.

My cheeks ache from how hard I'm smiling, even though they've embarrassed the shit out of me. The two of them look like absolute nut cases, but fuck, I love them. I pick up my pace, running at them as best I can with my monstrosity of a backpack in tow.

"Lara!" the girls yell in unison as they meet me halfway. Dumping my backpack in the nick of time, Mia launches herself at me. Thank god the girl is only 5ft with a tiny frame—she hits me with force. My attempt to catch her fails, and Harper collides with us.

The three of us hit the ground as one, resembling a twisted pile of limbs. Laughter bursts from all of us, mine almost hysteric. This *is* real.

I awaken with a start. Bolting upright, a level of uncertainty about my surroundings washes over me. I close my eyes and take a deep breath, calming my breathing before I burst a lung. Slowly opening my eyes, I take in the space.

It's dark. Heavy curtains hang drawn across a window to my left, rays of sunlight fighting a losing battle to break through the small gaps. A large, empty, built-in bookcase stands opposite me. Directly in front sits suitcases containing everything I own, waiting to be rehomed. My eyes roam to my right, and I see the entryway to my wardrobe and ensuite bathroom. The barn-style bedroom door next to this is closed, and I hear nothing but silence beyond it.

After my breathing and heart rate are under control, I lie back down. Staring at the ceiling, I grin to myself.

I'm home. My *new* home.

Feeling calmer than I did a few moments ago, I grab my phone off the bedside table. Damn, it's 8:00am already. My feet drag across the floor as I make my way into my ensuite, and shudder when I see my reflection. Good god I need a shower, and perhaps a makeover. Mascara smudges underline my eyes, complimenting the bags perfectly. My hair, which had been nicely curled yesterday, now gives off Hagrid vibes rather than the desired Hermione at the Yule Ball.

Mia and Harper are off work today to help me unpack and settle in like the good little housemates they are. We're hoping between the three of us, we can get most of it sorted today, leaving the weekend for sightseeing. Listening out, I'm greeted only by silence. I take that as a sign to have a quick shower and attempt to fix this mess.

The heat of the water streaming over my hair and down my body warms me from the inside out. I'll regret washing my hair as soon as I'm out and spending half an hour blow-drying it, but right now, it's exactly what I need.

Wrapping a towel around myself, I pop my earphones in and hit play on my current audiobook. Zade is doing unspeakable things to some lowlife as I stroll into the kitchen and run smack bang into Mia, who just stepped back from the cupboard.

"Ah!" Mia screams, and a cloud of flour plumes around us. It miraculously managed to miss our bodies, but it did hit almost every surrounding surface.

We stare at each other with wide eyes for a moment before bursting into laughter. Mia's mouth hangs open as the laughter bursts from her in fits.

"Jesus fuck, you scared the crap out of me," I respond, flour particles floating around us like snowfall.

As we pull ourselves together, Harper enters the kitchen and stops dead. Her eyes widen for a moment as they roam over the flour, settling back on us. Surprising me, Harper breaks into a wide grin. She lets out a slightly unhinged laugh before walking over to us.

"What on earth did you two do? I leave for five minutes to pick up coffees, and you've redecorated our kitchen as a winter wonderland."

The three of us spend the next 15 minutes cleaning up our mess, all still laughing at our mishap. I'm still trying to remember the events of last night, but I'm coming up blank.

"Gals, I have a problem."

Two pairs of eyes shoot in my direction as Mia and Harper pause, their brows dipping in confusion in unison.

"What the hell happened last night?" I ask. "The last thing I remember is dumping all of my belongings in my room, and then it's blank."

A moment passes, and both the girls grin. Harper breaks the silence.

"Lara, hon, that's because you passed out moments after."

"Welcome to jet lag, baby!" Mia adds, giving me a cheesy wink.

I've experienced jet lag previously, but damn it hit differently this time. I must have slept around 12 hours, which I've never done. I don't even think I slept that long as a child. Actually, I definitely didn't. My mother has spent many years reminding me of what a painful, sleepless child I was. A night owl from day one.

After a quick breakfast of homemade pancakes, courtesy of Mia and her latest fixation on cooking, we spend the rest of the day unpacking as much of my stuff as possible. By the time 6 o'clock comes around, we've achieved a lot: my books are restored to their former glory within the bookshelf, the smut, of course, having pride of place; my walk-in wardrobe is bursting at the seams from the sheer number of coats it's holding. For someone who lived where it rarely went below 20 degrees, I certainly own a ridiculous number of coats.

Exhaustion gets the better of me, and before I know it, it's 8 o'clock and I'm back in bed. As I snuggle into the blankets, I sigh. It's been a long and tiring twenty-four hours, but it's also been incredible. My cheeks hurt from the amount of laughter they've released. A sobering thought enters my mind: I don't remember the last time I laughed so many times in such a small time frame. Being around Mia and Harper has me embracing a carefree feeling, a feeling that's somewhat foreign to me.

The past six months have been a mental battle, to say the least. My friends back home are incredible, but they're all beginning to head down their own paths. Don't get me wrong, I'm so proud of them and endeavour to be each of their #1 cheerleader. But some days, it's harder to do so than others.

I've felt so lost recently, living day to day. I'd find myself always being the first to reach out in my friendships, whether it was to check in or to make plans. Every so often, I wouldn't. What happened then? We wouldn't speak until I gave in and reached out eventually. I know and understand we all have our own lives and our own priorities, but it sucked to feel like they were higher on my priority list than I was on theirs.

I've only been here one day, but it feels like it's *meant to be.*

Chapter 7

Lara

"Wakey, wakey!" a sweet voice booms. Hearing footsteps approach, I roll onto my right side and peek through my lashes to get a view of the culprit. My eyes widen when the door swings open to reveal Mia. Of the three of us, she's the least likely to be awake first, like, ever.

As Mia leans her shoulder against my door frame, I drag myself into a sitting position, rubbing my eyes. I check my watch and almost gasp. "Are you ill?" I ask. "It's only seven o'clock. Isn't your body clock set to nine at the earliest?" Mia scowls, and I grin.

She's already dressed and ready to go. It must be a reasonably chilly day outside because she's wearing a pair of beige corduroy trousers paired with her favourite chunky white sneakers and a soft pink sweater. If the locals are in trousers and sweaters, I'll be wrapped up top to toe in seven layers.

"I'll have you know I'm up before nine most days, thank you," Mia retorts, mirroring my grin. "Now, get up. Places to go! Tourists to check out!"

"I didn't move across the other side of the world to check out tourists, Mia. Take me to the hot Brits." This has Mia rolling her eyes and trying to restrain a laugh.

"Honey, you'll have plenty of time to see all the eligible bachelors the UK has to offer now that it's your home," Mia responds.

Harper's head appears over Mia's shoulder. She's curled her hair today and has on a light face of makeup. She looks so effortlessly stunning. Harper could pass as a tourist herself with her bronzed skin, uncommon for most Brits. I can see the top of a blue turtleneck knit peeking out from above Mia's shoulder.

Since the beginning of our friendship, Harper and Mia have been aware of my love for English men. I blame the likes of Henry Cavill and Tom Hardy for my obsession. Of course, I can't speak of hot British men without mentioning Orlando Bloom and Jude Law, circa mid-2000s. Thanks Mum for introducing me to the Lord of the Rings at a young age; it truly helped to shape my taste in men.

Perhaps it's because I have one, but I simply do not like Australian accents. Nine times out of ten, they sound bogan—the equivalent of America's low country-type accents for those unfamiliar—and I've yet to hear an attractive Australian accent. As a child, I used to tell my mother I'd endeavour to marry a British man so my children would have his accent. Failing that, I'd fake a British accent for their early years while their own real British accents developed as a result. If that doesn't show dedication to the cause, I don't think anything will.

"You make an excellent point, Harps. Alright you two, give me half an hour, and we'll be off. What time is the bus?"

We've bought tickets for one of the double-decker tourist buses, and I can't wait. I've visited London twice previously, but both were short trips. We have a whole day of sightseeing planned; I'm so grateful to the girls for being tourists in their own city with me.

"The bus will pick us up down the street at eight-thirty sharp, but we're visiting the bookstore first, remember?" Mia responds.

"Oh, I forgot! Okay, go, go. Let me get ready," I reply, hastily clambering out of bed and shooing the girls out of my bedroom.

I quickly dress in my favourite pair of jeans and throw on a red chunky knit over a cute thermal top. I pull on a pair of brown boots and hurry into the bathroom. My hair is in its natural state of dead straight, which works to my advantage as it requires absolutely no effort. I put on a light layer of makeup and accessorise with gold earrings and my favourite Burberry scarf.

Making my way out into the kitchen, I find the girls waiting for me with a homemade caramel iced latte and two slices of raisin toast. The sight makes me giggle. I forget I may have only lived here for a few days, but they've known me far longer.

After devouring our coffees and breakfasts, we set off. The cool air bites at my skin the second I step out of our building, and I'm thankful for the thermal undershirt. The bookstore, and my new place of work, is a few blocks over and a short five-minute walk. Chapter Nine Bookstore, aptly named given the building is #9, is a delightful place.

The store doesn't open until a little later, but we wanted to test out the walk and have a look from the street. The large bow windows lining the front of the store allow for the stray rays of sun to cast a glow on the books nearest to them. The front door is housed underneath a beautiful old arch frame, painted white to match the window frames.

Through the windows and to the left lie rows and rows of books, with aisles taller than most people. To the right is the counter, and nestled just beyond against the far wall is a little reading nook. It looks cosy, filled with bean bags, throw pillows and blankets.

We spend the rest of the day touring around London like typical tourists. The day's itinerary begins in Central London, visiting Big Ben, who I have affectionately dubbed Biggie. The refurbishments have finally finished, and Biggie is finally visible in all his glory. Why Biggie, you may ask, because who the fuck nicknames a global icon? Let's say one of the girls back home had a particularly questionable past with someone of a similar name. We don't speak of said person, and therefore, Biggie's real name seemed inadequate. Don't tell the locals; they'll have my head. Harper and Mia already stare daggers at me anytime I utter the nickname, and those two are scary enough.

After we've taken far too many pictures, we head over to Buckingham Palace. The last time I visited, the Common-wealth had a Queen, so it's a bittersweet feeling being here knowing there's no Lizzie. Not that she was within the palace walls when I last visited, but you get the point.

Continuing on with our quest to fill our camera rolls in one day, we take ample pictures at the gates and in the surrounding gardens. The day is filled with laughter, screams of joy, more steps than any of us were prepared for, and so much smiling. My heart is so full as we pass by places like the London Eye, St. Paul's Cathedral, and The Shard. Before we know it, we're on the bus once more and heading to our last stop of the day—Tower Bridge and the Tower of London.

We're sitting along the back row of the top deck, driving down Upper Thames Street with the Millennium Bridge to our right, and I have a little moment.

"Thank you, guys, for being tourists with me this weekend, it wouldn't have been nearly as fun alone."

Reaching my hands out to grasp each of theirs, I give Mia and Harper a teary-eyed smile and squeeze. They squeeze my hands in return, and we sit like that for a moment.

"As if we'd be anywhere else, Lars," Harper responds, grinning at me as the tears welling up in her eyes match my own.

"This has easily been one of the best days I've had in a long time," Mia adds. "Is it too early to start planning weekend trips away? There's so much of the UK we want to show you.

"And Europe!" Harper adds, leaning in closer to be heard over the hustle and bustle of the street below. "We can take the Eurostar to Amsterdam and Paris and venture out on our own from there."

The rest of the weekend is a blur of more pictures, cheesy grins, and laughs. Sunday brings Kings Cross Station and all of the Harry Potter sightseeing one could wish for. Madame Tussauds was also a highlight. Pictures with Captain America, the Star Wars cast, and the royals fill my camera roll, and I have no regrets.

The tourist weekend ends at the British Museum, pretending we know what the hell we're talking about when it comes to fine arts.

It's been the most wonderful weekend with the girls. Who knew being a tourist in your own new home could be so fun?

Today is my first day at the bookstore and excited is an understatement. Getting paid to discuss books all day with fellow bookworms? Seeing new releases first? Setting up staff pick displays, genre and trope sections? Simply sounds too good to be true.

When I arrived this morning, I was a healthy mix of excited and nervous. Marissa, the owner and manager, met me at the door. She's a little lady, probably somewhere in her mid to late 70s. I knocked once on the glass door before her head popped out from behind the end of a shelf.

Marissa is the epitome of a bookstore owner. White hair pulled into a loose bun at the nape of her neck, round-framed glasses sitting atop her nose, and arms full of books.

Placing the books on the counter, Marissa approached the door to greet me.

"Oh, you must be Lara," she beamed. Thanks to the phone calls prior to my move, her voice was familiar and wrapped around me like a hug. She smelt of book pages and something of a floral nature, but I couldn't put my finger on what exactly. Perhaps jasmine or gardenia? I don't pretend to know much about flowers, but she smelt homely.

"I certainly am. It's lovely to finally meet you, Marissa," I responded, a warm smile pulling up my lips. Marissa pulled me into a hug, and I felt the nervous energy evaporate.

"Oh please, sweetie, call me Riss." Her small smile wrinkled the skin around her eyes. She led me inside, plucking a small tin with baking paper peeking out the sides from the countertop and holding it out to me. "Just a small first day treat," she'd said sweetly. My heart squeezed in my chest in response to the kind gesture, so similar to something my own grandmother would do.

Following a cup of tea together in the reading nook, we spent the next two hours touring the store and each of its genre sections. Riss had drawn a little mud map for me with the layout of the bookstore. It detailed where each genre could be found, as well as prominent subgenres that were often requested. The gesture made my detail-oriented heart sing.

The conversation flowed easily between us. So much so that hours later, I don't think the stupid grin I'm wearing has left my face once. Riss, declaring her faith in me, has stepped out for an hour or two to run some errands and pick us up some lunch.

Deciding to be proactive whilst she's out, I tour the different genres. Pen and paper in hand, I make a note of any shelves with space for three or more in their stack. While wandering, I can't help but pick up some of the newest arrivals. I take in a deep breath and inhale the divine scent of new books —an aroma I can never explain, yet everyone seems to understand.

Happy with my list, I walk through the archway behind the counter and into the back room. Piles and piles of books tower over me, desperately needing some rearranging. The stockroom will be the second thing I tackle when I get a spare few hours.

I grab a cart, place my list inside, and get to looking. A mere two books on the list are secured before I'm rudely interrupted by a loud rumbling coming from my stomach. I glance at my watch. Damn, it's only been 15 minutes since Riss left. I contemplate whether I can hold off, but my stomach decides for me as it lets out another rumble.

"Okay, okay," I mumble to myself, "we'll get a snack."

My sad excuse for a book cart stands abandoned as I walk over to the cubby holding my bag, trying to remember if I'd packed any sweet treats. I swear I hear angels sing when I spot the tin Riss had handed me earlier. The lid is barely off, but the sweet scent of shortbread wafts through the air and I'm almost salivating in response.

As I take my first bite and moan in satisfaction, the doorbell chimes.

Chapter 8

Carter

"Dex!" I shout. My left arm secures most of my weight as I lean out the door frame of my office, preparing to yell again if he doesn't appear in the next five seconds.

"Yes, sir!" his voice booms from down the corridor.

Moments later, Dex waltzes out of his office on the left and makes his way toward me, grinning from ear to ear.

"Dexter, you are a right bastard. Have I ever told you that?"

Now standing before me, Dex throws a soft punch at my shoulder. "Only every day since college, mate."

My eyes strain from the sheer force behind their roll, which sets off Dex's laughter.

"Before you started your shit, I was going to ask if you wanted some lunch," I say, turning to walk into my office and gesturing for Dex to follow, "but now I think I'll revoke the offer."

"Oh, Mr Lawrence, you wound me." Hand shooting to his chest, Dex lets out a groan. "How will I make it through the day?" He leans against the doorframe, his other arm flinging up and behind him in an overly extravagant gesture.

"Has anyone ever told you you're a fucking drama queen, Ford?" I can't stop the incoming smile from pulling at my lips. The man is a twat, but fuck, I love him like a brother.

Straightening up, Dex pulls his wallet out of his back pocket. He rummages for a moment, then removes a £5 note and throws it onto my desk.

"I'll take a Buffalo with a side of chips if that's where you're heading." A wink in my direction, and he's gone before the chuckle even leaves my mouth.

I'm apparently far too predictable because Dex correctly assumed I'd be heading to Honest Burgers to grab our lunch.

I take the bike to Camden. Parking here is shitty at the best of times, and frankly, I don't have time to deal with the lunchtime influx. Thankfully, I manage to find a parking spot for the bike right outside the burger shop. Removing my helmet, I look through the windows and assess the situation. It looks relatively busy inside, which means I feel no guilt in making a pitstop nearby until the line dies down.

There are two places I frequent in Camden: the first being Honest Burgers and the second being a little bookstore. It's no Waterstones, but its character is half the experience. I secure my helmet on my bike and head towards Chapter Nine. My phone buzzes in my back pocket. Sliding it out, I see my sister's name across the screen.

"Hi, little sis," I answer with a grin, rounding the corner.

We chat for a little as I continue walking. As I reach the bookstore door, Emilia finally reveals the reason for her call.

"So, how are you since ending it with Molly?"

I chuckle, feeling the corners of my eyes wrinkle. Trust my little sister to check in on me after a break up—if you could even call it that. "I'm doing just fine Emmy, but thank you for checking." The bell chimes above my head on entry, and I head down the first aisle.

I stroll aimlessly through the aisles, absent-mindedly picking up and putting back down books, vaguely aware there's no one behind the counter.

"Oh, Carts, are you sure?" The worry in her voice causes my heart to ache faintly.

"Certain. Don't you worry about me."

"Alright done. It's not you I'm worried about anymore." I let out a small laugh as she continues, her tone more humourous. "I'm just disappointed I won't have a sister anytime soon. But I suppose it's okay. I've got the girls, so they'll do for now. I do just want you to be happy though, you know that, right?"

Wandering over to the Staff Picks section near the front of the store, a small smile crosses my lips. "Always, Em."

"Okay good, be—"

Emilia doesn't have the chance to finish her sentence as I let out an obnoxious "Ha!"

"What was that for?" my sister asks, confusion apparent.

"I'm at the bookstore, and you won't believe what's on the Staff Picks shelf," I say, incredulous. I pick the book up carefully as if it will bite me if handled incorrectly.

"What is it?" Emilia asks.

"It's paper porn Emmy, right up your alley. What the fuck?"

Emilia's answering laugh carries through the phone.

"I'm not joking, Emilia. It has a half-naked man on the fucking cover, smack bang in the middle of the display."

My sister's laugh stops as she gasps. "Oh, those are always the spiciest!"

"You've got to be kidding me," I respond. This was certainly not Riss' doing, so who the fuck has she employed?

Obviously, someone with absolutely no respect for the written word.

Before Emilia replies, I see movement in my peripherals. Turning towards the counter, I lock eyes with the woman behind it. I've never seen her before, of that I am certain. No one would ever forget her if they had. My mouth is dry, and I audibly swallow.

My sister's voice breaks through my trance, and I hastily turn back to the shelf, returning the book to its place.

"Carter, I have to go, the pub is calling me. Love you, talk soon."

"Love you too," is all I manage before the call ends.

I turn back towards the counter, once again locking eyes with one of the most breathtaking women I've seen. Her face looks simultaneously young and mature; I'd guess she's somewhere in her early to mid-twenties.

She has delicate features, with perfectly straight brunette and blonde strands framing her face. Where the brunette section nearest the crown of her head is almost a chocolate brown, deep and smooth, the blonde ends are light and honey-like. Her lips are plump and pink, coated with a gloss that makes them look downright kissable; her mouth slightly agape. She's as caught off guard by me as I am by her.

Only her top half is visible, with the large counter obscuring my view of the rest of her. She isn't overly tall, perhaps 5ft. 4 inches. A bright red knit hides her shape, and dainty gold earrings hang from her earlobes. I can't quite make out what they say, but they appear to be words, or at least letters.

Realising I'm probably staring, I offer her a small smile. She returns it, picking up the book she had lying on the counter. I can see a bookmark in it, so I walk closer to her.

"What are you reading?" I ask. My hands rest on the

counter, and I lean my weight on them. Too late. I realise I probably appear as though I'm attempting to cage her in. Her eyes widen ever so slightly, and I wonder what's going through her mind.

"Oh, a romance book. It's probably not quite your style."

The accent surprises me. *She's Australian? Unexpected.*

"Try me." My lips pull into a broad smile, hers only half as wide.

"It's called Dirty Truths. It's my Staff Pick." The alluring woman in front of me gestures to the stand I'd been in front of moments ago, and the pieces fall into place.

My eyes flit to the ceiling, and I scoff. This makes sense now. Of course she's the one who picked it; Riss would never choose to show off something like that. I knew the blue-eyed beauty standing before me was too good to be true.

Her eyes widen again, and this time there's no questioning what she's thinking—she's shocked and, quite frankly, pissed. As quickly as they'd enlarged, they're now narrowing in on me.

"Excuse me?" Her brows drawn dangerously close together. I blink. Was my scoff not clear enough?

"You can't be serious," I say simply, gesturing toward the book.

"And why not?" She *is* serious. Jesus fucking Christ. I hadn't planned on getting into an argument about paper porn today, but it seems the universe had other plans for me.

"Well, for one," I begin, holding up a finger for each of my arguments. "That's hardly a book, let alone something that should be promoted as a Staff Pick. Secondly, it certainly is *not* a romance novel, and labelling it as such is insulting to the entire romance genre. Lastly," I say as my middle finger unfolds to meet my thumb and forefinger, "it's porn on paper."

The woman is still staring at me, her eyes only narrowing

further with each finger I raise. Once I finish, she relaxes the crease between her eyebrows and cocks her head sideways.

"Let me guess," she finally says, the corners of her lips pulling up in a condescending smirk. "You read classics?" With the way her tone rises at the end, I assume it's a question.

"Yes, I do. Is that a crime?"

This time, it's *her* throat emitting the scoff.

She doesn't speak. I watch as her eyes rake slowly and deliberately up my body before landing on my own. My dick twitches in my trousers, apparently under the impression this attention is a good thing.

Crossing her arms across her chest, she beams at me. "Well, that tells me all I need to know."

I drop down onto my elbows, my eye line almost level with hers. Her eyes are what caught my attention initially. From afar, they were striking. But up close? They're something else entirely—the most unusual shade of blue. They are icy blue nearest her pupils but have a surprisingly thick ring of ocean blue encompassing the irises. I've never seen anything like them before, and I'm mesmerised by her almost immediately.

"And what would that be?" I ask, my voice dropping ever so slightly. She must notice because I glimpse her breath hitch. It's almost indiscernible, but it's enough to draw my gaze to the slight parting of her lips.

My facial muscles strain under the pressure as I fight to keep my expression neutral. Returning the gesture, I let my own eyes lazily roam over the top half of her body.

Her chest rises and falls heavier than before. I don't let my gaze linger, instead returning to meet her eyes. I register the way her pupils have dilated dramatically, the darker blue ring around them almost non-existent.

Fuck me, she really is a sight.

I've met a lot of beautiful women in my 29 years, but

there's something about this one that has me captivated entirely. But that doesn't negate the fact she has absolutely no taste when it comes to literature, which simply won't do.

Straightening to her full—albeit still small—height, she keeps her eyes trained on mine. "The only men who are intolerant of open-door *romance* novels are those who are intimidated by them." The word romance is practically spat at me. This only makes me grin in return. One look at the way her face drops tells me that wasn't the desired outcome. *Game on.*

Breaking eye contact, I notice the name badge attached to her blouse.

Lara.

"Lara, this has been delightful."

I see the confusion in her eyes as I turn and make my way towards the door. Poor thing clearly forgot she's wearing a name badge.

As I exit, the cool air feels like a bucket of water being thrown in my face. It wasn't that warm in the store, was it? Making my way back down the street and towards the burger shop, I replay the last ten minutes in my mind.

What the fuck just happened? I don't remember the last time, if ever, I had such a reaction to a woman. She rendered me speechless for a moment, at least until she opened her mouth and defended the monstrosity that is smut.

Chapter 9

Lara

"Honey, I'm home!" I shout in a sing-song voice as I waltz through our apartment door. My voice gives off cheery vibes, which is ridiculous, given I feel anything but. What the fuck was with that guy at lunchtime? Anger rises within me, mixed with a warmth I don't appreciate. I need to debrief with the girls, pronto.

At first glance, the apartment appears empty. The open-plan kitchen, dining and living spaces are devoid of life. As I walk inside and make my way towards the bedrooms, I find the first signs of life. Coming to a stop outside Mia's door, I watch her for a moment. Back hunched, head low and hand moving at an incredible speed, I'm entranced as I watch Mia work.

From the doorway, I'm unable to see what she's working on, but my goodness, is she working hard. Trying my best not to scare the shit out of her, I rap my knuckles softly on the doorframe.

"Hey, Mia," I say with a wide smile as she turns to where I stand.

"Oh, Lara! I didn't hear you get home." She returns my

smile before quickly turning to her desk, hastily shuffling items around. "Give me two minutes to tidy this crap up, and I'll meet you and Harps on the lounge with a wine. We want to hear all about your first day!"

"Did I hear talk of wine?" A familiar voice calls from further down the hallway. We let out a laugh. Turning my head in the direction of Harper's room, I shout back to her.

"Loungeroom, two minutes!"

A smiling head pops out from a doorway down the hall, and Harper gives me a thumbs-up before disappearing.

Exactly two minutes later, Harps and I are sitting on the lounge as Mia brings us each a glass of wine. Mia returns to the kitchen to retrieve her own glass and sets herself down by my side with a plop. Harper and Mia angle themselves against the arm of the lounge, both sets of eyes on me.

"So!" Mia exclaims after taking a sip of her wine. "How was our little girl's first day?"

Harper and I let out a sigh, followed by a laugh, while Mia smiles at us. The first time I met the girls, Mia declared I was the baby of the group. Imagine her shock when I reminded her that although I'm blessed with a baby face, I am, in fact, a year older than her.

Mia decided she didn't care for the specifics and has referred to me as the baby ever since. I don't recall when it changed from the baby to their little girl, but it makes me laugh and groan every time.

"It was excellent. Riss is lovely, and the bookstore is a dream." Taking a sip of my own wine, I let out a small breath.

"There's a but, I can feel it," Harper chimes in, raising a brow.

"Majority of the customers were also lovely. Well, all but one." The girls don't say anything, so I continue. "There was this guy—no Mia, do not smile" — I raise a finger in warning —

"this is *not* a happy story, remember—this awful guy, who came in while Riss was out for lunch, basically attacked me for promoting and enjoying open-door romance."

Mia's eyes go wide, threatening to pop out of her head. Harper's mouth drops open, and they both stare at me.

"That was almost my exact reaction too." I take another big sip of the Moscato in my glass that's going down far too easily.

"Fucking men," Harper mumbles under her breath, shaking her head once with a slow blink.

"You two will be pleased with how I handled him, though." A wicked grin tugs at my lips as they both look at me expectantly.

"Oh, do tell," Harper says, a mischievous look on her face.

"I may or may not have told him the only men who have that level of hatred for open-door romances are those intimidated by them."

Harper's eyes light up, and she breaks into the biggest grinat the same time Mia lets out a low whistle.

"You didn't." Harper's voice rises at the end.

"Absolutely I did." I grin at Harper, and she bursts into a laugh.

"Mia, honey, you're going to break your jaw if it drops any lower."

Realising what she's doing, she snaps her mouth shut and clamps her hand over it. Face turning pink, she tries and fails to hold in a laugh.

"I cannot believe you actually said that. Who are you!" Harper responds, Mia still laughing maniacally.

"I was pretty impressed with myself until his response was a smile." Truthfully, that part sucked. He was easily one of the most alluring men I've ever encountered. Scratch that; he was *the* most alluring man I've ever encountered. But in that moment? He was downright ravishing.

He was tall but not ridiculously so. If smut has taught me anything, it's that excessively tall men may be hot, but they don't make for the best sex in confined spaces. Nor do they make for suitable 69 partners. By my calculations, he'd be the perfect height. And by calculations, I of course mean the way I stared, unblinking, at his retreating form as he walked out of the store. Long enough to determine not only that he would make for an exceptional 6 to my 9, but also that his face would make for one incredible seat.

The dark hair atop his head had that sexy "yes, I woke up like this" vibe going on, and I had the strangest inclination to reach out and run my hand through it. His eyes were a stunning shade of green, as if someone had melted down an emerald and hand-selected it as an eye colour.

"Earth to Lara?" Harper's voice draws my attention, and I notice both she and Mia are staring at me with odd expressions.

"Yes?" I say, the word coming out is more a question than a statement. They giggle like little boys in response.

"He was hot, wasn't he?" It may be Harper who asks the question, but the look on Mia's face says she's wondering the same thing.

My mouth opens and closes like a fish trying to breathe on land, no words forming. The giggles only intensify.

"Oh, he was. He *so* was." Harper struggles to get the words out, doubled over from her giggling.

I stare at them both incredulously. Was it that obvious? *Yikes.* I need to work on my poker face. As I let out a sigh, two heads whip towards me. I sit back and run my hand through my hair, my fingers twisting through the blonde ends as I try to ground myself. I'm struggling to come to terms with how hot I found him. For me, hot men are few and far between. Call me picky, but I'm not one to find any old, tall, dark and handsome man *hot*. Which is why it's awfully jarring that this one had such an effect on me.

"Not only was he incredibly attractive, but he was wearing a suit. *A fucking suit.* I could've fallen to my knees right there behind the counter," I confess as my face heats from my admission.

"Fuck me."

"Lord have mercy."

Their synchronised replies turn me into the giggling Gertie. My hands come up to cover my face.

I, not dissimilar to many other women around the world, have a *big* thing for men in uniforms and suits. I can't explain it, but it's a thing, and it's *deadly*.

His suit looked like it was custom-made for his body. It fit like a glove, accentuating his broad chest and shoulders. I definitely did not check out his arse as he left, so I cannot confirm or deny if it was as incredible as the rest of him. There's just something about men with great arses.

"Even though he ended up being a dick, he does sound incredibly hot," Harper states. "Did you at least get his number?" My eyes shoot towards her. She doesn't look at me as she brings her wine glass to her lips and takes a large sip. Did the horny bitch even listen?

"Harps, I didn't even get his name. He only knew mine because of the name badge I forgot I was wearing. Anyway," I say, leaning further into the lounge and placing the toes of my sock-clad feet onto the edge of the coffee table. "I decided to refer to him as Mr Darcy henceforth."

I felt so confused when he said my name, and in *that* accent. The deep timbre of his voice made my thighs clench involuntarily, and the confusion was quickly replaced with embarrassment and a twinge of anger.

In that moment, I dubbed him Mr Darcy. It's unlikely I'll

ever see him again, so his real name is of no interest to me. Between his immaculate suit, the sheer arrogance seeping out of his pores, and his unforgettable face, he was the complete Mr Darcy package.

"A classic Bridget Jones moment, love that for you," Mia muses, nodding slowly in agreement.

"Oh, Mia." I have to pull my lips between my teeth to hold in my giggle. "I was actually referring to Fitzwilliam Darcy as opposed to Mark Darcy."

"Potato, potato," she replies, giving a flippant flick of her wrist.

Chapter 10

Lara

For the next four weeks, I'm left utterly baffled at the sight of Mr Darcy. Like clockwork, each Tuesday he visits the store, seemingly to peruse the Classics section. He never makes a purchase, which both intrigues and confuses me.

Riss is still here each of my three working days. We begin each day with a cup of tea and a sweet treat in the reading nook —a tradition that began on my first day. Riss claims she doesn't want to leave me on my own yet, "just in case". Watching the way she interacts with the customers, I tend to think it's more so because she doesn't want to be on her own. She knows almost every person who steps foot in the bookstore and converses with them all.

She's also bought me in some form of baked good each shift. Despite me insisting she doesn't need to go to that effort, she continues to show up each morning with a different treat. When I'd politely asked her why, she'd responded, "I always thought I'd be baking for my grandkids at this age, but life has a way of surprising us." I embraced her just a little tighter the following morning when she handed me a plate of brownies.

I haven't spoken to Mr Darcy since the initial encounter—unless you count the nonverbal communication, particularly eye contact. He alternates between throwing smirks my way and beaming at me. I, on the other hand, remain consistent by narrowing my eyes in his direction each time they lock with his.

Speaking of consistency, Mr Darcy has a little of his own. It's almost killed me each of the four times he's entered the store because he's in a suit. *Every. Damn. Time.* I'd be hard-pressed to remember the last man I saw who wore a suit as well as he does. I hate that I find him so attractive; it's appalling. I'm not normally one to be so affected by a man, but he's something else entirely.

I'm behind the counter, adding new stock into the system when the bell chimes. My eyes glance towards the door as the suit-clad man invading my thoughts materialises in front of me. The way he's absentmindedly running his palm up and down the stubble on his jaw makes me wonder how it would feel rubbing against the inside of my thighs.

My mind instantly shuts that thought down as he approaches me, and I struggle to keep the heat from tingeing my cheeks with a telltale blush. The last thing I need is for this arsehole to know I find him attractive.

"Lara." My name comes out softer than usual, and I decide not to think about knowing his usual tone.

"Hello, Mr Darcy," I say in response.

Shit.

Did I really say that out loud? Mother Nature, if you'd ever considered opening a sinkhole in London, I invite you to do so right beneath my feet. Attempting to quell the embarrassment trying to seep through my pores, I slowly glance up at him. He's already staring at me, the shadow of a playful smirk on his face.

"I beg your pardon?" The sensual tone in his voice is back, and I almost feel relieved. Deciding to just go with it, I pull my lips into a sweet smile as I continue to hold his gaze.

"Was I not quite clear enough for you, Mr Darcy?" I say the name with emphasis and watch as his eyes light up for the briefest of moments. *Game on.*

"You were indeed quite clear, Lara." His smirk grows as he holds my gaze. Every nerve-ending sparks to life at his words. Will his accent ever *not* be sexy as fuck?

"Good," I say, hoping this conversation ends quickly.

I grab the stack of books in front of me, praying the nervous energy isn't visible. Turning to head into the storeroom, his voice stops me in my tracks.

"What you weren't quite clear on, however, is why that name?"

I knew the conversation ending there was too good to be true. Slowly, I close my eyes and take a deep breath. Of course, it does nothing to help my nerves. This is *so* not ideal. How do I explain my way out of this? Do I tell him the truth and risk further embarrassment, or attempt to play it off some other way? Considering I'm a terrible liar, and even worse at improvisation, it seems the truth is the way to go.

Taking another deep breath, I open my eyes and turn back towards Mr Darcy, finding him smiling at me broadly. The sight has my stomach dipping, and I say a silent curse in his name. Why does he have to be so good-looking all the time?

"I thought it would've been obvious?" My voice is light, higher than its normal tone. Get it together, Lara; you're a strong, independent woman who is *not* thrown off by hot men.

His smile only widens. "Break it down for me."

Those eyes of his could harness the attention of a room full of people, and he wouldn't even know. The emerald green pools draw me in against my will, and I'll be damned if I fall prey to this man.

The books in my arms feel like a dead weight. Is this really happening? Jesus Christ, sometimes I really should keep my mouth shut. Perhaps then I'd avoid situations like this. I deposit the books onto the counter. In an act displaying far more confidence than I possess, I lean my elbows on the counter and entwine my hands in front of me.

My cheeks ache as I give him my best megawatt smile. I didn't exactly expect him to falter, but I certainly did not expect him to copy my actions, placing us in far closer proximity than necessary. Is this dick serious? Not wanting to show weakness, I hold my own.

"Where would you like me to start? Your categories are attire, attitude, and literary preferences."

His head tips backwards, a deep laugh reverberating through him. When his eyes lock back on mine, there's a glint to them that wasn't there before. I hate the way it makes my stomach knot. The way it has my mind whirling. The way it has me wanting to lean in closer to see his reaction. My eyes drift down to his lips momentarily. I think I've been subtle, but the smallest raise of his eyebrows tells me how wrong I am.

"Category A please, miss."

My breath hitches ever so slightly at the word "miss", and I know he sees it. Our proximity leaves no room to hide.

"That's an easy one—the penchant for suits. Truly, does your wardrobe hold nothing else, or do you enjoy the god complex the suits give you?"

My grandmother often tells me sarcasm is the lowest form of wit. I learnt it from my mother, who happens to be her daughter, and I strongly disagree with the statement.

In my humble opinion, sarcasm is hilarious, and I've always

enjoyed it. When I'm around the man in front of me, however, it jumps up a level. As does my attitude and sass level. I don't recognise myself with the words coming out of my mouth, but I can't help it. He brings it out of me like nobody else.

Apparently, he's unbreakable. He continues to beam at me as if I hadn't just insulted the shit out of him. "I assure you my wardrobe holds plenty; it's the god complex."

Taken completely by surprise, a laugh breaks free. Not a sweet little giggle, but a real belly laugh. Just when I thought he couldn't possibly have anything else going for him, the arsehole turns out to be funny.

Looking at Mr Darcy, his eyes are softer than they were a moment ago. I'd pay good money to know what's going on inside that head of his. Bloody hell, I need to stop. I don't care what he's thinking about; none of my business. Unless it's something about me, of course.

He pushes off the counter, standing at his full height.

"So that covers attire," he says, the corners of his eyes crinkling. My eyes once again trail down to his lips. He really does have a beautiful smile. "I think I can guess where the literary preferences come into it, but the attitude has me stumped. I don't think you know me well enough to judge me."

Arms crossing over his chest, Mr Darcy's eyes roam over my face as he continues. "But for you, Lara, I'll let it slide."

"It's hardly fair you know my name, but I don't know yours," I reply, knowing full well I'm wrong. I don't need to know his name, and the only reason he knows mine is because I wear a badge. There's really nothing unfair about it at all, but that doesn't stop me.

"I disagree, *Lara*." The jerk has the audacity to smile at me once more. It's a softer smile, and my god, it's even more gorgeous than the others. "You've named me all on your own. You don't need my real name."

The slight cock of my head allows for a far more *scrutinising* look.

"Is this really how you want to play this, Mr Darcy?"

At my words, he leans against the counter. Our faces are mere inches apart. I don't dare breathe for fear of pushing him away.

"I don't play games, Lara. I win them."

For the second time during this interaction, my thighs clench involuntarily. It's not only what he says but the way he says it. It's almost as if it's a promise spoken in a husky tone.

It feels like this conversation has taken a turn, and we're treading a dangerous line. I glance quickly around the store, noticing he's the only customer right now. Somehow that makes it worse.

With one last smile, he walks away.

Have I started a game I have no chance of winning?

Chapter 11

Carter

The cool April air caused goosebumps to form on my arms during my run this morning. Normally this time of year is beautiful for an early run, but this past week has brought in an unexpected cold snap. I ran faster than usual, attempting to outrun the cold, resulting in my far-earlier-than-necessary arrival at the firm.

It's a little while later when I start hearing the voices of my staff throughout the hallways, signalling the official start of the work day. Laptop in one hand and coffee in the other, I make my way to the boardroom and take my usual seat for the monthly Executive Meeting.

I'm vaguely aware of my colleagues filing in around me, but my gaze is fixed on the floor to ceiling window across from me, and the view beyond. If I look hard enough, I swear I can almost see the bookstore, despite the low clouds and it being tens of blocks away. An image of the striking woman with eyes reminiscent of the depths of the ocean fades into view clear as day. It's as though I've been transported directly to the counter, watching her share a carefree laugh with a customer.

"You good, boss?" Anna's voice removes me from the book-store. Concern mars her features as I meet her gaze. Glancing around the room, I'm caught off guard realising I'm centre of attention between eight pairs of eyes.

"Sorry, what was that?" I rough a palm along my jaw, completely taken aback that I was *that* lost in thought.

Anna lets out a small chuckle and a few of the others join in. "You're fine, boss. I was just askin' if you had any updates for HR." It's hard to supress my grin at the way *HR* sounds in her Southern lilt pronunciation.

"Right, of course." Tapping a key on my now-sleeping laptop, I force my straying thoughts to remain on the meeting at hand. *Not the time or place, Lawrence.* "Let's start with staffing updates, shall we?"

As I rise from my chair and exit the boardroom, I glance down at my watch. Stifling a yawn, I'm disappointed but not surprised to see it's far earlier than I'd thought. It feels as though I've already worked a twelve-hour day when it's not even midday.

I make my way to my office, smiling and greeting any staff I've yet to say good morning to. The past few months haven't been the easiest by any means, but I've really hit my stride recently.

The firm is busier than ever, which is excellent and exactly where we want the business. But it also means I've been working more than ever.

Sitting down at my desk, I flip through my diary to see what the rest of my day holds. Confusion seeps in as I look at the blank page. *Well, this is odd.* A moment passes before I realise—

it's blank because I forgot to write in it. It's only Tuesday, far too early in the week to be this dysfunctional.

When Anna, our HR department head, brought up the possibility of hiring me an executive assistant, I thought it was ludicrous. I'd told her that while I may be busy, isn't that expected as CEO? She'd laughed and agreed but also reminded me that my father, and my grandfather before him, always had EAs.

At this moment, staring at my wrongfully blank diary, I realise she may have had a point. Logging into my computer, I let out a sigh of relief when I see the small reprieve I have between meetings. I lean back in my chair, turn towards the window, and take in the bustling activity of Oxford Street down below. My mind wanders, betraying me with thoughts of that particularly feminine Australian accent, accentuated with the slightest of posh lilts.

Why am I thinking about Lara right now? Lord fucking knows, but I can't seem to shake her. Attempting a distraction, I send a quick text to Dex, asking him to meet me for lunch. His "aye aye captain" comes through almost instantly and has me rolling my eyes.

The sound of muffled footsteps approaching steals my attention away from the view. I turn to find Anna standing in my doorway; laptop beneath her arm and a coffee in either hand.

"You got a minute, boss?" Anna greets me with a smile, her faint southern accent as joyous as ever. The sweet scent of strawberries and cream wafts into my office.

"That would depend on the nature of your visit, Anna," I tease, motioning her to come in. Her light giggle fills the air as she takes a seat across from me, handing me one of the take-away cups.

"How'd you know I needed this?" I thank her, taking a sip of the steaming brew. One dark eyebrow raises as she regards me. Half of me is resisting the urge to squirm under her intense gaze, while the other half is suppressing a smirk.

"Out with it," I say finally, unable to withstand the silence any longer.

"We've known each other a while now, wouldn't you say?" Her brow raises imperceptibly with the question.

"Several years at least. What's that got to do with anything?"

"And you trust my judgement?"

This isn't a typical interaction with Anna, and it's throwing me off. She's typically quite fiery and will say what's on her mind without a second thought. "Anna, I've never known you to beat around the bush like this. What's going on?"

"I really think you should reconsider your stance on an assistant." I've barely opened my mouth to respond when she continues, holding up a hand. "Before you argue, I want you to listen. I watched you this morning, during that meeting. I say this with the utmost respect, boss, but you were so out of it, and that's not normal for you at all."

A few stray cinnamon strands have come loose from Anna's bun, and she tucks them neatly behind her ears. Through the tortoise frame of her glasses, bright green eyes bore into mine, expectant.

"Here I was thinking perhaps you'd just come to visit a friend without ulterior motives." Anna's eyes widen slightly, before she pulls her lips down in a dramatic frown. A deep laugh ripples through me. "As much as I hate to admit it, you're right.

A small gasp falls from her lips, and then her entire face lights up like she's just won the lottery. She claps her hands onto her thighs. The sound echoes around the office and her diamond engagement ring glints from her excitement.

"Finally, he listens!" Anna flips open her laptop, hitting keys and clicking buttons like her life depends on it. "I've only been trying to subtly persuade you for months. What made you change your mind this particular time?"

"First of all, you were as subtle as a cannon." A wide grin breaks out across Anna's face. "Secondly, I forgot to fill out my diary for today."

Anna's jaw drops slightly, and her eyes widen. Having known me for as long as she has, she's well aware of how Type A I am when it comes to my diary.

"Oh, Carter," is all she can say. "Don't worry, we'll find you the perfect EA. I'll put some feelers out and see if there's any potential from word of mouth before going through an agency."

Leaning back in the chair, I cross my arms over my chest. "You're simply the best; thank you, Anna."

Rising from her chair, Anna continues firing off emails as she walks out. A quick glance at my watch says I'm a few minutes late in meeting Dex downstairs.

I find him waiting by the front doors in the foyer, deeply engrossed in his phone. "What could possibly have caught your attention like that, Dexter?"

It seems he didn't have the slightest inclination I was approaching, if the way he jumps out of his skin is any indication. The item holding his attention so intensely goes flying upwards. Reaching out a hand, I manage to catch it before it falls to an almost certain death, as Dex recentres himself.

"What the fuck Carter," Dex says a little too loudly, causing some of the passing office staff to glance in our direction. "You don't sneak up on a man like that when he's watching porn."

My eyes almost pop out of my head. "You weren't, please tell me you weren't," I mutter.

Dex merely winks at me, turning on his heel in pursuit of a lunch spot. It seems I won't be getting an answer anytime soon. For a smart guy, my best friend does some dumb things. Which is precisely why it wouldn't be a huge surprise if he were telling the truth.

We wander down Oxford Street toward a local cafe, catching up on the week so far. Whilst the promotion has been a bit of a steep incline for Dex, it sounds like he's finding his feet. From what I've heard around the firm, the junior associates are stoked to have him leading them. I've known for a while that Dex would be a great leader; not only is he one hell of a lawyer, but he's incredibly personable, which is exactly what our up-and-comers need.

By the time we collect our lunch and find a table, I've finished telling Dex about ending things with Molly. With how busy things have been, we're hardly had the chance to catch up on a personal level.

"There's one thing I don't understand though, mate," Dex says around a rather large mouthful of baguette. "If you weren't even keen on Molly, why have you seemed so off with the fairies lately?"

Scoffing, I look up from my lunch and see Dex's eyebrows pulling together. I keep my face neutral as I respond, unsure where this is going. "Care to elaborate on when I've been off with the fairies?"

Now it's Dex's turn to scoff. "Oh, come off it." There's the smallest note of exasperation in his voice. "You've hardly been present in meetings. I can't count the number of times I've heard someone have to repeat themselves because you zoned out."

Dragging my fork through the Greek salad in front of me, it

dawns on me that the son of a bitch might have a point—especially given the way I completely zoned out this morning whilst picturing her. Then there's the whole diary mishap, although I could blame that on workload to disprove Dex's point.

Taking another mouthful without responding, my mind subconsciously drifts to the striking woman with eyes that could take a man's breath away. This isn't the first time she's crossed my mind since our initial meeting. Hell, it isn't even the tenth time. What is it about her that's left such an impression on me? So much so that I'm noticeably spacing out in meetings and work conversations?

Maybe it would be good to talk this out with Dex? It might get her off my mind.

I place my fork down and lean back in my chair. Purposefully not locking eyes with Dex, I finally speak.

"Don't overreact when I say this, but there's someone I can't get out of my head."

A dramatic noise comes from across the table, causing me to look up and see Dex's reaction. He's got one hand clasped over his mouth, failing to stifle the gasp that was probably heard down the street. The other hand has slapped down on the table, rattling everything it holds.

"Thank you for toning *down* the dramatics," I say, my voice dripping with sarcasm.

"You didn't really expect me to react calmly to this news, did you?" Dex asks, still shocked. "Carter, you're my brother and I love you, but sometimes I'm deeply concerned about the lack of interest you have in women."

Must admit, I'm a little offended.

"Dexter, you wound me."

"Can't even say I'm sorry, I wouldn't mean it." Dex smirks at me. "Is this someone a man or woman?"

Rolling my eyes, I let out a small sigh, which bleeds into a laugh. "How many times must we have this conversation? No matter how hard you attempt to sway me, I am a straight man, Dex."

He has the audacity to look hurt by my words, even though we've been having this conversation since our first year of law school. Huffing, Dex goes on.

"The bi's and gay's of London continue to have their hearts torn into pieces at the hands of one Mr Carter Lawrence."

I can't help but laugh. Dex has been trying to recruit me for almost as long as I've known him, even though we're both aware it doesn't work like that.

Whenever Dex mentions he's hooked up with someone, I have to confirm if it's a man or a woman to know how to proceed with the conversation. More often than not, the answer has been a woman. The best stories, though? They seem to be more prevalent when the answer is a man.

"Any who," I say, determined to continue this conversation with as little dramatics as possible. "She's an incredibly stubborn woman who works in the bookstore."

Dex's brows furrow as he studies me.

"Wow, she's really gotten under your skin, hasn't she?" he asks, not expecting an answer.

"I don't understand why she's affecting me the way she is." My words are coming out in haste. A sudden feeling of restlessness has me crossing and uncrossing my arms. "She has horrible taste in books, truly Dex. She's one of those uncultured heathens who believe written porn is a genre. She possesses an unmatched level of sass and sarcasm, her arse is incredible, and she's *Australian.*"

Dex lifts both hands with his palms toward me, preventing me from continuing.

"I'm sorry, but did you compliment her arse?"

I pause. "What? Why on earth would I do that?"

"I dunno, mate, but I'm quite sure you said, and I quote, 'her arse is incredible.'"

"Shit." Muttering under my breath, I glance away from Dex for a moment, then back at him. He's wearing the same smug expression, and I want to reach over and slap it off his face. "It would appear I did, in fact, say that."

Pure triumph radiates across his face, and now I want to slap him even more.

"Dex, mate, I think I had a minor stroke."

I'm surprised his mouth doesn't split up the sides when the grin on his face somehow widens even further.

"You've got it bad."

"No, I don't," I snap back defensively. Too quickly. Dex knows it too.

It's a fact. Lara has a really nice arse. One that makes you want to grab a fistful while she's sitting on your face.

Jesus, Carter, what the fuck man?

I've no idea where that thought came from, and I'm a little concerned.

I don't even like her.

"I don't even like her," I repeat out loud this time.

The arsehole across the table from me has the nerve to continue to grin at me, crossing his arms over his chest and mimicking my body language.

"You sure?" He raises a brow curiously.

The truth is, I'm not the slightest bit sure. The fact that my immediate reaction is to go on the defensive suggests that perhaps I like her a little more than I'm willing to let on. But I'm not about to let Dex have the satisfaction of being right.

"I've never encountered someone like her; we couldn't be more different. Yes, she's beautiful, that much is obvious, but we're complete opposites if you ask me."

"Might be an unpopular opinion, but I think you may like her."

My jaw drops ever so slightly, and I hit Dex with a "you can't be serious" look. Noticing, he holds his hands up in surrender.

"Hear me out. You're distracted in meetings, daydreaming like a teenager, and you've admitted you think about her more than you'd like." Dex looks me right in the eyes, leaning forward. His voice drops to a whisper. "I think you're *in love*."

I reach across the table and shove his shoulder playfully. "You are absolutely full of it." Dex bursts into a fit of laughter. "You've got to be taking the piss, Dexter. I just enjoy riling her up."

I've become addicted to the feeling I get when I rile her up. I find myself looking forward to each Tuesday, waiting to see those blue eyes narrowed in my direction, the scowl she loves to point at me.

"Okay, that last line might have been me taking the piss," Dex says through his laughs, "but I meant the rest of it."

I don't like the way his eyes soften as the laughter subsides. He looks like he truly means what he said, which is a cause for concern. No one, except perhaps Teddy, knows me as well as Dex does. For him to say I might like this woman who drives me crazy and has my cock stirring simply from the words she utters? Well, that's fucking terrifying.

We finish our lunch in silence, which I find to be slightly less than comfortable—the idea that I might *like* Lara plays on my mind more than I'd like. Dex doesn't question me any further, but I know him. He'll have a hundred and one questions swirling around in that head of his, dying to ask me.

The next few days are filled with far too many thoughts of Lara. Scolding myself didn't have the slightest impact, so I gave up. She continued to come to mind at the most inconvenient of times. A conversation with Emilia turned to thoughts of Lara when she'd mentioned the book of the month for her "Smut Club". I refuse to utter those words out loud, but that's what she calls it.

Even the most mundane of tasks had me thinking of Lara. I was standing in my office last week, contemplating ignoring the barrister performance reviews awaiting my attention, when an intrusive thought struck. One minute my mind was on my employees, and the next it was on Lara. Not just any Lara, but a naked one. Eyes skimming across the expanse of my solid mahogany desk, I pictured her bent over in front of me. Her hair twisted through my fingers pulled tight enough to have her breath straining. The twitch of my cock beneath my trousers had me snapping out of that daydream in an instant.

Lara had infiltrated my thoughts in the best and worst of ways. The firm was absolutely no place to be fantasising about that infuriating woman, even if she did have a body built to be bent over and fucked from behind.

Just yesterday, it happened again, this time during a finance meeting. One of our accountants had been going through numbers I most definitely should've been paying attention to. Instead, she'd uttered the word "books", and that had been enough for my thoughts to hightail it elsewhere.

Attending as many meetings as I do, I've learnt the art of appearing to pay attention whilst being worlds away in thought. That particular skill came in handy yesterday. To my staff at the table, I looked as if I were deeply enthralled by the numbers. What was I actually thinking about? How Lara would look pressed up against the boardroom windows. How she'd feel beneath my hands. What sort of noises she'd make as I toyed with her centre.

If I didn't sort my shit out soon, I'd need an intervention.

Ten minutes after I walk into the bookstore, there's still no sign of her. Acting totally cool and not at all like a crazy person, I circle the aisles several times with no luck. Am I really seeking her out now? Has it come to that? Oh, my brother and Dex would have a *field day* if they could see me now.

Rounding the front of the store on what I'd guess to be my sixth casual lap, I catch a glimpse of the blonde ends of her hair. Much too quickly, I stop in my tracks, turning in her direction. She's behind the counter, facing the wall behind it. Judging by the way she hasn't turned around, I don't think she knows I'm standing here.

From my vantage point to the side of the counter, I get the chance to really take her in, and without her berating me for it. Although I'd be lying if I said I didn't enjoy that. Lara has a deliciously sharp tongue for a young woman. Most of our encounters over the past couple of months have left me one of two ways: wanting to fuck her mouth to see how capable she is of insulting me with a mouthful of my cock, or wanting to devour her pussy until nothing but whimpers come from that mouth.

It's irrational how maddening I find her, yet in the same breath, I want to fuck her into oblivion. I want to invade her thoughts as thoroughly as she has invaded mine.

The first thing I notice: she's wearing a skirt. A reasonably short skirt, given the cooler weather we're still experiencing. The second thing I notice: her legs are fucking divine. Not because they're long and could belong to a supermodel. No, Lara is a little on the shorter side; I have at least a head on her. They're divine because they're hers. Seeing them on display for the first time has me feeling like a horny teenager.

Her calves are well-defined, probably from a childhood of dancing, and her skin looks unimaginably smooth. The desire to run my hand up her thigh to know how her skin feels beneath mine is almost painful.

Good god, this really needs to stop. Since I'm sure it would be in everyone's best interest if I cut today's visit short, I turn on my heel and move towards the door. A floorboard squeaks beneath my foot, and immediately I know I've been caught.

"Nothing to say today then, Mr Darcy?" Lara's teasing tone sounds from behind me. The one that makes me want to walk right back over there and bend her over the counter. Perhaps a good spanking is what she needs, some form of release she clearly isn't getting.

My eyes meet hers. Her pupils grow as I hold her gaze, the corners of my lips rising ever so slightly.

"You knew I was in the store, didn't you?"

Her eyes sparkle with humour. "Of course I knew, you're rather heavy-footed."

My jaw goes slack as I gape at Lara. A sly smirk is directed at me, her eyes narrow and feline-like.

"Rather heavy-footed?" I exclaim, quite taken aback at the accusation.

Lara bursts into a full-blown laugh, rendering her speechless. The look on my face really must have been something because tears of laughter stream from her closed eyes. I use her distraction to my advantage and stride right up to her side.

As if sensing me, she opens her eyes. Before I can stop to think, *what the fuck are you doing?* I reach my hand up and cup her jaw. My thumb brushes beneath her eye, wiping away the remaining lone tear. Our eyes lock once more, and my pulse races the same way it did that first day. Fuck, she has *such* an effect on me. The rapid beating of my heart radiates into my stomach and floods my ears. Her skin is soft to the touch, like silk beneath the pad of my thumb.

I decide to take a risk: up the ante of flirtation and get a *real* reaction out of Lara. "It would seem I'm not quite as heavy-footed as you believed."

It's as if the sound of my voice breaks her out of a trance. Lara blinks once and stumbles backwards, seemingly attempting to break contact. Her foot catches on a stray pile of books. For the second time in the past two minutes, I reach for her. This time, my hands wrap around her waist and pull her towards me. Face slamming into my chest, I inhale the sweet raspberry and rose scent of her. Lara's hands latch onto my biceps. Her warmth envelopes me, and I contemplate never letting her go.

Once again seeming to hear my thoughts, she releases me and pushes against my chest. I'm conflicted, as I often am when it comes to her. One part of me is still thoroughly gobsmacked that I'm thinking of her as anything but a pain in the arse, while the other part is utterly disappointed by the loss of contact.

Lara takes a step back, this time avoiding the now-fallen tower of books, and looks up at me.

"What was that about?" Her tone is stern as her arms cross over her chest, but the way her eyes roam over my body betrays her.

"Thought you could use a hand," I reply simply, the smirk from earlier developing in full. "You're awfully clumsy, Lara."

She stares at me, mouth agape. "I am not! I wouldn't have tripped over those books if it weren't for you in the first place."

"You're right," I admit. Lara's eyes flare briefly. "Next time, I promise to warn you before touching you. I'd *hate* for you to fall for me."

If eye rolls were audible, Lara's would've been the most obnoxious moan imaginable. I'd like to hear that noise under different circumstances, preferably my name, but a moan is a moan. I don't miss the way her cheeks turn a shade darker as I send her a wink over my shoulder, strolling unhurriedly toward the front door.

There's not a single doubt in my mind that this isn't one-sided. I've seen the way her cheeks turn crimson when I'm a little more adventurous with my flirting. The way her lips part and her eyes darken when my gaze skates across her body. She may deny it, but Lara is affected by me.

I need to find a way to prove it.

Chapter 12

Lara

"I can feel your eyes on me." Mr Darcy's deep tone jolts me from my daydreaming.

"I guarantee you can't, because they weren't on you." My eyes flit away briefly before roaming back in his direction, and I find him still enthralled by the classic he has in his hands.

Glancing towards the window at the front of the store, I notice an unfamiliar motorbike outside. It's sleek, black, and expensive looking, with a surface so clean I can see the store reflecting on the body. I don't know much about motorbikes, but I'd guess this one would cost more than my yearly salary at home. There's a thin sheet of rain falling—not unexpected on any given day in London—and I wonder how the poor rider is coping in the cold.

"Are you quite sure?" Mr Darcy continues slowly flicking through the pages.

My cheeks warm. How is he so alluring yet a huge dick at the same time? I move my head slowly to face the shelves he's in front of, hopefully giving myself time to pull it together.

"I'm sure about the fact you'd fit in perfectly as a Kane brother, with your arsehole-ish demeanour and penchant for suits." I don't say it loudly, but I don't exactly whisper it, either. Of course he hears, and the comment gets his attention. He looks up from the book, and our eyes meet across the store. Feeling the not-so-unusual spike in my heart rate that occurs whenever his eyes lock on mine, I avert my gaze, instead dropping it to the floor. For the first time, I clock that his usual dress shoes are missing. In their place are a pair of thick black boots covered in a wet sheen. Well, this is unusual. Obviously, it's raining outside, which explains the water, but boots?

"A Kane brother? From those dirty billionaire books?" The deep gravel of his voice draws my attention back to his face. And what an annoyingly good-looking face it is.

I suppress a groan before correcting him. "*Dreamland Billionaires* books, not dirty."

Mr Darcy pointedly ignores me and continues as if I'd never said a word.

"Correct me if I'm wrong, but I seem to recall you mentioning how incredibly attractive those men are?" Mr Darcy questions, slowly turning through the pages of *To Kill A Mockingbird*. I am stunned—he remembered our conversation?

Deciding not to overthink his memory skills, I settle for a suitably cutting retort. "Of course you'd remember that part rather than pay attention to the arsehole comment."

He shuts the book with a thud and turns his body towards the bench I'm standing—hiding—behind.

"I always remember the good parts, love."

Love.

What the fuck?

I cross my arms and open my mouth to reply with something smart, but find myself snapping it shut. He constantly throws me, and I don't know how I feel about it. If he continues to call me *love* with that beautiful London accent of his, we're going to have some *serious* problems.

The way the word rolled off his tongue so effortlessly is dangerous, *very* dangerous. Eyes drifting towards his mouth, my treacherous little mind goes into overdrive. I've got a list of approximately 132 other dangerous things his tongue could do. Whoever is pulling the strings in my brain produces something akin to a PowerPoint Presentation for each and every one of those things.

The way he not so innocently swipes his tongue over his lip causes goosebumps to form all over my skin. It's as if he can hear every thought I've had about him, the glint in his eyes teasing me. My thoughts quickly meld into something slightly less PG-rated as I imagine his tongue swiping over my neck in that same teasing way, trailing down my body until he reaches my centre. Would he be gentle, caressing me as he savoured every lick? Or would he be relentless, licking and sucking like a starved man until he wrung every last orgasm from my body?

Mr Darcy smirks at me as his attention returns to the book in his hands. Abruptly, I'm all too aware of my elevated heart rate. The strength with which it thumps against my chest has me worried it'll thump right through. My body threatens to overheat as my clothes grow tighter and my cheeks burn.

Way to play it cool, Lara.

Taking a beat, I mentally chant my new mantra to myself.

I am a strong, independent woman. I am not swayed by hot men in suits with British accents and dangerous tongues.

It is a little specific—okay, it's a lot specific—but I'll try anything at this point. As usual, he looks far too good in his perfectly tailored suit. The menace in me wants to grab a fistful of his shirt just to see it rumpled. He's also sporting designer stubble this week, which somehow makes him even more delectable. I'm not much of a beard girl—nor am I a bearded girl, just so we're clear—but there's something about the way his face matures with the presence of facial hair. Of course, even without it, he's still impeccably groomed.

"Lara, enlighten me." His voice is closer than before. "Did you hand-pick all of these titles?" I look up to see he's now browsing the *Perhaps Some Spice?* display I proudly pulled together last Friday. Riss was positively beaming when I walked through the door yesterday morning, claiming most of the weekend's customers had purchased from, or commented on, the display. I was happy with how it turned out. But right now, seeing Mr Darcy scrutinise it with narrowed eyes and pursed lips brings me even more joy.

"Certainly did; even categorised them myself." Grinning proudly, I give myself a mental high-five as I watch Mr Darcy's face twist with what can only be described as disappointment.

He turns his body in my direction, and I swear time slows down. It's as if the universe herself has seen the absolute specimen that is Mr Darcy, and has decided he deserves an extra five seconds of movement time. Eyes locked on mine, he runs a hand through his hair. I've come to know that's a move he does right before he's about to say or do something arrogant.

Right on cue, he promptly flicks his eyes over me. They shoot from my face to my legs and straight back up. If I hadn't been watching him like a hawk, I'd have missed it.

"Humour me, Lara," he says, one hand still in his hair, seemingly forgotten. "Is your life so devoid of male interest that any real action has to come from fictional men?"

Ugh! Is he serious? My *god*, he is beyond intolerable. He's like a sour patch kid in reverse; when you start to believe perhaps he's sweet, he sours and says things that offend, embarrass, or outright call you out. Looking into those dangerously green eyes, my thighs clench for the briefest of moments.

Oh, come on. We are not affected by him, stop that clenching this instant.

Regaining composure and remembering the pretty man behind the involuntary thigh movement offended me, I scoff.

"You are insufferable. Has anyone ever told you that?" He's also completely correct, but I'll take my last breath before I admit that to him. "This feels a little pot meets kettle, don't you think, Darcy?"

Collecting up a pile of books, I round the counter and make my way to the crime fiction section. He's on my heels, his presence warming me. Rather than give him what he wants, which is clearly my attention, I begin rehoming the books in my arms as I speak. "The same could be said for you; having to find love within the pages of decades-old works by authors long gone."

It occurs to me in this moment that the nickname I bestowed upon him several months ago has no effect on him. You'd think if a perfect stranger gave you an odd nickname and accidentally said it out loud, you'd tell them your real name, right? Wrong. Mr Darcy has never once even mentioned having a real name.

I don't even want to think about the ego boost he would get if I asked. As well as the fact it would make it seem as though I think about him or am interested in knowing anything about him, which I certainly am not.

I'd never be caught dead daydreaming about how smooth a seat his face would be when he's freshly shaven. Nor do I spend any amount of time considering what sort of dirty things would come out of such a clean-looking man's mouth. And I most definitely do not think of all of these things happening in the back office where every second would be filled with the thrill of someone walking into the store.

"I truly don't understand what you see in these books,

Lara." I hold in a grin, watching Mr Darcy hesitantly pick up one of the books on display with a finger and thumb as if it might bite him if he touches too much of it.

"What's not to see? They have plot, they have humour, they have romance. They certainly have more to offer than your precious classics."

Mr Darcy, still holding the book like it's diseased, looks over at me. The way his eyes roam slowly over me causes a tingling sensation to spread throughout my body. Not daring to think he likes what he sees, I keep a straight face trained on him. He flashes me a megawatt smile before returning the book to the display.

"Jealousy looks good on you, Lara."

"Jealous?" I scoff. "What are you going on about now?"

"Not everyone can appreciate real talent when it comes to story writing. People like you are essential—your simple taste keeps the classics as just that; classics."

I smile at him as sarcastically as I can. "Well, that's certainly one way to look at it."

I've never encountered a man this gorgeous with such flawed opinions on books and such arsehole-ish tendencies. But there's something about him that piques my interest. It leaves me with the desire to know more about him, about the person behind the handsome face. Is the cocky-confident thing a front? A coping mechanism? There's always the chance it's just who he is as a person, but the way he looks at me—like he can see right through me—says otherwise.

As if reading my thoughts, Mr Darcy speaks. "That's the glorious thing about opinions, isn't it? They're unique."

I roll my eyes at his words. "I'm aware, but thank you for the reminder."

The smirk lifting the corner of his mouth definitely

shouldn't have the effect on me that it does. Warmth spreads through my body; it starts in my cheeks and continues, unbidden, right down to my core.

As I watch him return the copy of *To Kill A Mockingbird* to the shelf on his right, I pray Mr Darcy didn't see the evidence of my body's betrayal seeping into my cheeks.

Chapter 13

Carter

"Men like you are typically one of two things." The words come out of her mouth in a slightly lower tone than usual. I mentally register confusion and a flicker of intrigue at the fact I know what her usual tone is—I'll analyse that later. Right now, I'd love to analyse the way her cheeks are reddening as she looks over at me. She really does have beautiful eyes; perhaps I should tell her to test her reaction? Not realising, or not caring, that I'm in my head right now, Lara continues.

"One." She raises her hand with her palm facing toward me as she unfolds her index finger to count. "You talk from experience. Cocky, but self-aware enough to know your words aren't unfounded."

As casually as I can manage, I make my way back over to the counter. There's a twitch in my trousers as I walk, and I pray Lara can't see the strain I feel. Diverting her attention in case seems like an excellent thing to do.

I cock my head to the side, a smirk forming on my face. Her eyes zone in on my lips, so I decide to show her just how cocky

I can be. Parting my lips, I lazily glide my tongue along my bottom lip. Pushing my luck, I rake my eyes over her face before they lock on her mouth. *Fuck, she is delicious.*

The faintest of pink tinges graces her cheeks. My smirk morphs into a shit-eating grin as she realises she's still staring at my lips. Her eyes shoot up to mine, instantly narrowing.

"Please continue, love. I'm very interested in option number two." I lean forward, resting my forearms on the counter. She jerks backwards, attempting to twist her facial features into a look of disgust. She fails miserably, and my grin only grows.

"Or two, you're all talk and absolutely no follow through. You're intolerable of smut because it's where you get your inspiration, and you're ashamed and intimidated by the fact men written by women are better than the real men on this planet." Her middle finger raises to join her index as the words tumble out with venom behind them.

Oh, this just got interesting.

I raise an eyebrow in a silent challenge. She has the audacity to stare blankly at me as if she didn't insult the shit out of me. I don't think before I stalk around the counter towards her. I stop mere centimetres from her, our bodies painfully close to touching.

"Do you trust me?"

Her confusion is apparent as she searches my face for meaning, but I wait.

"I hardly know you."

Something stirs within me as she crosses her arms over her chest and narrows her eyes, the trademarks of a woman who's been taught to stand up for herself. Recently I've noticed that the more I see of Lara, the more irresistible she becomes. But right now, the goal isn't defiance; it's surrender.

"That's not what I asked. Do you trust me?"

A startled look flashes across her face. She shifts her weight from one foot to the other, arms still firmly crossed. "I don't know why, but yes."

Anyone would think she'd accepted my marriage proposal with the sheer elation coursing through me like a white water rapid. Now isn't the time to think too deeply about that, though.

"Then take my hand."

It hangs in the space between us in invitation, my palm up with fingers slightly curled. Lara placing her hand in mine is the last thing I see before turning around, my eyes locking on the archway leading to the back of the store. Acting purely on emotion, I march us directly into the storeroom, my grip on her soft skin unwavering. The weight of her touch, along with the anticipation of what's to come, is almost too much to bear.

"What on earth do you think you're doing?" Lara asks, anger and confusion apparent in her voice. I seem to have committed her voice to memory over the past three months, and it's for this reason alone I'm confident there's a hint of excitement in there.

I don't say a word as I guide her to the desk in the far corner, stopping in front of it. Twisting towards her, I drop her wrist and look her in the eyes. Those blue eyes of hers are dilated, and the blood in my veins redirects to my dick. Apparently, my vital organs don't mean shit when my cock demands attention.

"Sit."

"Excuse me?"

"You heard me, Lara." Taking one step closer, I close the gap between us. "I said, *sit.*" The last word comes out more demanding than its predecessors. Wide eyes blink back at me before Lara gives in and sits.

Well fuck, that was easy. And hot. Why was that so hot?

Truthfully, I was half expecting her to slap me. I kind of still am. She doesn't strike me as someone who'd reject direction, but I also didn't expect her to be so complicit. Cheers ring out inside my head as I think of all the ways I can take advantage of that.

Lara's eyes widen still as I adjust my trousers around my knees and kneel in front of her.

"Have you completely lost your mind? What are you doing?"

"There are no security cameras."

"What? Yes there are? Why are you talking about security cameras?"

"There are no cameras, trust me."

I can almost see the wheels spinning in that pretty head of hers. I grasp the hem of her skirt in my hands and roughly push it up her thighs.

"Last chance; want to take it back?" Holding her gaze, I watch as her lips part ever so slightly. Her neck catches my eye as she swallows, hands coming to rest beside mine, which are still holding her thighs.

"What are you talking about?" Her voice is anything but uncertain despite the question she asks.

"Unless you take back what you said, I'm going to prove how wrong you are. My skills are the blueprint for fictional men."

As if without thinking, she lets out a scoff. Immediately realising what she's done, Lara's eyes go wide, and a hand slaps over her mouth. All I can do is grin up at her.

"I guess I've got my answer."

I don't wait for her to respond. My hands are on her in an instant, gripping her by the hips and pulling her to the edge of the chair. The sexy little gasp she lets out tells me she didn't mind the strength behind that pull one bit.

I gaze up at her from my position between her knees. My heartbeat slows momentarily as I take her in. Lara's gaze is filled with desire as her dilated eyes meet my own.

She'd never admit it out loud, but I've caught her looking at me with the same expression on more than one occasion. It's always when she thinks I'm not paying attention, but the joke is on her: I'm never not paying attention to her.

Refusing to break eye contact with the angel in front of me, I slide my hands up her thighs, stopping an inch below their apex.

"Tell me to stop, love." My self-control is wavering—and fast.

The light blue hue of her eyes darkens as she gazes down at me. That plump bottom lip of hers is pulled into her mouth, teeth raking over it as she gives the slightest shake of her head. If I blinked, I would've missed it.

With that, my self-control snaps. Fuck, she's going to undo me.

Left hand firmly planted on her hip, the fingers of my right hand gently trace down Lara's centre. I can feel the warmth emanating beneath her underwear, and my cock twitches in my trousers. Lara draws in an audible breath as I pull her underwear to the side with one swift tug. Fucking hell, she's so wet already.

Lara may act unaffected by me, but she can't deny this. The fact she's almost dripping with need, yet I've barely touched her, is concrete proof she's not as disinterested as she pretends to be. I fucking *knew* this wasn't one-sided. Now I need her to admit it. Perhaps a little old-fashioned edging will do the trick? Oh, who am I kidding? Once I taste this pussy, I won't be able to stop myself from devouring her.

Practically salivating at the sight of her bared in front of me, I bring my face within inches of her, breathing in deeply. Lara lets out a groan, her hips tilting closer to my face.

"Your eagerness is working wonders for my god complex."

"I wouldn't be getting too cocky if I were you, Darcy." Somehow, she manages to smirk down at me whilst batting her eyelashes. *Little vixen.* "In my head, you're not you. You're a combination of all my favourite book boyfriends."

Oh no she didn't.

"Is it customary down under to insult men knelt between your legs, or is that a Lara specialty?"

"Do you really want to go there right now? I mean I'm happy to discuss the men who've been in your position, but—"

"That's quite enough, you've made your point." My words come out lower and huskier than expected. "But once I've had my way with you, you won't even remember those arsehole's names—fictional or otherwise."

Lara lets out a nervous laugh. The sound is far too sweet and innocent for someone who's about to be wrecked in the least innocent of ways.

This banter-style foreplay is certainly a first for me. I've never had a woman challenge me the way Lara does. It's sexy as hell, but I think that's due to who she is and the effect she has on me as much as it is the actual interactions themselves.

Not wasting any more time, I slide my tongue out between my teeth and toward its goal. The moment the tip makes contact with Lara's clit, she whimpers. Fuck. I didn't think it was physically possible for my dick to strain any harder against my trousers. With featherlight touches, the tip of my tongue grazes her clit teasingly.

Lara lets out another whimper, and fuck if it isn't the sexiest noise I've heard. Keeping my tongue on her clit, I look up at her. She stares down at me with glazed eyes, the tension in her muscles visible as I peer up the length of her body.

"Could your fictional men do this?" I tease, flashing her a wicked grin. "I can't wait to feel you squirm beneath me." I don't hesitate, just devour.

I lap and suck at her pussy, as though it were my last meal. She tastes incredible. I've always enjoyed eating women out, but this is something else entirely. One taste of Lara is all it takes to ruin me; bring me to my knees, both physically and metaphorically.

Staring into her eyes, not breaking eye contact for even a moment, makes this feel even more intimate. My hand smooths down to meet my mouth at the apex of her thighs. Holding her gaze, my heart pounds beneath my chest as I plunge one finger into her core, not once allowing my tongue to leave her skin.

Her arousal coats my finger within seconds, her eyelids fluttering closed for a moment before boring into mine once more. There's a sharp hitch in her breathing, drawing in a ragged breath. Both her hands shoot out to the chair arms, gripping them for dear life as I flick my tongue over her clit. Her thighs contract against my shoulders, squeezing, but no amount of pressure will stop me. My gaze lowers to her throat as her pulse quickens, causing her artery to thump forcefully against the soft skin of her neck.

I can tell she wants more. She *needs* more. I plan to give her everything she desires. Sliding a second finger in, Lara lets out something resembling a sigh mingled with a groan.

"Look at you," I muse between strokes, the words sounding muffled against her skin. Lara stares down at me with an unreadable expression. *Well, that won't do.* I want nothing less than absolute satisfaction on her face, an undeniable look of pure bliss. "I think we can do better though, don't you?"

Upping the ante, I work my fingers faster. Lara's breathing begins to shallow with each pump of my fingers, but I'm not letting up. She has no idea what she's gotten herself into by saying yes to me; I won't stop until I've completely undone her.

Lara's walls squeeze around my fingers as she begins to squirm. My fingers draw out, and I sweep my tongue over Lara's pussy, taunting her with the gentlest pressure. Her hips buck slightly, bringing her even closer to my mouth. *God, this is hot.* Hotter than anything I've done before, and I had some wild nights during my university years.

Before I can get in my head about what Lara's thinking right now, she lets out the sexiest little whimper as her eyes roll back and close.

"Enjoying yourself?" I ask, mouth remaining on her.

"No." Her head is tipped back, eyes still closed, but there's the faintest smirk tugging at the edges of her lips. "I still despise you."

"I'm sure you do." My lips pull into a devilish grin against her clit as I decide to *really* push her to the edge. Pulling my lips in over my teeth so as not to hurt her, I close my mouth around her clit and bite down.

Her hands are in my hair in an instant, and she tugs on the dark strands, kneading her fingers into my scalp. My *goodness*, it feels incredible. It's taking a ridiculous amount of self-restraint not to grab her by the wrists, pull her up onto the desk, and fuck her senseless.

Patience, Carter. Rome wasn't built in a day.

Lara's grip tightens, and I mentally prepare to be pulled in deeper. Instead, I'm tugged backwards, away from the delectable meal I was thoroughly enjoying. Groaning, I reluctantly look up at Lara, making sure to keep my fingers firmly inside her, for good measure, of course. Lara raises a brow at me as her lips break into a soft smile.

"Okay Darcy, you've proved your point," she relents with

rasp, both hands still entwined in my hair. "I take back what I said, so you can stop now."

"Is that what you want?"

I need to know if she means what she's saying. As much as it would kill me to stop right now, I respect her too much to ever go against her wishes.

"What do you mean?"

"Do you want me to stop? Because I will, if that's truly what you want." I'm silently praying to any gods who may be out there that her answer is no. "But if you say no, I won't relent until you're spent beneath me in this chair."

A nervous little laugh comes from Lara, and my heart sinks a millimetre in my chest.

"That's unlikely."

Is she insulting me? Questioning my skills? Actually, she's not even questioning them. She's outright suggesting they aren't adequate. I reluctantly slide my fingers out. The last thing I want is to make her feel uncomfortable.

"Lara, I'd hate to sound like a dick, but the way your body was responding to my touch begs to differ."

She has the audacity to look momentarily taken aback, as if this is the first she's heard of it. As if she wasn't the one moaning and whimpering not one minute ago.

"I'm not disagreeing with that," she mumbles softly, her cheeks growing pinker as she looks down at her lap. "I don't have a great track record when it comes to men getting me off. Truthfully, I should say it's the men who don't have a great track record." With a gleam in her eye, she shrugs. "I've never had a problem getting myself off."

Well, shit, I did not think this was where the conversation was heading. I must admit, quite frankly, I'm astounded by this revelation. What sort of useless men are they raising in Australia?

"Hold on," I say, trying to put my reeling thoughts into words. "Are you meaning to tell me no man has feasted on you to the point of orgasm?"

Lara gives me a coy look. "Well, one or two may have." My eyes are drawn to her lap, where her fingers are fiddling with each other. Is she nervous? Or have I made her uncomfortable?

"But the odds aren't in your favour," Lara continues. Her eyes search mine briefly, and I wonder what it is she's looking for.

"I'm not usually one to bet, but I'd put my money on me." I give her my cockiest smile from my position between her legs. "I accept."

A laugh slips from Lara's lips before she quickly covers her mouth as if she can't believe she laughed. "I'm sorry, you accept what?" she responds, dropping her hand to her lap.

"I accept your challenge."

This time, the laugh is carefree. "That wasn't a challenge, Mr Darcy." Big blue eyes narrow in my direction. As much as it boosts my ego to know she's thought of me enough to give me a nickname, it might be nice to hear my name on her lips at a time like this. But if I want this to happen again—which I absolutely do—it's not worth the risk of her knowing my identity. Because if she knows that, it's only a matter of time before she knows how the media has portrayed me.

"No? That's too bad, I've already accepted. One does not simply back down from an accepted challenge."

"You're insane." The smile she's struggling to hold back, combined with the heat in her eyes, tells a different story. Now *that* I can work with.

Her legs have slowly come together, which simply won't do. Placing a hand on the inside of each knee, I yank them apart. A startled Lara lets out a small gasp as she looks down at me once more.

My hands trail up the inside of her thighs. "I vow to be the one to ruin those odds, Lara." Her name comes out in an unfamiliar gravel.

My hands reach their target, and I lean forward once more, refusing to break eye contact with the angel above me.

As my tongue makes contact with her clit, the unimaginable happens.

The fucking doorbell chimes.

Lara jumps in the chair, her hands twisting in my hair, attempting to push me away. The entire scenario makes me chuckle, even with the erection I'm sporting.

Aware we're no longer alone in the store, I rise from my position on the floor. But not before giving Lara one last languid lick, then adjusting the placement of her underwear. Lara stands, and I make sure to pull her skirt into place.

Before she can run, I place a hand on her forearm. She turns to face me, and I lean in. My lips graze the shell of her ear as I speak.

"If you think we're finished, Lara, you'll soon find yourself to be *very* mistaken." The words are more of a murmur than anything, but the answering goosebumps gracing her skin tell me she heard every word.

In no rush, I allow my gaze to trace each curve of Lara's rear form as she retreats to the shop floor, taking in each detail like it's the last time I'll have the privilege. Given the way in which the last ten minutes went, I think there's a good chance it certainly will not be the last time.

Dropping into the seat Lara vacated, I let out a deep breath. There's a dangerous play-by-play occurring at the front of my mind —the way it felt to have Lara gripping my hair and tugging. The way she writhed beneath my touch, her reactiveness lighting up something inside me. The way my cock ached to connect with some part of her each time she elicited one of those little whimpers.

As the front of my trousers threatens to become concerningly tight, my daydreaming is cut short. The overhead bell sounds, echoing throughout the shop—the telltale sign that we're alone once more.

I can't be certain how long I've sat here; it could've been two minutes or twenty. Time always seems to warp where Lara is involved, regardless of whether she's physically here or if I'm merely thinking of her. The latter has become increasingly more frequent, which both concerns and excites me.

Time to face the music.

Chapter 14

Lara

"It's been a pleasure, as always, Lara," Mr Darcy drawls, reappearing through the arched doorway. My name has never held such sex appeal until now. Before I can gather myself and respond, he's out the front door. Fixation sets in, and I'm unable to tear my eyes away from his retreating figure. He takes a few more steps down the path and stops alongside the motorcycle.

Sensing my eyes on him, he turns. Our eyes lock from afar, and I swear the faintest of smiles drags at the corner of his mouth. Without breaking eye contact, he reaches down and collects the helmet from its compartment. Ever so slowly, he lifts it above his head and lowers it over his face. I can't see his eyes anymore, but my *god,* I can feel them. The air feels stifling, and I abruptly turn from the window.

Did I really get all hot and bothered watching a man put on a helmet? Fuck, I need to get laid. Or go another round of whatever happened in the back room. Or both.

I'm also still trying to process the fact he rides a motorcycle, as if he wasn't hot enough already. Obscene images of those veined hands gripping the throttle flood my mind, causing an irrational rush of envy at the way it would be handled.

With Mr Darcy gone, I have a moment of reprieve. *What the fuck just happened?* I'm struggling to reconcile the person I know myself to be with the person who was willingly eaten out in her workplace by a man whose name is a mystery. I *do not* do things like this. I'm a rule follower who sees most men as nothing but disappointing. What was I thinking?

What's even more shocking is that I loved *every single second* of it. I've never been so close to the edge at the hands of a man before, and I'll be damned if I don't want to repeat it immediately. Not only that, but I'm now more intrigued than ever to know more about this man. It's a given that he's incredibly attractive, but I'm dying to see more of who he is on the inside. Our interactions are unlike any I've had with men previously. He challenges me, and I challenge him in return; he matches my sarcasm to a T; he looks at me as though he can't quite believe his eyes—I look at him and wonder *why me?*

After work, I arrived home with my mind still reeling. Do I look like I had a beautiful man's head between my legs mere hours ago? Am I going to be outed the second I walk through the front door? Is my arousal still evident?

The smell of freshly baked cookies wafts over me as I enter the open living space. Mia pops up from behind the bench. Looking every bit the modern-day housewife, she dons a frilly white apron and matching oven mitts.

"I made cookies!" she beams, greeting me.

"They smell divine." I attempt to mirror her smile as I make my way to one of the wooden stools at the bench.

Mia sets the tray down in front of me, meeting my eyes

with a quirk of her head. "Lara, are you quite alright? Your face looks funny."

Taking a seat, I let out a short laugh, caught off guard by her statement. She knows, she *must* know. She's looking at me like she's aware of what went down, or more accurately, *who* went down.

My thoughts stray to that talented tongue as I cross my legs, my insides clenching on their own accord. I rub a hand over my face, willing away intrusive thoughts of Mr Darcy. Another laugh escapes, and I have no doubt I appear unhinged right now.

"Harper!" she bellows, gripping the doorway to the hall and leaning her entire body in the direction of the balcony. "Help me! Lara's acting awfully peculiar."

The sound of hurried footsteps on the carpet announces Harper's arrival before her head pops around the doorway. She regards me for a moment, tilting her head to the side the same way Mia did.

"Mmm," is the only sound she makes as her eyes rake over me. "Something is certainly amiss."

Mia rounds the bench to join Harper in the doorway. They're looking at me the way Emma Thompson's character in *Love Actually* looked at her child when she announced she'd be playing the first lobster in the nativity play; utterly perplexed.

"What in the bloody hell happened at work today?" Mia crosses her arms over her chest.

Glancing between the two of them, I realise I have no idea where the fuck to start. I'm silent for a moment, staring at my friends without really seeing them. My thoughts are in complete disarray. How do I word this correctly?

"He ate me out."

It seems I don't bother with correctness, deciding instead to blurt it out like the answer to a quiz show question.

A high-pitched noise comes from Mia, sounding a similar frequency to a train whistle. My eyes dart to her first, and I stifle a laugh.

The oven mitts have fallen to the floor as she stands there wide-eyed. Her jaw hangs open, and the image of a laughing clown carnival game flashes in front of me. For someone with so much energy, it's almost frightening to see her so still.

Gaze sliding from Mia to Harper, I find a completely different reaction.

She's sporting the biggest grin I think I've *ever* seen on her face. The way she's able to appear perfectly poised at all times is an incredible skill. Especially now, leaned against the doorframe with her arms crossed over her chest.

"Lara, honey, please give us some context before she" — Harper glances at Mia, who's yet to move a muscle — "makes up her own nightmare-worthy story."

Still uncertain where to begin, I take a deep breath.

"He, as in Mr Darcy, was on his knees with his painfully beautiful face between my thighs approximately one hour and thirty-seven minutes ago. But who's counting?"

The sound of my voice brings Mia back to Earth. Her previously still body is now jumping up and down on the spot, hands clapping, and mouth warped into a smile so wide it would rival the Cheshire Cat. Tiny *oh my god*'s are being thrown out at an alarming speed.

"How? Why? Was it good? Is it happening again?" The questions leave Mia's mouth like rapid fire. "We need details, Lara."

"Perhaps if you took a breath, she'd have a chance to get a word in," Harper replies, rolling her eyes and grinning at me.

"Ah, you're right, I'm sorry, Lars. This is quite the revelation." Mia raises her arms above her head before pulling her hands down in front of her face, taking in a deep breath as they come to a stop in front of her stomach.

Amusement flickers in Harper's eyes, her gaze flitting between Mia and me.

'How' is a hard one, as is 'why' if I'm honest.

"Honestly, I'm not really sure how or why it happened. I know it sounds ridiculous, but it's the truth. It kind of just happened, you know? It wasn't good, it was *breathtaking*—literally." Heat rises in my cheeks.

The girls are quiet, still beaming at me.

"As for whether it's happening again, I highly doubt it."

"What!" Mia raises her arms in front of her, palms toward me in a stop-like motion. "Why?"

Before I can come up with a reason, Harper chimes in. "Darling girl, we can feel the sexual deprivation oozing from your pores. It's about time you did something about it."

"Harper's right, honey. Please fuck him, like as soon as possible. We need to live vicariously through you."

I can't control the burst of laughter that erupts in response; these two are something else. They aren't wrong, though; I haven't been out with even one guy since moving. Work keeps me reasonably busy, and when I'm not working, I'm exploring or hanging out with the girls.

Dating hasn't been high on my priority list, and I'm completely fine with that. Who needs a boyfriend when you have friends as great as mine? Casual sex, though, could be beneficial. I'd be lying if I said I didn't have a particular itch Mr Darcy could scratch.

Sort of like the way his stubble scratched the inside of my thighs.

Focus, Lara.

"The both of you are also single; why are we living through me?"

"Last I checked, neither of us had a suited man falling to his knees for us."

My lips twitch at Harper's response. Mia brings a hand up to stifle her giggle. It feels like a fever dream when you put it like that, but it's one I want to experience again and again. The man almost had me eating out the palm of his hand and certainly had me moaning. My cheeks heat at the memory. The only thing that could've possibly made it better would be having a name—a *real* name—to moan.

Chapter 15

Carter

It's been fourteen days since I tasted Lara, fourteen days since I learnt the sound of her moans. It's been fourteen days since I was last able to think straight.

From the moment she sat, I haven't had a single clear thought. Instead, I've mused over all the ways in which I can get myself between her thighs once more and finish what we started.

It's early, too early, but I'm already sitting in my office and have been for at least half an hour. A restless sleep last night led me to go for a run before dawn to clear my mind. It worked during the run, but the second I walked into the building, all thoughts went to Lara.

I found myself wondering more and more about previously unimportant details about her, like what she'd be wearing, how her night had been, and if she'd have on her signature scent— the delicate raspberry and rose aroma that invades my nostrils whenever I enter the bookshop, similar to the way Lara herself invades my thoughts. I'm glad Dex isn't in yet; the arsehole would be giving me an absolute earful if he could see the way I'm pining like a lovesick fool.

Although I've seen her since the stockroom excitement, we haven't touched each other like that since. There have been small touches here and there though, which I've been painfully fucking aware of.

I'd said something funny last week, and she'd placed a hand on my bicep while laughing in a way that had heat rising in my chest. Her face lit up so beautifully that it almost took my breath away. It was clear she was unaware of the captivating picture she made.

Lara probably hadn't thought much of it, but I certainly had. Anyone who may have overheard our exchanges for the remainder of my time in the bookshop would've had good reason to think I was trying to become a stand-up comedian.

The week before, we'd both reached for a book at the same time, and her fingertips grazed mine. It sounds awfully cliche, but *bloody hell*, it affected me far more than a simple touch should.

Keeping my thoughts from straying to that alluring woman is getting harder by the day, especially when sitting alone at my desk. Too many salacious ideas run rampant when I eye the edge of my desk—Lara bent over it, sat on it, spread open on it. I might be the CEO, but I wouldn't put it past Anna to fire me on the spot if I acted on any of those ideas.

Almost as if she knew I was thinking about her, an email from Anna pops up.

To: clawrence@jlsons.com
From: ataylor@jlsons.com
Subject: EA Update
Morning boss,

Quick update on the assistant front - I interviewed a few more yesterday, but unfortunately none seemed suitable. Majority of the applicants have been quite young, and a little too immature for the role. A few seemed more interested in knowing if the "pretty CEO" (their words, I assure you) was the executive they'd be assisting.

I have a few more lined up this week, so hopefully one is the perfect fit.

Kind Regards,

Anna Taylor

Head of Human Resources | J. L. & Sons

Running a hand through my dishevelled hair, I let out a sigh. I'm aware we haven't been searching for long, but I lose a little bit of hope with each interview that comes and goes.

When my father started the firm all those years ago, he never anticipated the rapid growth it would experience. What started as a small family law firm quickly transformed into one of the largest and most prestigious firms in the United Kingdom. And with that growth came media for the entire family.

Since the day I started university, my name has been well-known in the corporate and legal worlds. Anyone with the slightest knowledge of this world, at least in the UK, knows who my father is and usually who I am as well.

Naturally, as a young man in his late teens and early 20s, I thought it was the absolute best thing ever. I mean, who doesn't want their name on magazine covers? Or at least I thought I did until I learnt about the darker side of the press.

One night at the end of our first year, Dex and I had been at a party at a friend's estate not far from campus. We'd finished up exams, and the party was an excuse to let loose. I'd been casually seeing—sleeping with—a classmate for a few weeks, and she'd mentioned she may be at the party too. She was perfectly lovely, but something about her kept me a little on edge. Regardless, I'd kept seeing her on and off because I was nineteen and horny.

Long story short, she'd seen me talking to others and became overly territorial. To the point where she verbally attacked me in front of half the party, calling me a man whore, yelling about how I'd embarrassed her, and even threatening me with the press—a threat I had wrongly assumed was empty.

Flash forward an hour or two, and I'm in a more than compromising position with one of the girls I'd been talking to earlier. Without warning, the door slams open and in bursts, a hoard of press representatives, cameras and microphones as far as the eye can see.

My face, and more of me than I'd like to admit, covered the British tabloids for a solid week. Thankfully my father was able to quell it quite quickly, but I vowed then and there to keep my head down as best I could for the foreseeable future.

And that was what I did, until four years ago, when Teddy received that fateful phone call.

The memory of that day is as fresh as if it were last week. Picture this: you're the eldest son of a well-known family, loved by the British tabloids, and have just returned from a tour of Afghanistan. You receive one call from an unknown number, and your life alters beyond any of your wildest dreams.

Being the "fix it" middle child I am, I did the only thing I could think of to ensure the tabloids never found out. They may love my family, but they love drama and gossip even more. They'd throw us under the bus quicker than we could say "stop".

The next several weeks were spent finding a new woman to be seen with each weekend. What better way to distract the tabloids from sniffing around than to give them something to gossip about?

I'd made sure to have Emmy speak to her regulars at the bar about me, and in particular, what I'd be up to that weekend, ensuring the local photographers who frequented the bar overheard.

Every media article about me from then on had been in order to protect my brother and our family. Every picture with yet another gorgeous woman on my arm was staged.

Front pages were splashed with titles like "London's Law Prodigy has a Hot Study Date" and "Another One, Carter?" Each article made my parents more and more uncomfortable with the situation I'd brought on myself, but they knew why I was doing it.

It didn't matter to the media if I hadn't taken these women home; instead, opting to help my brother with his newly acquainted baby daughter, they decided the narrative.

At the end of the day, I didn't care what the general public thought of me, as long as it kept the attention off Teddy. My family, the firm—under strict NDAs—and those closest to me knew the truth, and that was enough.

I've spent the last four years keeping up the ruse in the public eye. Do I regret it? Occasionally, but only because of the ramifications on my personal life. If I had my time over though, I wouldn't change a thing.

Since then, the tabloids have known me as the player of the British Law World, which means women know me the same way. I've been on many dates over the years, all of which were photographed, of course, but the women I dated saw me as nothing more than a good-looking man in an expensive suit.

Not that I particularly minded; I spent a lot of that time seeing myself the same way and still do to an extent. But now, having taken over the firm, I wonder if I can make them see me as more. *I wonder if Lara could see me as more.*

The thought stops me in my tracks in a way that's almost comedic as I make my way through reception. It continues to rattle me how deeply this woman has invaded my thoughts and clouded my brain.

I'm trying my best not to burn myself on the baking tray when the music cuts out, and my sister's incoming call is announced.

"What took you so long?" Emmy sounds miles away from the phone as I answer. Placing her on speaker, I successfully remove the tray from the oven, sans third-degree burns. My mother may have had me baking from a young age, but I never quite mastered the art of safely removing things from the oven.

"Hello to you too, little one." I smile to myself at the smug tone of my voice. My sister *despises* it when I refer to her as 'little one'; something I've done since we were kids.

"Carter John Lawrence." It's never a good thing when she uses my full name. "Believe it or not, I'm actually calling for a serious reason."

"You've certainly piqued my interest, Emilia James." I listen a little more intently whilst continuing to tidy up my disaster zone of a kitchen after baking. A muffled "god, you're insufferable" comes through the phone, and I hold back the smile pulling at my lips.

Memories surface of all the times Lara has called me the same thing. Being called insufferable isn't exactly on my list of goals, but I can't deny the ridiculous flutter in my stomach every time she says it; proud of myself for eliciting a strong reaction from her.

"Are you even listening to me?" Emmy's voice cuts through my thoughts.

"Honestly? No. I'm sorry, I was somewhere else entirely. Could you please repeat that?"

Emmy lets out a sigh before continuing. "Oh, it wasn't anything vital, just how I may have found you the perfect assistant."

Stars appear in my vision from the speed at which I whip my head around. My brows draw together as I glance at my phone.

"By all means, please continue, dear sister."

I swear I *hear* the way her eyes roll. My sister has always had a bit of a dramatic flare, and rolling her eyes is something she does plenty when it comes to our conversations.

"Truly, there isn't much else to share. I won't tell you her name, in case she doesn't interview well, because quite frankly, you'd never let me live it down. But I'm positive she's the right fit."

I set free a small chuckle when I hear the smile in my sister's tone. It has me even more intrigued—I wonder who she's referring to?

Seemingly reading my thoughts in that comfortable way, she always has, Emmy adds, "You don't know her, so I wouldn't bother trying to figure it out."

Not unsurprising when it comes to my sister; she's known to be quite a sociable person. Her job at the bar emphasises this. Emmy is constantly telling us at family dinner about new friends she's made at work, and they're often colourful characters, to say the least. Is this "perfect fit" one of those friends?

Due to a schedule clash, my trip to the bookstore this week is earlier than usual.

The first thing I notice when walking into the store is an absence—there's no Lara.

Curiosity gets the better of me. "Where's the lovely Lara this morning?"

The smile Riss flashes my way is a little too mischievous for my liking, but I let it slide. I've found it's best not to question her motives.

Riss proceeds to tell me Lara had somewhere to be this morning and that she'd be in later. It's hard to ignore the slight drop in my shoulders as if my body itself is disappointed by this news. I'm caught off guard when Riss asks, "Something the matter, dear?"

"Oh no, everything is splendid." Glancing around the room, it's as if I need to prove it myself that she isn't here. I wonder where she is? "It's been great seeing you Riss, but I better head out."

After giving Riss a quick goodbye hug, I'm back on my motorbike. I'm struggling to process why I care *quite* so much that Lara wasn't there. Yes, I went down on her in possibly one of the hottest encounters of my life. Yes, she's been a constant in my mind since that encounter. Yes, she tasted like the sort of meal you'd request as your last. But none of that means I should care this much.

For the duration of the trip back to the office, one question is bouncing around my mind: what the fuck has gotten into me?

Chapter 16

Lara

"Credit where credit's due though, especially if you've given no inclination that you'll reciprocate the flirting. The man is persevering like an absolute champ."

An obnoxious laugh rips from my throat at Mia's words, which garners some odd looks from fellow restaurant-goers. The three of us are enjoying a meal out for the first time in weeks, finally having found a night we were all free.

I'm shocked but not surprised at Mia's praise for the man who shamelessly flirts with Harper most days. She makes a good point though. Regardless of the fact he's almost ten years her senior and they work on the same floor, he hasn't let up.

"Please don't encourage his behaviour," Harper responds with a tut. Despite her best efforts to hide it, I catch a glimpse of the smallest of smiles playing on Harper's lips. Mia just grins, shaking her head. "Anyway, enough about me," Harper continues. "Lara, honey, how's work going for you?"

It's not a hard question by any means, yet I'm stuck on how

to respond. Stalling, I take a sip from my water glass. "I love the bookstore, and Riss is a delight—"

"Oh, there's a *but* coming," Mia chimes in, prompting Harper to tap her hand and give her a warning look.

"Don't jump to conclusions Mia, let her finish."

Mia gives me an apologetic look. "Sorry, Lars. Continue."

A sad smile finds its way onto my face. "Actually, Mia's right. I love it there, but it just doesn't provide a high enough income for the weekend trips we planned that first week. When I got here, I had hopes of nights in Scotland, weekend trips to Paris, and perhaps an Amsterdam visit or two. Where have I travelled so far? The Tesco Supermarket around the corner."

"Hey now," Harper adds with a reassuring squeeze of my wrist. "Don't forget the Primark on Oxford Street. Surely it beats out our local Tesco."

A chorus of laughs rings out between the three of us. Cheeks tender and tears on the brink of spilling over, our laughter slowly dies down.

"Despite the wonderful Tesco and Primark trips we've embarked on, I want more. I *need* more. So I'm going to look for another part time gig to work alongside the bookstore."

Mia, who'd been watching the wait staff like a hawk for our dessert, whips her head in my direction with such tenacity I'm momentarily worried it'll fly right off her shoulders. "I know you love Chapter Nine, but would you be open to something full-time instead? Because I might just know of an opening you'd be a perfect fit for."

The June sun shining down on me as I make my way to my interview two days later makes me think of home. There haven't been an awful lot of sunny days during the three months I've been here, so I'm grateful for the warmth.

I've never been much of a summer person, which is laughable considering I spent most of my life in what's known as the "Sunshine State". Bearing in mind our summer days back home stay around the 32° mark; this 23° heat isn't exactly hot.

Where the locals are dressed for a day at the beach, and the smell of barbeques permeates the air, I'm in a Harper Original —as in borrowed from Harper's extensive winter wardrobe. It's handy having friends the same size as you for this exact reason.

Harper, well aware of the wardrobe I'd bought with me from Australia, whisked me into her closet yesterday when Mia informed us the HR Manager wanted to meet with me this morning.

"We need to pick you out a bombshell interview outfit, really make you leave an impression on them."

Harper is a firm believer of "dress for the job you want", which is precisely why I'm currently walking through London in a red pantsuit, as though the streets are my personal catwalk.

My hair is done up in a sophisticated ballerina bun, and my no-makeup makeup look will hopefully hide the nervous blush I'm sure to exhibit whilst simultaneously making my baby face look its 27 years.

Well, I absolutely smashed that interview, if I do say so myself. In my defence, Anna also told me as much. The Head of HR was easily one of the most delightful people I've ever encountered, as well as one of the best dressed.

The first thing I noticed as she strode through the lobby was her energy. It sounds strange to say I could see someone's energy, but it's true. The way Anna held herself commanded the attention of any and all in her vicinity.

She was tall, with legs that went for miles and curves I would pay good money for. The simple burgundy dress she donned hugged her in all the right places and made me desperately wish for a figure like hers. I wanted to be this woman when I grew up.

The interview was pretty standard; it included a brief history of the company, questions about me, questions about the company, etc. At the conclusion, Anna beamed at me.

"I had a feeling from what Mia had told me that you'd be a great match. Now I've met you, I think you're the perfect fit for our CEO."

CEO.

Mia hadn't mentioned the executive I'd be assisting would be the CEO, had she?

Anna had suggested we go upstairs to meet him, but unfortunately his office was empty when we arrived on the 20th floor. Regardless, I'd been offered the job on the spot and asked if I could start on Monday, at which time I'd meet their elusive leader.

Nothing but praise for Mr Lawrence came out of Anna's mouth, so I'm excited to meet him next week.

Although I have extensive admin experience in a variety of sectors, legal and executive assistance are two areas in which I have zero expertise. Given this, I'm kind of nervous. But *fake it til you make it*, right? Even though I wanted this job, I'm still a little shocked I was successful.

It's just after lunch when I arrive at Chapter Nine for my shift. Riss shuffles straight over as I walk through the front door.

"How did it go, dear? Did they love you?"

I don't get a word in before she pulls me in for a hug.

"Oh, what a silly question, *of course* they loved you. I wouldn't be surprised if they hired you on the spot."

Pulling away from Riss' affection, I give her a coy smile. I swear this woman knows *everything*.

"Actually, that's exactly what they did." I fiddle with one jacket sleeve, avoiding her gaze. "I'm meant to start Monday."

"Meant to?" she asks, eyebrows furrowed.

"I told Anna I'd have to confirm later today. I'm meant to open the store on Monday."

A small hand claps me on the shoulder. "Oh, Lara dear, don't be silly! My granddaughter can help me out; you're starting Monday."

Tears threaten to spill over my eyelids as I'm met with the sweetest smile. Whether they're tears of appreciation, joy, or sadness is yet to be determined. They're probably a combination of all three.

Riss has become somewhat of a fill-in grandmother to me, always checking in on me, asking for updates on the girls, and making sure I'm fed. Food seems to be her love language, so I'll be damned if I intervene.

"Promise me you'll visit for tea on occasion?" Riss' smile falters slightly as her eyes brim with tears, and that's my undoing. My nose wrinkles as I attempt to quell the emotions with small sniffles. Untrusting of my voice, I nod.

The petite lady reaches up a hand to cup my cheek, wiping away a stray tear from the tip of my nose. "This is a wonderful thing dear, you should be so proud of yourself."

My heart aches at the thought of not seeing Riss as often as I currently do. She's become an important constant in my life abroad, and mornings without our tea together won't be the same.

The rest of the day goes by in a blur, with more customers than usual, given a few new releases we've got in stock. Despite the rush, I haven't been able to shake the feeling that something is off today. What that is, I haven't the slightest clue, but the feeling doesn't wane.

I'm confirming the final details with Anna when Riss pops her head through the storeroom archway.

"Congratulations again, Lara. We'll see you at nine o'clock Monday." With a friendly goodbye, the call disconnects.

"It's official!" Riss beams at me from the doorway. "I'm off now dear, but I'll see you on Thursday."

"See you then!"

Collecting up her things, Riss blows me a kiss before disappearing from sight, the doorbell sounding moments later.

I glance down at my watch. Woah, it's four o'clock already. Where has the day gone? An unexpected pang of disappointment hits me in the chest as I realise what felt off: Mr Darcy hasn't shown his face today.

Disappointment sits heavy in my stomach. *Since when do I care?* A little voice chimes in from the back of my mind, sounding eerily like a mix between Harper and Mia.

You started caring from the moment he went down on you with more skill than Owen Gray.

Well, *shit*, the hybrid voice may have a point.

I go through the motions of closing the store for the day without really thinking about it. My thoughts are stuck on one tall, dark and sarcastic man and his lack of showing up today. I'd be lying to myself if I said I didn't enjoy our interactions, and I don't just mean the physical storeroom kind.

I hate to admit it, but the man makes me laugh. He also makes me scowl and roll my eyes to the point of pain, but the laughter side of things seems to be more prominent.

Last Tuesday comes to mind; it was as though he was enjoying seeing me happy. That can't be right, can it? The man usually gets on my last nerve, yet something was different that day. He was different.

"Well, well, this is certainly interesting."

The deep timbre of Mr Darcy's voice draws my attention away from the stack of books I've been pricing up. He's standing in front of the Staff Picks stand looking as dapper as always. On this angle, it's hard not to stare at the way his trousers hug his arse so perfectly. Something resembling a whimper escapes me at the sight. Heat blooms in my cheeks almost immediately. His gaze flickers to me, and I fumble the pricing machine I'm holding.

"W-what's interesting?" I hope the question makes him forget the noise he just heard.

There's a smirk on his face as he picks up one of the books, waving it in his hand like a makeshift fan. "This pick right here is very interesting."

Despite knowing he's purposely being vague to get my attention, I play along. I wander over to stand beside him, glancing at the book—The Bonus by T.L. Swan.

"He looks an awful lot like me, don't you think?" He quirks a brow.

I can't help it, I keel over in a fit of laughter.

When I right myself, I place a hand on his bicep. I didn't intend on touching him, but it doesn't feel wrong when I do. The moment my skin makes contact with his, my heart thuds once against my ribcage, then settles into its usual rhythm.

I feel his gaze on me before I see it. When I glance up, I'm met with the sincerest smile I think I've ever seen on that handsome face. There's never been any doubt he had a good-looking face, but when the corners of his eyes wrinkle and his signature dimple appears, my heart squeezes. I'm not sure I'll ever see someone more enchanting than he is right now, gazing down at me like I hung the stars.

Ignoring the strong desire to pull away from him and the intensity of his gaze, I keep my hand planted firmly on his arm. Mr Darcy studies my face for a moment before blinking and refocusing his gaze, the moment having passed.

On my walk home, disappointment flares again as thoughts of what could've been flood my mind. Given the fact there's almost ten million people living in London, there's a good chance I'll never see him again.

Chapter 17

Carter

The laptop in front of me whirs to life as my desk phone rings. Peering at the caller ID, I find myself sucking in a short breath. It's Anna.

This isn't a normal reaction I have when Anna calls me, but my new assistant is starting today, and Anna said she'd give me a quick call before she arrived.

Truthfully, I haven't decided how I feel about this whole situation. Do I really need a stranger coming in and attempting to keep me organised? I'm a grown man; I'm almost positive I can handle it by myself.

Reminding myself she's never given me a reason to doubt her judgement, I pick up the phone.

"Morning, Lawrence," comes Anna's cheerful voice through the line. "Are you ready for this?" I can hear the teasing tone in Anna's voice, and I have to try awfully hard to keep the breath I let out inaudible.

"Remind me again why we're hiring someone Emilia knows?"

A light laugh rings out.

"Humour me, please."

"Because she seems organised to a fault, something you need, and gave me the impression she'd be able to handle you, even on your foul mood days."

The last part has me chuckling while I close my eyes and lean back in my chair, deciding perhaps Anna has a point.

"She'll be here any moment, so we'll see you soon." As I reach to disconnect the call, Anna's voice sounds again. "Oh, and Carter? Be nice."

With that, she hangs up.

"Always," I say to myself with a smirk.

Some days I wish Anna didn't know me as well as she does, and today is one of those days.

The only thing I know so far about our newest recruit is her name—Lara. There must be thousands of Laras out there, but that doesn't stop me from wondering—what are the chances?

A soft knock interrupts my train of thought. Shit, I'm really not ready for this. How am I supposed to cope working with this Lara whilst mine occupies my every thought?

Mine? Where the fuck did that come from?

"Come in."

Standing in place, I slide my hands into my pockets and turn to face the window. The sound of the door handle opening has my heart skipping a beat. After taking a long, deep breath, I turn around.

"Carter, meet Lara—your new EA."

If I were a cartoon character, this would be the moment my jaw smacks onto the carpet, and my eyes bug out of my head.

Standing before me, looking dangerously good, is Lara. *My Lara.*

Again with the possessiveness, what is happening to me?

The answer is standing right across from me.

My whole body stiffens as if not one part of it knows how to react to this. Even the air in the room has changed. It's charged and thick with unspoken tension. My mind is racing. Is this some bizarre dream I'm about to wake up from?

Lara's expression morphs from a polite smile to one of sheer horror. Her eyes are wide, mouth slightly agape, and I realise she's probably the mirror image of me 30 seconds ago.

Whoever is pulling the strings of my brain cells makes the reckless decision to flood my mind with thoughts of the stock-room encounter with Lara. The way I feasted on her and how our time was cut painfully short.

As the initial shock begins to subside, my gaze rakes over her for a moment and really takes her in. Time stands still as our eyes meet. Those beautiful blues are most certainly still processing this development because she doesn't blink once.

I take in the black and white tweed blazer and skirt set; the way the latter hugs her figure so perfectly. I almost short-circuit picturing how incredible her arse must look right now. My mouth lifts in a half smile at the thought.

Anna clears her throat, reminding me of her presence. The moment Lara entered my space, it was just the two of us.

I'm entranced by Lara, and it's impossible to look away. Because of this, I witness the exact second Anna's throat clearing breaks her out of her trance. Right before my eyes, she processes that I'm standing here, her new boss.

Chapter 18

Lara

"**C**arter," the soft whisper escapes me before my brain is able to stop it.

There's a whirring sound throughout my head, and I'm pretty sure it's due to the fact my mind is going a million miles a minute, attempting to process the fact he has a name. A name other than Mr Darcy. A real name: *Carter*.

Vaguely aware of movement in my peripheries, it seems Anna is now directing her attention at me rather than her boss. *My boss.*

The fact I'm so caught up on his real name, instead of the fact he's my new boss, is laughable.

My new boss went down on me.

The man who will sign my paychecks is the man who takes up a little too much real estate in my thoughts. This is *not* good.

As my crazy thoughts begin to slow down a little, I'm finally registering I have this man's full attention right now.

The way he's looking at me is unnerving. It's as though his

thoughts are straying to *that* encounter as well, if the slight pull at the corner of his lips is anything to go by.

The intensity of his gaze has me slicking my palms down my skirt before returning them to a clasp in front of me. It's all I can do to avoid fiddling. Has someone turned the heat up in the past few moments?

Dragging myself out of my head and back into the situation at hand, I'm made painfully aware that Mr Darcy—*Carter*— must have spoken. His arm is outstretched in my direction, waiting, the delicious veins of his hand and forearm on full display.

A blush creeps slowly up my neck, and I send out a silent prayer that I don't end up looking like a tomato.

Ever so diligently, I reach my own hand out, taking his larger one in mine. Our gazes lock on one another. A handshake has never felt quite so inappropriate.

"Lara." *God*, his voice is as deep and authoritative as ever. "It's a pleasure to finally meet you."

Fuck, I hope the wicked glint I caught in his eye wasn't noticed by Anna, or the subsequent reddening of my face. The last thing I need on my first day is for the lovely Head of HR thinking I have a crush on my boss.

Did he know? He couldn't have known. Could he? Ugh, I wish I knew what he was thinking right now.

Carter's handshake is so much more than that; it's firm, and warm, and comfortable in a way no handshake has any business being. The silly little organ in my chest skips a beat when his fingers skate across the centre of my palm as he retreats, almost longingly.

The delicate contact sends a small zap of electricity up my arm, and I immediately miss the warmth of his hand in mine. My thoughts are yet to process the way they should, so all I can do is smile shyly at him.

It seems ridiculous to be shy around him when last fort-night, the man had his head between my legs. But alas, here we are.

"Carter, can I borrow you for a moment? I need to run you through what Lara and I covered this morning."

Anna flashes a warm smile my way before ducking out the office door. With a small glance in my direction, Carter follows.

I watch them silently for a moment, Anna speaking animatedly whilst Carter listens intently. Rather than continuing to stand awkwardly beside the door, I take a few steps further into the office.

Alone for the first time since this atomic bomb was dropped on me, my crazy thoughts ramp right back up again. He must have known, right? There's no way he didn't. It's his damn company after all. Bu then again, he looked as shocked as I felt when he saw me, so maybe he really didn't know? It's all too much.

Glancing around at the furniture and décor to distract my racing thoughts and rapid heartrate, I take in the simple yet sophisticated style of the spacious office. Two tufted cream occasional chairs sit centrally, across from a matching lounge, separated by a low-set deep walnut table. The crisp white walls are broken up by matching walnut bookshelves lined with what looks to be every law book known to man.

The main feature is clear: the dark mahogany desk sitting off to the right. It's situated so the sweeping view of the Thames is the backdrop, and any natural light will fall directly on it. The skin covering my arms prickles as my gaze comes to rest on the chair behind the lavish desk. My heart rate kicks up a notch as memories of Carter and me with a similar office chair float into my mind.

I'd deny it if I were ever asked, but I think about that

encounter far too often. I squeeze my thighs together as I reminisce about the feeling of his mouth on my skin. The heat of his breath at my core, his gentle touch on my inner thighs, the way his tongue knew precisely what I needed.

Feeling as though I'm being watched, I whirl around and meet Carter's gaze. Lost in the memory of him, I failed to notice him and Anna re-entering the room. His emerald irises flare briefly, and I'd put money on the fact that he can hear my filthy thoughts.

Jesus Lara, can you be a professional for five minutes?

My gaze remains firmly on Carter as I watch his flicker to the chair behind the desk, then to me, giving me a smile only I can see. And *holy crap*, what a devastating smile it is.

"Well, I think that's all from my end of things, so I'll leave the two of you to get acquainted." Anna beams at us, clearly happy with this pairing, before turning and walking out of Carter's office. My head swivels around as I watch Anna leave, but the door clicking shut softly behind her still manages to startle me.

Turning to face Carter, he's the picture of cool, calm and collected. He's reclining in his chair now, one ankle crossed over the other knee, and his hands come to rest against the back of his head. Oh how I wish I could appear as unaffected as he does.

I fight the urge to squirm as he regards me from head to toe, taking in every detail. I feel like an imposter in my pencil skirt and blouse because *I know* that *he knows* I don't dress like this. What he doesn't need to know though, is that I made a last-minute frantic trip to H&M over the weekend after a mini meltdown from having nothing to wear.

I now have several hundred pounds less to my name than I did on Friday. Carter's eyes lock on mine. The heat burning in them suggests perhaps there's one upside to my lack of funds.

I'd gladly spend every penny I have if it meant he'd never stop looking at me like that.

Woah, calm down, woman.

"Did you know—"

"What the fuck—"

Our questions fight for airtime as we both speak.

Taking a deep breath, I watch Carter do the same before diping his head slightly. "You first."

"Did you know?" I repeat, pacing the length of Carter's desk.

Reeling. I am *reeling*. It's the only accurate way to describe it.

"Lara."

My name on his tongue stops me in my tracks. One stiletto heel almost catches in the other as I turn to face him. God, he's so pretty it's almost painful. I smooth my hands down my blouse to calm my thoughts.

"Well, thank god that stopped your pacing," he says through a chuckle, and I'll be damned if it isn't a glorious sound. I really need to stop getting distracted by this man. By. My. Boss.

"No, I didn't know." Carter motions to the seat in front of his desk, which I slowly lower myself into. "I'd only been told your name was Lara. Although I'd hoped, I had no idea it would be you."

What did he say?

"Hoped?"

The word is but a whisper but loud enough for Carter to hear. Glancing at him, I notice a slight pink tinge to his cheeks that wasn't there a moment ago.

He clears his throat before continuing. "What I meant by that was, I . . ." Carter trails off as though he isn't sure where his sentence was meant to end. "I'd hoped for a suitable person for this position, and was a little wary when Anna told me the successful applicant knew my sister."

Well, this has me pausing. *I know his sister?* Considering I know approximately three people in London, one of whom is Riss, who's a little old to be Carter's sister, I'm stumped.

"I'm sorry, who's your sister?"

Carter gives me a funny look, sizing me up in a way I don't quite understand.

"Emilia Lawrence, she suggested you for the job." The blank look on my face causes Carter to cock his head to the side.

"I'm sorry, there must have been a mix-up. I don't know any Emilia's."

"Huh," is all Carter says in response. I can almost see the cogs turning in that handsome head of his. He gives it a small shake, eyes narrowing slightly. "Anyway," he continues, "that desk is yours. Feel free to make the space your own if you wish." Carter motions to the smaller desk on the opposite side of the room.

It's not quite as decadent as his, but is still clearly worth more than any piece of furniture I've ever owned. In the centre of the desk sits a descriptive how-to guide alongside a list of to-do items. Picking up the latter, I let out a small chuckle at how thorough it is.

"Anna left those for you; sometimes she's far too good at her job."

The level of detail and organisation Anna displayed was enough to cement that we'd be great friends. She's a woman after my own heart.

Carter doesn't speak again, and comfortable silence ensues. Considering I don't have any actual executive assistant experience, I'm happy with the lack of conversation. It gives me the chance to really focus on the materials given to me.

My first day passes by relatively quickly; learning new things makes time fly. Although minimal words were spoken, I'd need at least three hands to count how many times I felt Carter's warm gaze on me. But each time I looked over at him, he'd refocused on his computer, acting as though he'd never been looking my way.

Most of my trip home is spent trying to figure out how to tell the girls about *this* development. They're going to think I've lost my mind completely.

Chapter 19

Lara

That evening, the girls and I are seated on our small balcony, each with a wine in hand. One of Harper's signature charcuterie spreads sits half-eaten on the table. When I'd questioned the occasion, she'd referred to it as a "celebratory charcuterie for your first day in the big corporate world".

"So, Lara, tell us everything!" The girls beam at me, nothing but pride and support radiating off them.

It's times like these when I realise how lucky I am to have these two. In a place where I'm half a world away from my family, I've found a new, different kind of family in Harper and Mia.

Taking a larger-than-necessary sip of my wine, I decide it's best to start at the beginning; my new boss' identity.

"It was pretty great as far as first days go, except for a small mix-up. Carter, my new boss, was under the impression I knew his sister, Emilia. Oh, and Carter is Mr Darcy."

Two things happen simultaneously a single moment after the words leave my mouth: Harper does a real-life spit take, showering Mia and me in droplets of her Chianti, whilst Mia all but chokes on her mouthful.

Mouth gaping, I glance between my friends with the vigour of a die-hard tennis fan during a ten-point tie-break, trying to figure out what the fuck is happening.

My body seemingly stupefied, I can do nothing but sit here and watch the two of them. Harper wipes the back of her hand over her mouth, sweeping up the wine remnants. A sharp cough from Mia alerts Harper, and she's beside her in an instant, delivering several sharp blows to Mia's back. It doesn't make a difference though; Mia continues to choke.

Why hasn't she calmed down yet? This seems very odd.

My gaze turns to Harper. Her amber eyes meet mine for a moment before flicking between Mia and me.

"Come on you two, it's not even that bad. What the fuck is going on?"

A pair of sea green eyes avert my gaze, while Harper merely sits in silence. I'm starting to think there's something else at play here, and I have a feeling I'm about to find out what.

The girls look at each other, exchanging unspoken words, before returning their focus to me.

Arching a brow, I wait.

"I *cannot* believe I never told you this Lars, but Mia is a nickname." Bottom lip between her teeth, she absentmindedly chews as she waits. Out of the corner of my eye, I see Harper glancing between us, concern flickering over her features.

A slow blink is all I can muster. Oh god. *Oh. My. Fucking. God.*

"He's your brother, isn't he?"

The look on Mia's face tells me everything I need to know.

"He's my brother." The best way to describe the look Mia gives me is a kind grimace. "My birth name is Emilia, but my family usually refer to me as Emmy. I picked Mia in high school because kids gave me weird looks when they heard Emilia or Emmy."

I close my eyes as my stomach bottoms out. Mia continues talking, but I don't register a word she says. Her *brother*. I can't decide what's worse; the fact one of my best friends knows, in detail, about the places on my body her brother's mouth has been, or the fact that said brother is my boss. *Deep breaths, Lara.*

It seems almost ridiculous that I wouldn't connect the dots between Mia and Carter sharing a last name, but at the same time, it's not like I think about her last name often, if at all. Maybe subconsciously I assumed it was a common English surname so completely disregarded the coincidence? I guess I'll never know.

Can this day get any weirder?

"Oh my fucking god," I blurt out, scarcely aware of my own voice. Seems like those deep breaths did a fat lot of nothing.

"Oh my fucking god, indeed," Harper echoes, the sound seeming to come from miles away.

Opening my eyes, I'm met with a version of Harper who appears to have seen a ghost. The amber of her irises has been almost completely taken over by her pupils, and her eyebrows are inches from her hairline. Always the calm and sane one of the three of us, I have no idea how to react to this version.

The look on Mia's face couldn't be further from the woman next to her. With a hand over her mouth, I'm almost certain she's holding in a laugh. I think it's hysteria.

"Well, this is certainly not how I thought our evening would go." Mia's voice is at least an octave higher than normal, which is incredibly disconcerting.

Harper and I exchange a glance, both quickly looking at Mia.

"I don't even know what to say, I—"

"Lars, it's so fine. You weren't to know he's my brother." Her voice is still too high, which makes me wonder how true her words are.

"Are you sure?"

Mia sighs, resting a palm on my knee. "Yes, Lars, I'm sure. But let's not discuss the details."

We exchange small smiles, and all the while, Harper remains silent.

"Okay." I break the silence, crossing my legs beneath me and settling in for story time like a kindergartener. "I need the complete rundown on your family tree, please."

We spend the next hour gossiping about Mia's family history, and I'm slightly embarrassed by how little I knew about her family. I learn Mia's parents are still disgustingly in love after 35 years of marriage, and her other brother, Teddy, has a four-year-old daughter who's the light of his life. Mia doesn't offer up any information about the mother, so I decide it's best not to ask any questions.

After one too many wines, Mia turns in for the night. Although the conversation felt okay, it was clear Mia wasn't overly comfortable. I can't say I blame her; I can't imagine how I'd react if the roles were reversed. As night falls and the chill air begins to seep into our skin, Harper and I relocate to the lounge room, swapping wine for hot chocolate.

"I didn't want to bring it up in front of Mia because she gets a little defensive." Harper pulls her feet up beneath the throw blanket draped over us. "Have you ever seen the headlines about the Oxford Street Playboy?"

Headlines? Oxford Street who?

"Uh, n-no, I haven't." I rub a hand across my forehead, smoothing the frown lines my confusion has created. "Care to elaborate?"

She lets out a sigh, her face taking on a sombre expression. "I suppose you would've known who he was that first day if you had. Carter has been known as the Oxford Street Playboy across most of the tabloids in the UK for a few years now."

It all makes sense now. Of course he was too good to be a true gentleman. And far too skilled.

"That sounds unfortunate for him." Trust me to make light of any situation if it makes me feel slightly more comfortable. "That doesn't change anything, though."

There's a softness in Harper's expression, one that isn't seen often. "The man went down on you, so I imagine I'm right in assuming there's something there? Perhaps more than you've let on?"

A sharp "ha!" bursts from me, startling Harper.

"Harps, you do not need to worry about me. My heart isn't easily touched."

"It's too bad your vagina isn't as untouchable as your heart."

"Ouch." I throw a hand over my heart with a dramatic flair that would rival Pumbaa's iconic *"Oh, the shame!"* scene.

We break into a fit of quiet giggles.

Wiping a tear of laughter away, Harper gently places a hand on my blanketed knee and squeezes.

"I just don't want to see you get hurt, Lars." She gives me a small smile. "If the media is to be trusted, he's not exactly the relationship type."

Harper and Mia have been friends for over ten years, so of course she's seen more of Carter than what the papers show. But despite that, she's still warning me to be careful.

I pay little attention to the way something deflates inside me at that fact.

I take her hand in mine and return the squeeze, reassuring her.

"Harper, listen to me carefully. Whilst this may not be a one-time thing—"

"I beg your pardon?" Harper glares at me with bewilderment.

"Did I forget to mention the part where Mr Dar—*fuck*, Carter—told me we weren't finished yet when we were rudely interrupted? Oops."

"Big oops!"

I wave a hand casually. "Regardless. It's only physical, whatever *this thing* is between us. He might now be the relationship type, but then neither am I. At least not right now. Honestly, the less serious, the better. Plus, he's now my boss, remember?"

Harper's shoulders sag, her hand still wrapped beneath mine. "I just remember what it was like going through the heartbreak with you when that absolute wanker fucked you over."

Oh, but of course, my ex. What a piece of work he was, and probably still is.

Something must run in my mother's bloodline because now both of us have given our all to a man who turned around and laughed in our faces. Is this what they mean when they say "daddy issues"? My father's actions tore our family apart many years ago, and then I went and found a boyfriend who inevitably tore our relationship apart in the same fashion.

Their actions are a constant reminder that nothing is permanent, regardless of whether or not you want it to be.

"Between my ex and my father, I've encountered enough cheating arseholes to last me a lifetime. Trust me, Harps." Grabbing her other hand in mine and giving both a gentle squeeze, I smile. "I won't feel that pain again because I refuse to give anyone the power."

Harper squeezes my hands in return.

"Atta girl." Her face drops slightly. "I know Mia seemed pretty calm about this revelation, but—"

"It's fucking weird," I cut Harper off, finishing the sentence I knew was coming. "I honestly don't know how she managed to keep her cool so well."

"If I know Mia, and I like to think I do after ten years, she'll be processing for a little bit. She likes to act as though everything is fine and nothing phases her, but it's a front. Please don't take it too personally if she changes her tune in the coming days."

Despite already knowing this myself, I can't help the tiny niggling of disappointment. Not that I really have any reason to be disappointed—I'm planning to sleep with her brother—but it still sucks knowing things will be uncomfortable between us for a little bit.

Chapter 20

Lara

I'm fixing myself a cup of tea when my phone buzzes to life on the bench. Glancing over, I see my mother's name and a picture of us from my birthday on the screen.

"Hi Mum!" I answer cheerfully, placing the call on speaker and walking into my bedroom.

"Hi honey." I find myself smiling just hearing my mother's soothing voice on the line. It's odd how you can be around an accent your whole life, and yet it sounds so different when you hear it for the first time in a while. "How was your first week at the law firm?"

"It was pretty great. There's a lot to learn and many people to remember, but everyone is so kind and welcoming, so that made it a little less overwhelming."

"That's great to hear, honey. I'm sure you'll be thriving in no time."

Even from half a world away, Mum always knows what to say. My heart squeezes a little, wishing I could give her a hug.

"Thanks, Mum." Smiling to myself, I continue. "How's everything at home?"

"Oh everything's good, nothing too exciting to report. Your brother is being his typical painful self; he's too busy with work to catch up for coffee lately," she says, tutting her disapproval.

I asked one thing of my older brother before I left for England, and that was to make sure he made time for Mum. Spencer had given his standard "Yeah, yeah, I will" response, which didn't instil a lot of confidence. Despite this, I hoped he'd at least *try*. I love my brother, but work is definitely his number one priority. It would certainly benefit him—and Mum—if he spent a little less time on the field and a little more time with his family.

"Speaking of boys, have any nice British ones caught your eye?" The change of topic isn't exactly smooth, but she gets points for trying. I make a mental note to send my brother an admonishing text later.

"Mum, I'm 27. I'm hardly looking for *boys*."

"Oh, alright." There's a longer-than-necessary exhale on the other end of the line that has me stifling a grin. "What about men?"

The word 'men' comes out as though Mum hated the taste of it. She often hates acknowledging I'm no longer a child, mostly because it's a less-than-gentle reminder that she's not in her 20s anymore.

I huff out a laugh. "Unfortunately not."

It's as though Mum can hear the lie in my voice. "Are you sure about that, Lara Jane?"

Rolling my eyes as though my mother can see me through the phone, I continue. "Okay, fine. There's one attractive yet infuriating man who frequented the bookshop."

My mother lets out a high-pitched *eep* at my confession.

"He also happens to be the executive I assist at the law firm."

"Oh, how wonderful. Why don't you ask him to get a coffee sometime, honey?"

Apparently, the boss part fell on deaf ears.

"Mum, did you hear the part about him being my boss? As in, he's the person I work *for,* not just with."

"Oh Lara, you say that as if no one's ever fallen in love in the workplace."

"Love?!" I half shriek, half yell, repeatedly tugging off and sliding on the gold rings permanently adorning my middle finger. "I'm not looking for anything serious over here Mum, and certainly not *love.*"

"Why shut yourself off from something without even trying? I thought I raised you better than that." Her tone is teasing, but the words still stand to reason.

"I'm only here for a short while; what's the point? I'd rather not go through the ordeal of it ending." I take a sip from my mug as I wait for her to respond.

"How could you possibly know it'll end if you're not even willing to let it start? Plus, you and I both know you only bought a one-way ticket, meaning *technically,* you don't have plans to leave at present."

Well, she's got me there.

Despite everything she went through with my father, Mum has always been a romantic at heart. Not even a cheating husband could dampen her spirit permanently, and that's something I've always admired in her. I wish I could say the same for myself.

I've been cynical since the day I found out that nothing lasts forever; the day I learned my father might as well have ripped my mother's heart right from her chest. I imagine it would've hurt less than what he did.

It took years of asking until my mum finally told me the

truth behind the breakdown of their marriage. The official story, at least whilst I was growing up, was sometimes things weren't meant to be, and sadly their marriage was one of those things.

As I got older and had a better knowledge and understanding of the crueller parts of the world, I quickly realised there had to be something bigger at play.

When Mum sat me down and told me the heartbreaking truth, my first question was why. Why would he do that? Why didn't she tell me the truth before now? Why was he now happily remarried? Just plain *why?*

She'd looked at me then, and I saw years of sadness, hurt and anger within the small wrinkles around her eyes and in the way her brows sat lower above her lids. But there was something else too; acceptance. It was slight, and you'd miss it if you weren't looking for it, but it was evident nonetheless.

Her words have stuck with me since that moment. "Some things aren't meant to be."

Growing up, those around me had always considered me a Daddy's Girl. I've heard stories of how I'd follow him around the house, not worried about his attention but wanting to be in his presence. These stories made me smile in earlier years; I'd thought it was so sweet. Once I'd heard the full story of the divorce, I found them less sweet—my dad didn't have time for me. He had his daughter as his permanent shadow despite not being able to give me the time of day.

Over the recent years, my relationship with my father has become strained. We speak occasionally, but the conversation lacks substance. He gives me updates on his family without asking about me, so I find myself giving him the bare minimum in return—whether or not he realises this, I don't know. Nevertheless, I often find myself looking in the mirror, seeing only the little girl who longed for more, wondering why we weren't enough, why *I* wasn't enough.

On my 21st birthday, Mum had gifted me two of my most treasured possessions: her princess-cut emerald engagement ring and matching gold wedding band. In the almost seven years since, I could count on one hand the number of days I haven't worn those rings. While some may find it odd I wear rings representing a marriage that ended the way it did, they provide me with a level of comfort I can't quite explain. They also serve as a physical reminder to not let myself get attached.

The conversation turns to updates on other family and friends and general chit-chat. After we've said our farewells, I'm once again alone in my bedroom, left to ruminate on our earlier topic of conversation.

Sure, it would be lovely to have someone to come home to, someone to kiss me good morning and night, someone to hold me when I need it, and someone to laugh with . . .

But in saying that, my beautiful friends and roommates can offer me three of those four things. I wouldn't put it past Mia to offer them all, now that I think about it. Bless her; the girl just wants everyone she loves to be happy.

The point is, right now there's nothing any man can offer me that I can't already get through friends or from myself. What they *can* offer me though is orgasms. With any luck, they'll be better than the ones I deliver myself.

A face drifts into my mind, and I almost drop the ceramic mug I'm taking a sip from. Those pretty green irises of his flash a wink at me, tongue darting out to trace a plump lip.

I blink once, hard, and he's gone. My cheeks warm as I unclench my thighs, which I'd inadvertently squeezed together at the mental image I conjured of the Oxford Street Playboy.

Instant gratification—that's all this desire is for. I need to get this man out of my system, but do I really want to risk getting involved with someone with this level of media presence? I have no interest in that sort of attention, but my interest in the man himself might outweigh that.

The next day, as I stroll into the firm's lobby, I'm trying my best not to look as exhausted as I feel. Once I make it through today, I'll have officially been here for one week. It's a short amount of time in the grand scheme of things, yet my brain is that full it might explode. It probably doesn't help that I'm still dumbfounded about Carter.

He's been a perfect gentleman; no trace of the Carter from the bookshop. Weirdly, I find this a little disappointing. I thought he'd be a man of his word.

I'd love to walk right up to his desk and ask what happened to this not being over, but I think that may cross some HR boundaries.

"Lara!"

Startled, I look around and find the barista holding out my iced latte. The look on his face says that wasn't the first time he'd called my name.

With a mumbled, "Sorry, thank you," I grab my coffee, duck my head, and make my way to the lifts.

A ding from my coat pocket has me reaching for my phone, already knowing who it is. Did I give my boss a specific text tone so I'd know if a message was from him without looking at it? Perhaps. This is a great time to take some advice given by an old therapist of mine—don't overanalyse everything, Lara.

CARTER

Are you on your way up? My father wants to speak with us.

The man in question suggested we swap numbers earlier in the week. "Strictly for professional purposes, of course," is what he'd said. And I'd agreed, of course, but that hasn't stopped the intrusive thoughts from popping up late at night: what's the worst that could happen if I sent him an un-work-related text?

I hadn't yet decided if it was worth risking my job to find out.

His *father?* Wanting to speak with *us?* Oh, but of course, he's the '& Sons' part of J. L. & Sons. I briefly recall Anna explaining the history of the family-owned company on my first day, but a lot of the details went in one ear and out the other.

That first day was a whirlwind eight hours; I've honestly surprised myself by recalling anything at all that happened on Monday. I guess it's a little hard to forget that not only am I now working under the man who lingers in all corners of my mind, but I'm practically employed by his father too.

My first instinct was to assume nepotism when I heard the Managing Director's son was the CEO, but Anna quickly dismantled that thought by detailing Carter's extensive law background. It made me wonder why such a renowned lawyer would give that up to become a CEO? Perhaps I'd ask him one day.

Considering Frederick is Carter's dad, and the head of the company, my initial reaction is to overthink—one of my many useless talents. What have we done that's caused him to want to speak with us? Did someone find out about the bookstore encounter? Was I caught staring at Carter for longer than appropriate? I really need to stop doing that. Was he caught staring at me? It's unlikely but also quite possible, considering I myself have caught him staring on more than one occasion this week.

ME

Coming now.

The elevator ride seems to take longer than the build-up in a slow-burn romance. What if all of the above has happened and I'm being let go as a result, and his father is the one who's requested it? What if I'm walked out by security?

"Nice day, isn't it?" I blurt out to the woman next to me, whose name I'm yet to learn. I'm not typically one to engage in small talk with near strangers, but I'm not exactly firing on all cylinders right now. She hesitantly side-eyes me before muttering her agreement and dashing out of the elevator at the next floor.

Oh my god, does she know what Carter and I did? How could she possibly know? Does everyone know?

Taking a shaky breath as the elevator doors open on my floor, I rub my slick palms on my trousers, wiping away the anxious sweat.

Relax, Lara. Just relax.

As I walk into our office, I'm treated to a version of Carter I've not yet seen: relaxed. With his father sitting casually in the chair opposite him, Carter has an easy smile on his face. His gaze flickers toward me, his smile widening so that his dimple is on display, and the gesture has my insides warming.

Please stop reacting to him in ways like this; not cool.

The calm settling over my nerves is unexpected in the best of ways. Surely he wouldn't be so at ease if his assistant was being fired or if we'd been found out by his father, so I'm taking this as a good sign.

His father turns in his chair, standing when he sees me, giving me a friendly smile.

"Ah, Miss Matthews, lovely to see you." The pleasantness

he directs at me helps to calm my irrational thoughts, if only a little.

"Mr Lawrence, hi," I respond, beaming at him in return.

Carter's father, Frederick, is easily one of the sweetest men I've ever encountered. If you could capture the essence of a ray of sunshine and mix it with that of a Golden Retriever, it would be Frederick Lawrence. He's certainly not what I expected from a former CEO and lawyer.

Charisma isn't the only thing these two have in common. I'm not one to gamble, but I'd put money on Carter being the spitting image of his father at his age.

"Oh, none of that Mr Lawrence nonsense dear, Freddie makes me feel younger." He chuckles lightly as he gestures to the seat beside him. "Have a seat, Lara."

Freddie asks me all about how my first week has been, how I'm settling in, and if his son has me wanting to pull my hair out yet. Strangely enough, the last question has Carter glowering at his father.

"Pay no mind to his dramatics, Lara; he gets that from his mother."

We continue like this—Freddie engaging me in an unexpected game of 20 Questions and listening animatedly to each response I give, and Carter sitting quietly, observing the interaction—until his father realises he's yet to mention why he called us here.

"Right, I imagine you both have a lot on, so let's get to the point." Freddie rifles around in his trouser pockets. Phone in one hand and glasses in the other, he lets out a triumphant "aha" before continuing. "Son, Mason Devereux has requested to meet with you and a few other board members out in Norcaster. Lara, you'll also need to be present for note-taking."

Freddie pauses, no doubt awaiting some form of response

from his son. I use the moment to wrack my brain for where the heck I've heard the name Norcaster.

Of course! It's only been on my UK bucket list since I touched down at Heathrow. Norcaster is one of many quaint countryside towns within the Cotswolds region. It would look right at home in a Hallmark Christmas movie, which is precisely why it's on my list.

Honestly, is there anything better than a stereotypical cheesy Hallmark Christmas Classic? No, I don't think so.

"Mason would like to meet the Friday after next for a few hours." Carter's expression shifts; his brows furrow together, and a small grimace replaces his smile. At his son's evident displeasure, Freddie continues, "I know, Friday isn't ideal for a trip like this, but Mason is an integral member of the board, and it would serve you well to make a good first impression as our new CEO. Plus, it's a lunch meeting, leaving plenty of time for the both of you to return home that evening."

Carter begins tapping a finger on his deep mahogany desk, contemplating.

"Think of it this way; it'll be an excellent chance for the two of you to get acquainted with one another."

I stiffen at the mention of Carter and I spending time together in close, forced proximity.

Why has every word out of his father's mouth only caused Carter's furrow to deepen?

It hits me like a smack on the back of the head. Carter isn't displeased about the Friday meeting, but rather the fact I'm to accompany him.

Ouch.

I am to accompany him.

Unbeknownst to Freddie, this is easily the worst idea he'll ever have. The sum of Carter, me, a small enclosed space, and two hours can only equate to one of two things; disaster or desire.

Although I don't think I'm ready to put that equation to the test, it doesn't seem as though I have a choice.

Schooling my facial features into a look of nonchalance, I find myself fiddling with my rings as I think about the things Carter and I already know about each other. More specifically, the intimate ways in which Carter already knows me.

Chapter 21

Carter

"Come again?"

My father turns his head toward me, a smile brightening his face as he lets out a small laugh.

"Which part didn't you understand, Son?" My gaze bounces from my father to Lara as I attempt to assess her reaction. Her face, which usually hides nothing, isn't giving anything away right now. I don't know if that's a good thing or not, but I don't have time to ponder because Dad is looking at me expectantly.

"Sorry, not what I meant." My hand reaches to the back of my neck, and I rub it nervously. "Is it imperative that Lara attends? She's only been here a week and hasn't started taking notes yet."

The air in the room changes imperceptibly, and my gaze flicks from my father to Lara. The set of her shoulders has lowered slightly, and I can't help but think it's because of what I've said. I've offended her without meaning to. I'm fucking this whole conversation up, and I'm not even trying.

"Lara, I'm sorry, I didn't mean to offend you." Her eyes

meet mine, eyebrows furrowing minutely before she laughs lightly, the sound ringing out like the sweetest chime.

"I'm not offended." Lara's left shoulder raises and drops, her head tilting ever so slightly the opposite way. "You're right; I haven't taken any notes yet, but I'm willing to learn over the next two weeks."

Reclining in my chair to feign a nonchalance I certainly don't feel, I turn my head in Dad's direction and send out a silent plea—please decide it's a bad idea, *please.*

My father's smile widens as he stands. "Excellent, it's settled then."

Well, shit. So much for that silent plea.

"Victor can drive the both of you. Give him a call to let him know what time, Son." He claps his hands once, delight radiating off him. "Any who, I best be off. Your mother is expecting me for brunch."

Dad turns to face Lara from the doorway, raising a hand in farewell. "Lovely to see you, Lara, and good luck."

With a wink, he's gone.

The second the door closes behind him, Lara rises. She paces several steps away from the desk before proceeding to turn around and pace back. The sound of her heels on the tiles resembles the click-clack of Winnie's plastic princess shoes. She gives me a stern look as she stands across from me, trying her hardest to look authoritative with her hands planted firmly on her hips.

The smirk I'm trying to hold back slips free, and her stern look morphs into a scowl. It's gone as quickly as it came though, replaced by a reluctant grin.

"You're really not great at being serious, are you?"

Dramatic as ever, Lara slaps her hands down on the top of my desk, eyes pinning me in place.

"This isn't funny, Carter," she responds, still grinning like an idiot but valiantly trying to hide it. Her efforts really should be rewarded, and I can think of a few ways I'd like to reward her. I wonder if she has a praise kink? That would work wonders.

Not the fucking time, place, or woman. Pull. Yourself. Together.

"The smile on your face could've fooled me, gorgeous." I lean further back in my chair, surveying her.

Lara lets out an exaggerated huff, crossing her arms across her chest. It takes every ounce of self-control not to stop my attention from redirecting itself to that chest, but fucking hell, it looks divine.

For all the times I saw Lara at Chapter Nine, she'd never been wearing anything low cut or fitting. In her defence, the blouse she's currently wearing beneath her jacket isn't either of those things to any large degree, but it's certainly more than I've seen. And apparently, more than I can handle.

She's somehow managed to make corporate attire look intimidatingly sexy.

"Alright," Lara says, drawing my attention to her pretty face, "this is how it's going to go."

The whole time Lara is running through how she sees this meeting going, all I can think about is how unconcerned she is. She doesn't seem the least bit phased about spending a four-hour round trip stuck in a car with me, and I strongly dislike how that makes me feel.

Was she not as affected by the bookstore events as I was? It seems hard to believe at first thought, because if the roles were reversed, I don't think I'd be coping. Shit, I'm struggling to cope as it is.

What a humbling little realisation this is.

Do I test the theory anyway? *Yes,* yes I do. I can't help myself.

Lara stands before me, looking positively delectable. My legs take the lead as I stand and walk around my desk, invading the space between it and Lara. Leaning against the front, I keep my gaze trained on her face. A feeling of satisfaction sparks inside me, watching as her eyes flare momentarily when they track my hands gripping the edge.

Lara tightens her crossed arms, drawing my attention briefly to her chest. When it returns to her face, I stiffen as I watch her lick her lips.

Fuck. She has no idea what she's doing to me.

If she wasn't in front of me, I'd be tempted to readjust myself. Instead, I take one small step closer, hellbent on having any sort of effect on her. Lara doesn't react. Instead, she keeps staring.

Feeling braver than I have any right to, and knowing this is crossing *so* many lines, I take another step. When the tips of my shoes make contact with her heels, I finally get the slightest reaction from Lara. She lets out a tiny gasp.

From a distance, it's obvious she's gorgeous. But up close, she's exquisite.

The sunlight through the windows allows me to notice tiny freckles peppering her cheeks, evidence of her homeland. Her lips are set in a perfect pout, and their natural pink colour embeds itself into my brain.

"Can I help you, Mr Lawrence?"

Oh, *fuck me.* Fuck me all the way to Scotland.

There's a twinkle in her eyes as she says this, but it's gone in a heartbeat, replaced again by indifference. The way she's able to school her expression so quickly makes me think it's something she's had a lot of practice with. The idea of her having to hide her emotions for any reason doesn't sit right with me.

The way she says my name makes it feel like it belongs on her tongue, like no one else could ever make it sound as sweet.

This isn't the first time I've been called Mr Lawrence, but it's certainly the only time I've immediately wanted to hear it again, and again, and *again*. My hands flex at my sides, itching to touch her. Restraint is a heavy burden right now, but an essential one nonetheless.

Through no fault of her own, Lara is the most painful temptress I've ever encountered. She's not to blame for the way my body reacts to her, but *god* I wish she knew the hold she has over me.

My jaw ticks. The way her eyes flicker toward the movement is a pretty clear indication that she noticed.

"Mr Lawrence?" They're the only two words I can form; my mind unable to stop replaying the way she licked her lips, except to think about the unspeakable things I'd do to feel that tongue on my skin.

"That *is* your name, isn't it?" There's a teasing note to her tone despite the continual expression of indifference. "I must admit, it suits you better than Mr Darcy."

"I can't decide which name I prefer coming from your lips; Mr Lawrence, or Carter. I suppose it doesn't matter as long as it's my name."

Where the fuck did that come from? Have I completely lost my mind? I don't think a woman has ever caused me to cross so many boundaries, and yet here I am, ploughing through them like I have nothing to lose.

Her physical response is all that's needed to tell me this isn't one-sided. There's the smallest indication I'm having the same effect on her as she is on me—she draws in a sharp breath, pupils dilating.

"I've always prided myself on my self-control, but you push me closer to the edge than anyone ever has." She exhales, her breath like a whisper against my skin. It makes me want to crush my mouth to hers, consequences be damned. "The worst part," I breathe, struggling to hold on to my sanity, "is the edge has never looked better."

Lara's deep blue's gaze into my own, searching. For what, I can't be sure.

"The edge is a dangerous place to be, Carter. I don't imagine you're there alone, though, if the papers are anything to go by."

Christ, this woman knows how to strike with precision. I'm taken aback for a moment, wincing at the knowledge that she's aware of the tabloids. But she's right, of course. Each week, the papers and magazines continue to splash what they believe to be "scandalous" pictures of me with beautiful women.

What she doesn't realise though, is that these pictures were all taken in batches, weeks, and months ago. Not a single one has been taken since that first encounter with Lara. She can never know though. Honestly, I can't imagine how smug she'd be if she had that information. Not to mention how completely and totally fucked I'd be.

Lara inclines her head ever so slightly. My breath catches; is she about to—

My train of thought derails faster than a bat out of hell as Lara turns and walks away.

I'm left fucking rattled, positively rocked by the way she continues to break down my control one piece at a time. The sounds of her retreating heels make for a suitable soundtrack as I try to collect the pieces.

"Son."

Dad hardly ever greets me in any other way; no 'hello', no 'good morning', just 'Son'. Come to think of it, it's not all that often he actually uses my name when speaking to me.

The sound of my father's muffled voice through the phone fills the otherwise quiet backseat, the rolled-up partition blocking out the sound of Victor's classical music crescendoing.

Victor has been working for our family for decades now. He was Dad's driver for most of those years and became mine when I took over as CEO. He's more of an unofficial uncle to me than an employee, and we typically have great conversations about bikes while we drive.

"Dad, we need to discuss yesterday's conversation, please. Are you certain it's a good idea?"

"Well of course I'm certain," he responds confidently, as though he can't imagine how I could be questioning it.

"It's good for Lara's personal development within her role and it's good for your professional relationship with her. It also wouldn't hurt for Mason to meet your new EA in person."

He pauses, clearly trying to think of additional convincing reasoning.

"If I'm completely honest, I think spending time with a woman like Lara could really benefit you, Son."

I genuinely sputter at this. *What?*

"Wh-what on earth do you mean by that?"

There's silence on the other end of the line. Following this, Dad stutters out the beginning of a few incoherent words before finding his feet.

"What I mean is she's a lovely young woman, and it wouldn't kill you to spend more time with someone like that."

Is he quite serious? *That little meddler.* I really shouldn't be surprised, though; only a few months ago he was attempting to set me up with Kate from the cafe. The man means well, but *Lara* of all people? Naturally he doesn't know about our history, and she really is quite wonderful, but the last thing I need is my father involving himself in our relationship—or lack thereof.

"Is this some sort of ploy then? Your next attempt to find me a wife?"

"I refuse to confirm or deny. However, I will say your mother and I would desperately *love* another grandchild to spoil. Or a couple. We aren't fussy." I can hear the smile in his voice.

Typical; the grandchild angle. My parents love Winnie like nothing else. I'm certain they love her more than any of their own children.

All our parents have ever wanted for us is happiness, which is more than many can say for their parents. However, for them, happiness comes from family. They assume I'm enjoying doing my own thing while I'm still young(ish), but one day I'll settle down with a beautiful and loving wife, have a few children, and enjoy that next chapter. Though, what they don't realise is that their 'dream life' isn't necessarily for everyone.

I've not mentioned this to my parents, but I'm not certain I want children. I think the world of Winnie and would stop at nothing to protect her, but I'm not sure if fatherhood is for me. I could be perfectly happy and fulfilled spending my days with just the love of my life.

Perhaps I'll change my mind one day, but for now, it's not on the cards.

Before I can determine a suitable response, Dad continues.

"I can practically hear you rolling your eyes. I don't mean for you to go out and get married tomorrow; I just think it wouldn't hurt for you to be around her in a slightly different environment."

I can't help the sigh set free, accompanied by a small smile.

"Alright, Dad, you win."

"I knew you'd come around." God, he's one cocky son of a

bitch. Can't imagine where I got it from. "Don't forget to tell Victor when you'll need him."

Oh, Dad will have a field day with this.

"I'm going to drive us, figured it's easier. I'll give Victor the day off; he's been wanting to go for a day ride for a while, so he can make the most of a long weekend."

Dad doesn't say another word. He just laughs before hanging up.

Chapter 22

Lara

The list of despicable things I would do for a coffee is growing rapidly as I wait for Carter in the firm's reception. It was a joint decision to meet here, rather than Carter picking me up, because no one wants to deal with that interaction so early on a Friday morning. My phone pings incessantly from within my handbag, so I pull it out to see what I'm missing.

MIA

You've got this! Deep breaths!

HARPER

Please don't let him fuck you in the car.

Woah sorry. Ignore me, I clearly haven't had my second cup of coffee yet.

Stifling a giggle while simultaneously hoping my face isn't turning a deep shade of pink, I type out a response to my UK support system.

ME

Has anyone ever told you two that you're a lot?

MIA

Only every second day.

Harper has a point though. My brother is incredibly strong willed, it's annoying. He won't stop going after something he wants until he gets it. By the sounds of it, that could include you too.

Jesus, this conversation has gone from weird to fucked in the span of a few messages. I can't imagine Mia is loving this.

ME

Guys, I'm not concerned. Let's not forget I walked away from what would definitely have been a kiss.

HARPER

Need I remind you of the stockroom? If that man wants you, you don't stand a chance.

ME

It's a two-hour drive there, followed by a meeting, and a two-hour drive home - what's the worst that could happen?

Over the past two weeks, I've come to learn more and more about Carter. Like if he doesn't go for a run or work out in some form before work, he struggles to sit still. I genuinely thought he had a sugar high when I witnessed it for the first time.

"Are you alright?" I asked after watching him walk between his desk and the filing cabinet about four times. He grumbled something incoherent, let out a huff, and sat down.

It wasn't until the following morning, noting his typical cheery demeanour had returned, that I asked what was up yesterday.

"I missed my run yesterday morning, so I have pent-up energy," was his response. The man reminded me of a border collie, and I'd held back a chuckle at the thought.

I almost asked him why he missed it before remembering my boss was known as the Oxford Street Playboy within the media. I assumed a date, or perhaps several, was to blame. Plus, it wasn't really any of my business; it's not like we're friends.

The front doors open, and I know it's Carter without looking. Don't ask me how, but I can sense his presence. Call it intuition if you must. When I look up, my mouth forms a small *o*, not because I'm right, but because of what he's holding.

Carter has an iced latte in his hand. For someone who's strictly an Americano man, this is strange.

"Morning, Lara." His deep voice stuns me as I make my way to him. "Thought you might need this, morning attitude and all."

He bought me a coffee?

"Oh, thank you," I say in my smallest voice as I take the coffee from Carter's outstretched hand. As I take a sip, the sugary syrup hits my tongue. Shocked, I glance up at him watching me closely.

"Caramel?" I ask, sounding positively perplexed.

"That's how you like it, isn't it? You and your sugar obsession."

All I can do is nod.

Not only did the man buy me a coffee, he remembered *exactly* how I like it. It's a small, simple gesture, but I don't think any man has bothered to do something like that for me before. Certainly not my ex. He was too busy fucking other people to pay attention to my coffee preference.

But Carter's also thrown two small jabs my way, so I don't let the coffee thing get to my head *too* much.

Carter leads the way to the front door, opening it for me as

I approach. His gentlemanly actions are at odds with the sarcasm he typically reserves for me.

I'm caught up in reminding myself, *again*, about little things when an unexpected touch warms my lower back. It's light as a feather and gone by the time I've taken two steps through the doorway.

Risking a quick glance behind me, I watch as Carter's hand returns to his side. He averts his gaze, instead looking toward a sleek black Audi SQ8.

Don't be fooled by this knowledge. I'm the furthest thing from a car girl. I've just loved Audi's for as long as I can remember, and the one Carter is pointing to is sort of my dream car. I'd hate to sound corny—that's a lie, I couldn't care less—but it's definitely featured on a few vision boards.

This almost causes enough commotion in my head to drown out the memory of warmth against my back, but not quite.

I watch as Carter rounds the vehicle and stops on the passenger door side. As I approach, my heart flips in my chest at the sight before me. There's Carter, all tall, dark, handsome and suited, once again holding open a door for me. *For me.* What in the Uno reverse is this?

Looking up at him, I'm graced with a warm smile. The kind of smile that has the corners of his eyes wrinkling and his deep greens glittering beneath the rare sliver of British sunlight.

"Thank you."

I've almost completely lost the ability to form sentences, and it's ridiculous. Have men set the standards so low that I'm feeling all giddy over my boss opening doors for me?

Placing a hand on the top of the doorframe and attempting to not make a complete fool of myself, I throw my bag on the floor in front of the passenger seat. I place one leg inside, but the heel on my other foot catches in a pebble, and my life flashes before my eyes. In an instant, Carter is behind me. Electricity crackles through my veins at the connection between his strong hands and my waist.

"Watch your step next time, Miss Matthews."

The only people who've ever called me Miss Matthews were typically under the age of ten. Coming from young mouths, it made me feel older than my 27 years. But coming from Carter's, it has me feeling a completely different way.

If it weren't for Carter's hands still around my waist, my supporting leg would've buckled beneath those words. God, he's smooth. I can't imagine what he'd be like if he were actually trying to flirt with me.

Let's stop that train of thought right there. He's not flirting with me. Nor do I want him to.

Liar.

The word comes from somewhere deep in the back of my mind, from my inner validation and attention seeker. She can be such a hussy sometimes.

Carter's hands feel larger than I remember as they help me straighten. Embarrassed, I make quick work of climbing into the car and closing the door, narrowly missing Carter's fingers.

The hairs on my arms stand at attention as I watch Carter walk to his side, as cool and collected as ever. This is going to be a long drive.

Chapter 23

Carter / Lara

Carter

This is going to be a long drive.

For most of the two hours, we sit in comfortable silence. Except physically, I'm anything *but* comfortable. My entire body is practically vibrating knowing Lara is within arm's reach, yet I can't touch her.

I've never had this sort of visceral reaction to someone. It's causing a mess of my mind.

Stealing a glance at her, I let out a small exhale when I see her attention is focused out the window. Maybe I can get my shit together without her noticing the way my body reacts to her presence.

Refocusing on the road, I let my thoughts wander. Dangerous, with her in such close proximity, but it's all I can do to stop myself from reaching out and placing a hand on her thigh.

Since the first taste, the desire to have her again has all but consumed me. Right now, I'd love nothing more than to pull over, recline my seat, and drag Lara across the centre console right onto my face. My grip on the steering wheel tightens, my knuckles turning white from the force.

The thing I said about getting my shit together? Yeah, not happening.

"Well, that about does it. Thanks again for coming out for this meeting Carter. I'm very appreciative you took the time to visit." Mason's voice draws my attention, which has been lingering on one blue-eyed beauty across the room.

"Lara, thank you for note-taking. I look forward to seeing the outcomes of today's action points."

A timid smile graces Lara's lips as she gives Mason a small nod. "You'll have them by close of business Monday, sir."

Sir.

That word, coming from her lips, has two vastly different effects on me; my cock stirs, and my blood boils.

My trousers tighten almost imperceptibly. It's become somewhat of a recurring matter as of late when Lara's in the vicinity. It's incredible really, that one syllable from her can have this profound effect.

Now the formalities are finished, relaxed conversations begin around me. I'm at a loss as to how I managed to take anything in during the meeting, considering I kept one eye on Lara at all times.

The fact she's directly across from me is both helpful and a hindrance.

Fuck, she's pretty. Lara is still entirely absorbed in her notes, probably rewriting them into complete sentences. I've seen her do it several times at the office; she's far too attentive for her own good.

There's a thump in my chest as I watch her, cataloguing the

way her brows furrow as she furiously strokes a key, the way a smile tugs at the corner of her mouth as if she's impressed herself, the way she delicately tucks a stray curl behind her ear, the emerald adorned gold ring that never leaves her middle finger twinkling as she does so.

I should really look away, but I can't. If anyone in this room were to glance toward me, they'd see a man entranced. Good grief, I really need to get a grip. *Right, I'm looking away now.*

Of course, the moment I turn my head a fraction, those deep blue eyes bore into mine. Well shit, looks like I've been caught. Lara's eyes partially narrow at me, but the effect is negated by the look of amusement drawing her rose-coloured lips into an almost flirtatious grin.

Woah, let's not get ahead of ourselves, Lawrence; this woman is not flirting with you.

Lara

I break eye contact first. The man is intimidating enough normally, but add in some less-than-appropriate heated eye contact, and he's lethal.

A throat clears, drawing my attention to the end of the table where Mason is standing in his place.

"Carter, Lara," he addresses us, looking at each of us respectively. "Join us for dinner."

The mention of dinner throws me. It's still as bright as ever outside, certainly not dinner time. I'm left eating my words as I glance at my watch and realise it's 5:30pm. Shit, where did the afternoon go?

I notice Carter's face blanch slightly. He appears to be as unsure as I am on how to politely decline.

"As much as we appreciate the offer, we'll have to decline this time. We have to get back to the city."

"Oh nonsense," Mason responds with a chuckle and a flick of his wrist. "Think of it as more of an insistence than an offer. We couldn't possibly have the new CEO out in our neck of the woods and send him home on an empty stomach. And it's the Annual Norcaster Summer Festival; you simply can't miss seeing the festivities tomorrow morning." He pulls out his wallet, skimming through cards until he finds what he's looking for. Making his way over to where Carter's still seated, Mason hands him a card. "Here, this is where the group is staying. I took the liberty of reserving you a room just in case, but I'm sure they'll have another for Miss Matthews."

The way he speaks so matter-of-factly makes me think we might not have a way out of this.

Hold on, did he say tomorrow morning? And a room?

I don't get another second to contemplate any of that because one look at Carter distracts me entirely. Confliction flickers across his facial features before he regains himself and responds with a wide smile. "We'd be delighted, Mason. Thank you for your hospitality."

Well *shit*, I guess I was right about no way out. There's no way this is ending well.

Neither of us brought a change of clothes for this impromptu dinner. We were under the impression we'd be meeting and leaving, all within the space of a few hours. And *staying the night?* That's absurd. There's no way Carter was agreeing to that as well.

I look in his direction to find he's vacated his seat and is now laughing with Mason. He's wearing signature Carter attire: a pale blue long-sleeve button-up, tucked pristinely into a pair of navy slacks. His green eyes are lit up in a way that would make the sunshine on the ocean jealous. I'm almost transfixed by him.

In this moment, he looks carefree. His face is bright, mouth stretched into his classic businessman smile, and he's got a hand clapping Mason on the shoulder as they laugh. It's the most attractive he's ever been.

That isn't necessarily saying much though. He's got the sort of face that would bring anyone, man or woman, to their knees when turned in your direction.

Realising I'm staring at Carter and paying no mind to those around me, I politely exit the group I'd accidentally found myself in and decide we better get moving.

I'm careful to zig-zag through those still gathered in conversation as I make my way over to where Carter and Mason are standing, Carter's impressive side profile on full display.

As if sensing my approach, he angles his head in my direction. Carter's smile grows as he looks at me, and my stomach does a little flip. Goodness me, he really is far too handsome for his own good. As my stomach settles, Carter does the unthinkable and winks at me.

Winks. At me. Scratch the little flip; my stomach is somersaulting like the Olympic Gold depends on it.

"We'll meet at Hearth & Timber at six? That should be enough time for everyone to freshen up." The group around us sound their agreement, but Carter and I just nod. It seems everyone has a room up here. Everyone except us.

After packing up and saying quick farewells, we make our way to the car to deposit our work stuff. I'm utterly perplexed at how this is playing out. There's simply no way we're—

"It's not ideal, but it's in our best interest to take Mason up on the accommodation front." Carter's words come as a surprise, completely opposite to my previous train of thought.

"Oh?" is all I can manage in response.

"My father mentioned it would *serve me well* to make a good first impression as the new CEO with these guys, which is a polite way of saying there's no telling Mason no, under any circumstances. We'll head over to the bed and breakfast now to secure you a room."

The noise that comes from my throat is something between a scoff and a gasp; decidedly *un*ladylike. "I can't imagine he had *this* situation in mind when you had that conversation." Reaching the car, I pause. The cogs in my brain are turning at a rapid pace, so I continue. "Although, surely your dad must have known how likely a dinner would be, given his experience with these guys?" My words aren't pointed directly at Carter but are more out-loud thoughts.

He must have heard me though, because I'm almost certain I hear Carter swear under his breath, followed by a small chuckle. I think better than to question that. Not because I'm not intrigued, which I most definitely am, but because I don't think I was meant to hear it in the first place.

Chapter 24

Carter

It's too late by the time I realise I've laughed out loud at what appears to be nothing. All I can do is hope Lara didn't hear and wonder what on earth is wrong with me.

Of course, *of course*, my father would've known there'd be a dinner following the meeting. In fact, he was probably counting on it, the meddlesome little thing. Really though, I should've seen it coming myself. Of all the meetings I've been to during my time at the firm, it's rare for there not to be a dinner afterwards.

My father had been so blatant about his desire for me to spend more time around Lara, yet I still fell right into his trap. I make a mental note to berate him for this the minute I get back to London. The nerve on him both astounds and humours me.

We make the short drive to the Norcaster Bed and Breakfast in semi-comfortable silence. I'm still ruminating on the way my father stuck his nose where it didn't belong, and Lara appears lost in thought as well. I try my best not to stare, but I'm constantly in awe of her. She's beautiful, quick-witted, detail-oriented to a fault, and one of the most mesmerising women I've come across.

"You're going to cause an accident if you keep your attention off the road any longer."

And of course, she's as cheeky as they come. Her mouth has to be one of my favourite things about her.

There's a brief smirk on her lips as she turns toward me, meeting my gaze. Without a word, I direct my attention to the road and pull up in front of the B&B.

Lara walks toward the doorway, and I follow, subconsciously placing a hand on her lower back as I open the door for her. I'm painfully aware this isn't the first time I've touched her today, and I hope like hell it isn't the last. It's as though my skin craves contact with hers, and a spark of electricity pulses through me each time.

"Good evening, are you checking in?" The male behind the reception desk greets us with a warm smile.

"There should be a room for Carter Lawrence, but we need a second room too please."

The receptionist frowns slightly but quickly re-pastes the friendly smile on his face.

"I'm sorry, sir, but without a reservation we're completely booked. It's Norcaster Summer Festival week, you see, so we book out months in advance."

Great, just great.

"I understand. In that case, could I please request my room be Twin Share? We're heading back out for dinner, so wouldn't need an immediate turnover."

He taps furiously on his keyboard until something unseen causes his face to drop. Grimacing, he looks up at us. "Unfortunately not, sir. I do apologise, but you're booked in a Lake View King Room, which only has the one bed."

One bed. *One.* Between the two of us. There's no way Lara

will go for this. Absolutely not. Although, I suppose I can spend a night on the floor. I turn to her, seeing the mixed emotions on her face. "What do you think?"

She blinks once, a blush creeping into her cheeks. "I don't think we have a choice, Carter. Like your dad said, you can't tell Mason no."

A jolt runs through my cock at my name coming from her lips. It's utterly ridiculous and completely unwarranted; Lara uses my name all the time. But in this scenario, relating to sharing a room, and a *bed* for the night, it's completely different from ever before.

You are here for work, Carter. Cut the shit. No more thoughts of Lara going to your dick. This is getting out of hand.

It's only a short walk to our room, but each step plagues me. How is this going to play out? There's absolutely no way Lara will be fine with sharing a bed. I'm going to have to sleep on the floor; there's no way around it. I refuse to make her uncomfortable, no matter how badly my dick aches at the thought of nestling itself between that firm arse of hers.

Stop.

I let out a sigh of release as the door swings open; there's a small chaise against the window. That ought to be more comfortable than the floor, even if I'm far too long to fit.

"The bed is all yours. I'll sleep on that," I advise Lara, pointing toward the chaise.

"Don't be ridiculous," says Lara from behind me, stopping me in my tracks. *Ridiculous?* "This thing is huge. There's enough room for the both of us. We won't even know the other is in there, it's that large."

I huff; I can't help myself. It's incredible she really thinks I could ever forget being in bed with someone like her. I know full well that every ounce of my being would be continuously aware of her presence.

"I'm trying to be a gentleman, Lara. I'm more than happy sleeping on the chaise."

Lara gives me a once over, ever so slowly, as if completely taking me in for the first time today. Her eyes meet mine once more, and I pray to god she doesn't clock the twitch in my cheek as I give her a megawatt smile.

"What you're being is ridiculous. You and I both know you're far too long for that chaise, and there's simply no need for you to squash yourself onto it. I don't need you to be a gentleman."

I stop breathing. Not a single ounce of oxygen enters my lungs after Lara utters those last eight words. Staring at her, I'm at a loss. My heart thumps beneath my rib cage, my hands flexing of their own accord.

What game is she playing at? I've spent the past several weeks trying *hard* to get a reaction out of her, but the one time I'm being completely sincere, *this* is how she responds? Fuck, I might not have cracked the code for her yet, but Lara certainly knows how to push my buttons.

"Are you coming?" Lara calls from the doorway before turning and walking out.

Chapter 25

Lara

Norcaster's famous bread and butter pudding is sitting untouched in front of me. Not because I don't want it—I have the world's biggest sweet tooth, of course I want it—but because I can't stop gnawing on the inside of my cheek, anxious as hell about what I said to Carter.

"I don't need you to be a gentleman."

It was hours ago now, but I can't let it go. What was I thinking? Honestly, I don't know if I was thinking at all, and that's the problem. This is the exact reason I tend to overthink things on a regular basis; underthink, and I'll say something like "I don't need you to be a gentleman" to the one person I probably shouldn't say that to.

The pudding remains untouched for the remainder of the evening. I'm engrossed in casual conversation with our dinner guests whilst also trying to sneak subtle glances at Carter.

Every nerve ending in my body is on high alert with him beside me all night. For the most part, we don't touch, which only makes the small grazes of his trousered leg against my bare thigh even more unbearable.

Dinner is long but enjoyable, filled with too much food and a few too many wines, at least in some cases. A short while later, we're making the short walk to the B&B, and despite the fact it's summer, there's a slight chill in the air.

Wrapping my arms across my chest, I rub my upper arms in a feeble attempt to warm them up. Carter halts beside me. I turn to him, ready to ask what the hold-up is, but the question dies on my lips. Carter holds his suit jacket out to me, an unreadable expression on his face.

When I don't immediately reach for it, he looks at me quizzically. "Are you really going to be that stubborn as to not take my jacket? Your goosebumps can be seen a mile away."

It baffles me that his sweet gestures are constantly coupled with sarcasm. Deciding not to react, which is exactly what he wants, I simply extend an arm and reach for the jacket. "Thank you."

"I've never known you to concede to me so quickly, you really must be cold."

I slip on the jacket and am instantly hit with his strong sandalwood and vanilla scent. It invades my senses so completely it takes me a moment to remember Carter is standing right in front of me, and now is *so not the time* to be committing his scent to memory.

We continue on, and I take a total of two steps before a hand wraps around my waist and nudges me over. Carter appears on my left, having moved me further in on the path.

"Oh, don't tell me you've got a particular side of the path you have to walk on?"

Carter scoffs, giving me a tight smile as he begins walking again.

"As much as I'd like to humour you, love, no I don't; I was just raised right. A woman should never be made to walk on the side closest to the road."

There he goes, calling me *love* so nonchalantly again. What the fuck is his deal?

"Well, well, I suppose chivalry isn't dead after all. It's merely living in London in a suit."

Illuminated by the warm glow of the streetlights, Carter offers me a bemused smile before playfully nudging me on the shoulder.

"Watch out, Miss Matthews, that almost sounded like a compliment."

I nudge him right back, unable to stop my growing grin. "I assure you it wasn't, so don't let it inflate that already huge ego of yours."

With a shake of his head, Carter ushers me to continue with his hand on my lower back once more. Not that I'm keeping track, but this is the fourth time in less than 24 hours that Carter's hand has found its way onto my body. Like the first time, I'm lit up from the inside out, as if his touch has sparked a flame beneath my skin.

It's almost midnight as we arrive at the B&B. Despite the late hour, the streets are bustling with people out enjoying the Summer Festival, which leaves the inn deserted.

Luckily our room is on the first floor; my feet are beginning to ache from the walk back. I'm three steps in when my small heel catches in the carpet, causing me to stumble

Carter's strong arms wrap around my waist, holding tight, and I grab behind me at the first thing I make contact with. Given the rock solidness, it seems I've anchored myself to his thighs. Thank god I didn't reach any higher, or it would be incredibly uncomfortable for the both of us. Although, I've fantasised for weeks about how he'd feel beneath my fingers, so it wouldn't be *that* uncomfortable.

It feels like several minutes pass by before I realise I'm practically groping his thighs. Righting myself, I turn around to face the man who probably thinks I'm as coordinated as a newborn foal.

I flash him a small grin. I'm a step above him, which makes us almost directly face-to-face. It's only now I realise he's still got a firm grip on my waist despite the fact I'm steady once more.

I make a pointed glance at where his body connects with mine. "You can let go now. I'm fine on my own two feet."

His gaze shifts, following my own. His fingers flex against me, but still he doesn't break contact. The skin beneath his fingertips is burning up.

With each breath I take, they become shorter, almost ragged. There's a low, desperate hum vibrating throughout my body, like a volcano on the brink of exploding, waiting for one small spark to set it off.

"In my defence, that's twice now." His voice is low, taking on a commanding tone. "I think perhaps you enjoy having me catch you, like some sort of damsel in distress."

Any other time, a comment like that would have my eyes rolling until they hurt. But right now, that would be ingenuine. And the way he's looking at me, like he can see right through me, keeps me honest.

"I'm no damsel, Carter, but I'd be lying if I said I didn't enjoy being caught by you."

I stay quiet as I search his eyes for any hint of disinterest. Considering the man has been pushing my buttons for weeks and displayed a dangerous mix of chivalry and flirtation today, I figure the chances are slim.

The deep green pools staring back at me probably reflect what Carter sees in my own; desire and need—on the precipice of losing all control.

As my search comes up empty, two words ring out in my mind.

Fuck it.

Placing my weight on my toes, I lean forward and connect my lips to his.

For a moment, neither of us move. I've never had a kiss this still. Slowly, I reach a hand up to cup his cheek, desperate to feel his stubble beneath my fingertips. The small movement acts like a tripwire, and Carter comes to life.

Still keeping his hands firmly on my waist, he pulls back. Not much, but enough to see my face.

"What was that for?"

He's seriously questioning this? Good grief, this man is impossible. I'm struggling to discern how he feels, concerned I've somehow got it all wrong. That is, until he continues gazing into my eyes, his own softening ever so slightly.

"Do you have objections?" I raise a brow at him, daring him to tell me he doesn't want this. There's still a small part of me fearing I've read this entire thing wrong, but there's a larger part telling me to own it like the badass woman I aspire to be.

A smirk ghosts his lips. "No objections here; I'm merely hoping this isn't the wine acting on your behalf."

I'm momentarily stunned by his admission, by the fact he'd be less inclined to continue this if alcohol were behind it.

"Carter, I'd been drinking non-alcoholic wine since the second glass."

I revel in the way his pupils react to this; solid proof I made the right move. His eyes flare as heat emanates from them.

"I've been waiting for the perfect opportunity to continue what you started in the stockroom."

"Lara, you only had to ask, and I'd have dropped everything for you."

Before I get the chance to let a statement like that take over my thoughts, Carter returns his lips to mine, cutting off any chance of overthinking.

Blood thumps heavily against the artery in my neck, but there's a hitch in its steady flow as a thought occurs to me: that was the first time our lips have touched. It seems unbelievable, almost ridiculously so. The feeling of his lips on mine is somehow more familiar than any kiss that's come before.

The barely-there stubble is rough against my skin. A small moan elicits from deep within at the reminder of that feeling between my thighs. Carter nips at my bottom lip, spurred on by the sound, before smoothing his tongue over it.

Teeth and tongues fight each other for dominance. Carter sucks my tongue into his mouth, and I retaliate by latching onto his bottom lip and dragging my teeth across it. A sonorous growl flows from Carter's mouth into my own, the low hum wreaking havoc on my body. My legs threaten to bottom out beneath me, my breathing kicks up a notch in both speed and intensity, and my pussy attempts a vice grip on nothing but the sounds emanating from him.

Not a moment too soon, Carter snakes one hand around me and further up my back, planting itself firmly between my shoulder blades. My skin heats immediately at the contact, burning beneath his touch. His other hand slides up the column of my neck and rests gently against my wild pulse.

He must feel the way the blood pulses beneath his fingertips in answer to his unspoken question. Carter applies the slightest amount of pressure around the front of my throat in return, and I swear I see Heaven.

This is bad, this is *very* bad. We should *not* be doing this, and it should *not* feel this good.

It's just a kiss Lara, snap out of it. You've had plenty of excellent kisses; this is simply another tally on the scoreboard.

Of course he's a great kisser; he's had plenty of practice. So many women, even more kisses.

It's as though time stands still whilst our lips are pressed to one another's. The world simply ceases to exist outside of Carter. His tongue tangles with my own, fighting for dominance once more.

I let out a groan, but it's cut short by the sound of voices entering the inn's foyer. We break apart. Carter's wide eyes and heavy breathing match my own.

"We should probably move."

"I hate to say it, but I agree with you."

Our lips find each other again not a moment later.

Chapter 26

Lara

Our kisses are so all-consuming I fail to register how we make it from the stairs to our room. One minute we're on the staircase, and the next, I'm being ushered through the door and pushed up against the back of it as it closes behind me.

It takes what little self-control I have remaining to push lightly against his firm chest, breaking our kiss. My god, his chest is far harder than I expected. What I wouldn't give to see him naked, feel him skin to skin. Carter steps away instantly, a look of concern marring his beautiful face.

"Wait."

Carter's face falls momentarily before he realises, schooling his features into a more nonchalant expression.

"If you've had a change of heart, that's more than okay." His voice is filled with an unexpected level of sincerity. It throws me a little, not because he's not a genuine person, but because I'm not used to men being so candid.

Perhaps that says more about the men I'm interested in than it does about Carter, but that's not the point right now.

"No, it's not that, I just want to make sure you know this is a one-time thing."

"Oh?" He tilts his head, the ghost of a smile on his lips.

"Carter, you're my boss now, so it couldn't possibly be more. This" —I point between us— "is purely a means to an end for this crazy physical attraction, scratching an itch we've both had for weeks. Surely you know it can't possibly be more than that?"

"Please, tell me more about this itch we've both had." Carter gives me a wicked grin.

"Oh, come off it, we both know I'm right."

Carter snakes his arms around my waist, interlocking them behind my lower back. "I don't doubt that one bit, but I'm surprised you're so freely admitting it."

Given our proximity, I'm forced to look up at him to meet his gaze. The glint I see reflected back at me provides the confidence I need to take a step closer to him, bringing him flush against me. His thick erection is obvious through the front of his trousers, and it brings a smile to my face.

"Considering the kiss we just had, it would be a little insincere of me to say otherwise." I wrap my arms around his neck. "What I want to know now though, is if you're able to deliver on your words."

"I'm more than happy to show you I can do more than just deliver, *love*."

The name has no effect on me this time; I'm already bewitched.

"I should hope so; you talk an awfully big game."

Carter leans his head down, inches from my own. I can feel his exhales against my skin as he responds. "Such a smart mouth for someone who seems so innocent. I'm dying to put it to good use."

My stomach drops, akin to the sensation you'd feel as a rollercoaster begins its plummet to the ground.

Carter grips my waist and lifts me into the air. On instinct, I wrap my legs around him to stop myself from falling, and my skirt hitches up around my thighs. The positioning causes his dick to rub directly against my centre, a lacy pair of underwear the only layer between our bodies. A gasp escapes my lips, and Carter catches it with his own. He must be feeling exactly what I am because he tilts his pelvis as he walks us toward the bed, groaning into the kiss at the friction.

The breath whooshes out of my lungs as I'm unceremoniously deposited onto the king bed. Carter looms over me, looking down at me beneath hooded lids. His large frame blocks out the light above us, instead giving him an ethereal presence by casting a halo over his form.

Typically, I keep my sarcasm and mouthiness to a minimum when it comes to sex, but something about Carter draws it out of me. Propping myself up on my elbows, I cross one leg over the other, waving a heeled foot at the man above me.

"I'm ready when you are, *sir*." The last word was meticulously thrown in as an experiment of sorts. I'd caught a glimpse of Carter earlier today when I referred to Mason as 'sir'. At the time, I couldn't tell if the darkening in his eyes had been in response to that or if my eyes were playing tricks on me. I watch smugly as he has the same reaction now.

"Are you ever not sarcastic?"

Without waiting for a response, Carter leans down, grips an ankle in each hand, and tugs. The man must be stronger than I thought, given the ease with which he pulls me to the edge of the bed, once again lined up with his impressively hard dick.

The hunger in his eyes amplifies as he takes hold of my calves, raising my legs from where they're resting on either side of his hips. Carter places them against his chest, gaze still intently holding mine. His muscles flex beneath the heels of my feet, once again reminding me how badly I want to see beneath his shirt.

One at a time, Carter removes my heels with an unexpected level of care and grace. For someone with hands the size of his, he handled those tiny buckles with ease. The pad of his thumb brushes over the inside of my ankle, causing me to stifle a gasp.

He releases one ankle to adjust himself, and I lick my lips with anticipation. Normally I'm not too phased by dicks; size truly doesn't matter as long as they know how to use it. But there's something about Carter's that has me enthralled. I never thought I'd be so eager to put someone's dick in my mouth, but I guess there's a first time for everything.

My daydreaming is interrupted by the feel of Carter's hands snaking their way up my thighs and to my waist, pooling my skirt at my hips. In one swift motion, my skirt is on the floor, and I'm left with my underwear on full display.

Carter kneels down on the carpeted floor, reaching his hands around to my arse. He squeezes gently and pulls me even closer to him.

"Did you wear these for me?" The question is emphasised by Carter's finger tracing the outline of the black lace. My hips buck beneath his touch when he drags his thumb up the centre, stopping millimetres below my clit and trailing back down. This is the sweetest torture I'll ever feel; I'm torn between wanting him to stop immediately and praying he never does.

"In your dreams, Carter. I'm of the firm belief that a nice pair of underwear boosts your self-confidence by fifty percent."

He doesn't break contact as his slow torture continues, threatening to consume me.

"You've worked out the statistics, have you? I wasn't aware

you were such a number cruncher. I should put you in finance with skills like that."

"Oh shut up and kiss me, Lawrence."

Carter's laugh fills the air for a moment, but it's abruptly cut off as he draws himself up onto the bed. Hovering above me between my splayed legs, he places a chaste kiss on my lips. My hands find their way to his shirt-clad shoulders, holding him to me.

A chill goes through me at the feel of Carter's hot breath against my ear, my eyes fluttering shut.

"Would it be okay if I removed your underwear?" His voice is barely above a whisper as it caresses the shell of my ear, and I almost combust at the tenderness of his words. I open my eyes to find him watching me as if transfixed.

The way he's looking at me is doing something to my insides, and while I don't love the feeling it elicits, I don't think I hate it either. It feels too heavy right now, so I attempt to lighten the mood.

"If you don't remove them, I most definitely will." Taking my hands off Carter, I move to place them on the black lace sitting on my hips. Carter stops me in my tracks, both wrists in his grasp.

"Allow me, please."

Any fight I was going to put up is extinguished by the way he says *please*. Instead, I merely nod.

Carter gently places my arms by my sides, releasing my wrists. His gaze remains locked on my face while he trails a featherlight touch across my abdomen for what feels like forever before finally reaching the lace. He wraps his fingers around either side and slides them down at a snail's pace, lifting each foot in turn until I'm left bared to him from the waist down.

Without breaking eye contact, Carter bundles up my

underwear and slides them into his trouser pocket. My lips part in silent surprise, caught off guard by the caveman-esque action.

"I figured I'd hold onto them for you, since you won't be needing them again this evening."

"You're awfully thoughtful, aren't you? Now take off your shirt."

Straightening out my legs, I cross one ankle over the other. Not a second passes before Carter's gripping my ankle, throwing it across so I'm spread open beneath him.

"It's adorable you think you're in a position to make demands while your pussy is laid out in front of me like a main course."

It's astonishing that such a pretty face can utter such filth, and even more astonishing that it calls to my body the way it does, but I refuse to let him see the effect he's having on me.

"Please," I add, batting my lashes for good measure and hoping like hell I don't sound as desperate as I feel. Because fuck, do I feel desperate. The man fills out a suit like it's nobody's business, but right now, I want nothing more than for it to be lying discarded on the floor.

A grin stretches across Carter's face. "Only because you asked so nicely."

Satisfaction swells through me, but it's short-lived. Rather than going straight for his top button, as I'd anticipated, Carter reaches for his left cuff.

Asshole. I should've known he wouldn't let me win so easily.

At a leisurely pace, Carter proceeds to remove one cufflink, then the other, before unhurriedly undoing the buttons of each cuff. Against my better judgement, I let out the sigh that's been building.

"Something the matter?" There's a twinkle in his eye as he speaks, teasing me.

"Oh, not at all. I'm enjoying watching the slowest strip tease in history."

"You really do have quite the mouth on you, Miss Matthews."

I wait impatiently as Carter undoes each remaining button before tossing his shirt aside.

Holy fucking shit.

Carter, shirtless, deserves a place among the natural wonders of the world. He's divine. I trace each abdominal muscle with my gaze, transfixed by the way they ripple with each breath he takes. His chest is unbelievably broad, smatterings of dark hair spread across the surface. Snake-like veins run across his shoulders and into his biceps, weaving down through to his hands. I don't think I've ever seen a sight like this.

"Now it's my turn to talk." His voice breaks the trance his bare upper body put me under. Carter leans down and rests his weight on an elbow beside my head, his free hand moving to cup my jaw. "There are four words I need you to remember, love," he murmurs against my cheek, his lips caressing my skin ever so softly, only breaking contact as he speaks. "Harder." *Kiss.* "Softer." *Kiss.* "Faster." *Kiss.* "Slower." *Kiss.*

"Now, repeat them back to me." I'm trembling as he speaks again, the words reverberating through me. He pauses the course he's taking down my body, lifting his head to look me in the eyes, and I've somehow lost the ability to speak.

"Lara." My name comes out in a deep gravel that, mixed with the intensity of Carter's gaze, has the trembling derailing into near internal combustion.

"Yes?"

"Repeat. The. Words." Each word is punctuated with a nearly undetectable nip to the sensitive skin at the juncture of my neck and shoulder. The whisper of contact leaves me wanting to scream for more.

I'm given a moment to order my thoughts when Carter grips the hem of my blouse, dragging it up and over my head. His eyes flare when they lock onto the matching black brassiere, which he swiftly removes.

Steeling myself, I recount the words one by one. With each word out of my mouth, Carter continues his descent, kissing and caressing his way down my stomach and upper thighs. He purposely avoids my chest, the lack of attention making my breasts ache.

"Good girl," Carter breathes, breaking contact with my skin and leaving a cool chill in his wake. I want to whimper at the loss of heat, but I stop myself. "Keep going."

"S-slower," I say breathily as Carter reaches the apex of my thighs. I look down at him, our eyes connecting. Without a word, his tongue darts out, swiping directly over my clit. Something between a gasp and a moan makes its way out of my throat at the contact. He's somehow both demanding and tender at the same time. It draws me up off the mattress as if his touch is a call I can't help but answer.

The movement only spurs Carter on, and I suck in a sharp Breath as he draws me into his mouth, tugging. He lets out a carnal, primitive sound as he releases my clit and runs his tongue from one end to the other. It sends a deep vibration through each and every nerve in my body.

"Enjoying yourself?" Carter mumbles against my skin, and my eyelids flutter in response. Carter pops his head up, smirking at me. He's far too smug for his own good.

"You're doing an adequate job." That ought to knock him down a peg or two.

"I beg your pardon?"

"I said you're doing an adequate job."

"I heard you quite clearly the first time, you little deviant." Carter rises onto his knees and sits painfully still. His hands now rest flat atop his thighs, and I'm left spread out beneath him and missing his touch. The way he unhurriedly takes in every inch of me has my skin burning up. I'm not used to this sort of attention, but I think I kind of love it.

"What has me begging your pardon is your use of the word *adequate*." The last word comes out at a higher pitch, almost in questioning. "I'm used to being called many things love, but adequate isn't one of them."

Carter begins stroking my thighs with his fingertips, up and down the inside of them at a leisurely pace. It takes every ounce of self-control I have to keep my cool despite having the strongest urge to sit up, glide my fingers into his hair and drag his face down between my legs.

He's skilled, and he knows it. I've never experienced the sort of pleasure his tongue was providing, and I find myself craving it already. Either I've slept with amateurs, or Carter is the human form of "practice makes perfect". I don't think I want to know which statement is true.

Carter continues his lazy strokes as he gazes down at me.

"There's a first time for everything."

Head tipping back, Carter lets out a cold laugh. "God, what I wouldn't give to see you attempt this mouthiness with my dick down your throat."

"You keep making these threats with no follow-through, Carter. Go on, do it."

"Mark my words, I will. But right now is about you, and another first. I'm going to resume feasting on you, and I won't stop until you're coming apart beneath me, my name the only word leaving your lips."

Fuck. Me.

Carter has an incredibly dirty mouth, which is relatively

uncharted territory for me. Most of the guys I've slept with have been rather quiet, probably focused more on trying to achieve the unachievable rather than talking. But when it comes to Carter, the man can multitask.

If my pussy had a voice box, she'd be squealing right now. Or shouting expletives like her life depended on it. My inner walls clench at his words, and I fist the sheets beneath me.

Carter's eyes drop from my face to my waiting pussy, becoming hooded instantly. I watch with bated breath as he swipes two fingers through my slit, revelling at the sight of my wetness coating them.

"Fuck Lara, you're soaked. It seems my words are far more than *adequate* if this is anything to go by." A wicked grin plays on his lips, and I groan, angry at the way my body has betrayed me.

Carter leans his top half over my body, coming face to face with me. The feeling of his breath on my lips has a shiver rolling through me. His dick twitches against me beneath his trousers, and I'm reminded of the fact I'm completely naked whilst he remains entirely clothed where it counts most. Why is that so hot? It definitely shouldn't be.

"Are you ready? It's not too late to back out if you don't think you can handle it."

"Do your worst."

"Open your mouth for me."

I refuse to break eye contact as I slowly let my jaw drop open. Carter licks his lips in anticipation, and I try my best not to wriggle beneath him, desperate for any sort of release.

I don't even have a moment to gasp as the two fingers previously dragged through my centre are pushed into my gaping mouth. At the same time, two fingers on his other hand thrust into my pussy.

My back arches off the bed as Carter's fingers move in and

out of me at an agonising pace. I suck hard on the fingers in my mouth, rolling my tongue around them to wring a reaction out of Carter. Instead of speeding up, or slowing down, or reacting in any of the ways I expect, he stops.

I reach up, gripping his wrist and removing his fingers from my mouth with a *pop*.

"Why did you stop?"

"Why are you trying to distract me?" He raises an eyebrow in question.

Busted.

I give my best innocent look, batting my lashes. "I would never."

"You would, and you most certainly are, but it's not going to work. The harder you fight this, the harder I'm going to make you come."

Sheer hunger crosses his features as he slinks down the bed, coming to rest between my thighs once more. Lowering his mouth to my centre, his gaze remains fixed on mine. I'm hit with a surge of pleasure when two fingers re-enter me at the same time he sucks my clit into his mouth.

"Oh fuck. Carter."

It's a deadly combination. He doesn't even realise the power he wields right now. I'm on the brink of orgasm by another for the first time in my life, and it's both shocking and impressive.

My legs begin to shake, unable to hold out much longer against the large man between them. Carter doesn't let up even an inch, he simply perseveres.

I can *hear* how close I am, thanks to the rhythmic pumping of his fingers, and it's disturbingly dirty. I try not to imagine how it sounds to him. I let out a moan, failing to register how loud it is.

A fresh wave of arousal seeps out as I teeter on the edge.

Carter groans against me, releasing my clit long enough to lap up the evidence of his actions.

"That's it Lara, just let go."

His voice must be on the same wavelength as my body, because with each word from his mouth, every nerve ending tingles. My knuckles strain under the force with which they're gripping the sheets, and an unmistakable warmth is creeping up my spine at an alarming rate.

All rational thoughts have scrambled. There's only one word bouncing around my head: *Carter*. My head tips back on instinct as my orgasm begins to unleash.

"Oh . . . Carter . . . *oh*."

"You are magnificent."

Those three words out of his mouth are my undoing.

Chapter 27

Carter

Bearing witness to a woman's orgasm by my hands is the single greatest experience. Or at least, it was. But now, as I glance down at the beautiful woman beneath me, I have a new favourite: being the reason Lara comes undone.

Her eyes are closed, head tilted backwards as she tries to regulate her breathing. I watch as a sated smile graces her lips, feeling pretty pleased with myself. I lick my lips, the taste of her sparking fresh arousal. My cock is unbearably hard and has been since the moment our lips touched on the staircase.

It rattles me how strongly Lara affects me, yet she has no idea of the power she has.

"Shit." The word is said on an exhale. I can't take my eyes off her; the heavy rise and fall of her chest, the slow uncrumpling of the sheets from her fists, the way her eyelashes flutter open, and I'm greeted by two glorious pools of ocean blue.

Although the hotel room is dim, Lara's face glows brightly. She lets out a satisfied sigh, grinning up at me, and my chest almost explodes. She's breathtaking. It's hard to ignore the slight ache this causes, knowing she's only mine for this evening.

Despite wanting to stay there forever, I remove myself from between Lara's thighs, coming to lie beside her while she recovers. I prop myself up on an elbow, gaze raking over her pretty face.

"How are you doing down there?" I keep my tone light and teasing, but the question itself is genuine; I have this overwhelming urge to make sure she's okay.

"Carter," she exhales in disbelief, rolling onto her side to face me. "I really don't think you need the ego boost, but I can't lie, that was fucking incredible. *You* are incredible."

I shrug my shoulders, hoping it comes off as casual, even though I'm the complete opposite. Pride flows through me at the thought of being the only person to have brought her this level of pleasure. "Does that mean it was more than *adequate?*"

Lara chokes out a laugh, still regaining her breath. "Absolutely. The men back home could learn a thing or two from you."

"Watch out, you'll inflate my huge ego with that sort of talk."

"Speaking of huge things . . ." Lara trails off, pushing herself up from the mattress. She begins to slide a hand down my stomach, but I catch it before she can descend too far. Fuck, if her hand got any closer to my dick, all self-control would go out the window.

"You don't want to finish?" Lara glances at me curiously, the slightest look of concern detracting from her flirtatious tone.

"This was about you, not me."

I'm lying stomach down across the bed when Lara emerges from the ensuite bathroom. She tried insisting I shower first, given she'd take longer, but my persistence won out. My heart skips a beat—she's in nothing but a towel. Several water droplets cling to the delicate skin of her decolletage, but my attention is stolen by the few that roll down between her breasts. They beckon to me like a moth to a flame.

"As comfortable as you look, you're going to need to move over a little." Her voice, sweet as honey, pulls my gaze back to her face. There's a teasing smirk playing on her lips. It makes me want to yield to her every desire.

I push myself up, pulling my legs crossed beneath me. "I was serious about sleeping on the chaise, it doesn't bother me in the slightest. I'd rather you were comfortable."

With a tilt of her head and a dip of her brow, she pins me with her stare. "And I was serious about that being ridiculous. Given the way you were sprawled out, I think there's more than enough room for the two of us and a pillow wall."

A. Pillow. Wall.

This isn't how I saw the sleeping arrangement going, but I'll be damned if I let her see any disappointment or surprise on my face. I meant what I said about her being comfortable, and if that means I sleep up against a wall of fucking pillows, then so be it. Although I doubt I'll get much sleep knowing she's lying there, within arm's length but out of reach.

"We better get constructing then." I slide down the bed, pulling the duvet down with me. I'm about to reach for the pillows when I hear a muffled sound. When I turn around, I'm met with a red-faced Lara, one hand over her mouth and the other holding her stomach. Upon seeing my face, the howling laugh is set free.

"Oh fuck, the look on your face was *priceless*," she says

between heaving breaths. "I'm messing with you Carter, there's no need for a pillow wall."

I can't help but join in; her laughter is contagious.

Once we've gathered ourselves, I'm given a second of reprieve—she wants to sleep beside me.

Will she want to cuddle? Should I offer that? Would she slap me for even mentioning it?

A myriad of thoughts runs rampant as we stand here gazing at each other. Significantly reducing the space between us, I try to calm my racing heart as I lean towards her ear. "I'll remember this, Miss Matthews." A shudder flows through her, but I continue. "Do you have a preferred side?"

Our lips are painfully close as she tilts her head up. The ghost of a smile plays on her lips. "Left." Before I get the chance to do something stupid—like kiss her—she averts her gaze to my lower half, gesturing to the trousers I'm still wearing. "Are you sleeping like that?"

I couldn't think of anything worse than sleeping in these, especially after having worn them all day, but I'd do it without batting an eyelid if she asked me to.

"Will that make you more comfortable?"

She lets out a small sigh, her hand landing softly on my bicep. "I appreciate the consideration, Carter, but stop worrying about me so much. However you want to sleep is fine by me, but I'll judge you if it's in trousers."

"Spare your judgement because I'll be losing them quick smart." I make my way to the right side of the bed but stop short of undoing my button when I clock Lara still standing there motionless. That's when I realise she has nothing to sleep in, because there's no way her office attire would be comfortable. Luckily for her, I'm more than willing to give her the shirt off my back—literally. Reaching down, I collect up my shirt.

"Here," I say, bundling it up and tossing it in her direction, "you can sleep in this."

"Oh, thanks." Her cheeks turn a darker shade of pink. She returns to the bathroom, closing the door behind her. Except it doesn't latch, swinging open slightly. From where I stand, I have the perfect view of her in the bathroom mirror. Transfixed, I'm unable to tear my eyes away as she undoes the towel fixture, letting it fall to the floor. The moment it hits the ground, her eyes meet mine in the reflection.

Shit, I've been caught. Deciding to play it cool and deal with the consequences later, I hold her gaze. My breathing shallows when she smiles at me. It's a sexy, closed-lip smile, and it pulls at something deep within me. It's getting harder to breathe as she begins dressing in my shirt at a teasing pace, dragging her fingernails along the soft skin of her breasts when she pulls each side to the centre. All the while, her eyes never leave mine.

She leaves the buttons undone and turns towards the door. Without a word, she closes the door completely. I'm able to take a full breath for the first time since she emerged from the bathroom looking heaven-sent.

I'm still replaying the encounter five minutes later when the bathroom door unlatches. Something short circuits in my brain as Lara wanders out in my still unbuttoned shirt, rounds the bed, and climbs in. Lying her head on the pillow, she eyes me suspiciously. "No funny business, Mister."

Chuckling, I raise a hand in protest. "I'm sorry, which one of us is currently lying here practically on full display?"

"I didn't hear you complaining when I caught you staring," she says smugly.

"I'd be a fool to complain about a view like that." Her eyes flare briefly, and I continue before she can respond. "Agreed;

no funny business." That delightful laugh warms my heart as I give her a small salute.

"Sleep well, Miss Matthews," I say with a smirk as she rolls the other way. My cock strains harder than ever as I wander into the bathroom to shower.

Chapter 28

Carter

I don't know how long I've been lying here, sleep evading me, but I'm over it. I let out a huff, annoyed.

"I believe that huff is called sexual frustration."

Lara's unexpected voice startles me; given her stillness, I figured she was fast asleep.

With her back to me, I feel rather than see the self-satisfaction oozing out of her. It's in the way she wriggles her taut backside against my front, not enough to be blatantly obvious, but enough that I'm certain it's purposefully done. It's in the way she runs the ball of her foot along the inside of my calf, teasing.

"Funny. Did I wake you?"

"No, I can't sleep either."

"What's on your mind?"

Lara rolls over in my arms, her face now inches from mine. "Two things. But the main one is the uneven scoreboard. I'm an equal opportunist, Carter." Her hand comes up to stroke my jawline, her touch soft against the stubble.

Well shit. That's not how I pictured this playing out.

"You're really adamant about this, aren't you?" The intensity in her gaze has me picturing obscene images, like how incredible she'd look riding me. The way her breasts would feel in my grasp, bouncing in time with the rest of her. Would her head fall back, the euphoric feeling too much to bear, or would she refuse to break eye contact, gazing into my soul as she rides me into oblivion? The images do nothing to help the frustration; instead they worsen it. My cock has become agonisingly stiff within the confines of my underwear—the only layer of clothing I currently adorn—and given our proximity, there's no way Lara hasn't noticed.

"Abso-fucking-lutely. Now give in already so I can even the playing field."

Every drop of blood in my body reroutes straight to my already hardened cock as she dips her hand beneath my waistband, wrapping a smooth hand around it. She's no longer playing fair, and I like it.

Before I can state my case, Lara's up on her knees beside me. My shirt is completely open, exposing her breasts in all their glory. She's wearing a sly grin, one I've never seen before. It would almost be unsettling if it weren't so fucking *alluring*. It's dark outside, but the light of the moon casts Lara in an almost angelic glow.

"If you wrap that smart mouth around my cock, I guarantee you it won't make it into your pussy tonight."

"Bit of a one-hit wonder, are you?"

A chuckle escapes me before I can stop it. Lara's brows slowly raise as she looks me up and down with ease.

"I assure you I'm anything but a 'one-hit wonder' on any normal day, but considering I've thought about this moment every day since the stockroom event, I encourage you to choose your next move wisely."

Lara's eyes widen momentarily, and the hand stroking my dick falters, seemingly taken aback by my candour. I won't lie,

I've even shocked myself a little with that last bit. There's something about this woman that has me wanting to tell her every thought that's ever entered my mind.

Lara releases my dick, and I instantly miss the way she wrapped around me so perfectly. She leans her torso over me, her face coming to a stop mere inches from mine. The feeling of her breath on my lips sends a shiver down my spine.

"Unfortunately for you, I'm not known for my wiseness."

Lara places her lips on mine in a fleeting kiss, and I want nothing more than to hold her there. Before I get the chance, she's shuffling backwards and spreading her knees. Holding my gaze, Lara lowers her head to my dick, spitting on it. It's filthy and obscene and so incredibly fucking *hot*.

When she lowers her head, wrapping her mouth around me, something akin to a growl reverberates through me. Given the way she smiles around my dick, I'd hazard a guess she felt it too. I have to focus on keeping it together as Lara begins running the tip of her tongue along my length, swirling it around my tip with each stroke.

"*Fuck*," is all I can manage when Lara's movements increase in both speed and intensity. It's overwhelming in the best of ways. I reach a hand out, intertwining it into the strands of Lara's hair currently obscuring my view. There's something about watching her mouth on me. I never want it to end.

When I think she can't possibly make this any better than it is, Lara slows her movements. As she's almost deep-throating me, she unsheathes her teeth from her lips and drags them up my shaft with minimal pressure. There's an immediate warmth within my pelvis, the pressure building frantically.

"Unless you want me to spill into your mouth, I suggest you move, love." My voice is unrecognisable, heavy with arousal.

I expect Lara to move almost immediately, so I'm caught off

guard when she stays put, and even more so when she chooses to repeat the movement.

"I'm serious, Lara."

Finally, Lara heeds my warning and slides my dick from her mouth, wiping the back of her hand across her smirk.

"Thanks for the suggestion, but if it's all the same to you, I think I'll stay right here."

The vixen gives me a broad smile before sliding her mouth back over my throbbing dick. She begins to drag her tongue along my length again, keeping her eyes locked on mine with each lick. A shock goes through me when her free hand squeezes my balls, and I know I'm done for.

Despite my best efforts to hold out, my orgasm pulses through me, and I empty into Lara's mouth. Her cheeks are hollowed out, and she lets out the sexiest moan as I finish on her tongue. She gives me one last suck, and my head falls onto the pillow.

With my eyes closed, I focus on slowing my heart rate. There's a dip in the mattress beside me as Lara joins me. I lift my arm, allowing her to move closer, and lay it gently across her back. My hand finds the dip of her waist, conforming.

"That was, without a doubt, one of the best blow jobs I've ever received. It might even be *the* best if I'm completely honest." I'm still a little breathless.

"I'd hope so, that was some of my best work." Lara smiles up at me. Without thinking, I lower my head to hers, placing a kiss on her forehead. She looks a little dumbfounded initially before the smile returns.

"What was the second thing?"

"Huh?" Lara's brows draw together, creating a cute little crease between them.

"When I asked what was on your mind, you'd said there

were two things. Evening the score distracted me at the time, but I want to know the second thing."

The grin she flashes me looks eerily similar to Winnie when she's up to no good. "Hallmark movies."

"I'm sorry?"

"I was thinking about Hallmark movies. Those films are undoubtedly unmatched and completely underrated, and this place reminds me of the type of setting you'd see in one."

I can't help but laugh. "That's certainly not what I expected you to say, but I'm sure we can find one if you'd like."

Before I can reach for the remote lying on her bedside table, Lara responds. "Oh no, I didn't mean we have to watch one now."

"But do you want to?"

Even in the darkness, I don't miss the way her eyes light up at the suggestion.

"No that's okay, we should probably sleep."

The light in her eyes has dimmed. I'm hit with an unexpected thought—I'd do almost anything to see that light again. Without another word, I reach across her and retrieve the remote. It only takes a couple of minutes to find a film. Pressing play, I place the remote onto my bedside table. Lara rises slightly as I roll back over, so I slide my arm beneath her once more.

"Thank you," comes from her mouth in the softest whisper as she snuggles into my side. Her warm breathe against my chest provides a comfort I've never experienced.

I'm fairly certain I fall asleep smiling.

The small sliver of sun struggling to break through the clouds is the first thing I see when I awaken. It looks beautiful outside. Twenty-nine years spent in this country, and I'm still yet to get over how picturesque it really is.

Movement to my left draws my attention, and in an instant, the village outside doesn't hold a candle to the figure wrapped around my midsection.

She's rolled over, conforming her small frame to the side of my body. Her hair falls in waves across her cheek, dark lashes contrast sharply against her fair skin. I watch in awe as her body rises and falls in a steady rhythm, still sleeping soundly.

In this moment, with Lara's upper body draped across my own, my fingertips drawing soft circles on her shoulder blade, I decide anything with this woman, no matter how limited, is better than the prospect of nothing at all.

"God you're good at that."

The sound of her voice is spiced honey personified; it rolls off her tongue so effortlessly and swirls around me like liquid, yet sleep has given it the smallest of rough edges. It's glorious. I'd listen to it all day if I could.

"Good at what?"

She wiggles her shoulder. "That, the back tickles."

"I wasn't aware it was something you could be bad at, but thank you." Humour laces my tone as I smile to myself.

I don't dare let my hand still now, continuing the circles despite the slow developing cramp in my wrist.

Chapter 29

Lara

'F aster.'

'Harder.'

'That's it Lara.'

The sound of Carter clearing his throat pulls me out of my dirty daydream. Although, is it still a daydream if it really happened?

"So I've been thinking . . ." he begins. Carter's gaze slides to mine out the corner of his eye, assessing. I haven't the slightest idea where this is going, but if his thoughts have been anything like mine, it's nowhere good.

"Don't hurt yourself."

Is it possible to regret something as deeply as you are satisfied by it? That's how I feel about the three words I uttered. I don't know what it is, but there's something about Carter that causes any level of eloquence I possess to completely disappear. It's certainly no way to be around my boss, but in my defence, he's had this effect on me since the day I first met him.

"I offer to stop for coffee, twice, you insist we don't need to, twice, and *this* is how you repay me?"

He mumbles something, sounding oddly like, 'god, if I could put you over my knee right now', which sends an unexpected thrill through me. I'm tempted to ask him to repeat himself, but I decide it's far wiser to pretend I heard nothing.

"Please, elaborate on what you've been thinking."

Carter feigns a dramatic eye roll at my aversion to bite.

"Hear me out; last night should be repeated on a regular basis. Or, at the very least, a couple more times."

On instinct, I scoff. The second the sound leaves my mouth, I regret it. It wasn't intentional.

Dragging my gaze from the window, I turn to find Carter watching me. Thankfully we're stopped at a set of lights on the outskirts of London's city centre, so I can forgive the fact he's not looking at the road right now.

"Are you propositioning me?"

"Yes."

Now I really want to scoff, but I refrain.

"Really? While I'm stuck in a vehicle with you?"

"I can rectify that if you'd like?"

Before I'm able to form a response, we're going through the now-green intersection. Carter moves to the furthest left lane, turns down a side street, and comes to a stop.

"There." Carter gestures to our surroundings, arms spread wide. "Now you can flee if that's what you want to do." He turns toward me in his seat, his hand brushing against mine over the console and causing my heart rate to spike. He leans in ever so slightly, eyes bright. "But I don't think you want to flee, not really."

"No?" I hate the breathiness of my voice.

"No, not at all. Want to know how I know?" He looks so devilishly handsome right now. There's the ghost of a smirk on his lips, taunting me, and he's got the two-day stubble and bed hair combination nailed. There's no real reason as to why that combination is hot—in all honesty, it shouldn't be—but the man *cannot* look bad.

"No," I say again, with little conviction.

"I know because I watched your breath hitch in your throat just then when our hands touched, and I felt the heat radiating off you. I know because your voice is doing that thing it did last night when I had you repeat those four words to me. I know because—"

"Okay, okay, I get it." It's still baffling how full of himself this man is. I can't fault him on his observational skills though, unfortunately those are finely fucking tuned.

"Look, at the risk of sounding arrogant, it wasn't exactly rocket science to figure out what you needed last night. But apparently that's a lot more than the men in Australia can say. I'm merely offering a simple way for you to understand what you like and need in order to get the most out of sex."

I contemplate this for a moment. As annoying as it is, Carter's not wrong. He did have me figured out far quicker than anyone else I've been with, and certainly far quicker than my ex.

Even so, he must have some sort of ulterior motive. The man could, and does, get any woman he wants. Why me?

"What's in it for you?"

"I get to taste you again."

"I'm serious."

"So am I." Carter leans further over the centre console and snakes one hand along my jaw. "You're delectable, and it's addictive. I'd go down on you right now if you'd let me."

My thighs clench. Is it awful I'm considering his offer? God, of *course* it is.

"Carter, you're my boss. I can't imagine HR being too thrilled if they found out."

"I own the company, love. Who's going to tell me no?"

"You really are a dick."

"Is that a yes?"

"I really don't think it's a good idea." I'm lying through my teeth. The more I think about it and replay last night's orgasm, the more I want to say yes. "I live with your sister, remember? I can't imagine she'd take this well."

"You what?" He looks as though he's been slapped, mouth agape, eyes wide.

"I live with Mia. And Harper. I figured you knew, but I'll take your stunned mullet expression as a hard no."

One brow raises dangerously high, the space between them furrowing deeply. "I haven't the slightest idea what you just said, but no. I did *not* know that."

I slap a hand over my mouth to stifle the sharp laugh, but I'm not fast enough to hide it from him. "Sorry, cultural differences and whatnot."

This makes him smile, even if it resembles more of a smirk than anything. "I'd hardly claim cultural differences when it's England and Australia. But in relation to your living arrangements, I'm not concerned. Why would she need to know?"

"She's one of my best friends; there's no way she wouldn't find out. I don't keep things from her or Harper."

"She'll probably find it a little strange to begin with, but I think you need to give Emmy a little more credit. She's incredibly open-minded."

It's still so strange hearing Mia referred to as anything but Mia. I'm not doubting he knows his sister, probably better than I do, but he didn't see how the conversation went the other night.

"It's not that I don't think she's open-minded enough. I think it's a super weird situation to put her in."

Carter grabs my hand, cupping it between both of his. "Look, I completely understand where you're coming from. I don't doubt that eventually she'll come around to the idea of us, but it'll be weird for her for a little bit. But right now, this isn't about her. It's about you, and whether this is something you want."

Man, that was a solid speech. I'm running out of reasons to say no.

"It's not *not* something I want." I attempt to pull my hand away, feeling shy, but Carter tightens his hold. "Plus, it would be purely physical. It's just sex. It's not as though we're a couple."

"I didn't know you had such a dirty mouth. I'll have to explore that more next time."

I give him a stern look, brows knitting together. "Hey, I haven't agreed to your insanity yet."

"If you won't do it for yourself, then do it for me. Don't I deserve at least one do-over to state my case for not being a one-hit wonder?"

I stifle a laugh; he has a point.

"Strictly casual."

Carter nods, a faint twitch in his cheek as he speaks. "Strictly casual."

A rush of adrenaline courses through me at my decision. "Deal."

Carter doesn't speak. Instead, he flashes me that beautiful smile and slides the car into drive, taking off once more.

I'm still not convinced this is a great idea, but it's about time I let loose a little and did something for me. A few good orgasms never hurt anybody. As long as my heart stays out of it, I've got nothing to lose.

Chapter 30

Lara / Carter

Lara

"Start at the beginning, and don't you dare leave a single detail out."

Typically I'd at least get a 'hello' from Harper, but the second she picks up the call, it's straight down to business.

She and Mia spent the weekend in Mallorca for an old high school friend's bachelorette party, or 'hen do' as it's better known over here, so we've barely spoken since Thursday night. They landed back in Heathrow this morning, and I've been dying to tell Harper, if only to stop the constant state of over-thinking I've been in since Carter dropped me home two mornings ago.

"The beginning? Well, he greeted me with a coffee, exactly how I like it, and a snide comment."

"How strangely thoughtful. The coffee, of course," she adds, "not the snide comment. Men really are peculiar, aren't they?"

"You're telling me."

"Anyway, back to the play-by-play, please."

"My lunch break isn't long enough for that, but to cut a long story short—we spent the night in Norcaster. Together." Anxiety skyrocketing, I repeatedly click and unclick a pen. But it's no use—the constant clicking sound only makes me feel worse. I really should eat something, given I'm on my break, and some food might help the gnawing feeling, but I stay seated at my desk.

"Lara! Oh my god. You fucked him, didn't you?"

I cringe at the volume increase of Harper's tone. If she were anyone else, I'd be secretly praying she's not surrounded by people right now. The pen I'd been fiddling with drops to my notebook with a dull thud.

"Uh, not quite."

"Not quite? Sex isn't really something you can half do, honey."

"Please tell me you're not with Mia right now."

Harper lets out a partly suppressed laugh. "No, she's out for coffee. This is all you; you couldn't pay me to tell her you 'not quite fucked' her brother."

The way she says it so matter-of-factly has a wave of unease washing over me. I certainly wasn't thinking about his siblings when giving the best oral sex performance of my life.

"We didn't have full-blown sex, we just went down on each other."

Harper laughs lightly. "I'm not sure the distinction will matter too much to Mia."

"Shit, do you think she's going to react badly? She is, isn't she? Oh god."

The answering silence results in a dropping sensation in my stomach, and not the good kind. The tip of my heel taps rhythmically against the underside of my desk.

"Lara, honey, take a breath."

I do as she says, albeit roughly. My breaths are sharp and jagged, a reflection of the sudden wave of anxiety over telling Mia. Harper is silent as I get my breathing under control.

After letting out a sigh, Harper continues. "I want to reassure you, Lars, truly, but I just don't know. It's one thing to have the encounter you had at the bookstore without knowing who Carter was, but it's something entirely different to repeat it knowing their familial ties."

The fact she really isn't sure how Mia will respond is causing the anxiety to heighten. I've somehow failed to realise that this is completely different to the bookshop encounter—I'd like to blame sex brain, but I'm not sure it extends to two days later.

Just wait until she hears it won't be a once-off . . .

"Why are you always right?"

"It's a blessing and a curse."

"Is now a good time to mention I agreed to it happening again?"

For the first time since the proposition, I'm questioning my decision. Is this the dumbest thing I've ever done? Probably not, but it's got to be in the top five. I'm not sure what I'm hoping for with this call. Reassurance? Validation? A *go girl, get that dick?*

I suppose I just need her to be aware *now* so I don't have to watch both their faces as they process this.

I'm planning to fuck my best friend's brother, possibly numerous times.

Footsteps sound along the corridor, signalling Carter's return. Awful timing, given what I've dropped on Harper, but I can't continue this conversation right now.

"Hey Harps, I've gotta go, but I'll see you at home."

The call disconnects as Carter steps into our office, placing one hand casually on the doorframe in that indescribably hot way men do.

"Lara, could you meet me in the boardroom in five minutes? I need to discuss a potential upcoming project with you."

"Of course," I respond, but apparently Carter isn't looking for a response—he's turning on his heel and retreating before the words have left my mouth entirely.

Carter has been out of the office at meetings this morning, so this is the first I've seen of him since he dropped me home days ago. I certainly didn't anticipate the way my body would react to seeing him; it's hotter than a Queensland summer's day in this office. The need to adjust my blouse strikes me almost instantly, the fabric unexpectedly sticking to my body.

Unsure what this potential project is, I collect my laptop and a blank notebook. I pride myself on always being prepared, so it's a little out of my comfort zone to have no background information on the topic of this impromptu meeting.

My phone buzzes against my desk, revealing Harper's incoming text.

HARPER

I'm out for dinner tonight - talk to Mia x

Looks like I have about four hours to figure out how to tell Mia about this precarious situation I've found myself in with her brother. *Yippee.*

It's a short walk from our corner office to the boardroom, situated on the east side of the building. I make my way down the corridor, the open-plan cubicle spaces to my left and the glass-walled offices to my right. For an established law firm, the interior design is more modern than you'd expect. I return polite smiles to a few familiar faces.

The door to the boardroom comes into view as I round the corner. The only other time I've been to the boardroom was during the office tour on my first day, and the view certainly wasn't this enticing then. The room is framed entirely by windows. The blinds on the internal windows are drawn, shrouding us from anyone who may walk by.

Carter's standing at the head of the table, muscle-corded arms crossed over this broad chest. He's looking out the window until he catches sight of me in his periphery, drawing his focus as I walk in.

It's intimidating having his full attention. The urge to retreat overcomes me. My flight or fight instinct sets in unnecessarily, but really, it's only flight when it comes to me. Regardless, I stand my ground. The intimidation quickly morphs into a feeling of power; my presence has garnered his undivided attention.

His eyes light up, and he extends a hand to the chair closest to where he's standing. "Lara, please have a seat."

Carter's gaze roams over me as I sit, placing my notebook down and opening my laptop to a new document. "Does the project have a name yet?"

Wandering over to the door, Carter closes it with a gentle click. His gaze returns to mine as he makes his way to the head of the table. "Not officially, but I have some thoughts."

Carter grips the arms of the chair nearest me at the head of the table, dropping into it and crossing one ankle over the other knee. "For now, title it 'Bringing L Matthews Orgasms In-House.'"

"That doesn't sound like something concerning the firm, Mr Lawrence," I respond, my stare flitting from my laptop to the man next to me at the same rate my heart is currently beating. I'm trying my hardest to act naturally, but he's caught me completely off guard. I'm well aware he'd like to repeat Norcaster, but I certainly didn't expect him to bring it up so soon after, nevermind at work. He's already consumed too many of my thoughts since last week. The last thing I need to be thinking about right now is how his mouth felt on mine. Apparently, he disagrees.

Carter reaches forward, placing one hand over mine, stopping the absentminded tapping of keys I hadn't noticed I was doing. He doesn't move to grab my hand, just rests his atop it.

"Every time you call me Mr Lawrence, I find myself fighting a losing battle. A battle in which the loss is looking increasingly more desirable."

I'm so often astounded at the way he renders me tongue-tied with these little one-liners. It's nothing like the men—*boys*, really—I'm used to, with their cringe-worthy and often entirely laughable lines. Don't believe me? I once had a guy tell me I looked like I made my bed every morning. Another told me they wanted to call me beautiful, but beauty is on the inside, and they hadn't been inside me, so couldn't say for sure. *This* is the weird shit I'm used to and always had a response for, yet it's the things that come out of Carter's mouth that make me look like a fish trying to breathe above water.

"Come here."

For reasons unknown, or perhaps reasons I refuse to read into, he possesses a magnetic force that pulls me in inexplicably. I stand in place, noticing there's not even an inch between our knees. Carter spreads his legs, entrapping me between them, and I take an involuntary step toward him.

My heart skips a beat, and the ridiculous urge to run surfaces again when Carter lets my hand go, instead resting his hands on the outer sides of my thighs. The skin beneath his palms sears, but I can't tell if it's due to the increase in my core body temperature, his own warmth, or both. Despite the heat, I'm frozen in place.

Carter drags his hand up the outline of my body at a torturously slow pace, but when he reaches my waist, his soft touch turns possessive. He tugs me forward, making me straddle his lap, a knee either side of him. A spark shoots through my core at the feel of his hardening dick pushing against me. With my skirt riding up around my waist, my underwear is my only barrier. I can't stop my traitorous arms from snaking around his neck of their own accord, betraying the cool demeanour I'm aiming for.

Before I can open my mouth to ask what on earth he's doing, his lips find the soft skin of my neck. My body tenses momentarily before relaxing into his embrace, the air leaving my lungs.

"Good god, you smell incredible," Carter says on an exhale, his warm breath contrasted by my goosebumps.

His wandering hands slowly make their way around to my back, fingers toying with the bow, keeping my top secured. One fingertip skims the back of my neck. A jolt of electricity shoots through every nerve ending in my body.

I close my eyes and pray Carter doesn't notice the way my skin heats under his touch. Any hope is extinguished when I open my eyes and find him staring at me intently, the shadow of a smile playing on his lips.

"Why are you looking at me like that?" My voice is unrecognisable in this deeper-than-usual octave. I don't even have it in me to care right now, too turned on by the man beneath me.

"Like what, love?" Carter murmurs, his accent continuing to make *love* sound like the sexiest word known to mankind. I'd argue it is.

"Like a man starved." I just manage to get the words out, feeling overwhelmed by the way his mouth roams over my skin.

Carter doesn't respond right away. Instead, he continues his slow assault of kisses until a soft sigh escapes my lips.

"Because that's exactly what I am. I'm starved of the taste of you."

My breath hitches. The last rational cell in my brain gives out as he tugs on the bow he's been toying with. My shirt falls effortlessly from around my neck. The slightest of whimpers leaves my mouth involuntarily, and it's the wakeup call I didn't realise I needed.

"Carter!" I exclaim a little too loudly in his ear as he drags his mouth up the column of my throat.

A hum against my skin is his only response.

"Carter, you have to stop. Look at where we *are* for goodness sake."

Carter appears completely unaffected as his lips trail ever so slowly across my chest, getting dangerously close to my recently exposed bra.

Looking up at me, his lips barely leaving my skin, Carter's mouth stretches into a wicked grin. "And?"

"And? What do you mean 'and'?" I gasp, baffled at how utterly calm he is. "We're in the fucking *boardroom* Carter, anyone could walk in right now."

At this, he chuckles. He fucking *chuckles*.

"You mean to tell me this isn't our office?" Carter feigns confusion. Frustration heats my blood to a near boil.

"This is no time for jokes, Carter." Breaking the connection of my hands behind his head, I bring one arm around and slap his shoulder.

"If someone were to walk in right now, they'd get one hell of a show."

"Is that supposed to make me feel better?"

"Did it not?" Carter lets his hands fall to either side of my waist, gripping my hips. A gasp slips free when he drives his hips upwards, colliding with my increasingly aching centre.

"You're insufferable, did you know that? This is our *workplace*. Have you lost your mind?"

"I don't seem to recall you being this concerned in Chapter Nine. Correct me if I'm wrong, but I believe that was also your workplace?"

There's nothing worse than when Carter is so outwardly obnoxious yet right in what he's saying, especially when he's got that cocky look on his face. He's reclining in the chair now, the air around my face noticeably lacking his presence. His lips are curled up into a smile, his eyes slowly giving me a once over.

Carter has this infuriating sense of arrogance about him that I'm certain rubs me the wrong way. But as I look at him, *really* look at him, I'm doubting whether that was ever true.

Gaze still locked on mine, Carter unhurriedly draws his fingers to his top button. My attention is caught the moment he slips the button free, mere inches of his well-defined chest now exposed. I can't help but stare at the smattering of dark hair. It distracts me from my thoughts, dispelling each and every one of them. I pull my bottom lip between my teeth, causing Carter's shoulders to shake with laughter.

"It looks like someone's had a change of heart."

His gaze lingers on my lips, his eyes softening around the edges. It's unnerving, yet it unleashes a fire within me. My gaze flicks between those deep green pools, not an ounce of concern or hesitation in sight. The shadow of a smile plays on my lips before his mouth is back on mine in an instant.

Each heated and desperate kiss slowly but surely strips away my concerns. The boardroom fades away with every touch until it's just us, and I lose myself in him.

Carter

As lovely as Lara's navy bra is, I'd much rather see what lies beneath. Without breaking our kiss, my hands find the lace. Cupping her breasts, I give them a gentle squeeze, and I'm rewarded by Lara pressing herself even closer to me. My cock strains beneath my trousers, itching to touch her.

Our tongues remain tangled as I slide my hands up to the straps of her bra, slipping them off her shoulders with little protest. Returning my attention to Lara's chest, I make quick work of pulling down the cups of her bra, completely exposing her to the cool air. Her nipples are impossibly hard as I roll them between my fingertips.

I kiss her deeply once more, revelling in the way she fights me for dominance before standing. Lara startles, hastily wrapping her legs around my midsection, ankles locking against my arse.

"What—"

I cover her mouth with another kiss, silencing her, as I place her on the edge of the table. Her legs release their death grip, and I take a seat once more. The position change is completely selfish; I want easier access for what I'm about to do.

I place delicate open-mouth kisses from her lips to the edge of her jaw, continuing down the column of her neck. My tongue traces along the length of her throat, her pulse thundering beneath. A shudder racks through her as I reach her decolletage, teeth scraping gently across the bones.

Lara brushes her hand through my hair, pulling gently at the strands when I bite down on her collarbone, quickly replacing my teeth with my lips, sucking on the bite marks.

Testing Lara's limits has become my new favourite pastime. It's fascinating finding out what she does and doesn't like when it comes to intimacy, although so far, there haven't been any dislikes.

My slow descent down Lara's body reaches its climax as I drag my teeth across her left breast until I reach the nipple. I take my time teasing the hardened peak between my teeth with the other between my fingertips. A muffled whimper escapes Lara as she drops her head back, the hand that was pulling my hair now settled on the back of my neck and pulling me against her.

Unfortunately for Lara, that whimper signals it's time for this to end. I don't have to touch her to know she's close to dripping, and anything more from me would have her unravelling right here on the boardroom table. There's nothing I want more than to spread her legs and lick up every drop or fuck her seven ways to Sunday, but not here. Not now. I have to be smart about this if it's to continue, because *fuck*, do I want it to continue.

I pull away. Lara's head snaps up, tilting slightly as she searches my face. I say nothing as I reposition her bra, hoping my silence will encourage her own. I feel rather than see the way she continues to watch me as I reach for the ties of her top, replacing them around her neck. Once they're re-tied into a neat bow, I kiss Lara on the side of the neck. It's harder than I expected not to linger, but I force myself to stand upright and stroll away and out the boardroom door without a backward glance.

When I reach the meeting room adjacent, I dial a client's number and put my phone to my ear. Lara watches me with bewilderment as our eyes connect. I give her my best *'Can I help you?'* smile before I close the door.

It's ironic I'm the one leaving her wanting more, considering I've wanted everything she has to offer from the moment I laid eyes on her.

Despite my to-do list growing at an alarming rate, I've spent most of the afternoon entranced by the woman across the room. She's only looked at me a handful of times—spoken even less— but she has me wrapped around her finger. She just doesn't know it yet, and I'll be damned if I let on.

"I can *feel* you staring at me. Have you achieved anything this afternoon?"

The way she reads me so perfectly would be alarming if it weren't *so attractive*. Her entire face lights up the moment she looks over and sees the goofy grin I'm flashing in her direction, and it's enough to know I'd give almost anything to see that look again.

"I'll have you know I've added to my to-do list," I respond matter of factly.

This elicits a light laugh from Lara as she stands, gathering up her belongings. "I'm over here trying to make your job easier, yet you're sitting there making mine harder—make it make sense." Tutting, she wanders over and stands across from me, the desk a barricade between us.

"I'm only human, Miss Matthews." I stand, placing my palms flat against the desk and leaning my weight onto them. It gives me the perfect vantage point to look her directly in the eye, which will make what I'm about to say *that* much more impactful. "How do you expect me to get things done when the image of you in the boardroom is stuck on a loop in my head, accompanied by the soundtrack of your whimpers?"

I see the moment her eyes turn saucer-like, and her bottom

lip is pulled between her teeth. Those reactions alone are almost too much to bear; I need to get out of here before I act on any more impulses. With that, I pick up my laptop and walk out the door, leaving Lara utterly perplexed for the second time today.

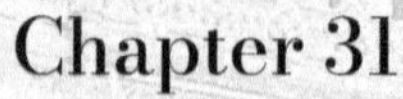

Chapter 31

Lara

Carter's retreating form and the downright sinful smile he gave me are still playing on repeat when I unlock the apartment door. He had some nerve leaving me high and dry like that, and I plan to make it known to him tomorrow.

I stop short in the living room at the clattering coming from the kitchen.

Mia.

The events of this afternoon completely threw me, resulting in no forward planning on the issue of telling Mia. Shit, shit, shit. I silently curse Harper for being out tonight; I could've used the buffer.

If I sneak past the kitchen and straight down the hall, I might buy myself some time to think this through. It might not be a great plan, but it's the only one I have right now.

"Oh hey, I thought I heard the door."

Mia's cheerful voice almost has me leaping out of my skin. My hand shoots up to my chest, attempting to calm my racing heart.

"Sorry Lars, didn't realise you were so jumpy. Are you good?"

I drop my hand to my side, trying to minimise the dramatics, and let out a small laugh. "Oh yeah, I'm fine, just didn't hear you."

Lie.

"You look like you've had a big day. Come, sit." She gestures to the stools at the breakfast bar. "I'll get you some wine. Have you eaten? I'm making Bolognese if you want a bowl."

"That sounds great, thanks Mia."

Following her into the kitchen, I deposit my things onto the counter and take a seat. I reach down to remove the new heels I was breaking in today and stifle a gasp when I sit up and find her standing right in front of me, two full wine glasses in hand.

Mia gives me a stern look, placing one glass in front of me. "Okay, what's going on? That's twice in the space of five minutes that I've somehow scared the shit out of you without trying. I've never known you to be skittish, so out with it."

My gaze drops to the floor, the white marble tiles becoming increasingly more interesting as I gather my thoughts. "I'd like to preface this by saying although I've spent all afternoon thinking about this, I haven't got the slightest clue how to say it delicately."

A half lie. Mia doesn't need to know her brother edging me in our office boardroom is the real reason I haven't come up with a good way to tell her this.

"Lars, whatever it is, just spit it out." She lets out a sigh, as though what I'm about to say couldn't possibly be *that* bad. Dread curls in the pit of my stomach.

"As you know, Carter and I had to go to Norcaster for a client meeting while you and Harps were in Mallorca." I drag my gaze to meet hers, waiting.

Mia quirks a brow. "Yeees?" she says. "Did the meeting not go well or something?"

God, this is painful.

"No, the meeting was fine. It actually went really well."

"But . . ." Mia responds, urging me on.

"But . . ." I close my eyes briefly, huffing out a breath. "Long story short, Carter and I slept together."

Mia's eyes widen comically, her brows shooting up towards her hairline. Before she can respond, I hurry to continue. "Not like that! I mean, we had to sleep in the same bed because of the Winter Festival."

"So you didn't sleep with my brother?"

I hesitate for a moment but instantly regret it when Mia's jaw drops open slightly, brows dropping down into a frown.

"Oh my god, you did." Her voice is quiet, much too quiet.

"No, I mean, yes, but n-not fully." I'm scrambling, tripping over my words.

"You either did or you didn't, Lara." Mia stares at me for a moment. When I don't respond straight away, she stands. "You know what, I'd rather if you didn't clarify what 'not fully' means. I think I've heard enough."

"Mia," I plead as she rounds the buffet and returns to the stove, her back towards me.

She places the wine glass down with force, drops sloshing out as she does so. "I just don't get it, Lara. There are more than four million men in London, yet you go and sleep with my brother?"

The emphasis on 'brother' has the dread I felt earlier turning cyclonic.

"I didn't plan to," I say quietly, but instantly regret it because it's not true.

"But you did!" Her voice booms across the small kitchen. Spinning to face me, she raises her arms helplessly. In the time

I've known Mia, I don't think I've ever heard her raise her voice like this. I brace myself as she goes to speak again, but she must think better of it, closing her mouth and eyes. She stays like this for a moment and my heart stops dead. "I need a moment," she says as she opens her eyes, far quieter than her last words. Mia leaves the kitchen, leaving me alone with my thoughts.

Sighing, I rest my forearms on the buffet, letting my head hang. The beginning of a pounding headache radiates across my forehead. I don't know what sort of reception I expected from Mia, but I really shouldn't be surprised—I can't imagine I'd react much better if it were my brother.

I don't know how long I've been sitting here when footsteps approach. Lead fills my skull as I lift my head, turning to see Mia has returned. Hesitantly, she wanders over and sits upon the stool next to me. We sit in silence for a moment, unsure how to proceed. Considering my actions started this whole thing, I decide to speak up.

"You're right. I could've said no, could've done what I did with anyone else, but I didn't." There's no point denying it. We may not have *completely* slept together, but Harper was right; the distinction doesn't matter to Mia. Honestly, I was naive to think it would. "I know this probably isn't what you want to hear right now—or ever—but I need to be honest with you from the get-go. It's not going to be a one-time thing."

"Oh my god," is her only response. I don't blame her, but my honesty right now is a must.

"I know, I know, there are four million guys to pick from, and yet I've chosen your brother. I'm not trying to make things weird, I just wanted you to know. I don't want to keep things from you."

"But why him? Of *all the men,* why my brother?" The earlier frustration has dissipated, leaving only perplexation in its place.

Why him? It's a valid question, and unfortunately one I'm struggling for an answer to. I need to dig deep and be truthful with not only Mia, but with myself. There are plenty of hot men here, why *can't* I pick another one?

"Honestly, no one has ever treated me the way he does. No one has ever had the effect on me that he does. At the risk of TMI, he cares in a way no man has before—about what I want, what I like, what I dream about but am too scared to ask for. In this way, he's kind of perfect for me. But if you ask me not to see him anymore, I can respect that. I just really hope you don't ask that."

Bracing herself against the edge of the bench, Mia hangs her head and lets out a sigh. She stays this way for a few moments, unspeaking. When she lifts her head to look at me once more, she looks disheartened. Her brows are low, and the corners of her mouth are turned down.

"I would never dictate who you can see, Lars. I'm sorry for biting your head off. As I'm sure you're aware, this isn't at *all* what I expected when I asked you what was wrong." She lets out a somewhat hysterical laugh before continuing. "But I know I can be hot-headed sometimes, and I'm very protective of my siblings, so I might have overreacted slightly."

"Come here," I say with a smile, extending my arms towards her. Mia leans into me and I wrap my arm around her, resting my hand on her shoulder.

"You have nothing to apologise for. I know you're protective of him, and I respect that so much."

"I just don't want anyone to end up hurt."

This has me pausing momentarily. I never thought Mia would be worried about that, given the nature of my relationship with Carter.

"I assure you, that won't happen. It's purely physical."

Regret over my choice of words smacks me on the forehead as soon as I utter them. We cringe simultaneously.

"What I mean to say is I'm well aware of Carter's public image, so this will never get to a stage where anyone would get hurt."

At the mention of the media, Mia's expression changes almost imperceptibly.

"It's more than meets the eye," she mutters, avoiding my gaze. "Regardless, be careful, okay? With your heart and his."

With that, she gives me a half hug, bids me goodnight, and retreats to her bedroom. Mia's bowl of Bolognese sits to the side of the stovetop, untouched. For a moment I consider taking it to her but think better of it. I'm sure she's had enough of me for one night.

Instead, I collect my own bowl and carry it into my bedroom. Once I've sat on my bed, I look up to the ceiling to fight the tears beginning to gather. All things considered, I think that went about as well as it could, but I'm emotionally spent.

Thirty minutes later, with a full stomach and dry eyes, I drift off to sleep, grateful that tomorrow is a new day.

Chapter 32

Carter

To: lmatthews@jlsons.com
From: clawrence@jlsons.com
Subject: Devereux Meeting Notes
Lara,
Please send through.
- C

To: clawrence@jlsons.com
From: lmatthews@jlsons.com
Subject: RE: Devereux Meeting Notes
Carter,
Notes attached.
It seems quite unprofessional for the CEO to sign off as 'C'. Where's your signature?
Kind Regards,

Lara Matthews
Executive Assistant | J. L. & Sons

To: **lmatthews@jlsons.com**
From: **clawrence@jlsons.com**
Subject: **RE: Devereux Meeting Notes**
Better?
Yours in Orgasms,
Carter Lawrence
CEO | J. L. & Sons

To: **clawrence@jlsons.com**
From: **lmatthews@jlsons.com**
Subject: **RE: Devereux Meeting Notes**
I hope you can feel me glaring at you through several solid walls all the way into the boardroom right now. Do you have such little regard for HR and professionalism?
Kind Regards,
Lara Matthews
Executive Assistant | J. L. & Sons

To: **lmatthews@jlsons.com**
From: **clawrence@jlsons.com**
Subject: **RE: Devereux Meeting Notes**
Unbeknownst to you, there are perks to being in

control of a company, and therefore, the company's HR department. They've been advised all emails between my executive assistant and me are not to be monitored unless explicitly requested by me; confidential content and all.

Does mentioning the boardroom have you reminiscing on how wet you were sitting on this table?

Missing Your Taste,
Carter Lawrence
CEO | J. L. & Sons

To: clawrence@jlsons.com
From: lmatthews@jlsons.com
Subject: RE: Devereux Meeting Notes
I have real work to do, Mr Lawrence, and you have a meeting to pay attention to.

Kind Regards,
Lara Matthews
Executive Assistant | J. L. & Sons

To: lmatthews@jlsons.com
From: clawrence@jlsons.com
Subject: RE: Devereux Meeting Notes
I'd much rather pay attention to the noises you make when you're close to the edge. Care to join me in here later?

Patiently Waiting,
Carter Lawrence
CEO | J. L. & Sons

To: lmatthews@jlsons.com

    From: clawrence@jlsons.com

    Subject: RE: Devereux Meeting Notes

I'd much rather pay attention to the noises you make when you're close to the edge. Care to join me in here later?

    Patiently Waiting,

    Carter Lawrence

    CEO | J. L. & Sons

Four Days Later

To: clawrence@jlsons.com

    From: lmatthews@jlsons.com

    Subject: Stylistic Choices

That tie really brings out the gorgeous green flecks in your eyes, but it would do an even better job of binding my wrists together.

    Kind Regards,

    Lara Matthews

    Executive Assistant | J. L. & Sons

To: lmatthews@jlsons.com

    From: clawrence@jlsons.com

    Subject: RE: Stylistic Choices

If you want me to tie you up, Miss Matthews, all you need to do is beg me nicely.

P.s. who has such little regard for HR and professionalism now?

Skilled Scout Graduate,
Carter Lawrence
CEO | J. L. & Sons

To: clawrence@jlsons.com
From: lmatthews@jlsons.com
Subject: RE: Stylistic Choices

Disregard my last email; I had a lapse in judgement.

Kind Regards,
Lara Matthews
Executive Assistant | J. L. & Sons

To: lmatthews@jlsons.com
From: clawrence@jlsons.com
Subject: RE: Stylistic Choices

On the contrary, I think you were finally open about what you want. Keep that up.

Eager to Hear More,
Carter Lawrence
CEO | J. L. & Sons

It's been six days since our last flirty email exchange, but not one of those days passed without thoughts of said emails. Lara's last email showed me the slightest glimpse into who she is behind the walls she's so meticulously constructed. But it isn't enough; I need to deconstruct the walls one brick at a time until I know her better than I know myself.

The more time I spend with Lara, the more I find myself becoming completely enchanted by her. Her presence in my life is unlike that of any woman before her. She's become the person I look forward to seeing each day. Regardless of whether she's giving me a small smile from across the room, moaning my name as she comes apart beneath me, or refusing to give me a lick of attention because she's working, I am in constant *awe* of her.

This is why, on a nondescript Tuesday evening, I'm sitting on my couch with my phone in hand, typing out a text message to my EA—something I have no business doing right now.

ME

So I've come up with an idea.

LARA

I never would've pegged you as an ideas guy.

Let's hear it then.

ME

Have you ever heard of the game Two Truths and a Lie?

LARA

Only every time I've opened a dating app. Are you fifteen? Why are you bringing this game up?

The muscle in my jaw ticks as I read over the words *dating app*. Truthfully, it's got nothing to do with me. Yet I can't help but feel an irrational annoyance at the thought of Lara having to endure the nightmare that is dating apps, and subsequently, the nightmarish men that would come with them.

ME

I think we should try it.

LARA

You have my number for work purposes Carter. Correct me if I'm wrong, but this doesn't seem very work related.

ME

You're wrong; hear me out.

We work in far too close proximity to not know more about each other.

LARA

I'm waiting to hear how this relates to a little game.

Man, she doesn't like to make things easy for me.

ME

Every Tuesday, we send each. other two truths and a lie. That way, we learn at least two new things about each other.

Those tortuous three dots appear, disappearing and reappearing several times. As the minutes go by, I fear I might've gone too far. I can't help it; I have this deep desire to know everything; her fears, her wants, the things keeping her up at night, everything.

Only when I place my phone down does a small vibration comes through.

LARA

I'm not convinced this is entirely innocent and it's an interesting way to go about it, but sure.

I didn't really believe she'd agree as suddenly as she has, so

I haven't prepared anything. Racking my brain, I start with three innocent things.

ME

I'm the middle child of three children, I broke my leg falling off a horse when I was 8, and my parents are grossly in love.

LARA

Second one is the lie.

ME

What makes you so sure?

LARA

You're far too sure of yourself to have done something like that, even as a kid.

A grin breaks out across my lips. I love it when she's fiery.

ME

Correct. But I did break my wrist as a child; I fell over my brother when we were racing. I've even got a neat little scar to prove it.
You're up.

LARA

I have an older brother, I've never broken a bone, and my parents are divorced.

She's purposely gone with three similar to my own, but I won't comment on that. I don't want to spook her when she's finally opening up, even if I did coerce her through a game.

ME

Second is the lie; surely everyone has broken a bone at some point.

LARA

Wrong. I have a younger brother.

ME

How old were you when your parents separated?

LARA

That's not part of the game.

I guess that marks the end of my coercion. One way or another, she'll open up to me in due course.

ME

See you tomorrow.

One Week Later

To: lmatthews@jlsons.com
From: clawrence@jlsons.com
Subject: Edwards Catch Up
L,
Please schedule time on Friday for a catch up with Edwards. I'll be in the office from 8:00am.
P.S. I hope you've got your truths and a lie ready.
Carter Lawrence
CEO | J. L. & Sons

To: clawrence@jlsons.com
From: lmatthews@jlsons.com
Subject: RE: Edwards Catch Up
Afternoon Carter,

Confirming Edwards for 9:00am Friday in the boardroom.

Shouldn't you be paying attention right now? This client meeting isn't due to finish for another two hours.

Kind Regards,
Lara Matthews
Executive Assistant | J. L. & Sons

To: lmatthews@jlsons.com
From: clawrence@jlsons.com
Subject: RE: Edwards Catch Up

Miss Matthews,

You should know better than anyone how skilled I am in the art of multitasking. Not only am I able to think about my part of our little game and remain an active contributor in this meeting, I'm also simultaneously able to reminisce about the way you looked spread beneath me in Norcaster.

Regards,
Carter Lawrence
Multitasking Extraordinaire | J. L. & Sons

To: clawrence@jlsons.com
From: lmatthews@jlsons.com
Subject: RE: Edwards Catch Up

Carter,

You should know better than to write things like that in company emails.

Kind Regards,
Lara Matthews
Executive Assistant | J. L. & Sons

To: lmatthews@jlsons.com
From: clawrence@jlsons.com
Subject: RE: Edwards Catch Up

Miss Matthews,

I think we're both well aware I could write far more scandalous things. Perhaps I should detail the way you went down on me with skills most men could only dream of experiencing. I think Anna would be impressed to read such things.

Regards,
Carter Lawrence
Spinner of Scandal | J. L. & Sons

To: clawrence@jlsons.com
From: lmatthews@jlsons.com
Subject: RE: Edwards Catch Up

If we're mentioning that, it's only fair we also bring up your own skills. The adequateness is really something to behold.

Kind Regards,
Lara Matthews
Executive Assistant | J. L. & Sons

To: lmatthews@jlsons.com
From: clawrence@jlsons.com
Subject: RE: Edwards Catch Up
Miss Matthews,

I'm looking forward to being back in the office if only to bend you over your desk and fuck you until you forget how to pronounce the word adequate.

Regards,
Carter Lawrence
Adequacy Eradicator | J. L. & Sons

To: lmatthews@jlsons.com
From: clawrence@jlsons.com
Subject: RE: Edwards Catch Up
Miss Matthews,

I'm now impatiently awaiting your 2T&AL.

Regards,
Carter Lawrence
Games Master | J. L. & Sons

To: clawrence@jlsons.com
From: lmatthews@jlsons.com
Subject: RE: Edwards Catch Up
Mister Lawrence,

Might I remind you I have a job to do here, which doesn't include babysitting a bored child (you).

1. I continue to find you utterly insufferable.
2. You've grown on me.

3. You're tiresome.

Kind Regards,

Lara Matthews

Executive Assistant | J. L. & Sons

To: lmatthews@jlsons.com

From: clawrence@jlsons.com

Subject: RE: Edwards Catch Up

Although I'm flattered to be the centre of your attention, you're missing the point of the game. Come on now, play nice. I'll start so you can have some inspiration.

1. I had my first kiss at 19.

2. You like me more than you let on.

3. The best job I've ever had is being an Uncle.

Regards,

Carter Lawrence

Chief Entertainment Officer | J. L. & Sons

To: clawrence@jlsons.com

From: lmatthews@jlsons.com

Subject: RE: Edwards Catch Up

Don't flatter yourself; the second is the lie.

Kind Regards,

Lara Matthews

Executive Assistant | J. L. & Sons

To: lmatthews@jlsons.com
From: clawrence@jlsons.com
Subject: RE: Edwards Catch Up
Keep telling yourself that Matthews, and I'll keep proving you wrong.
Regards,
Carter Lawrence
Knower of All Things | J. L. & Sons

Chapter 33

Carter

My fork is loaded with my last mouthful when my mother speaks. "Should we be concerned that none of you ever bring anyone to family dinners?"

Here we go.

It has been a while since this topic of conversation has come up at one of our dinners, so I really shouldn't be surprised it's being brought up now. What *does* surprise me is Mum waited until the end of the meal; Diana Lawrence doesn't beat around the bush.

In my siblings and my defence, the last person to bring someone to a family dinner was Teddy, but that was many years ago now and admittedly didn't end well.

I make a point of saying nothing, intent on enjoying the remaining mouthful of my dinner, when I feel my sister's eyes on me. Looking up, I see her giving me a pointed look from across the table. "Don't," is all I say in response, my voice low in the hopes only Emmy hears. Unfortunately for me, our mother has ears like a bat. She perks up, clasping her hands together with a big grin on her face.

"What's that, my dear?"

"Nothing Mother, I was just speaking to Emmy."

"Don't be shy, Cart," Emmy interjects, far too pleased with herself.

Our mother's head swivels between us like she's watching Wimbledon. I reach a hand across the table, grasping one of hers and giving it a squeeze. "I assure you, if there was someone in the picture, you'd know about it." I ignore the small twitch in my cheek as I speak, but my mother is far too observant.

"Okay sweetheart, if you say so." She gives me a wink and pats the hand encasing hers. Her words might say she believes me, but those two gestures say the complete opposite. One look in my father's direction says he's thinking exactly what she is: they don't buy it one bit.

But he isn't looking at me; he's grinning like an idiot at my mother. I turn back to her, and she puts her chin to her shoulder, stifling something like a giggle. *What am I missing here?*

"Sorry Di, I promise I tried to stay out of it, sweetheart."

"Oh I doubt that very much, Freddie. You've always been a meddler."

My father winks in response, and a lightbulb comes to life in my head. I know exactly what he's referring to: Lara. What the hell has he told Mum about her? Does he have something else up his sleeve? What does he know?

Fuck. Me.

I refuse to have this conversation.

Clearing my throat, I let go of Mum's hand and raise my wine glass. "I'm going to get a refill. Would anyone else care for one?" My family's responses ring out almost simultaneously.

"Yes please, darling."

"Thanks, Son."

"Absolutely."

"I'll help you, Cart."

Emmy is out of her chair and on her way to the kitchen before I can decline her offer. She corners me the moment I step foot into the large space.

"It must be so inconvenient having that little cheek twitch when you're not telling the truth." I reach for the door to the wine fridge, but Emmy blocks my path with her body. I place my hands on her shoulders and gently push her to the side.

"Why would you get Mum's hopes up when you know damn well there's nobody in the picture?"

"That's not what I've heard." Her tone is off. The way she throws the words at me like a weapon is so unlike her. Emmy tilts her head to one side and pops that shoulder up, the picture of smugness.

I'm momentarily stumped—did *Lara* say something?—before the obvious answer smacks me in the face. Undoubtedly, it came from Teddy. *Wanker.* Normally I can talk to my brother about things and know without a doubt it'll stay between us, but apparently that sentiment doesn't extend to conversations about women. Or more specifically, *Lara.*

"Oh, he's going to get it."

"Sounds an awful lot like he's right."

"Mind your business, Emilia." I leave my sister in the kitchen with my parents' wine glasses. With Teddy's glass in one hand and mine in the other, I return to the dining room to find his chair empty. My parents both give me a warm smile. "Emmy has your glasses, she'll be out in a moment. I'll take this to Teddy."

The library on the ground floor of my parent's home is where I spent a lot of my time during my childhood. Often I was reading, but Teddy and I also frequented the grand room because it served as an excellent space to play. Teddy also found it to be a haven when things felt like *a lot*, which is how I knew I'd find him here.

"I'd really like to kick your arse right now for whatever you told Emmy, but I don't like my odds."

My brother turns in place where he's sitting in one of the deep blue occasional chairs in the centre of the room. As he does so, I'm reminded of the sheer size of him. We might be the same height, but I've got nothing on his width. Shoutout to the British Army for being the reason I could never take Teddy on.

He gives me a once over, holding in a chuckle. "You'd be on your arse before you even got close enough to kick mine."

I make my way over to my brother, repressing my own laugh as I smooth a hand along my jaw and take a seat in the chair opposite him, passing him his glass in the process. "What have you been telling her?"

"Only the truth." Teddy leans forward, placing his elbows on his knees. He rests his chin on his thumbs, steepling his pointer fingers against his mouth. It's no wonder the rookies he trains are often terrified of him; I've known him my whole life, and he still intimidates me when he assesses me like this. Thick brown brows are drawn down over his narrowed eyes, and I resist the urge to squirm under the scrutiny.

"Sounds like it's your warped version of the truth. Why does she think I'd have someone to bring home to meet our parents?" Hopefully the casual persona I'm trying to portray looks less forced than it feels.

"Probably because she lives with the woman in question."

"It's casual with Lara, you know that. I'm sure Emmy does too, since, as you pointed out, they live together."

"But you don't want it to be casual."

"When have I ever said that?"

"You don't need to say it. I know you, Carter. I know the way you normally look at women, and it's got *nothing* on the way you look when you're merely *talking* about Lara. I can only imagine the puppy dog look you have when you look at her."

"You're a dick."

"Even so, I'm right, and we both know it."

There's no way I'm admitting it right now because I'll never hear the end of it, but he *is* right. The way I feel about Lara has snuck up on me like a lion to its prey, slow and unnoticed at first, but there's no going back once it strikes. I'm at her mercy. But I don't think I was ever *not* at her mercy.

We sit in comfortable silence for a while. My eyes skim over all the titles on the shelves, reminiscing on days long ago snuggled up on the adjacent lounge with Granny. It's because of her influence that I have a deep love for the classics. For years I sat in her arms, normally wrapped in a blanket or curled up by the warmth of the fireplace, as she read me the likes of Austen, Hardy, Orwell, and Bronte.

Their stories stuck with me, and over the years, they helped me through heartbreak and loss, including the tragic loss of Granny.

Teddy remains quiet but begins to tap his index finger against his lip and absentmindedly shakes his right leg up and down in quick succession. I wonder what's going through his mind. Just as I'm about to ask him, he gets in first.

"Ask her on a date."

"Excuse me?"

Teddy sits back, crossing one ankle over the other. His right arm rests on the chair's arm, his left closing into a fist and bearing the weight of his chin. "Ask. Her. On. A. Date." Each word is irritatingly punctuated by a tap on the arm of the chair, the thick cords of muscle flexing in his forearm as he does so.

"I can't do that, she's my assistant."

"Piss poor excuse; you're sleeping with her. Try again."

"She'll be returning to Australia in a few months."

"So your options are a) do nothing different, continue sleeping with her for a few months and wave her goodbye with nothing but regret when she leaves, or b) grow the fuck up, ask her out and enjoy whatever comes until you have to wave her goodbye, but with no regrets."

The temptation to pick option B is strong. But what about the image I'm portraying for the sake of my family? If we were to go on a date, the media would label her yet another woman through the revolving door of that is the Oxford Street Playboy, and I won't allow that. Lara deserves better. The least favourable option seems the easiest way to go.

"Option A, thanks."

"It was a statement not a question, arsehole. You really don't think she's worth it?"

"Of course she's worth it, but I can't."

"You can and you will." Teddy stands, taking two short strides to close the distance between us, his crisp white trainers now toe-to-toe with my Oxfords. He holds a hand out at me expectantly. "Give me your phone."

"Absolutely not."

"Give me your phone, Carter."

Teddy reaches into the back pocket of his jeans and pulls his own phone out. A picture of Winnie mid-giggle comes into view as Teddy waggles his phone in front of me. "If you're going to be a child about this, I'll text her myself."

"Fuck! Fine." I rip my phone from my trousers pocket, keeping a strong hold on it in case my brother tries to manhandle it from my grasp.

The arsehole sits down with an unnecessarily exaggerated casualty, making me want to slap the smirk right off his face. Phone returning to his pocket, Teddy crosses one leg over the other, wrapping clasped hands around his knee, and waits. If I weren't so pissed at him, I'd laugh at the dramatic display. Perhaps Emmy is more like him than I realised.

I glance over at my brother, quickly averting my gaze back to my phone when he sees. "So, uh, if you were to text her, what would you say?"

"Well," Teddy begins, rubbing his palms together, "I'd offer to cook her dinner."

"But you hate cooking?"

"You don't," he says simply.

The urge to slap him is replaced by the urge to pull him into a hug. He gets on my last nerve sometimes, but I'd be lost without him.

Although I refuse to admit it, at least for now, the way I feel about Lara isn't something I've felt before. It's unchartered territory, and I'm fucking terrified I'll screw it up.

Chapter 34

Lara / Carter

Lara

A vibration on the coffee tables rudely steals my attention away from the television, where John Krasinski and Colin Egglesfield are playing their little hearts out in a game of beach badminton. I fumble with my phone as the text notification lights up the screen.

A sharp laugh erupts from my throat. Harper is closing the front door on the retreating pizza delivery driver, the unexpected sound causing her to startle; the pizza box in her hand almost falling to the floor.

"What was that demonic sound for?" Harper takes a seat on the lounge next to me, placing our dinner on the table in front of us.

"You'll never guess who's asked to cook me dinner tomorrow night."

"Oh, I think I have an idea." Harper holds out her hand. "Let's see."

I place my phone into her outstretched palm. Harper scans over the message, not an ounce of surprise registering on her face as she hands it to me.

"I'm offended you thought I wouldn't guess this, Lars, as if it could possibly be anyone else. What's so funny about this though?"

"What's funny? What's funny is his joke because he certainly can't be serious."

"Because he's your boss?"

"No. Well yes, but that wasn't what I meant. We don't do dinner, Harps. We might do other things, but we don't do dinner."

Harper raises her eyebrows at me before turning away and bursting into laughter. "It's a good thing Mia isn't here right now; can't imagine she'd want the details on that one."

"Speaking of, aren't they both at their family dinner right now? That doesn't seem the best time to be asking to have dinner with me."

Harper pins me with a stern look. "You think he'd be discussing his text messages with his sister? I don't think so. And stop trying to change the subject. We're talking about your dinner with him."

"Harper, we don't do dinner."

"There's a first time for everything."

"There doesn't need to be a first time for this though." Even to my own ears, I sound ridiculous. I'm trying to argue my way out of having dinner with a guy who I quite happily let feel me up on a semi-regular basis.

"You can't sit there and honestly tell me you don't want to have dinner with him, can you?"

I'm shocked the word 'yes' doesn't immediately fall from my lips and even more shocked that the mere thought of outright denying it is almost painful. Noticing my hesitation, Harper beams.

"Ha, I knew it!"

"I think like you're forgetting two key facts here, Harps; one being this little game we're playing has an expiration date of just a few months, and the second being I don't want anything serious. Believe it or not, I kind of like things the way they are."

"Oh, darling Lara, you can be so naive sometimes." Harper takes a seat on the couch again, crossing her legs beneath her and turning to face me. "Every time you come home after seeing Carter, you're in a wonderful mood, regardless of whether it's after work, after sex, or both. Perhaps it's the post-orgasm bliss lingering, *or* perhaps there's something there to unpack." She taps me on the knee, raising a brow in question.

I swat playfully at her hand. "I think you're being a bit ridiculous, Harps. Did you ever think maybe I'm in a wonderful mood all the time since being in London?" At the same time the words leave my mouth, a part of me wonders if maybe Harper isn't being entirely ridiculous. But I shut that down right away because, *of course* she is. This is a bit of temporary fun and stress relief with someone who's become my friend. Nothing more.

"There's no doubt you seem much happier here than you did when you were in Aus, but there's something extra after you've seen him. And while we're talking about it, let's not forget you don't even have a return date, which makes your stay kind of indefinite right now."

I can't help but laugh. "You're looking too far into this; it's really not that deep." I pointedly ignore the part about not having a return date. I have no argument there, and Harper knows it.

"So you're going to turn him down then?"

Without thinking, I blurt out, "No." Her lips pull into a smug smile, and I want to slap myself. "W-what I meant is I'm not going to straight up turn him down," I say, failing miserably at backtracking. "I'll, uh, let him down easy."

"Is that what you want to do?"

"Well, it would be rude to just shut him down."

Harper pins me with a look that says *get a grip*. "That's not what I was referring to, and you know it. Do you really want to say no?"

I sit silently for a moment, playing it out in my head. What happens if I say no? Carter either continues to see me in a casual sense or moves on to other prospects, there are no hard feelings, and everything is as it was before we started sleeping together. Except now, the thought of Carter moving on to other women, as I've seen him do before me, puts my stomach in knots.

What happens if I say yes? I get a lovely home-cooked meal, get to spend time with Carter in his comfort place, and I'll probably have some of the best sex of my life—it's been like that with Carter since the night in Norcaster. Don't get me wrong, this all sounds wonderful because it *is* wonderful, but it's not tomorrow I'm worried about. If I say yes, it's what comes after that concerns me. Will he want more than one dinner? Will he make love to me and lie with me until the early hours? Will he do all the things I've always wanted from a man and make me fall in love with him, only to turn around and break my heart further down the track?

It's what comes after that has me overthinking his simple text, because it's really not simple at all.

"What are you thinking? I can see the wheels turning behind your eyes." Harper taps a finger to my forehead.

"If I say yes to dinner, he's going to think I'm saying yes to more."

"I think you're overestimating him; he's a male, after all. They don't tend to think too deeply into things."

"Good point; gave him too much credit for a second there."

We both giggle.

"Say yes, Lara. Let the pretty man cook you dinner and then have you for dessert; lord knows you deserve it."

I sputter out a cough as I almost choke on my mouthful of pizza.

"Has anyone ever told you you have a way with words?"

"Every day." Harper hands my phone back. The cursor flashes on the screen, taunting me. "Now, say yes before you overthink yourself out of it."

For the second time in a matter of weeks, I find myself muttering two words: fuck it.

ME

Does 7:00pm work?

Carter

Well I'll be fucking damned.

"I owe you a beer, brother. We're on."

After Teddy reads Lara's response, he claps me on the back, a smile breaking through his unusually overgrown facial hair. "I can't believe you worded it like that. Why the fuck is it so formal? It's like you forgot how to write a text message."

"Respectfully, shut the fuck up."

"You owe me more than a beer, bud. I'll accept your thanks in the form of Winnie duties next weekend."

"Ooh, has Daddy secured a hot date or something?"

My brother groans. "Stop. You know it's so fucking weird when you call me that. Also, mind your business."

"I hope you realise how hypocritical you're being; you've genuinely taken over my business these past ten minutes."

Teddy roughs a hand through my hair, the way he did when we were younger, removing it before I can smack him away. "I'm the big brother, I'm allowed to. Now hurry up and respond before she changes her mind."

I want to tell him he's being a little dramatic, but this *is* Lara we're talking about. I'm pleasantly surprised she's even agreed in the first place; there's every chance she'll revoke her agreement. I tap out an immediate, bold response.

ME

It's a date

The three little dots appear quickly, and I can't tear my eyes away from the screen, instead watching intently for her response.

LARA

I assure you it most certainly is not.

A cheesy as fuck grin pulls at my lips as I stare at Lara's message. Oh, it's *so* on.

Teddy knocks a knee against mine. "Right, little brother, what's your plan?"

"My plan?"

"Oh you, you've got to be prepared, Carter. You *cannot* go into this without a plan. How else do you expect to convince Lara this is a good idea?"

"Are you trying to say my incredibly good looks and irresistible charm aren't enough?"

"Don't forget your modesty." The whites of my brother's eyes are on full display as he rolls them. "You're spending too much time around Dex, his arrogance is rubbing off on you."

"Come on, don't pretend you don't love that arsehole."

"Oh I do, sometimes more than I love you, little brother."

Now it's my turn to roll my eyes. "Could we get back on track with this plan of yours, please?"

"No, no, not my plan—yours. I'm merely here to provide brotherly guidance."

"Such as?"

"Just making sure you don't make a complete arse of yourself, really."

I glare at my brother, but we both know there's no malice behind it. I wouldn't say I have a track record of making an arse of myself, but without Teddy's advice over the years, I very well could have.

More so than persuading her, I need to get her to come to her senses and realise there's more between us than we make out. I've known it since that first moment; I need to find out if she has too.

"Right then," Teddy says, breaking the silence and my train of thought. "If you've got nothing, let's start with hopefully an easy one." Teddy pulls a pen and paper from lord knows where and begins writing.

Rule 1. Keep it in your pants at the dinner table.

"I'm sorry, have you ever known me *not* to do that?"

"Mate, I don't know, or *want* to know, what sort of shit you get up to in your own home, but I do know the way you talk about Lara. And let me tell you, it makes that rule necessary."

We stare at each other for a moment before cracking smiles. Teddy starts to chuckle, and I can't help but join in.

"What on earth are the two of you giggling like girls about?" Our sister's voice has our heads snapping up to find her casually leaning against the doorframe, arms crossed with a smirk playing on her lips.

"None of your business."

Emilia looks at me with raised brows as Teddy's glare bores into the side of my face, but I refuse to look at him, gaze remaining locked on our sister instead. Her eyes slide to Teddy, then narrow as if waiting for him to spill.

"Lara."

If this surprises Emmy, she doesn't let it show as she lets out a sigh.

I turn my head to my brother, who's looking far too smug for his own good. "You're an arse."

"I merely answered our dear sister's question." Reclining in his chair, Teddy leisurely crosses his arms over his chest.

Our sister drops her arms and pushes off the doorframe with her shoulder.

"Teddy, would you give Carter and me a minute please?"

"For you, Emilia, certainly." Teddy stands, sending a wink my way, before striding out of the library.

"Wanker," I mutter under my breath. He can't hear me, of course, but it brings me a small satisfaction knowing I had the last word.

Emmy strolls into the library, taking the seat Teddy vacated. Her eyes narrow in on me, scrutinising.

"Please spare me whatever details you provided Teddy,

given she's my best friend, and it's already weird enough, but I do want to know what you're playing at here."

"Playing at?" I parrot back, wondering what's made her think any of this is a game.

Emmy nods, remaining silent.

"I'm not *playing* at anything. This isn't a game, Emmy. None of this is a game to me."

"Okay, okay, so you're not messing her around. What are your intentions then?"

I can't help but let out a chuckle. I wonder if she even hears herself. "Well, sir, my intentions with your daughter are completely and utterly honourable. And innocent, *very* innocent."

With lightning speed, my baby sister slaps my bicep. *Hard.*

"Ow!"

Emmy furrows her brows in my direction, arms crossing over her chest once more as she leans back in her chair. "Serves you right. Are you ever *not* a sarcastic shit?"

That question sounds familiar. Where have I heard it before? Of course, I've heard it from my own mouth, only it's been directed at Lara. I'm amazed it's taken me so long to realise we have that in common. *Perhaps we're more alike than I originally thought.*

Uncertain whether it's a rhetorical question or not and unwilling to give Emmy another reason to slap me, I just shrug and flash her a cheesy grin only she can pull from me. Whenever I'd piss her off when we were younger, I'd grin at her so intensely that my nose would scrunch, and my dimple would pop. For whatever reason, she thought it was the funniest thing in the world. Any ill feelings towards me would vanish, replaced instead by her contagious giggle—the same one she's eliciting now. My cheeks are aching from laughing with her, but I know my sister well enough to know she's still waiting for a real answer.

"Honestly, I just want to spend as much time with her as I possibly can before her visa expires and she's half a world away."

My sister has the audacity to laugh again.

"Here I am spilling my heart, and you're laughing?"

"I'm not laughing at you, Cart." I pin her with a look. "I mean I am, but not in the way you think. Who told you she has a visa?"

"Well, I-I assumed."

"You assumed wrong."

I may be many things, but wrong isn't typically one of them.

I'm restless, unable to decide if I'm more comfortable learning against the chairback or bracing my elbows on my knees with my chin in my hands.

"Before I begin jumping to my own conclusions, explain please."

"Lara has British citizenship by descent; her father is originally from Leeds but moved to Australia as a child. Initially she'd planned to stay for nine months, but she currently doesn't have a return date picked or flight booked."

"So you're telling me she has no real set date to leave?"

"Yes."

The feeling surging through me is one of pure elation. Lara has no set return date, by law or by her own volition. It's as though a small ember in my stomach has been set ablaze with this information. I'm not even sure I know what to say, except this change's things—for me, for her, for *us*. And boy, do I plan for there to be an us.

"You do realise this changes everything, right?"

"I feared it may." Emmy's words are in stark contrast to the bright smile she gives me. "Just do me a favour; don't fuck this up, yeah?"

I pull my sister into my arms, squeezing her tight. "I wouldn't dream of it."

Now more than ever, I'm determined to prove to Lara that this, what we have, isn't *just* casual sex—it never was. It was always going to be more, and it's about time she let go of any preconceived notions saying otherwise.

Chapter 35

Lara

"This place is incredible," I say, more to myself than Carter, as he exits the lift and strolls into the penthouse suite. *His* penthouse suite, apparently. I assumed Carter had money, but I never stopped to wonder where he might live. I suppose a penthouse in Kensington makes sense; I imagine a place like this would cost an eye-watering amount.

My attraction to the rear of a man never ceases to amaze me, but it's hard not to be when he looks like Carter. Tonight, he's paired a deep navy shirt with a pair of cream trousers that fit him like a glove. The muscles of his broad back ripple beneath his shirt.

Would it kill the man to wear a shirt that didn't always risk bursting at the seams? Or a pair of trousers that didn't make his backside look quite so slapable?

Realising I've spent too long checking out Carter's arse, I take a deep breath. As I step inside, I'm met with a floor-to-ceiling mirror on my left, and I take a moment to check myself over before continuing into the apartment.

The outfit I chose to wear is one of my sexier numbers. The entire trip over here was spent contemplating whether I'd made a huge mistake selecting it. This isn't a date, and it was never going to be, but my clothing choices might say otherwise.

The girls told you to wear something you feel good in, and you listened. It's not a date, and it's not a big deal.

The deep V-neckline burgundy blouse has me feeling a little out of my comfort zone, but my arse looks incredible in the black trousers I paired with it. The firm fit accentuates my backside better than anything else I own. Truth be told, that's the main reason I purchased them in the first place. Who says trousers can't be hot? Add in my favourite pair of black heels, and we've got the ultimate sexy and sophisticated ensemble.

I gather my hair in both hands and throw it over my shoulder, only the blonde strands framing my face remaining. With one final check of my favourite nude lipstick, I take a deep breath and turn to follow Carter. The apartment has a touch of his signature sandalwood and vanilla scent, but there's something else behind it—a rich, sweet smell permeates the air, similar to the aroma of burnt sugar and butter.

The expansive entryway is framed by sleek white oak wood panelling and opens up into a stunning open-plan kitchen and living room. A long granite benchtop flanked by plush emerald stools stands to my left, while a sunken charcoal lounge and decadent fireplace are on my right.

Unbidden images flood my thoughts as I gape at the wealth and beauty nestled within this room. Images of me, snuggled up in front of the fireplace with a good book, a glass of wine, and the man in front—no.

Me, here, with Carter, for something other than dinner and a fuck? Not going to happen.

As I make my way through the space, shaking off the lingering image of Carter and I snuggling, my eyes catch on what's possibly the most remarkable panoramic view I've ever seen; the London Eye lights up the sky, and Big Ben stands tall in the background.

"It's a little oversized for one person, but I like it all the same." Carter comes to stand beside me, a small smile on his lips as he turns towards me. The signature scent of his cologne is so inviting, the faint undertone of salty sweat giving him an 'I worked out today, but I also understand personal hygiene' vibe. "Let me show you around."

Clearly not having registered Carter's offer, I don't move, too entranced by the skyline. "And this view, my goodness, it really is something."

"It is indeed."

I turn toward Carter, the smile on my face faltering slightly as I do so. Heat blooms in my cheeks as I realise he's looking right at me rather than out the window behind me. He takes a step closer, and another, and I'm grateful the skyline is our main source of light as my cheeks burn.

Feeling a little self-conscious from his stare, I attempt to take a step back and return my gaze to the view. As my heeled foot moves, Carter grips my jaw with his hand to keep me from moving. "Where do you think you're going, love?"

"Nowhere, just wanted to admire the view a little more." Excitement and anticipation flood my veins, causing my lower belly to tingle from his intense gaze.

Carter smirks. "I didn't anticipate having to fight with the view for your attention." He leans in closer, voice lowered, lips mere centimetres from mine. "It appears I need to up my game."

Chapter 36

Carter

I feel rather than see the corners of Lara's lips pull upward as I close the distance and place a tender kiss on them. She's sweeter than sugar, a taste I've been craving for days. I snake my arm further around her body as my hand finds its new favourite resting place: Lara's arse.

She gently runs her tongue along the seam of my lips, a silent plea for entry. I oblige without hesitation and our tongues collide, deepening the kiss. I grab Lara by the waist in an attempt to direct her towards the bedroom, but she pulls back.

"Everything okay?" I ask, searching for signs of regret. What I find instead is an internal wall, just behind her eyes, that wasn't there before. I'm not sure what happened between kisses, but I'm not going to push her.

Lara smiles sheepishly. "It will be in a moment," she responds, her hands grabbing hold of my belt buckle. I place my hands over hers, halting her movements.

"And what do you think you're doing, Miss?"

"Please Carter, let me do this for you." Lara pulls her hands out from under mine and slowly drags them further south until they cover the bulge in my pants. "Do you not want me on my knees?"

Judging by our previous encounters, I'd assumed Lara was the submissive type. This new side of her though, the one who's mere seconds away from begging me to let her fall to her knees, is fucking intoxicating.

There's no denying I'm dominant, but *fuck*, there's something about a woman taking control. Every vein reroutes the blood within to my cock, and it's enough to stop my thoughts from lingering on the wall she's put up.

I let out a breath, and the resulting sound is something between a groan and a moan. Taking that as a 'please proceed', Lara unbuckles my belt, grips the waistband of my trousers and underwear, and pulls them down in one swift motion.

My cock aches as it stands to attention, no longer fighting its confines, and I tip my head to the ceiling in a silent prayer.

When I look down again, Lara is staring right at me, a gleam in her eyes. Ever so slowly, she lowers herself to the floor, and fuck if seeing her on her knees isn't the hottest sight I've seen. Without breaking eye contact, she leans forward and swipes her tongue along my shaft.

Fuck, this woman will be the death of me. When Lara giggles softly, I realise I've said this out loud. *Well done Carter, you fool.*

"Keep that up, and I'll make sure you can't walk straight tomorrow." My voice has a warning tone to it. Lara holds my gaze in a silent challenge. I'm not one to shy away, so I refuse to break first. We're still staring at each other when she takes me in her mouth, my tip touching the back of her throat. Lara makes a faint gagging noise, but it's enough for me to break eye contact, my eyes rolling into the back of my head in ecstasy.

Lara uses her left hand and her mouth in expert synchronicity along the length of me, her right hand grabbing my balls. Shit, it feels good, but I need to stop her soon, or this will be over far quicker than either of us would like.

"Is that a promise?" The words vibrate against my cock as Lara drags her tongue from base to tip. The deep exhalation I release only encourages the little minx, flicking her tongue back and forth over the tip of my cock before pulling me into the depths of her mouth.

When a familiar heat creeps up my spine, I gently grab Lara by her hair and pull her back, my dick popping out of her mouth as a satisfied grin spreads across her face.

"Is someone a little too excited, Mr Lawrence?"

Hearing Lara call me Mr Lawrence at work is already almost too much to bear, but in my house, whilst on her knees? It's my fucking undoing.

"No Lara, I simply refuse to come anywhere except inside that pretty pussy of yours."

The satisfaction from a moment ago fades from Lara's face, eyes darkening.

Yes love, two can play at this game.

"Come," I command as I hold out a hand to help Lara off the floor.

Chapter 37

Carter

The half an hour we've spent at the dining table would be in the top two most excruciating experiences of my life, second only to the broken wrist all those years ago.

With each mouthful of her dinner, Lara's been eliciting a sound that reverberates down to my bones. They started out innocently enough, to the point where she didn't even realise what she was doing. It wasn't until I had a knee-jerk reaction the third or fourth time that Lara noticed the effect her little noises were having. My knee colliding with the underside of the table caught her attention, a wicked grin drawing across her glossed lips at the look I'm sure was etched into my face.

From that moment on, it only got worse. I've never regretted a meal so deeply. I'll never again be able to eat chicken cacciatore in peace; it will always be accompanied by Lara's moans. And it's for this exact reason I decide it's time the tables are turned as I catch Lara assessing the lilies in the centre of the table for the third time in as many minutes.

Clearing my throat, I point my knife toward the vase that

belonged to my great-grandparents. "Do you have a problem with the lilies?"

Lara's head snaps in my direction, utensils motionless above her plate. She begins tapping her pointer finger against her fork, her eyes searching mine for context. Unfortunately for Lara, I'm not giving it away that easily.

"No, I do not have a *problem* with them, I just think they're a bit much for 'not a date'."

"I'm flattered you think I'd go to the effort, but I'm afraid they were a gift from my niece. I'm well aware this isn't a date; you've made that quite clear."

The way Lara's mouth drops open for the briefest of moments before she slams it shut shows I've won this round. If she's so hellbent on this not being a date, who am I to disagree?

"How's your meal?" I ask, popping the last spoonful of cacciatore into my mouth.

"It's quite lovely, but I'm sure you know that. And yours?"

I nod, finishing off the mouthful. "This used to be my favourite meal."

Lara looks at me quizzically. "You cooked me your old favourite meal rather than your current one?" When I nod, she asks, "Why?"

"Because my new favourite meal is sitting across the table from me."

From where I sit, I have the perfect vantage point for witnessing the exact moment Lara's pupils dilate, my admission hanging in the air between us. She visibly gulps down her mouthful, avoiding my gaze as a pink hue spreads across the bridge of her nose and onto her cheeks.

I lean forward and rest my elbows on either side of my empty plate, steepling my forefingers beneath my chin. There's something about the way Lara reacts that has me wanting to test the boundaries. "I can't wait to see what it's wrapped in beneath those trousers. Red lace? Perhaps black? Enlighten me."

Initially, I'm met with silence. Lara's focus is entirely on the remnants of her dinner. I wait, my patience thinning by the second as she finishes. Her utensils are placed ever so gently upon her plate before she meets my gaze—flames crackling in the iciest of blues.

"Why don't you come over here and find out for yourself? Remind me how good you look on your knees."

Fuck. Me.

Apparently my dick heard her as well, if the way it immediately hardens is anything to go by. This is *not* going to plan. Teddy would be pissed if he were to find out I completely threw out the fool-proof plan we spent the better part of an hour formulating.

Rule 1. Keep it in your pants at the dinner table.

In my defence, I technically haven't gone off track. Yet. But the desire to get on my knees and fucking *crawl* to the vixen across from me is increasingly hard to fight.

Snap out of it, Carter; you're no better than a horny teenage boy right now.

The corner of my lip pulls up into a half-smirk, causing the smug expression on Lara's face to falter. "Considering you've given a grown man the urge to get on his knees and crawl to you, I think it's time we take this elsewhere."

There. Kept it 'in my pants' *and* I was open and honest about my feelings. I think Teddy would be proud, so that's a win.

Leaving no time for her to argue or deliberate, I stand, round the table and hold a hand out for Lara, silently willing her to take it. She places her hand in mine, intertwining our fingers. "I think having you crawl to me would be rather enjoyable, don't you?"

I lead us away from the dining room and down the hallway to my bedroom. Opening the door, I stand aside and motion for Lara to enter. "Perhaps we'll find out one day."

"Ever the gentleman," she whispers in my ear, her voice laced with her particular tone of sass as she glides past me. I take that as the perfect opportunity to smack her arse. Her answering yelp brings a smile to my face.

Following Lara, I close the door behind me and reach out to grab her by the waist, turning her and pushing her against the door with a little more force than anticipated.

"Allow me to show you how ungentlemanly I can be, Miss Matthews." Lara's eyes connect with mine, and I can almost see the heat rising in them. Her brows raise, urging me to proceed. *Christ, she's a dream.*

"You are breathtaking in this outfit," I whisper hoarsely into her ear, running a hand down the deep V of her blouse. Her skin prickles beneath my touch, my fingertips drawing patterns across the bare skin of her chest. "But I'd much prefer it lying on my floor." I waste no time in delving my hand down the front of her trousers.

Lara rests her head against the back of the door, lips parted slightly, and I know this is my cue. My body moves closer to her of its own accord, and I trace a finger over her lace underwear right above her clit.

"Carter," she breathes, her voice nothing but a whisper.

"Yes, love?"

"Don't be a tease." It amazes me how she manages to retain her tone with my hand down her pants. Focusing on her breathing, I pull Lara's underwear to the side and languidly run two fingers the length of her pussy. Her breath hitches.

With each stroke, Lara becomes more aroused, and my

fingers move with more ease. But I know she's beginning to get antsy. On the next stroke down, I slide one finger inside her, stopping only when I can't push any deeper. Lara clenches involuntarily, and a whimper escapes her mouth.

"Fuck, you always feel incredible," I muse, sliding my finger in and out of her at a torturous speed. Watching her slowly unravel in my hands has become my new favourite thing. My lips find her skin, planting chaste kisses at the hollow of her neck and out along her collarbones.

Lara's heart rate quickens beneath my mouth. I slide my finger out, only to replace it with two on the next pump. The extra width startles her, the tightening of her walls rewarding me. My thumb finds her clit, and I apply the slightest pressure —exactly how I've come to learn she likes it. Her answering moan signifies the angle is *just* right.

"Oh, god." Her voice is unrecognisable beneath the weight of her arousal. Wanting to draw this out as long as possible, I withdraw my fingers from her pussy. Removing my hand from her trousers, I gaze down at Lara. Eyes hooded with desire, her irises are almost invisible. The scarcely audible whine tells me I wasn't the only one enjoying that.

Without breaking eye contact, I bring my fingers to my mouth and suck. "You taste like pure sin." I give my fingers one last lick as I remove them from my mouth.

Somehow Lara's eyes grow even darker, her eyebrows pulling together ever so slightly. "Holy shit. That was hot." Lara says breathily, her cheeks turning an adorable shade of pink as she squirms under my gaze.

Adorable, Carter, really? Get a grip. They're just cheeks.

Chapter 38

Carter

"Come here, you."

I don't give her time to respond, instead pulling her body against mine. I crush my mouth against her full lips. She moans into my mouth, the sound vibrating through me from head to toe. My arms slide from around her neck to grip her hips, rolling them into my own. Lara grins against my lips when my hard length rubs against her core.

My lips don't leave hers as I turn us around. We step in unison until the backs of Lara's knees collide with my bed, buckling beneath her. I take her weight in my arms and gently lay her down on the mattress, continuing my assault on her mouth as our bodies collide.

The hem of Lara's blouse is between my fingers. There's only one thing I want more than to rip it from her body right now, and that's to continue teasing her. The whimpers, moans and sighs she elicits are intoxicating in a way I've never experienced. Rather than pulling it straight over her head, I drag my fingers up her torso an inch at a time. The hem trails along her skin, and I bring my lips to trace the same route my hands take.

I'm rewarded with a strangled moan. Breaking contact, I look up to see Lara's head thrown backwards and the back of her hand pressed against her mouth, muffling the sounds that have burnt into my mind.

Well, that won't do.

Releasing her blouse, I reach up and grip her wrist, pulling her hand from her mouth and planting it next to her face.

"Don't let me see this hand covering your mouth again, do you understand? In fact, I don't want to see anything covering your mouth except my own hand. I want to hear every little noise you make."

Lara's pupils dilate as she watches me, motionless. The racing pulse in her wrist tells me she's as aroused by this as I am. Her tongue darts out and licks her lips as she gives one distinct nod.

"Don't get shy on me now, love. Use your words. Or has the cat got your tongue?"

My trousers grow impossibly tight against my cock as Lara bucks her hips against me. "The only thing that'll muffle my moans will be your dick down my throat or your hand around my neck."

Her words undo something within me, and all I see is red. The red in her flushed cheeks. The red blood thumping through her veins. The red in her lip where she bit it moments ago. The red lace peeking out through her undone trousers.

The burgundy blouse is over her head and on the floor within seconds, and my attention diverts to her waistband. My fingers move with expert speed, and Lara's trousers join her blouse on the floor before she can take a breath.

Taking a moment to soak up the sight beneath me, my breath catches in my throat. *This.* This is what it means to truly have your breath taken away. She's an absolute vision, but that's obvious to anyone who sees her. She's breathtaking in the sense that she continues to open up to me—emotionally and physically—despite claiming to not want to. It's in the way she matches my every move and the way she makes me want to do better, *be* better. There are so many things I want to say when I look at her, but I remain silent. Some things are better left unsaid. *For now.*

The lingerie Lara adorns is without a doubt the hottest I've ever seen. She's heavenly, the most alluring woman I will ever meet. If I had the photographic memory I'd always wished for during Law School, I'd happily give all the knowledge up if it meant I could keep an image of this forever.

My wandering gaze returns to Lara's face, and I find hers trained on me. Her eyes are soft, and there's something about the smile she's giving me. That smile would have me gladly doing anything she asked of me without a second thought.

"Doesn't your outfit look excellent strewn across my floor?"

"It looks a little lonely though." Lara lifts her foot and points a manicured toe toward my chest. "Your turn."

I lean forward to place a kiss on her lips, missing her taste the second I pull away. Kneeling over her almost naked body, I thread a finger beneath the knot of my tie. Lara's nostrils flare as she fixates on the way my hand pulls side to side, loosening the tie. She abruptly slides her elbows beneath her, desire burning in her gaze. I shuffle back, allowing her to swing her legs beneath her so we're knee to knee. Her fingers fumble with how quickly she's trying to undo the buttons of my shirt. I can't help but laugh.

"Need a hand?"

"Not from you, slowpoke."

"Slowpoke?" I tease, watching Lara struggle with the final button. "We'll see if you still think that when I'm fucking you senseless in about 60 seconds."

Lara's fingers briefly slip from the button, and I know I've won this round. Her gentle hands glide over my shoulders, taking my shirt with them and depositing it atop the pile of her own clothes. She looks at me expectantly. "Up, please. You're still wearing far too many clothes."

Giving Lara a smirk, I climb off the bed and stand in front of her, gesturing to my trouser waistband. "Be my guest."

The triumphant look on Lara's face has my heart thudding. I wrap my hands in her hair, running them through the strands and delicately along her scalp. A small moan slips from her lips. She makes fast work of removing my trousers, tossing them on the floor.

"Your outfit looks even better on the floor as well, don't you think?" I gently pull her back by the hair and see her eyes twinkling.

"My floor and our clothes; a match made in heaven."

Something flickers behind Lara's eyes, the way it always does when I say something that pushes the 'just sex' boundary I'm so eager to tear down with each passing day.

"I think your 60 seconds are up; time to put those words into action." Lara flops down onto the mattress, batting her eyelashes at me. Climbing onto the bed, I lean across Lara and dive a hand into my bedside table.

"You'll have to wait a few more seconds, unless you'd like to bear the heir to the firm?" Lara's eyes go wide, and she stares, unblinking. "You can breathe, love, it was a joke."

I rip open the foil packet, ready to roll the condom on when Lara reaches up and slaps me on the thigh. For someone so small, she certainly packs a punch.

"Not funny."

"I disagree, I thought it was quite hilarious." My movements halt when I glance down at Lara, lying there in that delectable red set. "As much as I love you in this, and believe me when I say *love*, you're still entirely too covered."

Lara raises her hips from the mattress in response. When I continue to watch her, she huffs. "Well, go on. They aren't going to remove themselves."

With a swift tug, her underwear is removed. Lara's eyes lock onto mine, mischief glittering beneath the surface. I lean forward and place a kiss on each breast through the lace, weaving my arms beneath her to unclasp the bra. The moment it releases, she lets out a small breath, and I discard it with the rest of our clothing.

"Much better," I muse.

Condom securely on, I spread Lara's knees and position myself between them. Fuck, the view from here is spectacular, and there's no denying it'll play on repeat in my mind for weeks to come. Not that Lara ever really leaves my mind.

Soft blonde waves spill across my pillow, framing Lara in a sort of halo. Her small breasts rise and fall with her breathing, peaked nipples taunting me. When she bites her bottom lip and looks up at me from beneath hooded lids, I can't hold out any longer.

Lara pulls her lower lip between her teeth as I prop each of her ankles on my shoulders. I hold her gaze, aligning my throbbing dick with her glistening pussy. She's so wet, it's making me delirious. The scent of her arousal fills the air; I can almost taste it on my tongue.

I take a deep breath in, trying to steady the pulse pounding in my ears at the sight of Lara spread before me and notch the tip of my cock at her entrance. Inch by inch, I slide into her. Her gasps fill the surrounding space as I slide in deeper, trying my damndest to hold back. I'm focusing on my breathing as I slide in and out a few times, but Lara's voice breaks my concentration.

"I still have all of my senses, Mr Lawrence."

Have I mentioned this woman will be the death of me?

"What have I told you about calling me Mr Lawrence?" I trace a finger along Lara's collarbone, slowly, my touch featherlight. I continue the path down the centre of her chest before moving toward one of her breasts. Tracing delicate circles around her peaked nipple but refusing to touch it is sure to teach her a lesson. If the way her body writhes beneath my touch is anything to go by, it's beginning to drive her crazy after only a few circles. I've pulled out almost completely, leaving only the tip notched in her entrance.

"If you continue to call me that outside the workplace, you might find yourself bent over the boardroom table, wrists bound in one of the ties you like to comment on. Tell me, Miss Matthews, would you be quite so mouthy then?"

My hands find their way to Lara's waist and grip her, hard. Using her body as leverage, I drive into her with force, stopping only when my hips collide with her round arse. Lara moans in response, encouraging me. I repeat the motion, but rather than stopping when we connect, I pull out and slam back into her. Fucking her like this, in my bed, is unmatched.

With each thrust, Lara's legs slowly slide off my shoulders. I'm relentless. Even as her legs fall to my sides, I don't stop, continuing to pump into her. Releasing her waist from my right hand, I glide it along the plain of her stomach, stopping only millimetres from her core. The pounding of my hips doesn't stop as I straighten up, my left hand holding Lara's waist tight enough to bruise.

I look down at Lara's pussy, stretched around my cock, and I salivate at the sight. Without a second thought, I spit on her clit. My thumb finds the swollen nub, and Lara sucks in a breath when I begin rubbing circles over it and spreading the moisture.

Chapter 39

Lara

I decide now is as good a time as any to step outside the safety of my comfort zone—the place that prefers to be instructed rather than to instruct—and take matters into my own hands. Plus, if I don't do it now, this'll be over before I get the chance. I'm so incredibly aroused, I can feel the beginnings of my impending orgasm building.

"Roll over." I intend for it to come out as a command, but instead it's no more than a breathy whisper.

Carter slows his pace, and the gentle thrusts are almost too much to bear. I have the sudden urge to slam my knees shut, but the weight of his body between them reminds me I'm stuck, spread open beneath him.

"Roll over, huh? Am I not doing an adequate job up here?" Carter flicks my clit with his fingertip, and I clamp my mouth shut to hold in the gasp. The wicked grin he dons tells me he's well aware of how much of an adequate job he's doing.

"Just do as I say." I don't typically display many dominant personality traits, but there's something about taking control in the bedroom that's making my insides do little backflips.

There's every chance I'll hate it or feel incredibly awkward, but it's a risk I'm willing to take with Carter. He has this unexplainable calm about him; I feel safe in his presence.

To my surprise, Carter pulls out completely and grabs hold of my waist. He obliges without another word, rolling us until I'm straddling his torso. One look at Carter's sheer size is enough to know he's got some strength behind him, but experiencing it firsthand the way I just did is something entirely different. I want to see all the ways he could manhandle me.

I can feel the evidence of my arousal seeping out onto his stomach. A sudden wave of embarrassment washes over me, urging me to clamber off him, but I don't get the chance.

"Don't you dare move." Carter pins me to him by the hips. I grimace, uncomfortably hyper-aware of the wetness pooling between our bodies.

"You don't find this weird or uncomfortable?" I ask, gesturing to the mess becoming more apparent with each squirm in my failed attempt to get off him. I can't bring myself to look him in the eye like this.

Carter places his thumb on my chin, carefully tilting it until I'm forced to lock eyes with him. "Lara, there's a gorgeous woman sitting on me who's about to ride my cock, and she's so aroused by me she's dripping. I'd have to be certifiable to find that weird or uncomfortable. On the contrary, I don't think I've ever been more turned on."

The sound of his voice alone could undo me. As if on cue, another wave of arousal rushes through me, heat rising in my neck and cheeks.

"Now, why don't you climb on and drench my dick instead?" Carter strokes my thighs while I rise, scooting myself down his torso until I'm hovering above his length. It's impossibly hard, with thick veins running the length of it. I stand by the fact it's good-looking. It's also one I enjoy having inside me.

With one hand wrapped around the base, I align his tip with my entrance. Carter sucks a breath in through gritted teeth when I drag the tip between my lips, signalling he can't take much more of this teasing. Hell, neither can I. It must be apparent on my face because Carter picks this moment to rock his hips up, pushing himself inside me.

We both let out a sigh of relief as he enters me inch by glorious inch. I bend, placing both hands on his hard chest as a brace. Guiding myself down the length of him until our bodies are flush, he lets out a strangled, "*Oh fuck.*"

Those two words are all the encouragement I need. I slowly rise up until we're almost separated and ease my way down, filling myself with him entirely. Finding my rhythm, I slowly increase the tempo and bounce harder. His moans of approval boost my confidence.

"Oh baby, *yes,*" Carter breathes. "Just like that."

I've never liked that pet name, but I could get used to it coming from Carter's lips and in his accent—his deep tone has an unfamiliar rasp to it, making it *that* much more alluring. I can feel myself constricting around him, inching closer and closer to release. Before Carter, orgasms never came to me this quickly, nor did they come from penetration alone. But a lot of things have changed since Carter entered my life. More than I'd like to admit.

A thrust from beneath me has my breath catching in my throat. "Car—"

My words are cut off as Carter throws our conjoined bodies sideways with all his weight. I yelp as we disconnect, and my back smacks onto the mattress once more. Carter lays his body atop mine, the full force of him feeling familiar and unchartered all at once.

He settles himself at my entrance and pauses, and I look up to see him staring down at me with an odd expression.

Carter's eyes trail over my face as if committing every detail to memory.

"Fuck, you're beautiful." His voice is soft, quieter than usual, but thick with an emotion I can't place.

Can't, or won't?

With widened eyes, I stare up at him, shocked at his admission. Has Carter ever shown this degree of candidness toward me? Before I can utter a response, he runs the tip of his cock against my entrance, up and down in a torturously slow rhythm. A small moan escapes my lips as Carter continues to watch me, his eyes dark and giving away very little.

I look down to where we connect and wriggle my hips, hoping for more. I need him. *All* of him.

"Are you going to be a good girl and come for me?"

All I can manage is a faint gasp. His words have left me speechless.

Carter presses himself harder against me. "What did I tell you earlier? Use your words, Lara."

"Yes. *Please.*"

The moment the second word leaves my mouth, Carter slams into me with such force all the air in my lungs evacuates in an almighty *whoosh.*

I don't recall the last time something felt like this; felt so *right.* As quickly as the thought enters my mind, it's gone.

If there were ever an inconvenient time to think about how right sex feels with your boss, it would be right now, whilst the aforementioned boss is six inches deep in my pussy.

His hand drags up my neck, fingers reaching beneath my ear while his thumb caresses along my chin. The gentle action is completely at odds with the way he's pounding into me.

Pleasure and pressure begin to build in my lower abdomen when Carter's thumb returns to my clit, circling. My breath becomes ragged, the blood pulsing through my veins at an alarming rate. A strangled moan escapes me. Carter pulls out abruptly, dipping his head to bring his lips to mine. His tongue runs the length of my lips before slipping between them, tangling with my own. Teeth clash, and moans mix as the kiss intensifies.

"Get on your knees." The words are spoken into my mouth, Carter refusing to break the kiss, but I push him back. I scan his face for an explanation, caught off guard by the demand. His lips pull into a grin, and he strokes my cheek.

"I've spent far too many nights thinking about your arse in my hands as I fuck you from behind and about how beautiful you'd look on all fours. So please, love, get on your knees for me."

It's the way he words it the second time that has me winding my fingers into the dark hair at the nape of his neck, kissing him deeply, and rolling onto my stomach. I look over my shoulder, eyes locking onto his as I pull my knees beneath me, momentarily jutting my arse into the air and wiggling it at him.

Before I'm able to lift up onto my hands, a sharp slap makes contact with my backside, sending a sting across the left side.

I let out a deep moan and drop my head forward into the mess of pillows, pain and pleasure mingling together in sweet sin. The burning sensation spreads, and goosebumps cover every inch of my skin. My thighs squeeze together so tightly it's almost painful, and I discover how wet I am. Again.

Raising up onto my hands, my head is drawn backwards by the grip he has on my hair. His fingers are curled into the strands, the rest of it wrapped around his wrist.

"Tap me on the thigh if it becomes too much." It's the only warning I get before a hand wraps around my throat. His fingers interlace where my chin meets my neck, and just the right amount of pressure is applied. Carter pulls up slightly on my neck, and my eyes roll backwards in ecstasy when he slides into me, bottoming out with a grunt.

The man has me in a chokehold, quite literally, but all I can think about is how disappointed I'll be when this ends. That's what happens; all good things come to an end. It's inevitable. Do we continue to do this regardless? Yes, yes, we do. I'm an absolute glutton for punishment, and he's the sweetest of them all.

Making the most of the little movement I have, I turn my head to the side, noticing our reflection in the mirror adjacent to Carter's bed. My eyes widen as they lock with his, pleasantly surprised to see he's already staring at the obscene image of us.

A mischievous grin tugs at his lips, causing heat to rise in my cheeks.

"Fuck, being able to look you in the eye whilst fucking you from behind is *otherworldly*. You look *so* good on your knees."

I'm about to tap his thigh when he releases my throat. I collapse forward once more, sucking in a deep breath, but it's cut short when Carter pulls out almost entirely, then thrusts back in with tenacity.

His hands glide down to grip my waist with bruising force as he continues to pump in and out, and I bite my lip to stifle the smile. I'm certain I'll have marks in the morning, serving as a reminder of this precise moment.

The feel of Carter's forceful thrusts in and out of my core, his firm grip claiming me.

The sound of skin on skin as the front of his muscular thighs continuously slap against my arse. My involuntary moans mixing with his grunts.

The intricate details of the chandelier hanging above us, glimpses of it bathing the parts of Carter I can see in a glorious glow.

The smell of sex. Raw, animalistic sex.

The taste of copper in my mouth from the laceration on my bottom lip. I can't be certain if it was Carter or I who bit down a little too hard on it, but I don't care either way.

Carter's thrusts slow, our bodies coming to an unexpected standstill. He remains firmly inside me as he lies his chest flat against my back, his lips caressing the shell of my ear. "Can I try something?"

Caught off guard, I resort to sarcasm—my preferred defence mechanism when I'm not in control of a situation's outcome. "You are *not* putting that," I push against him for emphasis, "in my arse. Not in this lifetime."

The arsehole has the audacity to laugh, which reverberates through our bodies and sends a delightful shiver down my spine. "Not quite what I was going for, but I'm glad we're setting ground rules. I was merely going to ask if I could add in a vibrator."

"You, of all people, own a vibrator?" It comes out more accusatory than it was meant to.

"Take down the judgement a notch, Miss Matthews," he tuts, withdrawing himself from my body and reaching over to a small gift bag on the floor I'd failed to notice. "I purchased it yesterday after asking you to come over."

"Well, that's awfully sweet, but my birthday isn't for several months."

Grabbing my chin between his thumb and forefinger, he tilts my head in his direction once more, and I love the way he eyes me hungrily. "Oh, how I'd like to put that bratty mouth to better use again," he murmurs, running the pad of his thumb across my bottom lip. "But that will have to wait."

He releases his hold, but my gaze remains on him, watching intently. The vibrator packaging is discarded with expert speed, leading Carter to return to his place behind me within seconds.

I'm still watching our reflection when Carter's hand snakes under me, coming to rest on my clit. I jerk forward at the sudden cold sensation as the unmoving vibrator touches my skin.

"Same rules as before," Carter says, tapping his thigh with his free hand.

"Noted." I don't make the mistake of nodding this time.

Carter gives me a pleased look in the mirror. "You're learning."

Without breaking eye contact through our reflection, Carter spits on his dick, coating his length until it's gleaming. He winks. "Don't want to hurt you, love." Without another word, he glides inside me until his hips are flush with my arse. The click of a button sounds, but it isn't warning enough for the jolt of arousal that pulses through my clit as the vibrator comes to life.

"Fuck," is all I can manage with a soft moan, overwhelmed by the sensations.

"How does that feel?" Carter's voice is huskier than usual and somehow even hotter. Another moan escapes me when he kicks the vibrator up a speed, causing my hips to buck into him as he drives into me. If I thought I was overwhelmed before, this shit is next level now.

My arms wobble, and then I collapse onto the sheets from the weight of the pleasure. I manage a few deep breaths before an arm wraps around my midsection, hauling me up and pinning my back against his bare chest.

"Keep your eyes on me, baby." The hand wrapped around my stomach slides its way up my body, pinching and twisting each nipple as it climbs.

That familiar warmth begins creeping up my spine, radiating from the apex of my thighs. With my face turned to the mirror, my head falls against Carter's pecs. Our gazes never stray, the fire within each of our eyes fighting for dominance over the other. My hot breath caresses the underside of his jaw with each sigh. Knees buckling beneath me, Carter's body becomes the only thing keeping me upright.

The inner walls of my pussy tighten around Carter. Any doubt around whether he felt it is ripped to shreds when he increases the setting on the vibrator once more. My entire body lights up, pure ecstasy flowing through my veins.

"That's it baby," Carter croons. With one hand between my legs working the vibrator with expert synchronicity to his thrusts and the other caressing my small breasts with a bruising touch, Carter paints the filthiest picture in our reflection.

If the general public could see him now, there'd be no reason to question whether men can multitask.

The feeling of my impending orgasm returns with a vengeance, but I'm adamant I won't go down without a fight. I've always been a little on the competitive side, but never in my wildest dreams did I think I'd be fighting not to come first. I'm running out of time and options, so I resort to playing dirty. I've witnessed firsthand the effects my moans and sighs have on Carter, so it's time to kick them up a notch.

On his next deep thrust, I let out my sexiest moan, complete with a high-pitched 'ah' as I snake a hand around to the nape of Carter's neck. I tangle my fingers into his short hair, tugging. Another exaggerated moan leaves my mouth, and my free hand reaches up to pinch my sensitive nipple.

"Oh, fuck Carter, right there." I don't even recognise my voice; it's far more sultry than ever before. It seems to hit the spot though, because Carter goes harder and deeper more rapidly than ever. The movement of our bodies has the headboard slamming up against the wall, but we don't care.

Instead, his eyes close, and his head drops back. Satisfaction rolls through me like a wave breaking on the shore as he gives one final deep thrust, letting out a strangled moan. When I feel Carter fill the condom, imagining how it would feel to have him fill me instead, I come undone.

All coherent thoughts slip my mind, one word remaining in their wake—Carter. He continues to surprise me in the most unexpected of ways. Although on second thought, this orgasm isn't unexpected at all. I'm well versed in his oral skills, so it would be remiss of me to assume any less of his other skills. And *fuck*, is he skilled.

Every inch of my skin tingles with adrenaline. Every nerve ending continues firing on all cylinders. Every brain cell is fighting with another; half are trying to piece together how to repeat that orgasm pronto, while the other half are rebuilding the walls that came crumbling down the moment he held the door open for me.

We collapse onto the bed in a pile of entangled limbs and sweat-matted hair, but neither of us care. We're too busy trying to catch our breaths and lower our heart rates. I'm genuinely surprised my watch didn't start some medical alert with the way my heart was racing, practically trying to beat its way through my sternum.

Unsurprisingly, the runner among us regains his breath first.

"Fuck, Lara. You are exquisite."

A delirious laugh echoes from my throat. Meeting his eyes, I see a glint in them I haven't noticed before. The effort I'd put into lowering my heart rate only moments ago is thrown out the window, the hussy ramping it right up after seeing that look.

"You're not too bad yourself." The words come out muffled as I stifle a yawn.

"Someone's worn out." Carter pokes my side. I try to slap him away before he realises I'm ticklish, but he moves his hand before I get the chance. "Should I rule out round two?"

Rolling my eyes, I fail to hide the smile that breaks through. "I should probably get going unfortunately, it's quite late." Before I can roll away, an arm loops around my midsection, tethering me to his side.

"It's late indeed, which is why you can't leave now. I simply wouldn't feel comfortable with you driving home in such a spent state."

I can't help but laugh as I try to get up. "Please, I'll be fine. I'm a big girl."

My attempt is futile, and I'm rolled back to face Carter. The laugh dies on my lips when I see the earnest way he's looking at me. There's something in his eyes.

"Please stay." His voice is soft, calling to somewhere deep within me. The plea throws me; it's so unexpected from someone so confident, which only makes it *that* much more impactful.

"If that's what you want, okay."

He lets out an audible breath in response, his body relaxing. We're both silent for a moment, still looking into each other's eyes. The tension is too much to handle. With Carter relaxed and unsuspecting, I'm able to sit up and draw in a few deep breaths.

"I'm going to use the bathroom. Would you mind lending me something to sleep in?"

"Of course." He rolls out the other side and pads over to his wardrobe. With the curtains yet to be drawn, his naked body is lit by the moonlight. Cords of muscle ripple through his back and along his shoulders as he reaches for a t-shirt and a pair of his underwear. He turns to face me, and it's almost too much to bear. His front is even more glorious than his back; thick abdominal muscles fan up into his broad chest and his deep V line has me salivating.

"Hey, eyes up here." His playful tone pulls my attention

back to his face. "You'll be swimming in this, but it'll have to do. You don't have to wear these if you don't want to," he holds up the underwear, "but in case you didn't want to put yours back on."

This man. This thoughtful, beautiful man.

"I'll take both, thank you." I catch the items tossed my way and wander into Carter's bathroom. The entire time I'm freshening up, the fearful-avoidant part of me rears its ugly head.

Do not let yourself get attached to him. You're already too close. He'll leave. All men leave. Even when they claim to love you, they leave. Even when they shouldn't, they leave. Why would he be any different?

By the time I climb back into Carter's bed, I've all but shut down. Not even the feeling of his arm draped over my waist is enough to pull me out of it. Closing my eyes, I will sleep to take me quickly. I think I hear Carter say something, but I keep my eyes shut and say nothing. Soon after, I hear his breathing even out.

They leave. Why would he be any different? All men leave.

Chapter 40

Carter

With her cheek resting against my bare chest, Lara sleeps soundly, the slow steadiness of her breathing filling my bedroom.

I'm absentmindedly stroking her hair with one hand whilst the other rubs small circles on her exposed shoulder blade. In these quiet moments, Lara curled up in my arms, I find myself wondering how anyone else could ever possibly compare to her.

Sleep evades me. I'd love nothing more than to be exactly how Lara is right now, yet I can't seem to shut my mind off. It's hard to be bothered by it though, when it's Lara's unexpected takeover earlier playing on repeat. Once she let her guard down, the confidence and dominance oozed out of her.

It was easily one of the hottest things I've witnessed.

"So you're telling me she has no real set date to leave?"

"Yes."

Yesterday's conversation with my sister floats through my mind. Is it crazy to consider the possibility that this really could be more?

I'm in the kitchen when I hear Lara padding down the hall. When she rounds the corner, I'm awestruck by how beautiful she is. This isn't new information to me; I've known it since the moment I first laid eyes on her, but it's a different kind of beautiful at four in the morning.

It's in the way her hair is unruly, cascading around her like a waterfall. It's the puffiness of her sleep-deprived eyes, and the way she rubs them as she walks. And it's especially prevalent in the way she dons the shirt I discarded last night, the material leaving little to the imagination with every button undone. *My god, my shirt has never looked better.*

"Hey, you."

Lara covers her mouth as a yawn escapes. "I woke up and you weren't there."

The expression on her face is one of vulnerability, but then her brows furrow as though she isn't impressed she said that out loud. Her fingers begin fiddling with the rings on her middle finger, a telltale sign of her nerves. But why? Is she worried I'll leave? It's my house, after all, so there's little chance of that.

Don't be an idiot, Cart.

Unbidden, the sound of my brother's voice enters my thoughts. Of course, he's right. Over the almost six months I've known her, I've discovered Lara has an almost innate desire to keep people at arm's length. I'm yet to find out why, but I'm hopeful she'll open up one day. But this is at complete odds with what she's said—she almost sounded worried that I left her. Some parts of her are still a mystery.

"Don't worry, love, I'm not going anywhere."

She looks up at me then, her features softening. Her lips part slightly, pulling into a small smile as my words sink in. I can't be sure whether she caught the double meaning or not, but the way she looks at me gives me hope.

"Tea?" I ask, wanting to break the tension.

"Please."

As I make up our cups, I picture a lifetime like this. Evenings filled with candlelit dinners, quiet moments, her head on my chest as she sleeps soundly, and all the laughter, love, and orgasms my heart desires.

Though unexpected, the thought doesn't scare me. If anything, I welcome it. I'm not quick enough to quell the hope that surfaces at the thought of spending every evening, and the early hours that follow, the way I've spent this one.

Chapter 41

Lara

From my spot on the couch, I have a clear view of three things: the romcom currently playing, the bay window overlooking the little alleyway, and 80% of the time-telling devices in the house—the latter are all making me painfully aware it's 9:00pm, and I haven't heard a peep from Carter today.

I'm sure he has a valid reason for not being in contact. He's in Paris on a business trip after all, and it's not unusual for him to be a little silent whilst he's away, but it's Tuesday, AKA our Two Truths and a Lie Day, and he's never missed one since he instigated it. He has a pretty heavy schedule whilst in Paris—I'd know; I booked most of it—but I can't help the deflated feeling coming over me.

Perhaps he ended up having a free night and found a beautiful Parisian woman to spend the evening with. Perhaps I'll see them in the tabloids tomorrow morning. Perhaps the way he makes me feel when I'm with him isn't special, it's how he treats everyone. Perhaps I'm just an idiot.

I'm not quick enough to stop the lone tear from sliding

down my cheek. I watch as it lands silently on my thigh, the physical manifestation of my spiralling thoughts. Without warning, the floodgates open, the tears streaking through my makeup at a rapid pace.

The noise of the front door opening sounds worlds away. Not even the fear of being seen like this can break me out of the trance I've found myself in. I only look up when white sneakers appear in front of me. Mia stands over me, her face etched with concern. Rather than speaking, she plucks the tissue box from the coffee table and places it in my hand.

"I'll be right back," Mia says after I've dabbed at my face within an inch of the tissue's life. She gives my shoulder a small squeeze before retreating into the kitchen.

Ten minutes and several tissues later, Mia returns with a bright blue cocktail in each hand.

"I figured we could use these." Handing me one of the Screaming O drinks, Mia takes a seat beside me, curling her feet up beneath her. She takes a long sip, humming her approval, before turning toward me. With a sad smile, she places a hand on my knee and asks, "What's going on?"

The small gesture pulls at my heartstrings. Looking up at the ceiling to quell the fresh onslaught of tears, I dab at my lower lash line with a fresh tissue before answering. "I just feel so lost."

Mia doesn't say anything. Instead, she waits for me to continue. I sniffle, folding and unfolding the tissue in my hand. Mia's hand closes over mine, halting the fidgeting.

"I thought I'd have my life figured out by now, but I'm somehow the complete opposite. I enjoy my job, but it's not my dream job—I don't even know if I have a dream job. Or a dream life. Shouldn't I have it figured out by now? God, younger me would be so disappointed in the lack of progress I've made."

I'm halfway to 28, but somehow I'm less sure of myself

than I was at 22. I can't help but feel as though I've let my younger self down by not having achieved certain things by now. Growing up, I always thought I'd be married to the love of my life by this age, living in the home we'd created together over the years, and maybe even with a baby. Now? I'm single, casually sleeping with the perfect guy, and I can't even say for certain I want children.

Beside me, Mia lets out a small sigh. "Has anyone ever told you you put far too much pressure on yourself?"

I let out a wet laugh. "A couple might have."

"I'm going to give you a piece of advice. It might come across as harsh, but please know it comes from a place of love."

It still humours me Mia thinks she needs to preface her advice this way as if she's ever not straight to the point. Although it's often a harsh truth, it's always meant with love. I brace myself, truly unsure where this is about to go.

Mia reaches for my cocktail, placing them both on the table. She grabs my hands in her own and places them on her knees.

"You need to let go of the unrealistic expectations you put on yourself as a child, because you were just that—a *child*. We had no idea what being an adult was really like when we decided our dreams at seven years old."

"You should consider a career in psychology."

"Stop deflecting with humour, this is serious." Mia smacks our intertwined hands against her knees. "You need to embrace the unknown, my girl. Despite your beliefs, life doesn't have to be meticulously planned out all the time."

It's times like these I'm reminded of how well this girl really knows me. It goes to show time is only a number. Someone who's known you for less than two years can learn to know you better than someone who's known you your entire life.

"We're still young, Lars. We have so much time. And as for

disappointing your younger self, need I remind you that you've moved *halfway across the world*? You left your comfort zone in the largest way possible, and that shit takes serious courage. Young Lara would be so damn proud of the strong woman she's become. Your mum is always so proud of you too, don't forget."

Great, now I'm crying again.

I run my hands through my hair and let out a sigh, tears silently streaming down my face. I don't even want to know how ridiculous I look right now; a splotchy mess for sure.

Mia pulls me into a tight hug. "Sorry, I didn't mean to upset you further," she mumbles into my shoulder. I press my wet cheek against the side of her head.

"It's not you, I'm just an emotional mess right now." The words are half choked by a laugh.

"Is the general lost feeling all, or is there something else?" When I don't immediately respond, Mia pulls back, placing her hands on my shoulders. "Is it Carter?"

I grimace, and Mia's shoulders drop. "We don't have to talk about this."

"Lara, you're my best friend, and he's my brother. You are two of the people I care about most, of course I want you to be able to talk to me about him."

"I don't want to make things uncomfortable between us. I know how close you guys are, and I'd hate to make that weird."

"Don't be ridiculous, Lars. I love you both, and I want to know what's going on. Just do me a favour and spare me the dirty details, please. I barely get by knowing the stockroom situation was actually my brother; anything else and you might send me to an early grave."

"So you didn't tell her about the boardroom?" Harper said, causing Mia and me to jump out of our skin.

We turn in unison to find Harper standing by the living room doorway, her own Screaming O in hand.

Mia whirls back in my direction, her blonde ponytail almost taking my eye out. "Boardroom? What about the boardroom?" Before I can determine an appropriate response, Mia's speaking again. "You know what, don't answer that. I absolutely do not want to know." She turns to face Harper once more. "Harps, you suck for bringing that to my attention."

"Oh please, no details were given."

"I might be blonde, but I'm not *that* dim. I can put two and two together and get boardroom."

Oh, kill me now, please.

I slap a hand to my forehead, dragging my palm down my face.

"Harps, so glad you're home." The sarcasm is thick. I pat the small square of unoccupied couch next to me. "Come, sit."

A grin stretches across Harper's face as she makes her way over, But the grin fades the moment she gets close enough to see the tear tracks down my face. Harper's head swivels between Mia and me, searching for information. "What on earth did I miss?"

Together, we proceed to catch Harper up on the evening's events. By the time we get caught up to the point of her entrance, our glasses are empty.

"Right, refill time. If I'm about to analyse the feelings one of my best friends has for my brother, I need more alcohol. I think this calls for a round of Homerun Lane's."

Mia takes our empty glasses, leaving Harper and me slack-jawed at her reference. The cocktail is aptly named after Maren Moore's *Homerun Proposal,* a best-friend's-brother romance.

After Mia's left the room, Harper pulls her legs up onto the couch, crossing them beneath her and turning toward me. With hands clasped in her lap, she mirrors an eager preschooler.

"You left one part out—what was it that upset you to the point of tears tonight?"

Oh, just spit it out you baby.

"At the risk of sounding like a complete fool, Carter didn't text me today."

Before I'd even uttered the words, I knew she wouldn't know how to respond. Not because she thinks I'm a complete fool, but because this is *so* unlike me.

Harper leans against the arm of the couch, assessing me, then taps a finger against her lips, contemplating. "First things first, you're not a fool, and that isn't a foolish thing. Your feelings are more than valid, okay? Secondly, let's clarify—the lack of a text from Carter is what got to you today, is that right?"

"That's what started it." I slump against my end of the couch, pulling my knees up against my chest. "How did I even end up in this position? I've never had an issue with casual sex before; why now? And why him?"

"Before the overthinking takes complete hold of you, let's talk it all out."

I groan. "Mia does *not* want to hear that."

"What do I not want to hear?" Mia pops her head out from the kitchen, holding a finger to her earlobe.

"Nothing—"

"Lara talking about your brother—"

Harper and I speak at the same time, and *of course* she's gone with the truth rather than a harmless 'nothing'.

Mia casts her eyes toward me, narrowing them slightly. "Lara Jane," she says, taking on a tone eerily reminiscent of my mother, "we've been over this already. I've had time to process this over the past few months, and I'm okay with it. Happy with it, actually. So long as you—"

"Don't talk about the dirty details. I know," I finish her sentence, knowing exactly what she was about to say.

"So," Harper begins as Mia returns with our next round of cocktails. "What do you feel when you're around him?"

"Way to start off easy, Harps." From her spot on the adjacent armchair, Mia playfully kicks at the foot Harper is swinging along the carpet.

"I figure it's best if we go straight to the guts of it," Harper says matter of factly.

What do you feel when you look at him? Mia's reaction makes it sound as though it should be a hard question, but it's quite the opposite.

"Safe." The word slips out effortlessly as though nothing had ever felt quite *this* right.

Two sets of eyes shoot in my direction; one set almost identical to the man in question. All this time living with her and I've never noticed before now. Those eyes have burned their way into my memory as vividly as if they were my own.

Harper pulls her bottom lip between her teeth, and I swear she's trying to hide a smile. "That was quick, Lars." She may have only said four words, but the knowing look she gives me tells me everything she doesn't say. I look across to Mia, sitting there with her arms wrapped around her drawn-up legs and her chin resting atop her knees, with an expression mirroring Harper's.

"Too quick," I respond. Despite their positive demeanours, I can't stop the wave of discomfort washing over me.

"I happen to think it was just right," Mia says, her face bright. "Can you elaborate though? What is it that makes you feel safe?"

I take a moment to mull this over; how do I answer?

"I know it's easier said than done, but you can't look at me as his sister right now. Right now, I'm your best friend."

The way she can read my mind so effortlessly is incredible; I've never felt more grateful for that skill than I do right now.

"Honestly, I don't know if I can describe it without sounding incredibly fucking cheesy."

"Then don't. You could be a whole arse wheel of camembert right now, and we wouldn't bat an eyelid."

"Speak for yourself, Harps, I'd be running in the opposite direction."

"Emilia!" Harper exclaims. "That's not helpful."

I'm doubled over in stitches before I can hear Mia's response. These two never cease to entertain, especially during those moments when you'd least expect it.

"Oh god Lara, are you okay?" Harper's voice sounds much closer than before, and there's a hand on my back. "She's shaking," Harper continues in Mia's direction.

"I-I—," is all I can manage through silent laughter. I draw in a breath, straightening up. "I'm fine, I was laughing." It's a miracle I'm able to get the words out.

"I think it's hysteria," Mia states, to which Harper hums her agreement. "Hysteria aside, we're getting off track. Lara, you were saying?"

"Right, yes, Carter." My fingertips swiftly find my rings, twisting them absentmindedly. "I look at him and feel the sort of safety and security I longed for as a child. I feel like the things I dreamt of when I was younger might be possible with him. But there's a small part of me that feels fear. I wasn't looking for something like this. I didn't want something like this."

From childhood until my pre-teen years, all I'd longed for was to be loved. Whenever I came across someone—particularly males—who showed me anything remotely akin to love, I attached myself to them; teachers, classmates, and sports coaches alike. But once I hit my teen years, it was like a switch had been flicked. The longing I felt had been replaced by the strong urge to push away anyone who tried to get close to me.

Although I still craved that closeness, I struggled to let people in. My therapist identified it as a fearful-avoidant attachment style—apparently it's quite common among children of divorce, especially under the circumstances of my parent's split. Despite working on it over the years, it's never truly gone away. Which is why it's both confusing and unnerving that I've taken to Carter the way I have.

"We know." Harper's voice is soft, almost soothing.

"It's bound to end in heartbreak; I can't do that again." I concentrate on my breathing, willing the tears to remain at bay. Too many have already been shed tonight, and I'll be damned if I let even one more slip for a man. Even if the man is Carter.

"But what if it doesn't? Isn't that a risk worth taking?" This time it's Mia who speaks. I look up at her, trying to keep the shock out of my expression.

Lying in bed, my thoughts are almost overwhelming.

I have feelings for Carter.

I have feelings for the man who's not only my boss but the brother of one of my best friends.

I have feelings for a man who lives half a world away from my home.

I have feelings for a man who is guaranteed to break my heart.

I have feelings for a man, full stop.

Maybe if I continue to repeat this like a mantra, it'll force some sort of reality check on me and shock the feelings right out of me. It's highly unlikely, but it's worth a shot.

The longer I lie here, the more sleep evades me. This man could be everything I dreamed of as a child; everything I ultimately decided wasn't real when I learnt of the cruelness of the world.

You could spend 20 years with the love of your life, and then one day, they turn around and say they don't love you anymore. Or you can have two beautiful children with him, and then out of nowhere, the three of you aren't enough. The things they once found endearing and unique about you are now seen as irritating and inconvenient.

They say the only things guaranteed in life are death and taxes, but I believe heartbreak and disappointment should be on that list too.

Chapter 42

Carter

He'll never tell us now.

BIG TED

Thank god.

ME

Lucky for you, dear sister, I am too delighted about said news to hold back because of Big Ted the Party Pooper.

BIG TED

Oh goody 🙄

ME

We'll need to prepare another place setting for dinner next week.

BIG TED

Back up, does this mean you actually succeeded in locking her down? Or have you lost your mind and married some Parisian woman in a drunken haze?

EMMY

Teddy, you are so troublesome sometimes.

If by 'her' you mean Lara, is she aware she's coming? Because this is news to me. BIG news.

ME

Well no.

But she's about to, as soon as I get home.

Chapter 43

Lara

"Hand on my heart, those were the best potatoes I think I've ever eaten," Carter says with far too much enthusiasm.

I awkwardly swivel my upper body in his direction, elbows deep in the sink full of dishes from tonight's dinner. He's giving me that goofy smile where his one dimple pops and the golden flecks within his green irises reflect off the kitchen light. I have to turn away after a few seconds, finding it a little hard to breathe.

"I don't understand how you can say that so sincerely; they're just potatoes with a bit of seasoning."

"'*Just potatoes*' she says," he mutters with an almost imperceptible shake of his bowed head, I think more to himself than anything. He finishes off with a tut. "Are you sure I can't help you with something? As much as I'm enjoying the view of your arse in those jeans, I'd much rather be put to work than stand here watching you do it all."

The second Carter had gone to collect our plates after dinner, I stopped him. It's one thing for him to clear up after me at his house but in my own? Absolutely not. That's not his job. Plus, I'd already cooked us a late dinner after having worked up a serious appetite in my bedroom—I think we've reached our quota of couple-y business for one Saturday night. Thankfully the girls are out with some friends from school tonight, so we're awarded some privacy.

Over dinner, Carter told me all about Paris. I'm still yet to visit myself, but the way he described it so vividly made it feel as though I was right there with him in the memories—a place I had no right to be.

"I'm sure; I'm done." The water drains from the sink with an awful sucking noise as I dry my hands and turn to face Carter with a smile. "Could you refill our glasses? I'll be right back."

"With pleasure." The way he prolongs the vowels in his glorious accent sends a fresh wave of heat right through me. Not to mention the way his lip quirks at the corner, tempting me the way a siren's voice would a lonely fisherman in the deep sea.

I turn on my heel and race down the hallway at breakneck speed. I had two glasses of wine over dinner with no bathroom break, and it wouldn't be wise to jump a man with a full bladder.

After the fastest pee of my life, and more than ready for round two, I return to the kitchen to find Carter muttering to himself, wine glasses in hand. It gives me a rare glimpse into Carter beneath the suit. Those moments might not come around often, but they strike me in the chest every time. He may be painfully good-looking, with forearm veins for days and an arse that won't quit, but he's also human, just like me. Although they manifest in different ways and for different reasons, we've both had feelings of uncertainty, self-doubt, inadequacy, and apprehension.

Leaning against the doorframe, I clear my throat. "You good?"

"Shit Lara, you can't sneak up on a man like that. Especially when he's holding wine." He lets out a breath.

I can't help but smirk, entirely amused by him.

"Wow, you're jumpy. Are you alright?" Strolling toward him, I reach for my glass still clutched in his grasp. The movement, or my proximity, seems to shake him from the strange stupor. He shakes his head faintly once before wandering past me and into the lounge room. Carter takes a seat, and I plant myself beside him.

His gaze burns into the side of my cheek as I take a sip. "Come to dinner with me next Friday."

The last word catches me off guard, causing me to almost choke on the mouthful of wine. Friday is the unofficial-official Lawrence Family Dinner Night. Every Friday, the Lawrence siblings descend upon their childhood home for a family dinner. I learnt about the unspoken tradition not long after I moved here, but Teddy and Carter were simply nameless older brothers then.

"Friday?"

"Yes, Friday. As in the day between Thursday and Saturday."

If he wasn't so pretty, I'd want to punch him right now. I turn to face him, feeling the growing frown mar my forehead. "Is Lawrence Family Dinner cancelled?"

Carter looks at me blankly. "What?"

"What?" I parrot back to him, aware I probably sound as though somewhere a village is missing their idiot. I think he's caused something to short-circuit in my brain.

"No, I'd like you to accompany me. In fact, I'd love for you to accompany me if you're free."

"To your family dinner?"

"Are you hard of hearing all of a sudden?" There's a teasing tone to his words, yet the insult is all but lost on me. I'm too consumed by rage and bewilderment. Sure, half an hour from now there's every chance I'll realise the rage is possibly a bit of an overreaction, but right now, it feels justified.

"Are you losing your mind? Why would you invite me to your family dinner?" Blood is pumping through my veins at a rapid rate, the sound almost deafening. I stand quickly, feeling like there's not enough air on the couch for the both of us. Carter's aftershave hangs between us, a commanding scent threatening my willpower and overloading my senses.

Carter remains seated, looking up at me curiously. If there's one thing men have, it's the *audacity*. Who does he think he is, looking at me like I'm the crazy one when it's him who's inviting his sex friend to family dinner? What the *fuck* is that about?

"Because I thought it was about time you met the rest of my family, and for them to know the *real* you, rather than the nonsense Emmy and Dad have no doubt told them."

"Carter, are you hearing yourself? Have you even thought this through? What sort of crazy person invites a friend with benefits—who also happens to work for them, need I remind you—to something like that? Why not take one of the many women you've dated? There are always pictures splashed around of you and some bombshell woman. I'm sure any of them would jump at the chance to have dinner with a family like yours."

I'm rambling a *lot*, but there's little I can do to stop. If I asked a Magic 8 Ball, never in a million years would it have predicted *this* response, and that's saying something because those things manage to predict almost anything.

"Lara," Carter murmurs as he rises from the couch, standing almost a full head taller than me. Despite my heartstrings being pulled taut at the sound of my name falling from his lips, I can't meet his gaze. Instead, I choose to keep my eyes trained on the beige-flecked carpet beneath us. His arms move slowly toward my sides, taking hold of my hands. My heart skips a beat at the connection. It doesn't matter that he's touched me countless times, the reaction is always the same.

"I don't know what you're playing at, but I want no part of it," I say, still unable to meet his gaze.

Carter gives my hands a small squeeze before he responds. "Nothing is a game to me where you're concerned."

The words are unexpected, drenched in a vulnerability I haven't heard from Carter before. He's usually so sure of himself—like annoyingly sure—so this unshielded display catches me off guard. But it does nothing in the way of making me look up at him. Call me cowardly, but I can't bring myself to see the softness written across his features. It's overwhelming and confusing and too much for my overthinking brain to process right now. It's also completely at odds with the Carter Lawrence portrayed in the papers, something akin to whiplash.

"Look me in the eyes and tell me you feel nothing for me."

My gaze snaps up from our interlocked fingers to meet his eyes. Those emerald pools hold so much emotion. There's a fire somewhere within them, smouldering away until the timing is right. I let out a sigh, trying to find the words to make him understand.

"That's irrelevant. This isn't about my feelings; it's about you trying to make this into something it isn't, and for the life of me, I can't understand why." I try to pull my hands from his, the contact feeling too intimate. My attempt is futile, but Carter relinquishes his grip in response, and my arms fall limply to my sides.

"Stop deflecting, Lara." His tone is both authoritative and soft as he holds my gaze. "Tell me you feel nothing for me."

It's a command and a plea, and I have no idea how to respond.

There's a dull ache in my chest as I stare into the deep green of his eyes, wishing he could understand my inner turmoil. There's so much I feel for him, but what does that matter when it's going to end? There are a million reasons for this—whatever *this* is—not to work out: I'm from half a world away, he's got a reputation preceding him, I have no idea what I'm doing with my life, his whole future is laid out ahead of him. And it's not like they're small reasons with quick fixes; it's never that simple.

Some things aren't meant to work.

Despite this, I can't help the single tiny butterfly flapping to life deep within me at the thought of this working.

"Carter . . ." I say softly, begging for him to understand. My eyes drift across his body, a body I've come to know as well as my own, as I take in every inch of him.

I can practically *feel* the scratch of stubble lining his sharp jaw, regularly making his presence known on the skin of my inner thighs. His throat works as my eyes coast over it, and I wonder what he's thinking right now. My knees weaken when I look at his broad shoulders, memories of my legs thrown over them threatening to erase all rational thought.

Before I can continue the agonising visual tour of his body, Carter cradles my chin, tilting it up with his forefinger and thumb until my gaze is gently pulled to meet his. His hand flattens against my cheek as he looks at me, heat radiating right beneath the surface where his skin meets mine. Instinctively, I raise my own hand up to meet his, my palm fitting perfectly over the back of his hand. I lean into his touch, letting out a breath I didn't know I was holding.

Carter holds my gaze, and my chest squeezes at his expression; it's a painful combination of admiration, hurt, and what I can only describe as adoration.

"Lara." He says it as if it's a promise. "Should you feel nothing for me, tell me now and I'll leave."

"You don't get it, Carter, I can't do this." I drop my hand from where it connects with his, expecting him to do the same. Rather than breaking contact altogether, Carter tenderly wraps his hands around my elbows, softly tugging me toward him.

"Lara, please." The pleading in his eyes only worsens the squeezing in my chest. "Help me understand."

I open my mouth to say something, anything, but I realise I don't know where to begin. My jaw hangs open for a moment, my brain not immediately processing the fact there are no words coming out.

"It can't be real." My voice cracks on the last word, and a tear escapes through my lashes as I attempt to blink back the imminent onslaught.

The rings on my middle finger feel heavier than ever.

The moment Carter notices the tear, his face crumples. "What can't be real?"

Steadying myself, I take a deep breath. There was always the possibility this conversation would happen, but I'm still unprepared. My knees wobble at the thought.

"It can't be real," I repeat, closing my eyes and summoning every ounce of courage I can, "because if it's real, I can be broken. I don't want to break Carter. I refuse to."

I open my eyes once more, noticing the furrowedness of Carter's brows through a tear-blurred vision.

"Talk to me. *Please*." His voice is so soft it threatens to pry open the restraint I have on my tears. "I can see this isn't easy for you, but please talk to me. I want to understand."

"Can we sit?"

Immediately, Carter lets go of my arms, nodding, and takes a seat once more.

I feel like I need more time to prepare for this conversation. Or more alcohol. Perhaps both? Unfortunately, there's a severe lack of both, so a deep breath will have to do.

I join Carter, tucking my legs up beneath me and resting my shoulder against the back of the couch.

"There's a reason I don't say much about my dad." I twist the rings around, finding comfort in the familiar feel of them. "My parents had been married for ten years when he decided we weren't enough for him anymore; my mother wasn't enough. Thirteen years together, ten years of marriage, two children, and all it took was one decision made by my father to ruin it all."

I've given up fighting the tears; it was always going to be a losing battle. Concentrating on my fingers rather than Carter's steady force in front of me, I continue.

"People say love conquers all, but that couldn't be farther from the truth. Love destroys. It destroyed my mother the day my dad went home with someone else. I refuse to let it destroy me."

My gaze remains trained on my fingers fidgeting in my lap. Locks of hair cascade around me as though someone's drawn the curtains over my face.

"You can't spend your entire life keeping everyone at arm's length, love."

My heart skips a beat as Carter reaches out to tuck one of the stray strands of hair behind my ear. His fingers draw from the shell of my ear to the underside of my jaw, his touch lingering. In the blink of an eye, my heartbeat is as steady as ever. As if his touch grounds me.

"You push people away, telling yourself it means nothing,

and I'd agree typically it would mean nothing. But *I* know *you* know this is different. *We* are different."

I want to argue, to tell him he's wrong, but I'm losing the fight I had in me before. His words terrify me, but somehow they're also clarifying. Everything he's saying is true, as though nothing has ever made more sense than the two of us, together.

"This was never meant to be more than a casual thing," I continue with a sniff. "I didn't want anything serious, but you managed to take down my walls and let yourself in without me even noticing."

"That's where you're wrong. This was never going to be just a casual thing, Lara. I knew from the moment I met you, when I was simultaneously mesmerised and mortified, that we were brought together for a reason."

I let out a wet laugh as more tears stream down my face.

"I know you're scared. Fuck, so am I. But if there's one thing I know for sure, it's that there's nothing we can't face side by side."

This man has come to know me better than I ever imagined he would. The world certainly works in mysterious ways.

"You're somehow everything I never wanted, and yet the man I dreamed of one day meeting. I'm a contradiction within myself; I spent so many years believing I needed to settle down, marry, maybe have a few children, and everything would be right, yet I've avoided anything that felt remotely serious."

"That's why you threw a wall up that night at my house."

"What?"

"The first night you came over, when I invited you for dinner. I'd taken one step toward my bedroom, you pulled back, and I saw the shutters go down behind your eyes. If it weren't for the fact you were on your knees and begging not a moment later, I would've brought it up then."

"I've done a lot of work in therapy over the years to build

fewer walls, but you caught me off guard that day. The look in your eyes seemed so loaded, and it scared me."

Carter wraps his arms around me, pulling my body against his, and as he rubs small circles on my back, warmth and comfort settle over me, somehow almost bone deep.

Tears prick my eyes, but they're different this time; tears of contentment. I've never really understood the saying about how a person could feel like home, but I think I'm beginning to.

"I promise you there's nothing to be afraid of, love. If anything, I should be the one who's scared. Something tells me I wouldn't survive heartbreak at your hand."

"And what makes you think I have the power to cause you heartbreak?"

"There's yet to be a day since we first met where I haven't thought about you. I don't recall a time where I've felt this comfortable, to the point I can't imagine not knowing you, now that I do."

The sincerity in his voice is startling.

God, some of the things this man says make him seem as though he were written by a woman. Surely no one is this smooth without being cringeworthy?

Oh, but of course, someone with a lot of practice could be. Someone like the Oxford Street Playboy.

The little voice in the back of my mind rears its ugly head, determined to throw me off kilter just as my guard is coming down. Unfortunately for Carter, it succeeds.

"As wonderful as everything you're saying is, it's also incredibly at odds with the image you seem to portray in the media. So tell me, which one is the real Carter?"

Chapter 44

Carter / Lara

Carter

From the moment I curated the Oxford Street Playboy persona, I knew one day it would bite me on the arse. I just never expected it to be a bite from the most incredible woman I've ever known.

"At the risk of sounding incredibly cliche, it's not what you think. Please let me explain?"

"I'd love to hear you explain how never being seen with a woman more than once 'isn't what I think'." Lara scoots back slightly, pursing her lips with her arms crossed against her chest.

When I don't immediately respond, she gives me an incredulous smile. Fuck, I've really got my work cut out for me, and I've no one to blame but myself. Given my time again though, I wouldn't change a thing.

"It was a ruse I formulated to protect my family. I created this playboy persona and fed it to the media outlets, knowing they'd swarm on it like vultures to a carcass. Only my family and those closest to me know the truth, because they were the only ones who mattered."

With each word out of my mouth, I watch Lara become more and more perplexed. She sits and stares for a moment, her mouth silently opening and closing.

"You—it . . . wh-what?" The words tumble out incomplete, her utter confusion apparent. "What? Why?"

"For Winnie."

"Your niece?"

"Yes, for my niece. She was an unexpected surprise for our family, and more specifically for Teddy. For the first year of her life, we had no idea she existed."

As expected, this causes Lara's jaw to drop.

"How is that even possible?"

"It's a long story for another night, but for now, let's say her mother was never going to be in the running for the Model Citizen Award." Lara nods absentmindedly, pressing her lips together and pulling them between her teeth with an under-standing hum.

"Once Teddy knew about Winnie, he called me and was completely freaked out. Not about Winnie herself—he was thrilled to find out he had a daughter after the initial surprise—but about the scandal that could be brought to light. Our family is often in the media given our status in society and wealth, and he couldn't afford the bad press in his position with the Army, nor did he want his baby daughter to be the centre of a scandal."

"As soon as he explained the situation, I knew I had to do something, *anything*, to help my family. That's when I came up with the playboy-image ploy. I figured if I could capture the media's attention with pictures of different women on my arm every week and feed them *just* enough tidbits for their imagina-tions to run wild with gossip, I'd be able to take the brunt of their focus. That way, Winnie's past would never be found out."

"So all of those pictures in magazines and online articles were, what, fake? Or had you been dating *that* many women?"

"Yes Lara, they were fake."

"You didn't date a single one?"

"No, they were all amateur models who were more than happy to pose for some candid pictures with me in exchange for an introduction with Lisette Manuel."

"Woah, sidebar—you know Lisette Manuel?"

"She's an old family friend; we spent holidays together in the countryside as children."

"And you really didn't date a single one of those *beautiful* models?" She cocks an eyebrow.

"No, I really didn't. Besides a slightly awkward but brief period seeing the daughter of my parents' friend that I ended not long after meeting you, my last relationship was a whirlwind two-month summer romance when I was in my mid-20s."

"Before Winnie." I struggle to make the words out from beneath her breath, apparently a thought unintentionally spoken aloud. Her eyes have widened slightly, resembling a deer in headlights.

"But isn't Winnie, like, four now? Why continue with the ruse? Especially given everything you've said to me tonight. About me, about us." She ducks her head as she speaks the last words, avoiding my gaze in favour of her rings.

"Oh, love." My palm finds the juncture of her cheek and jaw. It's subconscious at this point; something within me has an almost innate desire to touch her. "I stopped feeding the media staged images the second I began having feelings for you. I couldn't bear the thought of you thinking any less of me. From that moment, you've been the only woman on my mind and in my arms."

"It's easy for you to say that, but how can I be sure you're telling the truth? I want you to prove it."

I blink, slightly dumfounded. "Prove it? Okay, just give me a moment." Pulling my phone from my pocket, I scroll and tap ferociously on the screen, searching for proof. "Here." I flash the screen toward her so she can see the image.

"Uh I'm sorry, what is this proving?"

"Look there," I say, pointing to the top of the image. "Look at the date—March 16th. Correct me if I'm wrong, but that was only a few days before we first met." I look down at her, those deep blue eyes boring into mine with an intensity that's almost too much to bear. There's understanding there too; she's coming around.

"That's correct." Something unseen by me suddenly catches her attention, her eyes cast downward. But it's not enough to hide the ghost of a smile floating across her lips.

"This was the last picture I had orchestrated. Once I met you, this incredible, beautiful, powerhouse of a woman, no one else mattered. There's not a woman out there who could hold a candle to you, Lara."

She lets out a wet laugh, looking up at me with tears brimming again.

"How do you manage to make the cheesiest things sound so un-cheesy?"

"It's the sexy British accent," I respond with a wink.

Lara

I'm failing to reconcile the man in front of me—the man saying the sort of things younger me could only dream of—with the man I've seen plastered all over magazine covers and across various social media outlets.

How could someone with a reputation like his possibly mean everything he's saying?

"But the news articles—"

"Were fabricated. By me."

"All of them?"

He gives me a warm smile. "All of them."

I'm aware I'm making him repeat himself, but Carter is nothing if not patient. I have no doubt he'd repeat himself until the cows come home.

I sit in silence for a moment, turning this over and over in my mind. The longer I ruminate on it, strangely, the more it makes sense. The way Carter has been towards me since the moment we met has never been anything less than sincere, and yet it was always a contradiction to what I'd seen about him in the media.

At the beginning, I didn't really think much of it, nor did I have a problem with the image portrayed—after all, I hadn't been looking for anything serious. But looking back, as July and August rolled into September, I became increasingly aware of the contrast in the versions of Carter.

"You make it impossible for me to even *look* at another woman, Lara, let alone consider touching one. There is only you." Carter continues to speak, utterly unaware of the realisation I'm coming to.

The back of his fingers trails over the dampness coating my cheek. Reacting on instinct, I lean into his touch. He cups my jaw, his gaze locking on mine, and there's a quiet confidence behind it.

"There will only ever be you." Carter's words are strong and steady as if they're the only thing he's ever known to be true.

But how do I accept the kind of love I've never believed in?

"I tried so hard not to feel anything for you." The words escape so quietly, to the point I fear Carter hasn't heard them. Though, the fear is short-lived. Carter lets his hand drop from my face, resting it on my exposed knee. He stares at me unabashed before an uncontainable grin breaks out across his face, his eyes alight.

"You can't give me that smile right now."

"And why's that?"

"Because it makes me nervous. I'm trying to have an adult conversation here, and the smile does something distracting to my insides."

The grin only widens.

"Carter, I'm serious."

"I know, I'm sorry." But he doesn't look the slightest bit sorry as he casually flicks his wrist. "Just don't look at my face then."

After a deep breath, I continue. "I fought hard against developing any feelings for you. There are so many reasons we shouldn't work. Firstly, you're my—"

"Boss? That's easy. I'll move you into any other suitable position within the firm that you desire. But I know this isn't your dream job, so I'll help you into any industry I have connections with. Whatever will make you comfortable, I'll do it. Next reason."

If I didn't know Carter as well as I do—the way he has to exercise in the morning or he's unbearable; that he orders his black coffee extra hot but then lets it cool for five minutes before taking a sip; that he's the most organised male I've ever encountered—I'd be gobsmacked by his prepared response. But I do, which is how I know he's someone who will do whatever it takes to get what he wants. If that means exhausting all favours with professional connections in the hopes I give in to him, he'd do it in a heartbeat and ask what's next.

To hide the smile playing on my lips, I roll them between my teeth and rub a finger along my cupid's bow.

"Mia."

"I know her as Emilia, but I'm familiar with her."

"God, you're insufferable. Mia is my next reason."

His hand remains firmly on my knee, encouraging as ever. "I don't believe you can claim my sister as a reason to place a tally in the con column of us."

"And why not?"

"Out of the three of us, she's really the only one who should be allowed to have an issue with this, given I'm her blood and you're her best friend—"

"You just proved my point." Lounging against the arm of the couch, I give Carter the smuggest look I can muster. I'm a little thrown when he mirrors it.

"You didn't let me finish. I was going to add that, last I spoke to her, she wasn't against it at all. I'd go as far as to say she was encouraging."

"Encouraging? Are you sure we're talking about the same Emilia Lawrence?"

"Unless you've befriended and moved in with another of my sisters named Emilia, I believe so."

"There's no way. There was a moment when I first told her where I worried for my life, Carter."

"Come on, Lara. I'd expect you of all people to know how

she is—dramatic and reactive straight off the mark, but she always comes around."

"Even so, *this*" — I gesture between us — "isn't really the sort of thing you could expect her to come around to."

"Lara."

I take a deep, grounding breath. Yet again, I'm feeling slightly overwhelmed. I look over at Carter, who's sitting beside me with his most sincere smile and those gorgeous green eyes, and I know there's no word of a lie in what he's telling me.

Mia is okay with this, encouraging it—*us*—even.

"I don't understand why you didn't tell me the truth sooner. I mean I do, but I don't, you know?"

"Because you spook easily."

My jaw begins to drop, but Carter is quicker. "I'm kidding."

Carter lets out a yelp mingled with a chuckle when I smack him on the knee. "You deserved that."

"You're right, I did."

There's something different about holding Carter's gaze. He looks at me as though he can see everything; my past traumas, our present, and my future, and there's nothing he wants more than to be just that—my future. Perhaps that's how it should be.

The longer we look at each other, the more I notice the way his eyes begin to water. Ever the physical touch type, he grabs my hands and wraps his own around them, cocooning them.

Carter

A tear slips down my cheek unbidden, but I don't move to wipe it. I'm not afraid of showing emotion around Lara.

"You must know, I'm deeply sorry for not coming clean about the whole facade sooner. My family needed to come first. But if there's one thing I've come to know is true, it's that I can so clearly see you being part of my family as well."

"Doesn't that scare you? Having those feelings about someone who could break your heart?"

"It is scary; quite frankly, it's fucking terrifying. If I'm honest, I think my exact words to Dex were, '*fuck, Dex, I think I'm falling in love with her, and that scares me more than almost anything.*'"

Lara's head flicks up, those tear-brimmed deep blues looking into my soul. Her eyes soften as a small smile pulls at the corners of her glossed lips. She blinks, a lone tear rolling down her soft cheek. I'm mesmerised by her.

"Carter . . ."

"Yes, love?"

A gentle giggle escapes, Lara's hand coming up to stifle it before wiping the stray tear away. "You have no idea what you just said, do you?"

Oh no, what did I say? It can't be anything too horrible, given the giggle.

Oh fuck.

I just told Lara I think I'm falling in love with her without actually telling her.

As someone who prides themselves on the way they're able to handle any situation thrown at them with a smile, satire, sense, or all of the above, I'll be the first to admit I *royally* fucked this one up.

Lara looks at me expectantly, no doubt wondering if I'll freak out or double down. This is far from the way I imagined telling her, but there's a silver lining—I'm going to tell her. Any agonising over timing is out the window. That initial 'oh fuck' feeling subsides, and a wave of calm washes over me. *I'm going to tell her.* Wrapping my hand around hers, I look deep into those beautiful blue eyes that I've come to know so well.

"It might not be the way I'd have liked to tell you, but that doesn't make it any less true—I'm falling in love with you, Matthews." Her hand trembles in mine, becoming clammy. Despite every part of me wanting to break eye contact from fear of rejection, I don't. Instead, I hold her gaze like it's the last thing I'll ever do. I catalogue each variation of blue, the varying thickness of the darker rim, and the almost imperceptible flecks of green, committing it all to memory on the off chance this is the last time. But as I witness the tears welling again and the tiny pull at the corner of her mouth, I know with absolute certainty no one will ever look at me the way Lara is in this moment.

"I'm not expecting you to say it back or even reciprocate the feeling, not yet anyway. But I don't doubt one day you will, and it'll be the second greatest moment of my entire existence." I lean in closer, my mouth inches from hers. "Second only to any occasion where I find myself between your thighs, drowning in that—"

"Oh, shut up and kiss me, Lawrence." Her tear-stained cheeks develop her signature blush as the most captivating smile reels me in.

I can't wipe the smile off my face as I crush my mouth to hers, kissing her with everything I have. Running the tip of my tongue along the seam of her lips, she opens herself to me.

It's the type of kiss you'd expect to see at the end of one of those holiday Hallmark movies Lara's been forcing me to watch right before it fades to black. She doesn't need to say a word; this kiss tells me everything I need to know. She's falling for me, too.

Chapter 45

Lara

You are a strong, independent woman, and you can do hard things.

You are a strong, independent woman, and you can do hard things.

You are a strong, independent woman, and you can do hard things.

"Did you say something?" Carter's hand finds the spot between my shoulder blades that I'm certain was custom-made to fit his comforting touch. I look up at him as he leans his face closer to mine, smiling sweetly.

"Sorry, talking to myself."

We're standing outside his childhood home, except *home* is a loose term. I think *small mansion* would be a more fitting description. The exterior is bright white, with floor-to-ceiling arch windows dispersed along the length of the front. A stunning portico stands above us, with cherry blossoms housed in built-in planter boxes on either side. The front door is a deep navy, adorned with a floral wreath beneath the half-moon window.

Despite the beautiful home, I'm on the verge of a nervous breakdown while struggling to comprehend why I'm so nervous —Mia is my best friend, and I've come to know Freddie quite well. Together, they make up half of the family beyond the double oak doors looming before me. But it's the other three who are making me nervous—Carter's older brother, Teddy, his mother, Diana, and the infamous Winnie.

"I know you're nervous, but you're going to do great. My family already loves you." Carter places his other hand over mine, halting the subconscious ring twisting.

"Half of them don't even know me; they can't love me."

"You don't think I've told them almost everything there is to know about you? Everything there is to love about you?"

"Almost everything?" I question with a quirked brow.

"Well, I figured there's some details my family don't need to know. For example, the little breathless noise you make when I do this." Without hesitation, Carter runs his palm down the curve of my back and over my arse. When I think he's finished, and I'm confused about the point he's trying to make, he delivers a sharp slap to my backside.

I draw in a quick breath, the cool air burning a pathway from the back of my throat right into my lungs. Before I have the chance to respond, the front door swings open, revealing an older but no less beautiful version of Mia.

"You're here!" she exclaims, a warm smile lighting up her delicate face. Carter's mother whirls away from us. "See Freddie, I told you I heard a noise at the front door." Attention returning to us, she continues. "Goodness me, you're even more beautiful than my son let on! I'm Di, it's wonderful to finally meet you, dear."

Di steps forward, wrapping me in a warm embrace, and there's no denying who Carter inherited his hugs from. My senses are encircled by a mixture of citrus and floral as she pulls back to look at me, still holding onto my shoulders.

"It's wonderful to meet you too, Di." Hopefully the nerves I feel aren't portrayed in my shy smile.

The genetics in this family will never cease to amaze me. If we were ever to have children, I hope to god they'd inherit their father's genes. Her blonde lob is perfectly styled, the ends curling up slightly where they graze her shoulders. Her makeup is light, emphasising her high cheekbones, and a pink hue is expertly swiped across her lips.

Impeccable style is clearly another hereditary trait in this family. The black and white A-line dress swishes around Di's calves as she ushers us inside, her heels clicking against the hardwood floors.

The house is a statement piece from the outside, but the interior is something else entirely. We enter the open-plan foyer, and I have to make a conscious effort not to gape. To the left is a formal dining room, the grand table in the centre set for seven. The navy decor rivals that of a showroom, and I think I've found my dream home. To the right is the most spectacular kitchen I'll possibly ever see. The navy theme continues in the cabinetry lining the far wall, contrasted with brushed brass fixtures. I'm in complete awe of this place and beyond jealous Carter grew up here.

"You look lovely as always, Mother." Carter bends to give his mum a kiss on the cheek, and she stands on tiptoes to meet him halfway.

"Thank you, my sweet boy. Come, the others are in the drawing room."

I don't think I've ever been in a home with a drawing room. I'm fairly certain it's another name for a fancy living room, or at least that's what my Bridgerton knowledge tells me. Judging by what I've seen of the house so far, I imagine it'll be meticu-lously designed and decorated.

Di wanders down the corridor ahead of us, but I find myself frozen in place. Carter, ever the observer, notices my hesitation. "We'll be two seconds, Mum." He raises his arm toward her, two fingers up. "See, she wasn't so scary, was she?" He gives me a cheesy grin, his dimple popping. "One down, one to go."

"I don't recall saying they'd be scary," I retort, giving Carter a pointed look. "I won't lie, though; your brother sounds a little intimidating."

"He is."

"Ooh, it's a good thing you're pretty because you're a pain in my arse."

Carter ducks his head, his lips featherlight against mine as he gives me a chaste kiss. "Let's go introduce you to Big Ted."

Chapter 46

Carter / Lara

Carter

I'm falling more in love with Lara with each passing moment.

I wasn't sure it was possible, but as I watch her interacting with the people I hold dearest, I realise it is.

Teddy lived up to his Big Ted nickname, introducing himself to Lara and wrapping her in a huge bear hug, almost lifting her feet off the floor. She let out a sweet laugh, the sound hitting me square in the chest like an arrow.

My brother then proceeded to call me out in front of everyone, telling Lara he hoped this meeting would mean I'd stop gushing about her every time I opened my mouth. Lara's face flushed pink, her hand coming up to cover her mouth, but it was clear she was smiling beneath it. If anything, at least it proved I wasn't lying when I said I told them almost everything about her.

It doesn't take long before Lara and my niece become best friends. As soon as she saw the book in Winnie's hand, Lara sat with her and asked if they could read it together. My heart threatens to burst right out of my chest at the sight. We haven't spoken about children yet, and probably won't for a while, but the way she's talking animatedly with Winnie tells me she'd make an excellent mother if or when the time came.

Winnie was easily the most excited to meet Lara. She's been obsessed with her Aunty Emmy for weeks now, constantly wanting to talk to her, see her or dress like her, so it's no surprise she's completely enamoured with Lara now.

"Dinner is served!" My father announces with a clap from the doorway, happiness radiating from him. His family is his pride and joy, and Friday Dinner has been the highlight of his week since we started the tradition.

Lara stands, holding out her hand for Winnie, helping her up. Lara takes a step toward me, but a small tug on her skirt from Winnie stops her. "Can you sit next to me, Lala? Uncle Cart can sit next to you too."

Bless her tiny soul. We tried telling her several times it's *Lara*, but Winnie's stubborn and doesn't like to be wrong.

"I'd be honoured," Lara replies, grinning down at her, then glancing at me. "Looks like our places have been chosen for us, Uncle Cart."

Winnie starts toward the dining room, hand still firmly clasping Lara's. When she doesn't move, my niece lets out an adorable huff, dropping her hand and continuing on alone, leaving just Lara and me in the drawing room.

"Would it be odd to admit that hearing you call me Uncle Cart has almost the same effect as when you call me Mr Lawrence or sir?"

Lara grins at me, eyes bright. "Odd? Yes." She takes a step closer, coming almost chest-to-chest with me. "Hot? Also yes. It makes me wonder what other names would have the same effect. *Daddy*, perhaps?"

This woman.

But two can play at this game.

"How about we leave that one until there's a tiny two-legged reason to call me that?"

Her eyes widen. I can't help but mirror the grin she donned only moments ago.

"Come on, our dinner will get cold."

Lara is still gobsmacked as we make our way to the dining room. Winnie enthusiastically smacks the chair next to her when she sees us approach. Her dad sits across from her, trying and failing to hide his amusement at her excitement. Next to him is my father, followed by my mother, and Emmy sits at the head of the table. I pull out the chair, and Lara takes her prearranged spot next to Winnie. All eyes are on us, and it takes effort to fight against the blush rising on my chest.

Spirited chatter begins around us, making me realise I forgot to warn Lara about how lively the conversation can get at the dinner table. But when I glance over at her and notice the gleam in her eyes, it seems the warning would've been a waste of time. She's completely enraptured by my family. I reach over and place my hand on her knee; the need to touch her is constant. If it annoys her, she doesn't let on, instead giving me a shy smile.

My sister's stare burns a hole in the side of my head, observing the whole thing. I look over at her, expecting to see judgement, but I'm instead greeted with a knowing grin. I can't help but return it, knowing full well my sister can see right through the casual palm on Lara's knee. I'm completely smitten, and Emmy knows it.

Naturally, my brother would pick right now, when I'm enjoying a wholesome moment with our sister, to stir shit.

"Hands where we can see them thanks, Carter. There are children in the room."

There are many varied reactions to this: Mum and Lara chuckle and Dad whisper-shouts, "Theodore!" before giving him a light smack on the crown of his head. Emmy and I roll our eyes. Winnie's reaction is my favourite, though; her eyes dart down to where my hand still rests on Lara's knee and up to meet my gaze. Her little blue eyes narrow in my direction before returning to their normal size when she redirects her attention to Teddy.

"I'll watch him, Daddy," she says, ever so seriously before continuing to chomp on the stick of carrot in her hand.

I lean into Lara, my lips mere inches from her ear. "On second thought, maybe we should try out the Daddy thing—"

"Lalalala," blurts my sister, who's sticking her fingers in her ears like a child, eyes squeezed shut.

A blush ascends the column of Lara's throat, and she lets out a small, startled cough.

This gets the attention of the rest of the table once more. "Emilia, whatever are you doing?" My mother half shouts in an attempt to be heard through Emmy's dramatics.

"She's clearly trying to block out whatever filth was pouring from young Carter's mouth," Teddy answers. Oh, how I wish he were close enough to smack.

My mother's mouth is agape, and my father is giving me a stern look. "Son, please. Rein it in at the dinner table for your sister's sake."

Lara begins laughing to the point her eyes water. Everyone else is silent, and when Lara notices, she stops abruptly. "Sorry, I'm finding this very entertaining." She wipes a stray tear from beneath her bottom lashes.

Winnie looks at her with bewilderment before breaking out into her own laughter, causing Lara's fit to start again, and soon, the entire table joins in.

Lara

The rest of dinner went off without a hitch, full of laughter and stories of the Lawrence siblings' childhoods. It was all kinds of wonderful. The smile hasn't left my face, even as I lie in Carter's arms several hours later.

"Your family is incredible."

With my head resting on his chiselled chest, his heartbeat kicking up a notch is palpable.

"I think they'd say the same about you."

I smile against him, rubbing my nails lightly against his bare skin. "I mean it though, thank you for inviting me tonight. I've never experienced a family dinner like that, or a family dinner full stop really."

"I know they don't know you overly well yet, but they think the world of you, love. As do I. You are the most divine woman I've ever had the pleasure of knowing. I'm looking forward to not only every moment I get to spend with you—which'll be *many* moments, by the way—but also everything you're going to achieve in life. You are destined for greatness, and don't you ever forget it."

With a kiss on my forehead, Carter leans over and turns out the light. As I snuggle into his embrace and blink away the emotion rising to the surface, the pieces slide into place.

I love this man.

For weeks now I've felt myself falling for him more and more, so this doesn't come as a huge surprise. The complete calm I feel at the revelation is what surprises me.

"Carter?"

Well aware he's the type to fall asleep almost instantly, I don't move for fear of waking him.

"Yes, love?" he murmurs against the crown of my head.

"I love you."

I'd expected my heart rate to double upon saying those three words out loud. Instead, it beats steadily. Carter's heart beats in tune beneath my palm. He covers my hand with his own, giving it a small squeeze.

"I was beginning to think you'd never admit it."

Looking up at him, everything I feel is mirrored in his eyes. Where I expected to see a smirk or smug look, there's nothing but genuine adoration.

"I love you too, Lara."

The lack of light only highlights his misty-eyed gaze.

A feeling of divine serenity washes over me.

Perhaps I don't need to have everything figured out yet. In the most unexpected of ways, I've found a man who's in love with me and, more importantly, one who believes in and supports me wholeheartedly. With him by my side, I'll find my way.

Epilogue

One Month Later

Lara

"Are you coming, or do I need to come and get you myself?" Carter drawls from the ensuite, his head popping around the edge of the door. He's wearing one of his signature smirks, and as always, it does something dirty to my insides.

"I'll be in in a moment," I respond sweetly from where I'm still sitting in the middle of his bed, in no rush to move.

"You have five minutes, otherwise you're coming by force. I haven't tasted that pussy for days, and I'm ravenous." Carter disappears, and the shower runs a few seconds later.

For a moment, I want to drop everything and run to meet him beneath the hot stream and let him eat me until I can't take it anymore. But then I remember myself and shake my head.

Earlier this evening, before Carter returned from a work trip, I began writing a letter to my younger self. It sounds kind of wankery, but I think it's necessary. I've been in the UK for just shy of seven months now, and my life looks remarkably different from anything I could have imagined. The little girl with abandonment issues would be *so proud* of who she is today.

Carter and I have officially been together for a month, but it feels far longer given the unofficial lead-up. In the letter, I've detailed everything about Carter, starting with the fact he's a giant pain in the butt sometimes and ending at the realisation he's someone I didn't think existed beyond the pages of romance novels, yet here he is.

Most importantly, I made sure to include a paragraph dedicated to his love of Hallmark movies. Sure, I might have started it that first time in Norcaster, but Carter has instigated most watch sessions since then. He continues to tell everyone that I force him to watch them, but we both know that couldn't be further from the behind closed doors truth.

I'm still working at the firm, but I'm now under Anna in the HR department. Given I'm a stickler for rules and rights, I thought it could be fitting and felt like a change. It's only been a few weeks, but something about it feels *right*. I've put all of this in the letter as well, explaining there's no rush to have everything figured out at such a young age, which is something I've come to accept in recent months. It's incredibly tough to let go of expectations you put in place when you were merely a child with dreams, but doing so comes with a sense of freedom I can't put into words.

I'm about to sign off the letter when the shower shuts off abruptly. Hurried movements sound from the ensuite. Carter walks out a moment later, a towel wrapped low around his hips, bare from the waist up. I peruse his body, the muscles rippling beneath the surface as he moves in my direction. The expression on his face stops my perusing. He looks awfully stressed, staring down at something on his phone.

"Carter." I pause, waiting for him to look at me. "Is everything okay?"

He rubs his free hand over his face, his telltale sign something is troubling him.

"The papers, they know." He looks at me then, concerned, and a flicker of fear ignites in those deep green irises. I don't need to ask to know what he's referring to—Teddy.

Handing his phone over to me, Carter climbs onto the bed and lies against the headrest. I skim the article, seeing a few pictures and details I already know, but that the public was never meant to find out.

This is *bad.*

Carter sits up beside me, running his fingers through his dark, towel-dried locks before dropping his hand to rest on my bare thigh. "I know I need to explain everything to you—and I will—but I'm not ready yet."

I place a comforting hand on his knee and squeeze. "Whenever you're ready, my love."

"What's this?" he asks, reaching forward to pluck the letter from where it lies between us. He reads aloud, "To me."

"Hold on." I scramble to retrieve the piece of paper from his grasp. "It's not finished yet. You can read it in a moment."

I add four more words to sign off the letter.

There, now it's complete.

From London, With Love
L x

Acknowledgments

When I think about all the people who helped me get to this point, it overwhelms me in the best possible way. There are so many people deserving of acknowledgement, but I've stuck to the core list so this section isn't 50 pages long.

You, the reader—thank you from the bottom of my heart for taking a chance on my little book. It's still kind of crazy that there are strangers across the world reading about the people I made up in my head, but I'm grateful for each and every one of you.

Mel D Designs—thank you for bringing my vision to life. You took a draft a child could have made and turned it into the beautiful thing it is today. Endlessly thankful for the time you put into finding me the perfect loopy L.

Elena—arguably the single most patient person when it came to this book (read: me). I'm immensely grateful for the patience, grace and professionalism you've shown me throughout this process. I look forward to working with you again!

Zarin—you saved me in the days prior to ARC distribution, and I'll never be able to repay you for the support and assistance! This book wouldn't look nearly as professional without you.

The End of 2024 Accountability Group—you guys really saw me through the last 20% of this book and beyond and cheered me on every step of the way. The weekly check-ins had such a big impact on my productivity when things got hard. Thanks for being the big sister authors I always wanted.

To my Beta Readers—Brookelyn, Brooke, Caitlin (bestie), Danielle, Emma, Erin, Hannah, Rhianne, Ronnie, and Sian—you guys are superstars, and I truly mean that. I could never thank you enough for your feedback, encouragement and love for FL,WL. From its early stages to the final version, each of you played a part. A special shoutout to Rhianne for being my personal hype girl and to Ronnie for being the reassuring author sister I often really needed.

The Editorial—I can't even put into words the impact the two of you had on this book, and, by extension, me. You were there to give feedback at the most obscure of times, you were there to scour through my manuscript for eye colours I'd long forgotten, and you were there to validate me when I needed it most. I love you guys and your love for my fictional men. Danielle, Teddy is yours.

Bonnie—I don't mean to be dramatic, but believe me when I say this book wouldn't be out in the world if it weren't for you. The support and guidance that you've offered not only me, but this book, is something I will forever be grateful for. It's wild to think that one of my biggest supporters is someone I've never met, but I hope to change that one day.

Mum—I'm not sure if I'll ever allow you to read this, at least not in its entirety, but in case you do—thank you. Thank you for being my built-in best friend, for being the wonderful woman you are, and for raising me the same. I hope you don't mind that there are pieces of you sprinkled throughout this book. You are strong, you are resilient, and I love you to death.

About the Author

Em Hardy is a romance writer from Brisbane, Australia. If you're looking for sarcasm and spice with a side of suits, you've come to the right place: these are Em's self-proclaimed areas of expertise.

When she's not writing, Em can be found losing herself in a good spicy romance or thriller, attempting to run, or planning some form of extravagant Christmas event year-round.